LILLI'S CHAIR

A. BAXTER

This book is historical fiction. The author has attempted to recreate events, locales and conversations from her memories of them and research. The opinions expressed within this book are solely her own. The author does not assume and hereby disclaims any liability to any party for any loss, damage, or disruption caused by errors or omissions, whether such errors or omissions result from negligence, accident, or any other cause.

Cover Design: Wicked Whale Publishing
Interior Design: Wicked Whale Publishing

Copyright © 2020 by Alvina Baxter Moran

All rights reserved. In accordance with U.S. Copyright Act of 1976, the scanning, uploading and electronic sharing of any part of this book without the permission of the publisher / author is unlawful piracy and theft of the author's intellectual property. If you would like to use material from this book (other than for review purposes), prior written permission must be obtained by contacting the author at alvinab@comcast.net. Thank you for your support of the author's rights.

Baxter, A. pp 500

Lilli's Chair/ A. Baxter

Summary: A German girl's life is forever changed after a terrifying accident and her family's journey to America.

ISBN: 9798693038080

Printed in the United States of America

I dedicate this book to my family.

DISCLAIMER TO LILLI'S CHAIR

The author, A. Baxter, grew up in the City of Boston, the middle child, in a family of 7 children. As a child in a loud, active family, she discovered that books provided insight, took her to imaginary places, and opened doors to long ago times. Lilli's Chair, her first novel of historical fiction, was based on conversations, stories and memories heard around her family's kitchen table. These stories, told and repeated throughout the author's childhood, created a sense of family folklore, struggles and strength. Poetic license has been applied when referencing real life individuals, incidents, and places, they were strictly from the author's imagination. References to real people, actual events, places, and times were intended to provide a sense of authenticity and are fictitious. In some cases, names have been changed to protect the privacy of the people involved. Throughout the narrative, the author's intention was to provide a story about the power of vision, courage and most importantly love.

CONTENTS

Chapter 1 — 1
Lilli, Brooklyn, New York, 1901

Chapter 2 — 25
Lessons

Chapter 3 — 37
Differences

Chapter 4 — 55
American

Chapter 5 — 75
The Introduction 1901

Chapter 6 — 89
The Gift

Chapter 7 — 107
Wedding Day

Chapter 8 — 115
Home

Chapter 9 — 127
Wilhelmmine, Germany, 1864

Chapter 10 — 145
Not Breathing

Chapter 11 — 157
Heartbreak

Chapter 12 — 175
Family

Chapter 13 — 197
Christmas Eve, 1914

Chapter 14 — 213
The Knock, Winter 1915

Chapter 15 — 235
The Patriot

Chapter 16 — 245
American Doughboy

Chapter 17 *Boston, Massachusetts, 1917*	253
Chapter 18 *Marion, October 1916*	261
Chapter 19 *The Train Station*	267
Chapter 20 *Letters*	279
Chapter 21 *The Front, 1918*	293
Chapter 22 *Burning Up*	305
Chapter 23 *Everything Changes*	313
Chapter 24 *A Time to Heal*	323
Chapter 25 *Boxes, Summer of 1919*	331
Chapter 26 *Ripple Effects*	339
Chapter 27 *Forest Street, Boston, MA*	355
Chapter 28 *Perceptions*	365
Chapter 29 *Eggs, Chickens, and Church*	377
Chapter 30 *Butterflies*	387
Chapter 31 *Commitments*	399
Chapter 32 *Boston, Massachusetts, 1921, Hairpin Turns*	413
Chapter 33 *The Art of Conversation*	423
Chapter 34 *Putting the Pieces Together*	435
Chapter 35 *Choices*	445
Chapter 36 *The Visit*	459

Chapter 37 *The Gathering, November, 1921*	469
Chapter 38 *Silent Night*	479
Chapter 39 *In Her Own Words, Boston, 1987*	489
Epilogue	511
References and Sources	515
Acknowledgments	523
About the Author	529

"We must be willing to get rid of the life we planned, so as to have the life that is waiting for us." - Joseph Campbell

1

LILLI, BROOKLYN, NEW YORK, 1901

"Ow!" Lilli winced, twisting her ankle, as a lightning bolt of pain shot up her left leg. The thin soles of her black high buttoned shoes offered meager protection against the searing heat from the cobblestoned sidewalks. Its intensity burning right through to her aching and tired feet. Lilli doubted her ability to continue, grimacing she gulped, forcing a meager drop of moisture down her dry throat, her stomach commiserated by groaning loudly. She was thirsty, tired, hungry and hot, shaking her head, she told herself to shape up, she would be fine, none of this was new, she'd felt this way before under circumstances far more arduous.

The bulky bundles she carried had become awkward and heavy causing her to question, "What was I thinking? I've bought too many things. I can't carry it all." The desire to drop everything was enticing, and becoming too much to bear. Exhausted, sick of being bumped, jostled, pushed and banged into, Lilli strategically tried to navigate her way through the busy and crowded New York City street. The only thing she wanted to do right now was to stop and take a break.

Furtively she looked around, hoping to find an empty spot, knowing that this was practically impossible in one of the most populous cities in the world. Remembering not to be dismayed, Lilli remained steadfast as she continued to search, hoping to spy just one tiny oasis. Not disappointed easily, she was starting to think this effort futile. The street was incredibly hectic, along with possessing an overbearingly foul smell that hung thick in the air. Then, she saw it, like a true oasis, miraculously it appeared. Without a moment's hesitation she quickened her pace rushing to it. Quickly she staked her claim, only then did she carefully lower her packages trying to avoid the dirtiest of the soiled cobbled stones.

Confident that her parcels were protected she reached her hands behind her and pressed them down on her aching back. Then she slowly straightened up rising inch by inch, arching her chest forward until she stood perfectly straight. Exhaling with a sigh, she pushed her back into the solid hardness of the cast iron post. The soothing warmth of the metal's heat immediately sent heavenly comfort to her muscles and into her slender bones, enjoying this welcomed bliss for several minutes, Lilli let out a long exhale.

Relaxing her shoulders, she thought, "Oh, my aching feet, my ankles, my sore toes. Why are all of these darn city streets made with so many lumpy, bumpy and rounded stones?" Her brows furrowed as she remembered their stories and promises. "Those men told us that these streets were paved with gold. I haven't seen any gold anywhere, just cobblestones like back home." Hoping for needed release she wiggled her toes which were squeezed tightly together in her shoes, immediately she felt the laces tightening more as the movement she craved was further constricted.

Badly wanting relief, for one brief moment she thought, I might just take them off. She desperately wanted to remove her shoes and for a brief second, she thought she would. Defiantly, she stated, I'm taking off my shoes, going to wiggle my toes in the air and rub my feet. I don't care. Quickly though, she heard her mother's voice in her head, "No, Lilli, absolutely not. Nobody ever removed clothing in public, not even shoes." So compliantly the shoes were kept on.

The afternoon summer sun was high in the cloudless blue sky and she felt the hot blaze of its heat penetrate through the light cotton material of her white blouse and black gored ankle length dirndl skirt. Being a professional seamstress and having a confident sense of style, Lilli knew the correct attire for each and every occasion. A light white blouse and full length long black skirt were the appropriate and perfect attire for a proper young lady whose day was going to be busy and full of shopping. Her parents had raised her well; Lilli was always a proper young lady.

As the crowds rushed by her, she protectively drew her packages even closer shielding herself and her bundles. Cautiously, she shifted, readjusting her precious parcels as she precariously moved even closer to the thin narrow edge that separated the sidewalk from the filthy gutters below. Suddenly, a whiff of the stench floating by flew up her nostrils causing her to gag as the foul smell permeated the air around her. Gasping she held her breath, as her hand flew up to cover her nose and mouth. Looking down she noted the stinking refuse, garbage and floating excrement in the gutters that were just beneath her. Quickly turning her head, she composed herself until she was confident that neither she nor her precious contents were in harm's way. No longer able to hold her breath in, she exhaled and breathing cautiously, slowly stretched her arms overhead as her legs tightly and protectively straddled her bags. To an observer she appeared to grow even taller as she drew her crown to the sky lifting and raising her chin slightly upward.

It felt good to stretch her body, she hadn't realized how tightly she had been holding herself and how sore her muscles had become. Flexing her hands open she spread her fingers as wide as possible. Just then a smile crossed her face as she remembered his words from long-ago and heard his voice as he watched her practice her lessons. Lilli had placed her hands on the piano keys spreading her long slender fingers as wide as she possibly could. "Lilli," he gasped, "Your fingers are so long, they are beautiful, I believe that you could play an octave." Lilli could play an octave, she loved music and was proud of her God given ability to play a piano. Thinking of her piano lessons she felt a relief spread over her body and a smile to her face. For one split second she lowered her eyelids closing them shut as she heard the beginning notes of Mozart's Piano Concerto play in her head. Shaking her head slowly from side to side, Lilli whispered, "I can't believe this; I can't believe how my life is changing again."

Lilli Von Holtzapfl was absolutely correct, all of these changes were hard to absorb but incredibly, life was changing again. For the last few years, it changed with the speed of a rapidly spinning kaleidoscope with each change being separate, distinct and unique. Lilli believed that her life mirrored this kaleidoscope because it had become increasingly clear that it was exactly these separate and unique changes alone that had become the only real constant for her.

Yet, it was this incredibly important and latest change that would truly change all of her tomorrows. Meeting the handsome, charming and shy young man, Walter Von Vetterlein, this one individual had changed everything. To Lilli it seemed like only yesterday, but it had been several months since she was introduced to Walter. Thoughts of her future husband, brought a sweet content smile to her lips, she knew that yet again change was happening. Enjoying this respite, she pushed herself back further pressing deeper into the solid strength and warmth of the streetlamp. Then slowly she turned her head from side to side as if in disbelief of all that was happening. Lifting her face, she looked up and raised her eyes, now moist, to the heavens above with a look of gratitude. The weight of her thick, curly, brown hair gently swept across her shoulder blades and back. This gentle sweeping motion brought a comforting wake where once pinching tension had been.

"I could relax here all-day." Lilli thought. Closing her eyes shut, her long, dark lashes tickled her cheeks and brought a sparkling panorama of visions to flash before her. Memories brought her back to that day, time, and place when she believed finally, everything would turn out all right.

Feeling a sense of calm and contentment flow through her bones a slow, shy Mona Lisa like smile, spread across her face, so much like her father's. Her keen dark brown eyes opened, they sparkled and twinkled brightly, those from her mother.

She looked out upon her world with a powerfully renewed hope, faith and a grateful heart.

Feeling this peaceful calm wash over her, she nodded her head and whispered, "This is all good, these are all good changes." Lilli was thankful because for a while it had seemed that so many of the changes in her young life had not been good. "Hopefully now life would be better." Optimistically, she assured herself, because it hadn't been just the changes; it was the speed of the changes that stunned her.

So much had happened since that autumn day in 1898 when she, Lilli Von Holzapfel, age 16, and her mother, Wilhelmine Von Holzapfel, age 34, left the only home they had ever known to come to America.

Courageously, they traveled across the continent of Europe by horse drawn cart and them by train, finally by boat they crossed the wide expanse of the Atlantic Ocean, with one goal in mind, to come to a new land, a new world and a new life.

Her mother had tearfully confided to her that she had tried, but since her father's death living in their home town had just become too painful, harder than she could ever have imagined.

Every place she went he was there; his touch was everywhere. His extraordinary skill and craftsmanship were evident on the buildings, the uniqueness of his designs, and the superb quality of his work. She could see what might have been his future, their future, all shouting his great artistry, talent and vision. Every time she looked up, at a spire, a rooftop, or a gable she felt her heart stop and a lump in her throat. Again, and again so many times she was reminded of his tragic death and of their irreplaceable loss. She saw him falling, she imagined him grabbing, reaching for help, for a hand, but none came and no matter where she looked, he was there and the pain she felt had become too much for her to bear.

During these times Wilhelmmine had heard talk of America, conversations were everywhere she went, no matter where she was. People were being told that in America there was opportunity, possibilities and a chance to begin a new life. Even though the promises seemed unbelievable, the stories appeared to ring with truth, everyone believed them. Wilhelmmine wondered, could it be possible. She asked herself," How can I begin again, when everything around me pulls me back?" It was Stuttgart, Germany, where Lilli and her mother had known the support of family, the comfort of friends, and the security of close neighbors. Yet, the aching pain of their loss was too much.

With Wilhelmmine's vision, courage and faith she and Lilli left their home. Leaving behind them the town where for many years their families had lived. They left where generations before them had been born, where Lilli's mother, father, aunts and uncles had been born. They left the village where her parents married, and where Lilli had been born and raised. They left where her cousins now lived and were raising their families.

Their family had roots, deep roots, thick, long and sinewy that spread like an old English Beech tree traveling far, wrapping, locking and intertwining. This was the place where Lilli was connected and grounded, where she felt safe and secure. She knew this place intimately, she called it home, a place so familiar, that when she walked down the unpaved country roads she knew the people who lived in each of the houses she passed and then again in the next house, she knew their families, and the families who had lived there before them.

In her hometown, Lilli, talkative by nature, loved to converse with those she met, often she was greeted by name, neighbors made inquiries asking about her mother, cousins, aunts and uncles and often her grandparents. Stuttgart, Germany, was the home she and Wilhelmine had left, leaving behind them security, comfort, shelter and safety. They left for an unknown future leaving every yesterday they had.

What they knew of America had come from stories and rumors heard from others. Men from America traveled to the local villages, drinking in the taverns, standing on the streets, and sitting in the shops, telling stories of plenty, of opportunity, and a land of promise. These men traveled from America to the homes of the villagers sharing a meal and telling tales of opportunities, of streets paved with gold, where there was no hunger and enough work for everyone. Their stories were weaved with drinks, laughter, and hearty slaps on the back, as they told of an amazing land of plenty. Their vivid tales engaged the hopes and dreams of all who heard, these were generous men, easily showing their largesse as they bought drinks and shared meals. They told of prosperity for everyone, large tracts of land for farms and even of cities named after their own beloved German Chancellor Otto Von Bismarck.

They spoke with such confidence describing how everything was bigger, better and more plentiful. These stories made it all seem true, real and possible. These weren't fabrications, why would they lie? They spoke of abundance, and prosperity, they promised it was all there for everyone.

Lilli straightened her long slender back, lifted her face and squared her shoulders, she looked up and spoke to the heavens above. This time she exclaimed out loud for her ears and for those of anyone else listening, "That was only three years ago." As if the heavens had not heard she repeated even louder, "Three years ago." Several people passing paused, some stopped, some stared though only briefly giving Lilli curious and quizzical looks then shrugging they continued on their own way. To them, she was a stranger, they didn't know her, they didn't know her family, they didn't know where she came from and they didn't want to become involved. Her family was not here, her history was not here, nor were her yesterdays, but her tomorrows had come.

The rays of the afternoon sun penetrated deeper into her skin sending warmth directly into her bones. She glanced from side to side quickly looking around at the crowded and bustling streets. Lilli relished this warmth from the far away sun as she thought how everything and everyone in life was really connected. She thought of how events and occurrences that may appear to be far from you can truly impact you and change your life without you even realizing it. Already at her young age she comprehended the importance to truly listen, to appreciate time and not take events or people for granted, to see clearly without judgment and to be open to life's possibilities.

Slowly, Lilli took everything in, the sounds of the street, its hustle and bustle, its diverse population, its promises and its lies. Everything it offered and everything it took back, all of it, wrapped around her. She watched as many, like herself, were rushing forward to their tomorrows, focused on where they were going, not looking back at where they had been, not seeing their present and maybe trying to forget their past.

Then her ears heard their voices, the voices of men, the loud and deep calls of the street vendors hawking their overflowing produce from their two wheeled push carts. Their bulky and awkward carts brimming full, smelling of fresh ripe tomatoes, onions, garlic, squashes, rutabagas, potatoes, carrots, parsnips, cabbages and many other types of fruits and vegetables, all squished and crowded together, one on top of the other. These carts offered a variety of vegetables, the kind which Lilli had never seen in her own home town. Each vendor strained to operatically raise his voice to shout over the others, as magically their voices blended together creating a symphony of accents and languages unlike anything heard anywhere else in the world.

As a sale was completed the sounds of tank you, grazie, a dank, danke, and merci would complete it. Then the chorus would begin anew, creating its' own crescendo and rising up again. Lilli began to gather her packages, then paused as she overheard a loud conversation between a pushcart vendor and his worker. He was shouting at a scrawny, dark-haired boy of no more than 13 years of age. The man was yelling, "Sean boy, c'mon now start ya shouting as loud as ya can. We gotta get rid of these damn tings before tonight." Lilli peeked around the corner to see a large push cart brimming full of extremely small round bright red berries. Staring at them she had no idea what they could possibly be, never had she seen the likes of these in Germany. She didn't know how they could be used as a food. She thought, "Humph, I'm certainly not going to buy any." The conversation became louder as the young boy asked,

"But sir, Mr. Quinn, sir, what are they? Tell me what it tis I am selling? What do I say?" Mr. Quinn, with apparent annoyance raised his voice louder screaming, "Damn it boy, whatsa' matta wit you? Look at them, they are little round red tings, can't you see it? C'mon, just shout out, little round red tings fer sale, little round red tings!" Plainly dismayed and holding back tears, his voice high pitched Sean, timidly yelled out as directed, "Come on, get your little round red tings, get them now, fresh, ripe round red tings." Lilli smiled as she wondered if anyone was about to buy some little round red tings for dinner tonight.

Standing there, she suddenly felt her ankles wobble as her feet pressed harder into the rounded cobblestones, she felt the vibrations before hearing the sounds. It was the quick and heavy rhythmic clip clop, clip, clop of horse drawn carriages as they came rapidly galloping down the cobblestoned streets. Then suddenly, she heard the chug, chug, chugging sound of a motor car as its wealthy inhabitants were being bumpily but genteelly chauffeured to their next destination. Listening to the sounds, she heard the grating of metal wheels on the tracks of the newly installed electric trolley cars as they carried passengers on the public transportation system from one end of the city to the other.

She knew that the people, the sounds, the smells, the old morphing and blending with the new, all of this mirrored her life; reflecting exactly how she felt. This city possessed an energy, excitement and promise that was uniquely American. Never before had she felt this sense of excitement and energy anywhere else, knowing that she wasn't separate from it, for her life too, had become part of it all.

Lilli thought, "Just like this city my world is spinning faster and faster. Excitedly she raised her voice, her eyes moistening with tears and this time unabashed she loudly exclaimed, "Here I am, living in Brooklyn, New York. I am living in one of the greatest cities in the world. I'm working as a seamstress, planning my wedding, its 1901, the beginning of a brand-new century and I, Lilli Von Holtzapfl, I am here in the United States of America."

But then as quickly as she had begun, she abruptly stopped closing her mouth tightly, aware that she really was attracting attention. This time people were beginning to turn, stop and stare at her with dubious curiosity. She definitely didn't want to attract attention from these strangers or make a scene. She didn't want to embarrass herself or her mother. "Oh gosh," she thought, "what would mother think? What would she say?" As thoughts of her mother came to her Lilli smiled, feeling a sensation of love and admiration fill her heart. Yes, Wilhelmine, her gentle, beautiful, kind mother, so determined, smart, loving, and very courageous.

Thoughts of Wilhelmmine brought Lilli back, causing her to pause. Inhaling deeply, she drew in a breath. A slight smile crossed her face as her memory traveled back to Germany, knowing that in reality, she never could have dreamt this, this American city could never have been a life that she envisioned. How could she when there were no roots to connect it to?

She wondered, how did this all happen? I know how I got here, sure by that slow moving, foul smelling and crowded boat, but how did it really come to be? When did this plan get put into place, when did those first steps begin, when did living in America become my reality? This Lilli pondered as the events of the last few years rapidly blended into each other like the bright colors of a changing kaleidoscope they rushed through her mind.

Relaxing her shoulders, she dropped her arms to her sides, her hands opened widely. She stretched, extending her long fingers allowing her palms to turn outward facing upwards as if beseechingly to the heavens. "Yes, that octave." She thought and smiled. In whispered tones she asked "How did all of this happen. How did it happen so quickly? Is this how it is here in America? Everything just keeps moving. Nothing stops, nothing slows down, everything just keeps moving forward."

Everything did seem to be moving forward and as Lilli stood on this busy cobblestoned street, she heard the vibrant cacophony of the sounds of life itself. The noisy rhythmic clattering of streetcars, the symphony of accents, the shouting of vendors, the high pitched crescendo of mother's calling their children's name and of the children shouting back. All of this in languages so very different and yet the words all sending the same messages of hopes, dreams and promise.

Preparing to leave she was again jostled and bumped by crowds hurrying to work, by women carrying babies and holding children's hands protectively as they rushed to their destinations. Hearing yells and the sounds of a commotion Lilli moved quickly to avoid being stampeded as gangs of running children ran past her. They appeared to be of all ages, shapes, and sizes, all running at top speed, helter skelter, uninterrupted and unchaperoned through the city's streets.

It was apparent they had no regards for anyone as they swiftly maneuvered through the crowd pushing and shoving everything and everyone in their path. Their clothes were ragged, their bodies filthy, and their faces gaunt, they seemed to come from nowhere and to be going nowhere. Lilli was struck by their squalid appearance and the gaunt hungry looks of their faces. She noticed that they didn't look at you directly, just their eyes darted from left to right as their bodies shifted and swerved. These children were too much to take in, and Lilli felt an ache in the pit of her stomach for them. Like a mother protecting her own she pulled her bundles closer moving them out of the way. For several seconds she stood frozen, not able to stop watching, as she found her eyes following them until they ran out of sight and their pounding footsteps could no longer be heard.

Blinking her eyes Lilli glanced around as if it all was new to her, she noticed the sundry and various businesses tightly lined up like soldiers in a row, shoulder to shoulder, side by side. They stood supporting, holding each other up, all connected one next to the other along the crowded street like dominoes; if one fell, they would all collapse, if one caught fire, they would all burn.

She looked at the rooftops of the factories which dotted this ever-expanding city. She noted one factory in particular, remembering that once she and her mother thought about looking for work there. Now she knows of so many young women, newly arrived immigrants like herself, who had taken jobs at that very factory. "What is that place called? "She pondered, "Oh yes, it's that really big factory, the one called Triangle Shirtwaist, something or other." She wondered if maybe Mother and she should apply there but rumors were that the girls were chained to their machines and exit doors were locked. That can't be true, she thought, besides, I really do love working at Emma's Dress Shop.

Moving on, she glimpsed another very large brick building advertising a shop for men's dress shirts, the sign on the front proudly stated the owner as a Herbert Cole and another bigger sign indicated that his shirts sold for $1.00. Hmmm, Lilli thought that's quite pricey, but at that price they must be really nice shirts. She knows how often value represented the quality of an item. She remembered the lessons her mother and father had taught her that sometimes when you pay more, you are actually saving money. Thinking of this lesson she smiled, appreciating so much all the lessons of life they taught her.

She heard the push cart vendors hard at work selling their wares. Then Lilli's ears picked up as she heard different voices emerge, younger and higher voices than those of the vendors, she recognized their call, their anthem, "Extra, Extra, read all about it. Hot off the presses!"

It was the shouts and yells of the gangs of newspaper boys. These boys often slept in alleys and under stairwells or were crowded together in tenements with orphans and homeless urchins. Sometimes if lucky and available they shared floor space with larger combined families, but most often they were cramped together in filthy flats and damp basements. Together they lived, worked and competed against each other every day. Trying to earn a living, they hawked their daily papers, purchased with their own hard-earned pennies, as they protectively staked their claims to their precious turf, their own jealously guarded spot on these their coveted corners. These boys yelled, hollered, and shouted over each other, trying desperately to raise their voice above the next, as they called out loudly to compete and attract attention.

Desperately, they hoped to sell their newspapers before the next boy did. Their daily survival and often their families depended on them. As their calls rang out, they frantically looked around. Searching, they knew exactly who they wanted to see, their customers and upon seeing them, they possessively called out; sometimes even calling out to known customers by name.

Taking this all in, she suddenly heard the strong lilting accent of a Celtic brogue. It was from a young boy as he recognized a fellow country man, "Mr. O'Malley, halloo there Mr. O'Malley over here, sir, it's me sir, its Kevin, Kevin Moran sir, yes Kevin, County Mayo, County Mayo sir." he repeated, "Sir, Mr. O'Malley, remember me? Hallooo, I've got ya paper sir, yer news sir. Got it here fer ya, sir. It's the latest news. Right here fer ya. It's hot off the presses fer ya. Been holdin' onto it fer ya sir."

Enjoying and taking this in Lilli stopped to watch as Kevin, a handsome lad with thick dark curly hair and a strong muscular build cheerfully beckoned to his customer, a regular as they say. Hearing the familiar lilt of his countryman's voice, Mr. O'Malley quickly turned, and looking around he flashed a broad friendly grin, his step quickened as he waved and shouted back with the same lilt lifting his voice. "Hey, halloo there lad." Quickly approaching the boy, he happily purchased his paper, while offering a tip of the hat. Then before departing, his smile broadened and his eyes twinkled, as he shoved his free hand even deeper into his coat pocket and leaned into Kevin, offering the lad an extra coin along with a friendly brisk pat on the back. Then he shouted, "See ya tomorrow lad." as he waved his paper in the air and bid good bye, turning briskly, he walked away.

Standing there Kevin smiled at the back of his regular, tapped the brim of his Scally cap and quickly shouted "Tank you, Mr. O'Malley, tank you sir. Oh yes, right here, see you tomorrow sir." His dark blue eyes sparkled with delight while his free left hand protectively patted the outside of his pocket as he quickly turned to look for his next countryman.

As Lilli watched she noticed how young and painfully thin many of the boys were. But there was one boy in particular who caught her eye, she paused to look his way. She had noticed this one particular boy was standing at a distance a little farther away from the others. She noticed that he raised his voice a bit louder stretching his arm to hold his papers up a bit higher with one hand while his other hand cradled a crutch tightly under his arm. He had a crutch because he was standing on his one and only leg. Lilli suddenly realized, he had only one leg and yet he too was trying his best to make it in this new country.

Awed by this boy's courage and filled with compassion, she knows that nothing would stop this young man; telling herself that this was the land of opportunity no matter where you came from, who you were, or what had happened to you.

With empathy welling inside her, Lilli lifted her chin, and reached into her pocketbook for change. Grabbing her bundles in her arms, she quickly lifted them up. Not taking her eyes off this young man she walked over to him. He noticed her approaching and offered her a guarded one-sided smile as she spoke softly to him saying, "I'll have one of your papers, bitte."

Extending her coins, she thanked him, consciously pronouncing each word clearly and precisely using her newly learnt English words, "Thank you," instead of her native "danke." But still she noticed that her English words were strong with her natural German accent.

The boy, dropping his eyes downcast, politely bowed his head slightly forward unable to tip his hat as he stammered and replied in his native tongue, "Gr, gr, grazie, grazie." She noticed too that the brown Scally cap he was wearing like many of the other boys was worn and soiled and that his voice stuttered then faltered, thick with an accent from a faraway land unlike hers but still an accent.

Beginning to leave, Lilli paused then turned back to face this young man again. Looking directly at him she asked, "What is your name?" Hearing her question, he slowly raised his head up. Lifting his eyes, he looked directly into hers, and replied, clearly and distinctly, "Francisco, signorina, Francisco." Leaning in towards him slightly, Lilli replied, "Thank you, Francisco." As she turned towards home, she assured herself, that Francisco would be fine, as she nodded her head affirmatively.

Lilli looked down both sides of Atlantic Avenue, she saw shops owned and run by the families who lived right inside them. This was so similar to her home in Stuttgart but also in many ways, very different. In Stuttgart all of the lettering and advertising was in German, Lilli's native tongue. In Stuttgart many of the shops had been owned by one family for many years, maybe generations but here the shops were owned for the very first time by new owners, new Americans. Many of the signs and letters were in different languages too, some German, some Italian, some Polish or Yiddish, and English. But some of the letters were actually different looking altogether, apparently from a different alphabet. Lilli remembered that in Germany the language was the same for all of the shops, not so in this American city, she thought.

Tilting her head back and looking straight up, Lilli's gaze shifted from side to side as she took in the crowded brick and wooden tenements which lined each side of the street. She noticed how the wrought iron fire escapes which resembled a large letter Z, crisscrossed from one side of the building to the other all the way down the fronts of each building and how each stairway stopped approximately twelve feet above the sidewalk. Drawing in a breath she thought that was still an awful drop to the ground.

Then she leaned further back to look up at the clothes lines which were strung from one building to the next. These lines, many on pulleys, drooped precariously as each line was full with the garments worn day after day. Each item draped over or hung onto the line secured with clips or pins, strung across the ropes from one building to the next.

She noticed that these clothes too resembled the brick and wood buildings that were squeezed tightly one next to the other. These ropes were covered with shifts, bloomers, nightshirts, diapers, infants' clothes along with blankets and sheets.

Lilli thought that like the clothes lines the people too were crammed full into these tenements, families, sometimes more than one generation often two or even three generations living together, trying to carve out their daily existence, as they tried to make a new home in their new country.

It took blind faith strong enough to believe when there was no proof to believe, packing up only what could be carried in their two hands. It took hope that their future would be better as they left the known and traveled to the unknown. Leaving pieces of their lives, dropped and scattered in towns and villages all over Europe, never to be retrieved again. Leaving everything, just as Lilli and Wilhelmine did, they left everything behind and moved with faith, courage and hope to the American promise.

"I know," Lilli thought," It takes more than a dream, it takes a profound faith and a resolute courage to leave everything you know for a future you cannot even imagine to come to this new country."

The future for Lilli and Wilhelmine was Brooklyn, New York, this was where they now called home. Lilli wondered, "Is it here where we will always live? Is this where I will raise my children?"

Understanding that all of these differences were becoming her new reality, she took it all in; she listened to the symphonic sounds of the different voices, accents, languages. She inhaled the sweet, the strong, the odorous and the bitter scents of the people and their foods. She felt the energy of this moment, time, and place, everything it offered, all of it in this very different, amazing country. Softly closing her eyes, her lips moved as she quietly uttered a heartfelt prayer to God, "Dear God, please look down upon us, protect us with your love, keep us safe, as you guide us. Be with us always providing strength and courage no matter what faces us tomorrow.

Amen." Blinking her eyes open she inhaled deeply knowing that these sounds, noises, and smells were the heartbeat, pulse, and breath of this busy, thriving American city. Lilli breathed it all in as she drew its vibrant energy into every pore in her body.

The sun had moved behind the buildings, no longer shining directly down on Lilli. Seeing the shadows, she sensed the passing of time, and felt a coolness where only moments before there had been sunshine and warmth. Knowing that she must get home, she headed in that direction. Shifting and adjusting her packages, she walked briskly as she heard the loud clattering sounds of horses' hoofs on the cobblestones. This sound brought a different kind of chill down her spine as it triggered a frightening memory from long ago. Shaking it off Lilli assured herself that she was fine, there was nothing to worry about. Then suddenly she felt a slight mist of spraying water, that quickly brought her memory back from the past to the present, she knows now what is coming. Ducking into the first doorway she saw, a smile crossed her face. Protected on the steps and peeking out from behind the door jamb she spied one of the city's many street cleaning carts drawn by horses. Its hoses spraying water in all directions, drenching sidewalks and pedestrians alike regardless of whatever was in front of them. Moving like a leviathan the strength and power of its hoses attempted to spray clean the filthy streets and sidewalks of Atlantic Ave. Lilli watched as it moved deliberately, slowly and purposely from one street and on to the next. "Yes, moving on to your next victims." she thought. Chuckling and noticing that some others were not so quick, Lilli was pleased that this time she was fast enough not be sprayed by one of those huge hoses. As she left her protective doorway she thought, "I'll bathe in private if you please."

Her pace quickened as jumbled memories of her life passed before her. Juggling the packages, she was relieved to know how close she was to home. Even as both her thoughts and strides rushed Lilli forward, she couldn't help hesitating to catch her breath and enjoy each beautiful memory knowing these were events and times she would always remember and cherish.

"Your beliefs become your thoughts, your thoughts become your words, your words become your actions, your actions become your habits, your habits become your values; your values become your destiny." - Mahatma Gandhi

2

LESSONS

As she approached her home, a third floor flat on Atlantic Ave. Lilli saw her mother, Wilhelmine, outside on her hands and knees bending over their front stoop. A smile crossed Lilli's face, and her pace slowed as in a trance she watched. Her mother's long sleeves were pushed and rolled up to her elbows, her curly dark hair was pinned back from her face. Lilli gazed at her mother as Wilhelmmine first swept and then scrubbed the stone steps of their home with soapy water. Then satisfied she bent forward and wiped dry each of the several steps on their stoop until they all sparkled like new.

Standing there, Lilli was transported to a moment in her childhood she was back home in Stuttgart; she was 8 years old. This was the time when her mother taught her this exact chore. It all came back so quickly, as she remembered that day, for it was much more than a mere memory, she remembered how the event felt and she remembered how she had felt.

Much like today the sun shone brightly in the clear blue sky. She heard her mother's voice calling her to come out onto their front stoop, "Bitte, Lilli, Lilli komm hier." As Lilli approached her mother explained, "Lilli your father and I believe that it is time for you to begin to do chores. This is your first lesson, so every Saturday morning you will do this chore rain or shine." Lilli asked, "I am only 8 years old; how can I do this chore?" But her mother persisted, "Oh Lilli, you will and you can, now, listen carefully and watch as I teach you. First, you will need to get your supplies, a broom, and a small shovel. Also, a bucket filled with hot water, a dry rag, a scrubbing brush, and soap. Then you will start at the top of the stoop. First you sweep from left to right making certain to get into the crevices and corners of each stoop before you go down to your next one. Only then do you step down with your broom using the same approach for each stair until you are at the bottom of the flight. When you have swept all of the dirt to the ground below you then sweep the dirt into a pile and using your small shovel you collect the dirt and throw it in a barrel out back."

Lilli's eyes were wide as she listened and watched while this new task was explained. Her mother turned to her and said; "Now it is your turn." Lilli tried to sweep as her mother had shown, but her arms were small and the broom handle was unwieldy and long. Lilli struggled — it was difficult to move it easily on the stairs. Wilhelmine stood back watching as her daughter wrestling with the long-handled broom tried to learn this new chore. Her arms folded across her chest she smiled and nodded knowing that soon this would be as easy for Lilli as it was for her, but right at that moment Lilli was challenged. After several minutes watching, Wilhelmine slowly walked over to her daughter. She stood behind her and wrapped her arms around her daughter's shoulders. She placed her larger hands over Lilli's smaller ones. "Now meine Liebchen, let me guide you." Feeling her mother's warmth and inhaling her scent Lilli leaned back into her mother's bosom, her eyelids lowered, she felt loved and safe. Exhaling deeply, Lilli smiled as Wilhelmine with her longer fingers and wider hands gently covered the smaller ones. In unison together they moved, and guided the long handle of the broom. Within no time they were working in tandem as Wilhelmine and Lilli swept their front stoop together.

Lilli felt as if they were dancing and after a while, with patience, guidance and lots of laughter Lilli began to understand how to complete step one of her new task. Then smiling at her daughter Lilli's mother told her, "Now here is the real fun part, again you start at the top of the stairs. Take this scrubbing brush, dip it deeply into your bucket of hot soapy water, and swish it around. First you scrub across the top step, then the second and so on, until you get to the bottom of the stairs. Now Lilli, this is the grand finale as they say, meine Liebchen. Taking your rag, you begin at the bottom and now go up the stairs wiping each stair dry. When you reach the landing at the top stair, you know you are done. You have finished your chores for the day. Now, I will share with you a very special secret, Lilli, turn around and look at your work. See how shiny these stairs look. See how clean they are and how they make your home, our home sparkle and shine. You know they are sparkling because of you, because of what you have just done, this is your work." Lilli remembered looking and seeing the approval on her mother's smiling face but she still needed more assurance. With eyes wide with hope, she asked imploringly in her soft childlike voice, "Did I do good, mommy? Did I do good?"" Yes Liebchen", her mother's voice softly cooed, "You did real good, you've done a very good job."

Many years later those words filled her memory, as Lilli remembered exactly how that moment felt. She had been a child, yet she remembered how it felt to do a good job, to be proud of her work and to be appreciated for her efforts. From that moment on Lilli was aware of the power of words and of your surroundings. She understood that often a person's fate was impacted simply by how one was taught and how one lived. She remembered how grown up it felt to learn this new chore. She believed that she was helping out in the family and she felt pride in doing a job well done.

But most importantly she remembered her mother's smile, the gentle laughter of her soft voice as she taught and guided, teaching this chore. But it wasn't the task she remembered; it was the feelings of that moment. She felt safe, eager and confident in her newly developed skill. She knew that learning this task was important to her and her parents. She even felt a little grown up, taking pride in knowing that her efforts too were appreciated. She knew that her mother cared, was concerned and interested in teaching her. She knew now that it was through her mother's loving guidance that she learned, grew and became the woman she was today.

Lilli was grateful knowing that this scheduled chore brought from their homeland was completed by the tenants living in their apartment building. Lilli reminisced how it seemed like only yesterday that she had learned this chore in

Germany. But now it was yesterday that she was completing this exact process in America. To be responsible and do your chores was an expectation that always happened in the old country and one that was brought here to America. In Lilli's head her mother's words rang out, "Lilli, this is our home, no matter how little money we have, soap and water are not expensive nor an extravagance. "

Smiling Lilli approached her mother calling out to her in their native tongue, "Mutter, mutter." Hearing her daughter's voice and that familiar word Wilhelmine turned, her face beamed as she smiled and replied, "Liebchen, mein Lilli." As Lilli approached Wilhelmine dropped the scrub brush into the hot soapy water and picked up her bucket, "Just in time, I am finished." she said, as she wrapped her free arm around Lilli's waist. Lilli shifted the bundles in her arms, and together they entered their home.

Climbing the stairs Lilli noticed how spotlessly clean and shiny everything appeared, the neat and clean vestibule at the entry and in the hallway as it opened into the apartments. She felt the coolness, the peacefulness and the calm that it immediately invoked. She inhaled the aroma of the polished wood as it sent out its rich, comforting, aromatic scent. She became aware of a sense of calmness, cleanliness and order so strikingly apparent because of the stark difference to the hot, busy, chaotic world she had just left outside.

Their apartment was small, but sparkled with neatness and cleanliness. There were only three rooms, a small kitchen area, a sitting area and the bedroom they shared. This orderliness was not only pleasing to the eye but comforting to the soul. As Lilli and Wilhelmine entered their cozy home they smiled at each other. Exhaling, they relaxed looking forward to the time they now would share together. Placing her hand on Lilli's arm Wilhelmmine told her, "Now Lilli, I will put on the water for our pot of tea and you will show me all that you have bought."

Neither Lilli nor her mother could have dreamt, the type of challenges and changes they would encountered in this new world. Yet, there was strength in Lilli; you could see it in her eyes and how she held herself. It was not bold or pretentious but a resolute courage infused in her genes, nurtured in childhood and modeled by her parents. As Lilli was growing, she learnt by watching and listening. It was through the daily actions and words of her family that she understood she was loved, protected and wanted. As she listened to her parents, they in turn listened to her.

Often in the evenings Lilli would snuggle onto her father's lap, lighting his pipe he would share his projects with her, the challenges he encountered and the problems he resolved. She grew up hearing his sage advice, "Lilli, when you come to an obstacle, don't let it stop you. Consider it an opportunity to learn, to be creative, or to find an alternative solution. Sometimes Lilli, what at first sight appeared to be a problem turned out to be an opportunity."

Then he would go on telling her, "That is what I always try do when confronted with a problem or even an apprentice who was having difficulties. "He proudly confided to Lilli that when a project was completed, he would inspect every corner, every frame and every bit of delicately carved trim for perfection. When satisfied he would take out his sharpest blade, ascend the stairs to the rooftop, and at the highest peak of the building he would meticulously carve his initials deeply into the wood. WFH, inscribed there forever, leaving a little bit of himself at every finished job. He told her that someday people would find his initials, recognize his work and remember he had been there. Remembering her father's secret Lilli too, would find a small corner or a narrow seam in the material of a completed project and delicately embroider her initials LAH.

She held onto those words from her father forever, hearing his comforting voice in her heart and his advice in her head. He taught her to believe in herself and for this she was forever grateful. In the past it was her parents who represented the team; they were a united front raising their daughter. Too soon Lilli thought as she closed her eyes and drew in a heavy breath, too soon, he was gone. So instead of the three of them it was now the two of them, Lilli and her mother. Lilli expected that she would have obstacles and challenges; she was prepared for them; she would not retreat or even give up. She would always remember her father's advice, keep on trying.

For Lilli there was comfort in knowing that her mother would be there for her and knowing that she would be there for her mother. Lilli certainly understood that life could be hard, that they would face sorrow and struggles. Already, she had been tempered, her heart had been broken and her spirit had been crushed. Yet, she had faith that the only answer was to believe in your own ability to survive, to keep striving towards your dream. She knew that she was stronger because of what she had already endured and survived.

Lilli was naturally optimistic and planned to stay that way, it was in her blood. Her mother was always strong even after losing infants during pregnancy, losing children at birth and losing Willi her husband, from an apparent accident at work. Her mother remained resolute and refused to succumb to self-pity or despair. This was the example Lilli saw growing up; this was her model for life. Wasn't it her mother's strength and courage that Lilli depended on when she had none herself?

Lilli's thoughts race back to that one night, back in Stuttgart as she and her mother sat before the kitchen fire, her mother reaching out to cover Lilli's hand with her's saying, "Lilli we will begin again. There are too many memories here, it is too hard. We will start a new life together in America. I know we can do it and I know you can do it with me." Lilli and Wilhelmmine had heard the stories of opportunity in the new world, of the right to determine your own future, to purchase property and decide the direction for your life, and not have it mandated for you. Lilli swallowed back the lump forming in her throat, inhaled a deep breath and thought, "This is America, anything is possible, we'll be fine." Then placing the heavy packages on the floor in front of the kitchen table, she watched her mother as she struck a match to light the gas and bring the water to a boil. Turning to the packages, Lilli asked, "Mutter, did you make any of that sweet dessert from the mold we received when we first arrived? I love its sweet sugary taste as it melts in your mouth." Wilhelmmine nodded yes, quickly opening her ice box to remove the smooth dessert. With dishes and spoons in front of them they began carefully and gently to remove the contents of Lilli's heavy bundles. Watching her mother's expression at everything she had purchased, Lilli smiled confessing, "I just have to purchase a couple more finishing pieces, but most everything is here." Wilhelmmine nodded as her eyes moistened seeing the contents of Battenberg lace, cream colored silks, yards of organza, flowing tulle, and Brussels lace being removed from the bags. Finally, reaching down to the bottom of the last bag Lilli pulled out hooks, eyes and fasteners as the once heavy bags laid empty, scattered and strewn like fallen leaves across the polished kitchen floor.

"Whether we are Christian or Buddhist or Jewish or Muslim or of any other faith tradition, if we are truly a part of one another's breath, then we can breathe into a deeper, wider, welcoming universe in which everyone belongs and everyone is beautiful."
- Patricia Adams Farmer

3

DIFFERENCES

*L*illi was a believer, she believed that without a doubt there was no other place like America. It was that belief along with the hopes and dreams that inspired so many to come to America to build the kind of life they could not imagine anywhere else. With a fervent belief in the possibility of America's amazing story, strength was garnered and courage was found to make it a reality. Lili knew it wasn't guaranteed but it was promised, and the dream had a name it was called the American Dream.

Lilli hoped that she would meet a special someone, just like her mother did. Fall in love, like her mother did, get married and have a family, like her mother did. Maybe more children than her mother had, big families seemed to be the trend and since Lilli was an only child, she knew that there were times when it had been lonesome.

Before Lilli and Wilhelmine arrived in New York, already many people from their mother country, had fled to America like so many others from all over Europe and the British Isles. They fled following revolts and uprisings in their towns and villages, after deadly famines, or to escape religious persecution in their homelands. Many young men came to avoid being conscripted and forced to fight in continuous and horrific European wars. In America was the promise of freedom from economic hardships, religious persecution and continuous battles.

Everyone heard the stories that in America there was no hierarchy or an aristocratic class predetermining the ceiling for individual aspirations. It didn't matter how wealthy your ancestors had been or what titles they carried, here you were judged on your own merits, there was no aristocracy, everyone was equal under the law. In America it didn't matter if you worshipped on Saturday or Sunday or if you didn't worship at all.

This was the story that so many had heard in their villages. They heard it in the taverns, on the streets and in their homes. The message was loud and clear not only from Americans themselves but from letters sent from relatives, friends and neighbors who had gone before them. It was that encouragement proving potent enough to convince so many hopeful people just like Lilli and Wilhelmmine to cross the seas in search of new beginnings. In America they believed that anything was possible. "And it is, yes, it is." Lilli told herself.

With determination and courage Lilli and Wilhelmmine packed their boxes cramming them as full as possible leaving for this new country. But they brought more than their possessions to America, they brought a can- do attitude. With intense effort, they assimilated into their new American life quickly looking for gainful employment.

Talking with others they heard of the limited choices for women, whether working in a large factory with seamstresses lined up next to each other row upon row as they had heard about or look for employment in a smaller seamstress shop.

Wilhelmmine believed that they could have their own shop someday, as she told Lilli, "We had a following in Stuttgart maybe we can build one here too. We can start in a local shop and then decide our next steps." They were hopeful that they would find just the right place, but first they needed to get started.

They started out, walking down Atlantic Avenue and saw the roofline of a large factory where many other seamstresses worked. Lilli wondered if maybe this would be the best beginning. Just as she was about to mention it to her mother, they turned a corner and noticed a small dress shop, the entryway tucked cozily in a brick building. Its appearance was more European in style, it felt familiar and welcoming, there was something reminiscent about its feel. Lilli mentioned to her mother how it reminded her of a shop where they had once worked back home.

Simultaneously, they stopped at the entry way and with a nod to each other Wilhelmmine knocked gently. Then slowly feeling as if she was stepping back in time, Wilhelmmine turned the doorknob. As the door opened a bell rang softly, and compared to the brightness outside the inside of the room seemed very dark. It took several seconds for their eyes to adjust and focus before they saw an older woman sitting towards the back of the room.

Sitting at a high table on a tall stool, she looked up with curiosity at the two neatly dressed and attractive women who had just entered her shop. She wasn't sure if they would be customers or not. Wilhelmmine noticed that this woman's gaze was both discerning and welcoming. Carefully placing her work on the table, the owner, Emma Shapiro, quickly stepped off the stool, and walked over to Lilli and her mother. As she approached them, Wilhelmmine began, in broken English, to introduce herself and her daughter. Emma looked directly at them, nodding, as a slight smile crossed her lips. All of a sudden, Wilhelmmine felt a sense of calmness come over her, all of the outside noises disappeared. She knew immediately that they had found the perfect place.

With her keen eye and deep insight Emma felt that too.

She listened intently as together they told their story. Many times, Lilli would interject interrupting her mother to add information and even a humorous anecdote. At those moments, Wilhelmmine would smile and wait for her daughter to finish before going on. She knew that Lilli felt the need to add more details and intimate information of their journey and their life in Stuttgart. After several minutes of conversation Wilhelmmine gently placed her hand on Lilli's arm as she looked towards Emma and said, "My daughter, she loves to talk, hasn't stopped since she was a baby." Smiling, Emma replied, "And when she does, you should worry." Wilhelmmine understood how true those words rang, for memories quickly came to her of the time when Lilli's voice was silent. At that moment, Lilli looked at her mother, her smile radiant, she knew too that this was the perfect place. Emma liked them both and asked them, her voice thick with an eastern European accent, "So tell me, do you want to work here?" immediately offering them the employment they sought, she knew that she had found a perfect team. Responding simultaneously, they said, "Yes, we want to." Sliding off of her stool to gather the necessary paperwork, Emma turned as she nodded her head, replying in sotto voce, "Want is good."

Lilli and Wilhelmmine were hired and the following day they began working as professional seamstresses at Emma's Dress Shoppe, a local, dressmaking shop on Atlantic Ave with a coveted clientele of very well-heeled women. They never did make it to that large building with bolted doors, locked floors and women chained to their sewing machines from dawn to dark.

Emma was a solidly built middle aged woman. She had a quick smile and sharp deep blue eyes which shone with compassion as she spoke. Lilli and Wilhelmine quickly learned that Emma owned and managed the shop with Saul her husband. The couple had escaped from Eastern Europe, arriving in the early 1890's. Unlike Lilli and Wilhelmmine who left their home for a better life, Emma and Saul fled their home in Russia to save their lives. "It was the pogroms." Emma told them," Savage and violent pogroms against people of my faith. God forbid, you even try to imagine the vicious, cruel and unrelenting attacks backed by my own government." Emma described nights of horror when the Cossacks would stealthily attack villages where those of the Jewish faith lived. People would awaken to screams and cries of horror. Her body visibly shivered as she spoke of babies being slaughtered; children massacred en masse; homes consumed in fire as the heart wrenching screams of the inhabitants filled the air. Whole families murdered in their sleep. Emma's heart beat faster and her breath became shallow, her memory became vivid as it brought it all back to life. Speaking of these events, she relived every frightening and terrifying moment. The horror and circumstances were unimaginable to Lilli and Wilhelmmine. They listened holding each other's hands; their mouths open, and their hearts beating faster as they tried to breathe. When Emma finished her eyes were filled with tears, she cried for what they once had, for who they had lost and for what would never be again. A solemn shroud of silence filled the space broken only by the sound of quiet weeping. Emma had never spoken of these atrocities to anyone but only to Lilli and Wilhelmmine. For her it seemed a catharsis, that was the past, this would never happen in America she thought.

Emma and Saul came to America to practice their faith in peace and because they were Jewish, their shop would be closed before sunset on Friday and all day on Saturday to celebrate their Sabbath. The three women's friendship developed quickly and after a while Lilli or Wilhelmine would leave the shop early on Friday helping to prepare Emma's home for Shabbat by lighting candles and cooking the evening meal of Challah, roast chicken and sometimes chicken soup. Then the shop would be closed on Saturday until sunset opening for 4 hours allowing the women to catch up on any leftover work and then again it was closed on Sunday to offer Lilli and Wilhelmmine time to attend their religious services too.

Lilli and Wilhelmine enjoyed this arrangement for it allowed them an extra day to enjoy their own Sabbath. After weekends spent honoring and celebrating their faiths the shop would open early and promptly on Monday morning, the workday beginning at 7 a.m. and ending at 6 p.m.

Even though the hours were long and the work laborious, neither Lilli nor her mother complained. They enjoyed working together delighting in each other's company and relished working for Emma. They were also glad that as the shop became more popular, Emma hired other young women not only from Germany but other European countries. They became a diverse group of women, representing all ages, with much in common; yet they had their differences.

Sitting together around the large work table they shared scissors, pin cushions, needles and spools of thread as well as their stories. In the background there was always a soft humming or click, click, clicking as the sewing machines created a gentle repetitive sound muffling the noise from outside. The women worked easily together teaching each other lessons and skills brought from lands far away. Emma always supervised walking around offering guidance and assistance where needed. Sometimes she would spend a longer time with an employee who was having difficulty but no one minded, they knew she would assist them too. They waited patiently for her guidance or choosing to asked assistance from another. Without hesitation guidance was offered as sometimes many hands stitched the threads into delicate silks, heavy brocades and tulle fabrics. Frequently strong friendships developed even before the stitches were completed. As each piece was completed the women would present their finished work to appreciative exclamations of oohs and ahhs around the table.

Each one of them took pride in the quality of their own

work and in each other's expertise, as together they created beautiful wedding dresses, exquisite silk blouses, flattering evening skirts and warm heavy coats for their wealthy clientele. Emma's shop developed a reputation, respected by her peers, while clientele would boast that a particular item they wore had been designed and created exclusively for them at Emma's.

As they worked on their projects conversations around the table would begin. Telling stories of the old countries, speaking of the families that traveled with them and of the families that were left behind. It seemed that each story was filled with vision, and courage. They told of tearful departures, and of frightening dangerous journeys that had been taken to come to America.

Even though each woman's story was unique and personal, many times their stories sounded familiar. In spite of their apparent differences they found it helpful and comforting to hear that in reality they shared so much. In the beginning their stories were told in their native tongues, with interpretations that often-provoked outbursts of laughter and giggles, but as the days and weeks went by the stories became peppered with English words. Again, laughter would ensue as the women nodded and smiled at one another's efforts to sound more American. As time went on more and more English words replaced the German, Greek, Polish, Gaelic, Yiddish and Italian languages.

It seemed to happen without anyone noticing, but before long their stories began to change less about where they had been as they shared hopes and dreams of the future. Their conversations became more personal, sometimes even more intimate. Eventually no topic was off limits, as giggles and blushes spread around the table. Often Emma and Wilhelmmine would not respond but simply raise an eyebrow or glance at each other with a knowing nod and smile. As the late afternoon sun shone through the clear glass windows, they felt cocooned encircled in a warm glow as they worked together. Over time coworkers became friends and then friends became family. Slowly their conversations began to focus more on their tomorrows with less time devoted to their yesterdays. As they spent more time working alongside one another obvious differences faded in favor of blended similarities brought on by shared circumstances and a shared new language. Slowly, stitch by stitch, they were becoming Americans.

The women of Emma's shop fell into a pleasing and familiar routine. Their lives were becoming less stressful at times even easier, and they were adjusting to their full demanding workdays, while looking forward to their restful nights. There was a palpable feeling of contentment among them. A passerby looking in would see smiles and hear laughter as the work never stopped.

Lilli and her mother began thinking that maybe someday they could open a shop of their own. Wilhelmine told Lilli, "If Emma could do it so can we. Your father ran his own business and I helped him so opening our own business is not out of the realm of possibilities. We can do it." Many of their neighbors owned their own shops and stores, "Yes." Lilli thought, "Opening our own shop is a possibility!" Lilli thought it made sense. She asked, "Wasn't this the reason for coming to America, to carve out our own destiny? To Lilli and Wilhelmmine, it seemed as this was how their lives would be, the two of them working and living together. They began to spend their nights in discussions of the obstacles they might encounter and how they could make their dream a reality.

As time went on their days took on a familiar rhythm, their schedule was manageable, and life seemed to be calming down, settling into a comfortable routine. So, it was until, like the turn of a kaleidoscope, everything changed.

It was an ordinary Sunday in the month of May, the early spring warmth comforting, as it whispered hints of the coming summer's delights. The sweet aromatic perfume of blossoming Viburnum trees permeated the air. Finally, at last, winter's cold and snow had melted away as it quickly became a distant memory.

For Lilli it began as a typical Sunday morning, as was their practice Lilli and her mother attended the Lutheran Church services. Both Lilli and Wilhelmmine had volunteered to assist at the annual church picnic following the services. Lilli always remembered how the warmth of that day seemed a gift from the bitterly cold winter that had preceded it.

Walter's favorite younger cousin Henry Schonfeld invited him to attend his church's annual picnic, for a second time, Walter had declined the previous year. Although Walter had been raised in a very large family, he was shy and not a big fan of crowds. He found that he usually kept to himself. However, for some reason even he did not understand, this time he accepted his cousin's invitation.

Henry's own large family the Von Schonfeld's had been attending The Evangelical Lutheran St. John's Church in Brooklyn since they first arrived from Stuttgart several years before. In his letters home to Walter and in their shared conversations Henry enthusiastically mentioned this church, naming the families who attended and the many activities offered hoping to entice his cousin's interest.

Meeting new people and embarking on new adventures was something Henry relished and loved to do. He also loved to share his adventures and escapades with whomever would listen, so, from the time he was a young boy Henry was a prolific storyteller, if he couldn't tell then he would write. Anxiously looking for his letters, Walter found Henry's stories enchanting. He looked forward to receiving them, especially delighting in reading about his cousin's endeavors in his new country. Although Walter's replies were often less verbose and more succinct than Henry's, their exchanges inspired Walter to join Henry in America. When Walter decided to come to America, he specifically wanted to be near family and near Henry in particular.

Upon first arriving in the spring of 1896, shortly after he celebrated his 18th birthday Walter spent several months at a farm in Schenectady belonging to distant relatives of his family, the Hufnagles. This beautiful farming community was about 250 miles from Brooklyn. Their homestead was a large, rambling farm with fields of corn, rolling fragrant apple trees, grape arbors and blueberry orchards along with cows, pigs, chickens and a random goat bleating here and there.

Walter enjoyed and appreciated his time with the Hufnagles, rising before dawn to help with the chores, working in the fields and sitting around the large crowded dinner table after a long hard day. He cherished the time spent talking and laughing with his cousins, they were warm hearted and welcoming so much like his family back in Germany.

Walter's natural tendency was to be quiet, more of a listener sitting back and not demanding attention. Though his reserved nature did not mean he wasn't paying attention; instead, his silence allowed him to be an astute observer of people. Walter noticed that it was always the father, his Uncle Paulus, who would sit down first at the head of the table, followed by his sons and then his daughters. Finally, Walter's Aunt Genie would join the family always sitting down last at the opposite end of the table.

"This is so much like home." he thought. "The head of the household always sat first and always at the head of the table, that was a place of honor."

Even the chair for the father was more decorative and had arms like a throne. Though, Uncle Paulus's chair did not need to look like a throne; anyone watching could tell that he was the master of his home. He was a tall slender man yet muscular from years of hard work; gentle and kind but also a stern disciplinarian. Walter thought that is the kind of father I want to be.

Sitting at the table Walter noticed how everyone would sit waiting patiently, no matter how hungry, for Uncle Paulus to bring his hands together, bow his head and say grace. Only after grace was finished, would forks be picked up, platters passed, and voices raised.

Yet, there was one very curious thing Walter noticed each and every evening. As the meal was being eaten and the events of the day were being discussed, in the left hand of every person at that table was an object. Sometimes the curled left hand rested on the table and sometimes it laid on the persons' lap. Walter wasn't quite sure what the hand held or why.

Maybe it was a napkin or rags, even a wipe cloth for potential spills. Walter smiled to himself as this thought struck him as humorous, "Everyone holding a cloth, well that would be more of a deluge than a spill."

He didn't say anything, just observed but then one evening, Uncle Paulus noticed that Walter was glancing at his cousins' hands around the table. Suddenly, placing his fork down, his booming voice crashed through the sounds of the utensils scraping, dishes being passed, food being chewed and drinks being swallowed.

"Excuse me, but Walter, let me ask you, do you know if you were born left-handed as a baby?"

Startled Walter looked up. "You know Uncle Paulus, actually I don't know,"

He looked down at the fork which he was holding in his right hand. "Why? "He asked.

"Well," Uncle Paulus began, "Back in the old country if a baby began to use his left hand to reach for something, to pick up toys or to feed himself, indicating that his left hand was his dominant hand it would be slapped and the object taken away.

Being left-handed was a serious problem, no one wanted their child to be a left hander not at all." Uncle Paulus went on, "Often the parents would need to tie the child's left arm behind them or wrap a sock on that hand making it difficult to use. Well, I decided right then and there that none of my children would even consider being left-handed. And to make sure that didn't happen I established a rule in my house. This rule was put into effect when our first child, my son, Alan was born and this rule has been kept ever since."

Upon hearing his name, Alan looked up, proudly displaying

his fork in his right hand, as he continued chewing. Looking over at Walter he nodded, then he smiled shyly at his father, prideful of his first-born status. Uncle Paulus nodded back acknowledging Alan and then continued explaining his rule.

"When eating at the kitchen table, the left hand had to have something in it. Maybe at first it was a soft doll, maybe a wooden block, and as our children grew it became a cloth or maybe a ball of ribbons but it had to be something, because if I ever saw a left hand being used, I'll tell you that one of these heavy utensils here on this table would be thrown directly, and I mean directly at the culprits head. And you know what Walter?" he asked. Opening his mouth to reply Walter was quickly cut off as Uncle Paulus proudly stated, "None of our children ever became left-handed."

With that everyone roared with laughter, even Walter. Aunt Genie added, "And Walter, the item we hold in our left hand is called a clutchie, because we clutch onto it for dear life." This time the laughter was even louder punctuated with giggles, guffaws and snorts. Walter smiled and chuckled nodding as he realized that this was how family traditions began.

After the meal, as the dinner dishes were being cleared by Aunt Genie and her daughters, Walter wondered why being born left-handed was really so bad. "How could it be such a character flaw? He pondered, "Why were children born left-handed if it was so wrong?"

He also wondered if someone could choose to be left-handed or was it simply a part of who they were? Wasn't a child born with the tendency to be either right or left-handed? This was curious to Walter; he just didn't understand what difference it really made. It didn't change the soul or the character of the person. Why should it make such a difference? But it did make a difference. Being left-handed was just not acceptable. Not acceptable to Uncle Paulus and as Walter understood not to anyone else either.

These thoughts continued to bother Walter, because he understood that often children were born with inherited characteristics. He had been born with a cleft palete causing him to speak with a lisp. Growing up this had often made him the butt of jokes with the other kids. He knew that this was one of the reasons that he was probably more of a listener then a talker and he was relieved when eventually he grew a small mustache that covered his top lip, the cleft palate was still there, it was still a part of him, but nobody saw it.

Walter enjoyed his time with the Hufnagles, they were a loving, and caring family. But he knew that farming was not his chosen career path so as winter approached Walter decided that it was time to move to the city where his cousin Henry waited. Walter again packed his bags, taking with him, his own clutchie a special gift from Aunt Genie. As he tucked his clutchie into his left side pocket, he hugged and thanked everyone, then bid farewell to the Hufnagles, promising to keep in touch.

"Know Thyself" - Plato

4

AMERICAN

Prior to 1898 Brooklyn existed as an independent city, then on January 1, 1898 it was incorporated as a borough joining the noisy, busy, thriving metropolis of New York City. This populous cosmopolitan community was very different from anything Walter had ever experienced. He had grown up in a rural German town, later spending time with his Hufnagle relatives on their farm. He always enjoyed nature, often taking solitary walks, he walked everywhere, continuing this habit in America by rising at sunrise to begin each day by taking a long brisk walk. However now, instead of walking in fields and forests he walked on cobblestones, brick and mortar. Undaunted by the change of scenery, with an eagle's eye he surveyed the shops, the tenements and the churches. He specifically enjoyed the architecture, structures and designs of many of the buildings on his way. In Germany he had been an apprentice to an architect and his dream was to become a professional architect in America.

During these solitary walks he discovered that there was one place where he would stop, it was St. John's Lutheran Church. Walter found himself intrigued by this unique and historic looking building; it was reminiscent of many older buildings in Europe. He felt comforted as he recognized the Rundbogenstil period of architecture which he knew by its rounded arches and historic revivalist style.

In the 19th century approximately seven million German immigrants arrived in America, many entering through New York City. Most of these newly arrived immigrants followed the religious teachings of the Protestant religion, particularly Lutheranism, founded by Martin Luther, the 16th Century, German Augustinian Monk.

To satisfy this growing population a number of Lutheran churches featuring various designs had been built in the Brooklyn area. Walter enjoyed the structures of them all, but there was something about this one particular church St. John's that pulled him in, causing him to pause and catch his breath as he admired everything about it. Even subconsciously Walters' pace would slow down as he approached it. Over time as he stood in front of this church, he began to feel an overwhelming pull to enter, but he resisted. He was intrigued by the intricate design of the façade, finding it similar to many churches of his home town. He noticed also a feeling of tranquility overtake him as he stood in its massive shadow. It wasn't long before St. John's Lutheran Church became an important and integral aspect of his early morning walks. No matter the weather he always stopped and admired this spiritual building. On one early morning as he reflected, he felt compelled to offer a prayer of gratitude, and from that time on his practice became to stop, quietly pray his morning prayer, then continue on his way, his day having begun.

Even from the outside he enjoyed the welcoming solace of St. John's Church. So, on a warm Sunday morning he accepted Henry's invitation to join his family and attend a Sunday service.

To his delightful surprise he chose the perfect Sunday, because immediately following the service the members were gathering together for their annual May celebration and picnic.

Happily arriving just before the service was to begin, Walter quickly climbed the steps to enter, but suddenly a strange sensation overtook him which caused him to pause. This sensation was so powerful that he reverently placed both feet on the top granite step taking note of every minute aspect of this beautiful building. After several minutes he solemnly entered the vestibule. Upon entering he stopped abruptly for a second time having been instantaneously transported back to his youth.

The interior of the church was familiar, the cool peacefulness of the sanctuary, the rich aroma of the freshly polished oak panels, the ornately carved wooden alter, the softly cushioned voices of the congregants buzzing in the air, all of it wrapping around him enveloping him in its memory. Yet, there was something else that he sensed, something which resonated from deep within his soul raising the hairs on his skin impacting his senses before revealing itself to him. Voices, words, language, it was hearing his native tongue that stole his breath away. Suddenly all of his senses were on fire, the language, sights, sounds, and smells were everywhere, rapidly spinning around him. Looking from left to right, everywhere he turned he saw his childhood come alive.

It was the Teutonic language, which proved so powerful to Walter. He believed that there was a strength and directness in that language that gave him a sense of pride, not only hearing it but speaking it. These guttural sounding words came from the back of the throat, quickly and sharply appearing to express authority and order.

Suddenly he heard the large church organ in front of him bellow out its opening chords. The notes seeped through his skin and into his bones tightly spinning themselves around his soul. Closing his eyes for a moment everything around him ceased to exist, save for the music. Breathing it all in he felt the majestic notes sink deeper into his core, quenching a thirst he hadn't realized was parched. It was as if this music was blessed water flooding dry land renewing him as it filled his every pore. Each note containing a story, a memory of what once was. The sounds of the organ pipes rained over him as the music of Beethoven penetrated deeper and deeper into his core. He was enraptured, feeling an inner peace he had not known for a very long time. As the voices of the choir rose singing Beethoven's Eroica, Walter's emotions rose along with them. Tears sprung to his eyes bringing him back to a different church in a different land at a different time filling him with bittersweet joy.

Standing at the sanctuary, Walter offered a prayer of thanks to God, for allowing him this moment, this gift, for it was truly a gift, this piece of his past made present again. He desperately longed to hold onto this feeling, as his yesterday's blended into his todays, but the service was about to begin.

Standing in silence a moment longer he wiped a tear from his eye and quietly took a seat in the very last pew. Looking towards the front he noticed that Henry and his family were sitting a few rows ahead of him. He decided to remain where he sat, needing to be by himself, not wanting anything or anyone to distract him. Prayerfully he folded his hands, as he tightly held onto his yesterdays.

During the service he thought, "This is so similar but still not the same." He noticed that the congregation was less formal, more friendly than back home, as they greeted each other in their old language, saying "Guten morgen;" "Guten tag;" even just "Tag." He noticed the sermon was in German but shorter and ended on a far more optimistic and upbeat message than he remembered. Standing to sing the last hymn he waited for the conclusion of the service to walk down the center aisle and greet his relatives. He overheard the members talking about the upcoming church picnic later in the day, and he noticed too that many people were greeting Henry by his new American nickname "Hank".

He was surprised by other differences some stark, particularly the surnames, in the old country many names included the title von, a sign of a noble heritage; but it seemed now that in America the title was no longer being applied. Walter's brow furrowed as he considered this, how could he not use von? That would be incredulous he thought. The title of von had been in his family forever. He felt pride when he said, "von Vetterlein" remembering that in Germany if your last name was prefixed with von it meant you were of an aristocratic lineage, maybe a member of royalty, a baron or baroness.

Back home when his aunt and his father told stories of the

old days and of their families, they would always mention with pride the importance of having von in their name. Yes, it was a title and he knew that in America titles were not considered important because everyone was created equal. "But it meant something to my father." he thought, "So, I will keep von in my name." He was not yet ready to lose that connection with his heritage, his homeland or his father.

"Maybe someday von will not be used but I must." Walter thought. "I don't know. I just don't know! I am an American, but how do you feel American when everything you know and understand is in another country. Walter asked himself, "What does it really mean to be an American." His answer came quickly, "Why can't I be American and German too?"

Walter had learned his history not just from school but from his family, to Walter there was pride in being German. There was a value in holding onto where he came from, holding onto traditions he had learned as a boy. Those traditions were his foundation, his story. He also felt a responsibility to respect and honor those who helped make Germany the country it had become. Much like America, Germany was a newly unified country and was becoming a major influence in Europe. Previously, as Prussia it had been divided into separate provinces, but in 1871 under the leadership of Chancellor Otto von Bismarck and the North German Confederation many of the Bavarian provinces had been unified into one country to form the new German nation.

Reflecting, he thought, "I really like America, I like all of these new ideas, I like the opportunities, I like being here, but I liked the old ways too." And at times he missed them immensely.

Life in Brooklyn, in 1901 was completely different from Stuttgart, it was populated with people, many immigrants from all over Europe, just like Hank and Walter.

During the walks around his new neighborhood he heard many different languages and dialects spoken, including German. Walter mused that this was part of what made America so special. The different languages, the air around him rich with fragrances and aromas that had never touched his nose before. Many of the people passing by had skin colors and facial bone structures vastly different from what he knew in Germany. These sights, sounds and smells now became part of the fabric of his days and soon they became his norm.

Walter thought, "Things are very different here, but does becoming an American mean you had to leave behind everything you had once been? How do you even do that? How do you let that go? How do you forget?" He asked, "Can't you assimilate into America, be an American but still honor the land where you were born? He had heard that using the term German-American was disparaged and frowned upon. But Walter believed that remembering where you had come from didn't mean you weren't proud to be an American.

Walter thought, "You shouldn't have to lose who you were before coming to America, instead being an American expands you, it connects you with others. It's about honoring and respecting each of the differences as you embrace your newly blending heritage. We might be different nationalities but now we are all Americans."

Reminiscing, he remembered how leaving Germany had been an extremely difficult decision, much harder than he thought it could be. "Almost everyone I know and everything I'm familiar with is back home." he lamented.

Yet, home had been tough too; Walter was born in 1878, the seventh son of a seventh son, his mother had died while delivering him. He understood that many women lost their lives in child birth, but often he felt guilty wondering if he was responsible for his mother's death. He kept trying to bury this feeling of guilt deeply in his soul but it was always there, eager to rise up and remind him. His father's sister Frida raised him, wet nursing him at her breast right along with his cousins, often they introduced him as their milk-sibling. Growing up he thought of her family as his family and of her as his mother. Yet, he knew the emptiness in his heart at the absence of his true mother. Sometimes when he was little, he tried imagining that he knew her, that he could hear her voice, smell her scent or feel her touch.

He sorely missed the mother he never met and didn't know. He knew that his brothers and his father missed her too. He remembered many evenings late at night when they all would gather around the fire in Aunt Frida's kitchen. Often as shadows grew larger on the wall a story would begin. Sometimes it would begin as a memory of his mother, with the older brothers and cousins adding to it, telling their memories, he noticed how his father's head would lower and a faraway look would come to his eyes. Walter would listen, there was nothing he could add, but at these times he would reach out rubbing his father's slumped shoulders or place his small hand on the strong calloused hand of his father's and gently keep it there.

It wasn't fair, he thought, that all of his older brothers

carried memories of their mother, because for him there were none. He wished if only he had a memory to hold onto, a hand holding his, a hug, a kiss, a whisper. Walter's lack of connection to his mother made him feel just a bit different from his brothers and also from his cousins.

Often, he felt as if he was just on the edge of everything, not quite fitting in and not really being left out. Yet, growing up in his aunts' large, boisterous and loving family he knew he was safe, nurtured and loved. There were times though when his aunt would reach out to grab and hug her children. To Walter it seemed that those hugs lasted just a bit longer than the ones he received as he felt a throbbing ache wrap around his heart.

He dreamt of what it would be like to feel his mothers' arms around him, to laugh as she nuzzled his neck or tickled his belly. He wondered what it was like to have his mother tuck him into bed at night and give him good night kisses, tell him a story, to say I love you, he would never know. He remembered often having a sensation, a feeling of not being quite tethered to this earth, not being anchored and not having anyone there to pull you back if you went drifting out too far.

Thankfully, he still had his father, although he was ill, he was still with him. He couldn't begin to think of how it must be to have neither a father nor a mother. "How lonely and how lost such children must feel," he thought. He knew of children in the old country who had lost both parents, their lives were hard and they seemed so very alone. Often times he would see them shivering and begging for food or a place to stay. Sometimes these children lived with relatives, more likely they lived in almshouses or orphanages. Often, they worked as servants, in factories or on farms. They had a broken and bewildered look in their eyes, a look that still haunted Walter to this day. He knew he was loved and because of that he felt blessed.

Walter was proud of his father and his father's service. Edward von Vetterlein had fought bravely and had been severely wounded in the Franco-Prussian war of 1870-1871. He never fully recovered from the injuries he sustained which made it difficult for him to pursue a profession or trade for very long. He tried his hand at being a shoemaker but it was too hard for him to stand or sit up for long stretches of time and often the fabrics and materials he used made him even sicker.

As the years passed, his father's health deteriorated causing him to spend more and more time convalescing at home. Eventually, as his breathing became raspier and shallower, Edward spent the last years of his life confined to bed.

With Aunt Frida's help Walter took on much of the responsibility of taking care of his ailing father. Even though Edward grew weaker, it seemed that through Walter's love and nurturing he was able to keep his father alive longer than anyone had predicted. Whenever Walter entered the room where his father was resting, Edward would light up, his complexion would brighten and he would become more animated. At times he even seemed to have more energy.

Walter would sit by his bedside and listen while his father told stories of the war, stories of the early years when his mother was alive, when his brothers were little and dreams could come true. He had often heard these stories, he even knew them by heart, but he never told his father, he loved hearing them again and again. Yet, in spite of his efforts, when

Walter was 18, his father closed his eyes one night, never to open them again. It was as if he knew that it was Walter who had kept him alive and he was letting him go.

After his father's death, Walter knew it was time to begin life in a new country. He was a responsible and dedicated worker; he learned quickly as a draftsman and aspired to become an architect's apprentice while in Stuttgart. He believed that these skills learned in Germany would be skills he could use to create opportunity in America.

Working long hours, he saved as much money as he could. Then with Aunt Frida's guidance and blessing, he mustered the courage to write to the Hufnagles and soon received their welcoming reply. Packing everything he could carry in his box, he set out for America, the promise of a better life his inspiration.

Walter shook his head coming out of his reverie, "I still even call Germany home, when will I feel like Brooklyn is home and that I am an American? "he wondered, "Did I make the right decision to leave Germany, is this the right place for me? Will I be successful? Will I be able to find someone I love, and who loves me? Will I be able to make my own home and raise a family, to have a wife, children, and happiness? He wondered if he was asking too much. Having a wife who loved him, children to hold, and a family of his own, meant so much to Walter, more than he even realized.

He thought of how back at home they spoke of the amazing opportunity in America; you just needed to work for it, to go after it they said." I'm shy but I'm a hard worker", he told himself. Walter had always been shy, his aunt Frida and his father use to speak to him about his shyness, being the youngest of 7 boys in his family along with 6 cousins it was easy to fade into the background and not speak out. Walter wondered if his quietness and shyness was just because everyone else was always noisy and talking or was it because of his difficulty speaking. Plus, Walter loved hearing the stories they told, often after listening to Aunt Frida and his father he would think about a particular story for days on end.

He loved so many things about his Aunt Frida, from her welcoming voice and ready smile, to the way she always greeted anyone who entered her kitchen with a warm embrace, the way she would tilt her head to listen intently to anyone who spoke to her, and how she would nod in understanding. Yes, he thought, there were many things that he loved about his Aunt and his cousins but that one thing in particular, it was the stories. He loved sitting around the kitchen hearth listening as tales were spun and memories repeated, often many times embellished. Chuckling out loud he remembered the hot summer day when his cousin Frederick ran through the hen coup yelling at the top of his lungs and waving his hands high in the air. Boy, those hens flew off their nests with feathers flying everywhere, their loud squawking was heard throughout the farm. Well, no hens laid eggs for quite a while and Frederick didn't sit down for days either.

Or the time Fritz deliberately knocked over the outside privy with Aunt Frida sitting inside. Walter remembered how everyone laughed so hard; everyone except Aunt Frida. No one took pity on Fritz, when he was forced to clean up a stinking mess. But Walter particularly liked it when Aunt Frida told him of the folklore around being born the seventh son of a seventh son. She would always boil water for tea then begin the story holding the mug in her hand, telling Walter that in some cultures it is believed this particular son, the seventh son of a man who was also a seventh son with no daughters in between had powers that could heal. Aunt Frida told Walter that having been born in February and with a galea or caul on his head he brought good luck and was destined for greatness. Walter felt that this seemed more like a burden than a benefit. He felt a strong responsibility for his actions, giving thought to what he said and did. This behavior made him gentler and more considerate than most boys. He was also more of a listener than a talker. Everyone in his family loved his thoughtful and kind ways. They believed it made him better able to understand things since he listened with an open heart. Frequently, it was Walter who intervened and stopped his brothers and cousins from fights or mishaps which were always happening. He was definitely able to ease tensions, calm things down, or bring peace where there had been mayhem. It was the memory of these stories that made Walter's eyes fill, as a smile appeared on his face while homesickness filled his heart at the same time.

Hoping to find new friends and kindred spirits Walter tried reaching out by attending several events in his neighborhood. Shaking his head, he remembered one disaster in particular, it was on a Monday evening in April, he had attended a young people's social held at the local Baptist Temple. He remembered the date, the 19th because he had heard about a marathon being held for the first time in Boston, Massachusetts on that same day. He had read that the running distance was 24.5 miles, accustomed to taking long walks he thought, "I could do that, maybe Henry and I could do it together, if they repeat the event, and if they let us walk instead of run." He definitely would have preferred being there rather than at a church social. His palms were moist and sweaty as he held his ticket stamped, Monday, April 19th, 1897. Printed on the front in cursive script was his introduction, "Hello, my name is Walter." Entering he looked at the crowd of young men and women gathered in the hall, and quickly realized that he didn't see anyone he knew or recognized. He felt out of place as his heart beat faster and his palms began to sweat. He wished that he hadn't attended and thought about leaving as quickly as possible. Chuckling to himself he thought, "Maybe I should take up running. It seems a popular activity in America," As he stood near the exit, he noticed that he didn't hear anyone speaking German and he didn't recognize the accents. He felt alone, and it seemed everyone besides him were in groups talking with friends.

His feet felt as if they were in cement and his heart pounded, he couldn't wait to leave. As quickly as possible he exited through the nearest door, tucked his ticket into his pocket and headed straight home. As these memories came back, Walter drew in a deep breath, remembering how awful it felt being all alone even though he was in a crowd.

"Come on Walt," he chided himself, "straighten up," looking around he asked, "Where is that cousin Henry now?" Then he spotted him, you could see Henry easily as he was tall and lanky with blond curly hair. Even if you didn't see him you would definitely hear him. Henry was always laughing, his laughter would start slowly, rolling up from his stomach, as his head would drop back and a deep baritone sound bellowed from his throat. It was a contagious laugh, it brought all around him to join in and laugh, even if they didn't know what he was laughing about. As Walter walked towards his cousin, he noticed how relaxed and comfortable Henry appeared, standing in a circle amongst several other young men. He had one hand in his pocket while the other gestured with gusto captivating everyone's attention like a true raconteur. The young men chuckled as Henry spoke with animation. He had the ability to make friends anywhere at any time, people felt as if they had known him for years rather than just being introduced. When Henry met someone, he would shake their hand with a strong hand shake and look straight into their eyes. Often people described Henry as a hearty fellow well met.

Walter wondered, should I try harder, maybe I could be a little like him. He smiled, noting how easy mannered and comfortable his cousin appeared and admired his ability to make friends everywhere he went. People just liked being with Henry, I like being around Henry too, we always laugh. Nodding his head affirmatively Walter thinks, "Fine, I'll go to the picnic; I can always leave early if I want, it certainly won't be the first time."

Walking over to his cousin, Walter straightened his shoulders and looked up at him. Henry greeted Walter with a nod and without saying a word in lock step, they headed towards the food, noise and activity. Walking and talking together Henry joked poking at Walter. Not being able to help himself Walter found that he was laughing out loud too, they were laughing in unison as they headed towards the church's large and bustling picnic area. Even though Henry was several years younger than Walter being with him reminded Walter of his older brothers; a smile crossed his face as that thought made him relax even more.

They began talking about all the different food they would be eating at the picnic. Walter was feeling better, being with Henry was like a tonic, just walking, talking and laughing with him. He felt the melancholy of nostalgia fade as his smile broadened. Suddenly, a breeze tickled Walter's nose, he inhaled a blend of wonderful fragrances. His spirits lifted more as he glanced over at Henry; who too seemed to be inhaling the delicious aromas. He was grateful for his cousin, there was something about simply being with him that made Walter feel comforted. Being with family, recognizing similar smiles, hearing familiar accents, laughs or noticing similar gaits, it was a real feeling; it made Walter relax and content. "I bet most people feel this way." he thought. This is what family is, a familiarity and a common history; knowing that your foundation is the same even without saying a word the connection exists.

Walter believed that being connected to a family was so important. Knowing that you are with people who love, respect and support you just for being you becomes a keystone in life. He understood, it's not always perfect, you are going to have disagreements and misunderstandings. But it is for forever that you are bound to those who came before you, those who are with you now and those who will come after you.

Walter believed that the meaning of family meant each ripple your story created was dependent on the one before it, then the next ripple was dependent on that one and so on and so on until the ripples disappear as everything is blended.

Family tethers you and when things are not working out for you, hopefully some, maybe all, or maybe simply one will help you out and hold you up. Someone like Aunt Frida, she was there for her brother and her nephews. Walter truly believed that you become who you are by standing on the shoulders of those who have come before you, have held you up and have been silent guides for your life and you continue the process as you help raise those who have come after you.

It was these values which Edward, his father and his Aunt Frida possessed.

They supported, helped and loved each other because they were family. When Walter's mother died at his birth, it was Aunt Frida who nursed him keeping him alive. When his father could no longer take care of his family, it was Aunt Frida who invited them to move into her farm house, her home became their home. In this home there was laughter, tears, hugs, kisses, loud voices and hushed tones. He knew that being part of a family, no matter how extended or how distant you were it meant that you were never, ever alone. No matter where you were or what you were doing you were never alone.

He wondered whether he had these feelings and beliefs because he lost his mother at his birth, because he knew the power of being loved by his cousins and Aunt Frida or maybe it was simply because he was the seventh son of a seventh son.

Approaching the picnic area memories of home flashed before him, for Walter home was Stuttgart not Brooklyn. He knew that accepting this change would take time. Looking over to where many of the congregation had gathered, he noticed that people were standing, talking and mingling around large picnic tables. His gaze stopped as he noticed a young woman, or was it the aroma of the sweet-smelling apple breads, strudels and cobblers that caught his attention. He continued to observe her, as she offered fresh baked pastry to several children crowded up to the table, their little hands outstretched. He noticed her gentle graciousness, how lovely she was, how she smiled sweetly, laughing with the children as she placed pastries in each of those eager outstretched hands.

For a moment, Walter took a deep inhale, closing his eyes, he was back in Stuttgart. It was the aroma, the smell from his aunt's kitchen every Sunday morning; recognizing it he inhaled deeper hoping to keep it for a very long time.

"Gosh, I miss them," he thought as he eyes misted and his heart ached as he saw them all, every one of them, brothers and cousins all crowded around the kitchen table. He saw his aunt and his father. The vivid reality of it gave him a jolt as he braced himself, allowing the memory of yesterday wrap around him like a heavy shroud. He wanted to remain in that memory longer but his stomach grumbled loudly, loud enough for Henry to hear, and he did. Walter was quickly brought out of his reverie by the laughing voice of his cousin saying "Hey, Walt, hungry man, come on over here." In a blink, he's back, he's in America, at the Lutheran church, at a picnic in Brooklyn, watching a beautiful young fraulein offering pastry, Walter looked at his cousin and smiled, "Danke, Henry, danke kleine cousin."

"It was love at first sight, at last sight, at ever and ever sight."
- Vladimir Nabokov

5

THE INTRODUCTION 1901

*L*ooking up Walter noticed she was gone; his heart skipped a beat as he asked himself, "Who was she? Where did she go? "Quickly, his eyes scanned the picnic area as he looked around. Then he saw her. "Phew," he said, surprised at realizing how important it was for him to find her. Relieved to see her again a slight smile crossed his lips as he observed that she had gone to assist others at a different table. He felt intrigued by her and wondered who she was, what was her name?

The young woman that intrigued him was Lilli von Holzapfel, she and her mother had recently begun attending St. John's Church. Lilli, just as Walter had been, was drawn in by the design and architecture of this unique building. It reminded her of the old country, but more importantly it reminded her of her father. She knew that he would have been struck by the beauty, structure and architectural design of this very special building.

To Lilli, the elegant style was resplendent, as she looked at the pointed steeple windows and entrances, she noted how the design of the steeple represented two palms coming together, as in prayer mode. Each time she looked at the steeples Lilli would place her finger tips together noting that this was exactly how she prayed each evening as she knelt at her bedside. There was so much about this church that made Lilli feel comforted, hearing the German language, singing the familiar songs and listening to the sermons in their native tongue. Remembering how important the holidays were at home, Lilli couldn't wait to celebrate them at this beautiful church. Ever since she was a child, she looked forward to her most favorite holiday of all, December 24th, Weihnachten. Christmas Eve in America was not the same as Lilli remembered so she and her mother kept many of their old traditions. Lilli particularly loved hearing the Christmas Carols especially the ones that she had grown up singing with her parents and their family, her most favorite of all being Stille Nacht, known in America as Silent Night.

Sometimes even when it wasn't that holy time of year Lilli would hear her mother humming tunes like Stille Nacht or O Tannenbaum, throughout their flat. No matter in what language Stille Nacht was sung the gentle, peaceful, calming vibrations of the tune were universally recognized. Often when her mother began humming, she would join her, then other times she might simply prefer to listen to her mother's beautiful soprano voice humming or even singing out loud. Entering her reverie Wilhelmmine would become oblivious to anyone around her. She could be working at Emma's Dress Shoppe or in their flat humming softly as she did her chores or prepared the family meal. No matter what time of year it was, hearing her mother's beautiful voice singing these songs always brought a smile to Lilli's face. Especially when she heard the tune of Stille Nacht coming from her mother's voice Lilli knew that all was well.

Even today in the spring of 1901 as Lilli moved about the table, she softly hummed Stille Nacht. The words came to her in her native tongue, "Stille Nacht, Heil'ge Nacht" as she placed a large dish of warm apple strudel on the wooden picnic table covered with a deep blue and white checked tablecloth. Stille Nacht; that was truly her favorite Christmas Carol of all. It was also her Uncle Herman's favorite too. Uncle Herman was her mother's older brother and Lilli's favorite uncle. When her mother told her stories of growing up in Stuttgart, so many included the times she spent with her older brother Herman. Wilhelmmine would regale Lilli as she told her of the adventures Herman and she went on, or the toys and furniture he carved for her, and of course, even the trouble they got into together. Hearing these stories, they would laugh out loud, sometimes tears fell from their eyes. Thinking of Uncle Herman made Lilli smile and without even realizing it she was becoming just like her mother. Like Wilhelmmine, Lilli was oblivious to everyone and everything around her, as she continued to sing softly the words of Stille Nacht while placing the deliciously smelling desserts on the wooden picnic table.

As Walter watched Lilli, he noticed how different she appeared from the other young women. Lilli Von Holtzapfl, was 5ft 6 or 7 inches and stood several inches taller than most of the young women her age. Many of the girls had creamy pale complexions, blond hair and blue eyes, Lilli was different, her eyes were a dark brown, her complexion a deep olive and her hair was the darkest brown he had ever seen, almost black, which she wore pulled back from her face and tied at the nape of her neck with a brightly colored ribbon.

Walter also noticed that she moved gracefully and comfortably among the women, exuding confidence as she guided some and offered assistance to others. Her attire was formal wearing the popular Gibson Girl style of the day with eyelet lace around the neck and a yoke of eyelet lace across the bodice. The soft cotton lavender material draped comfortably over her slender figure and the long sleeves pushed up slightly from her wrists were gently gathered. The dress cinched in comfortably at her small waist and was tied in the back with a long tapered sash which hung almost to the hemline at Lilli's ankles.

When Lilli looked up, she noticed Walter watching her and automatically she smiled a demure shy smile; however, her large dark brown eyes twinkled and her heart skipped a beat. Unlike Walter, Lilli was not shy; she never had been. Being an only child, growing up with her doting mother and father, along with all of her aunts, Uncle Herman and many cousins, she had always been the center of their world. This upbringing had given Lilli confidence where Walter was withdrawn. Lilli often knew what she wanted and would figure out how to make it happen, where Walter was often willing to acquiesce to another's wishes or wants before his own. As an only child Lilli didn't have to share; but for Walter being in a large family everything was shared. However, there were similarities too, and one very important thing in common, both of them had been raised in a loving home where respect, responsibility and moderation in all things was taught. They both understood that your family and home were always the center of all your interest.

Walter thought, "How could I not notice her?" For the first time in a long time Walter was glad to be right where he was. Little did Walter know but Lilli too thought, "Hmm, I wonder who that handsome young man with Henry is? I've never noticed him before. Maybe Henry will introduce him to me." Having recently met at church, Lilli and Henry had become quick friends. She enjoyed his fun loving and carefree manner, along with his keen sense of humor and wit. It was easy to be friends with Henry. Already, Lilli felt as if she had known him for a long time. "Phew, thankfully we're here in Brooklyn." Lilli thought. She was glad that things were more casual in America; back in the old country, as her mother called home, in order to meet a young man a formal introduction to the parents was required and only upon approval would there be an introduction to their daughter. Quietly, Lilli chuckled as she thought, at the ripe old age of 19, I certainly don't have time for all that.

Henry looked over at Walter, his eyes narrowing in amusement as a broad smile crossed his face. Walter obviously was interested in meeting Miss Lilli von Holzapfel. Clearing his throat Henry pulled himself up even taller than he was, and asked, "Um, excuse me Walter, but would you like me to introduce you to that lovely lady, Miss Lilli von Holzapfel?" "Von" Walter thought, as a broad smile crossed his face. He gave his cousin a quick nod and without hesitation along with apparently forgetting him altogether, quickly began walking towards Miss Lilli von Holzapfel.

Realizing Walter would get there before he did, Henry took longer strides rapidly joining his cousin. Then side by side they headed off in Lilli's direction. Sensing their arrival, Lilli looked up tilting her head to the side; she smiled as she watched them approach her. Taking in the moment Lilli observed them both as the cousins, Walter and Henry walked in her direction. Suddenly she felt her senses peak as she inhaled the sweet-smelling blossoms of the apple and viburnum trees. She noticed how bright and vibrant the tulips and yellow daffodils were as they grew in the picnic area. She inhaled the sweet smell of pastry and warm baked apples permeating the air. Lilli noticed too that the chill of the early morning air had evaporated and been replaced by the warmth of the sun as it penetrated through the light lavender material of her dress. She heard the melodic chirping sounds of birds and looked up through the spreading branches mottled with buds to the cloudless deep blue sky and thought, "What a beautiful day today is."

Sensing their approach Lilli greeted them saying, "Guten Tag," Returning Lilli's greeting and without hesitation Henry began the introduction, but before he finished, Walter, stepped forward holding out his hand to take Lilli's. "Mr. Walter von Vetterlein may I introduce you to Miss Lilli von Holzapfel." Henry finished quickly as Walter had already taken Lilli's hand in his thinking, "I don't want to let go." Lilli smiled, cleared her throat as she gently released her hand. Walter was immediately smitten, he smiled directly at Lilli looking into her brown eyes. At that moment Lilli knew that yes, today was definitely going to be a beautiful day.

Neither Lilli nor Walter seemed to notice that Henry turned away to leave, smiling he waved saying, "Auf wiedersehen. "Then he walked away, joining the rest of his family as they gathered around a long picnic table talking, laughing and enjoying the delicious treats.

For the remainder of the afternoon Lilli and Walter were inseparable. First Lilli would talk, Walter would listen, then Walter would talk and Lilli listened. Laughing easily together they spoke of their old country and of their new country. They exchanged thoughts about the difficult decision to leave their homeland, of the voyage to America and of the families they left behind. At times tears from laughing too hard or from feelings too deep would fill their eyes. Sharing their thoughts with each other their sentences were peppered with both the English and German languages. Often it seemed that both languages were being spoken simultaneously, with the translations coming straight from their hearts.

As the morning passed into afternoon, it seemed as if they had known each other for a very long time. There was so much they had in common, much that was familiar and much that was new. It seemed that together they could have the old and the new, their memories and their dreams. They understood the other with no judgments, no misgivings and instinctively trust was growing.

They shared the fears and hopes of their lives in this new country, full of its opportunities and risks. Walking together a sense of companionship enveloped them. They both knew that from this time forward together they would be fine, their dreams were possible.

The brightness and warmth of the day faded with the sun setting into the west as the air became cooler, Lilli shivered as a cool breeze blew. Walter knew she needed to leave and asked if he could see her again. Lilli felt the warmth of the day return and eagerly complied.

From that moment on they saw see each other as often as possible. Before long both Lilli and Walter having so much in common, knew that they were meant to be together. Coming from the same part of Germany meant they shared similar memories and traditions. They both believed in honoring their parents, their families, their homeland and their Lutheran religion. They were both ambitious and wanted to be successful, but they also understood the value of living a life of moderation, and the importance to always keep the home and family the center of their lives. They understood and felt a keen sense of pride in their heritage but also a sense of excitement in calling themselves Americans. They believed in each other and understood each other's dreams for the future. They felt the energy and excitement of building a life in a new country together but also not wanting to let go of their deep roots in the old one.

Immediately they felt right together, it made sense to them, there was no one else for them, they believed that together anything was possible.

As time slipped by it wasn't long before they had become each other's best friend, not only did they like each other, they loved each other, and they were falling in love. Lilli noticed that through her observations of Walter and his patient ways she was also learning to become more patient herself. And Walter noticed that through Lilli's belief in him and in their future, his confidence was growing.

They saw themselves not only as a couple but as a team, two people forging one future together, each one of them making the other a better person, a more complete person.

They believed that often things happen which you can't plan, predict or even control. They wondered if maybe they were destined to be together and might it have happened in Germany also? They believed in the power of their shared faith, they believed there was a higher power that moved in their lives, this power didn't control events but inspired them to be open to welcome and embrace them. Cousin Henry introducing them to each other at the church picnic was such an event, one that Lilli and Walter would forever be grateful.

As their love grew, they knew there would never ever be anyone else. Lilli told Walter of her parents and of being raised in a home where moderation in living and valuing each other was the foundation of her childhood. As she had grown her parents had shown her the importance of selfless love, of bringing joy into everyday activities and making the home the center of all your interests. These values spoke to Walter; he understood them for this was what he always wanted for his life and family. This was what Aunt Frida had shown him and he loved her for it.

Time passed quickly, and two months later Walter asked Lilli's mother for permission to marry her daughter. Wilhelmmine liked Walter; there was something about his calm, gentle nature that was comforting. Without hesitation, she granted her approval and permission. Ecstatic, Lilli was now planning a wedding, a union that would bring not only her and Walter's New York families together, but also their families from Germany.

Lilli was delighted; she had never known such happiness. Her heart overflowed with joy and each night as she knelt to say her evening prayers, she placed her palms together, fingers pointing upwards to heaven, saying, "Thank you God, for the memories of yesterday, the beauty of today, and the hope for tomorrow. Please bless my family, both here and in Germany. Please bless Walter, his family here and in Germany. And please bless our family and the children we will have, each and every one. Danke, God, Amen."

"Wow," Lilli flushed as she thought, Walter von Vetterlein, loved and wanted to marry her. To Lilli, he was the most intelligent, thoughtful, kind and gentle young man she had ever met. He was quiet and patient where Lilli was forthright. Lilli smiled knowing that her mother described her as persistent and determined, yet in a gentile manner.

But these were qualities that Walter didn't seem to mind, often he would laugh as he found these characteristics appealing. Lilli liked it when he laughed, his eyes would sparkle, and he would bring his hand up to cover his mouth. As if he didn't want the laughter to escape because he was enjoying it so much, or maybe to hide his cleft palete.

Walter was a handsome man; he was taller than Lilli at approximately 5 feet 11 inches. His hair was light brown with a slight curl which made it appear a little tousled and when he smiled which was now quite often a dimple on his left cheek gave him a roguishly handsome look. But it was his mustache that Lilli could not get out of her mind, that soft mustache tickled her whenever they kissed. This of course was not very often because they were not yet husband and wife. Lilli's face flushed becoming warm as she thought of Walter's kisses, "I definitely like kissing Walter." Quickly flustered she tried to release the image from her thoughts.

It seemed as if time was spinning in a whirlwind from that Sunday afternoon when Henry introduced them. Even though she hadn't admitted it Lilli had been worried about becoming an old maid and being called a spinster. She was relieved knowing that she was soon to be married and begin a family telling herself, "I am going to be called a fraulein or a married woman as they say here in America and then I'll become a mother."

This was the life that she had observed, her mother, aunts and cousins living, being a wife and mother was something Lilli believed she would do also. She had always helped her mother with chores around their home so she felt confident in her ability to keep a home, do the shopping, the cooking, sew the clothes along with nurturing and loving all of their babies. However, she did harbor one concern, doing all of these chores had been with her mother's guidance and assistance. Now, she wondered how she would accomplish it alone.

"All the happiness there is in this world arises from wishing others to be happy." - Geshe Kelsang Gyatso,

6

THE GIFT

August 15th 1901, was an especially warm summer day, as Lily purchased the final pieces for her wedding gown, hurrying from store to store on the bustling streets of Brooklyn. Her arms were full as again she carried bags of Battenberg lace, cream colored silks and yards and yards of organza. Street vendors called out their wares as people hustled and bustled about them. Recognizing their voices, she ignored their calls, she was in a hurry.

Her arms ached with the weight of the packages, Lilli heaved a deep breath and shifted the packages protectively so nothing would drop onto the filthy pavement below.

"Yuck!" Lilli thought as she looked down at the ground beneath her feet. She wondered, "Why are these city streets so filthy?" She remembered how in Stuttgart the streets were swept each morning by the vendors or even the apartment dwellers. For some reason no one seemed to think about sweeping the streets here. "Well," Lilli decided, "I'll always sweep and clean my walk."

Thinking of living with Walter in their own home, a huge smile crossed her face as she felt her heart expand in joy, she wondered if it could burst. Quickening her pace, almost skipping, she thought, "I am so happy, I've never felt this happy before. Dear God, please I never want this feeling to end."

Lilli and Walter's wedding day was set for September 1st 1901. Almost all of the preparations had been completed, invitations had been sent via post across the ocean to friends and family in America and Europe. Even though both Lilli and Walter lived in Brooklyn NY, many of their relatives still lived in Europe and some would be arriving from across the ocean. Walter was grateful for his relatives the Hufnagles in Schenectady and their large farm. They had offered its many rooms as one of the places that the families could stay.

It seemed longer than 3 years since she had seen so many of her relatives. Neither she nor Wilhelmmine could contain their excitement at the thought of seeing them again. Lilli and Walter dreamed that this was only the first of many visits they would share. Along with the relatives they were thrilled at the number of wedding gifts arriving by post for them. The small rooms in her mother's home were becoming full with gifts of cuckoo clocks, steins, china, linens, cookware and even books. But the gift Lilli appreciated most was not the material ones just the person being there was more than anything. This made her think of one particular invited guest, her favorite, Uncle Herman. She loved him so much. He didn't need to send or bring a gift, just his being there was truly gift enough for Lilli.

Hurrying down the busy Brooklyn streets memories of Uncle Herman came to mind. Herman Von Holtzapfl was a very unique person, kind, thoughtful, and even unpredictable. Lilli remembered how at dinner time he always ate dessert first before he ate his dinner. Lilli would sit at the table and laugh out loud as Uncle Herman enjoyed his piece of apfelstrudel before his dinner. As Uncle Herman would say, "I might be full after dinner so I want to make sure I enjoy my dessert first." No one ever corrected or tried to change his practice.

Lilli laughed out loud remembering this conversation from years ago. Even though it was only a year before that he had visited America from Germany, she couldn't wait to see him again. Lilli remembered how excited she was to see him and talk with him. When looking up, she had to tilt her head back ,because he was so very tall, well over 6 feet; with deep blue eyes and hair so blond, that when he was young, his family called him schleppkopf, she learned that in America the term was towhead. To Lilli, he seemed magical, he could do anything, he was smart, creative and artistic, he could carve toys and make furniture. Often, he would chisel wooden toys and figures for gifts to give on Weihnachten eve when many people in Germany celebrated the night before Christmas. He loved to read too, doing research on mythology, history and literature and frequently the gifts you received had a story attached to them.

Lately Uncle Herman was working right in Berlin, Germany's capital. In the past he had written about his activities as he worked closely with the Kaiser and the Chancellor Otto von Bismarck. Lilli's uncle was so proud of how

Germany was changing. It was under the leadership of Chancellor Bismarck that a German national healthcare system was established, as well as old age pensions for the elderly along with insurance coverage. Many people credited Bismarck with Germany being considered a very progressive country. For much of the world it appeared that Germany was even more progressive than most of Europe and even America. Eventually due to differences in opinion with the Kaiser, Bismarck resigned leaving Uncle Herman devastated. He had considered about coming to America and staying with his sister Wilhelmmine, but his loyalty was to his Kaiser and to his country.

Uncle Herman believed that Kaiser Wilhelm truly wanted to make a difference for his country. Frequently, he had written to Lilli and her mother about the many changes and reforms that had happened under Bismarck. There were several chancellors after Bismarck, but they didn't seem to bring the progressive ideas Bismarck had.

Even though Lilli missed her home in Germany she knew that if she had not come to America, she would not have met Walter. Just recently they had received a picture of Uncle Herman dressed in his new uniform as a member of the elite guard for the Kaiser's Gardes du Corp.

She had read the inscription on Uncle Herman's belt buckle, "Gott Mitt Uns." Lilli believed that no matter where you were God was always with you. She loved the new photograph of her uncle, as did her mother who displayed it proudly on the table in their small parlor.

Everyone in the family understood that this was a very special promotion and the entire family celebrated his success. Lilli remembered from her lessons back home that the Gardes du Corps began long ago in the early 1700's by the Emperor Frederick II. The Gardes were the emperor's personal bodyguards, the elite of the elite and now Uncle Herman had joined their ranks. A personal body guard to the Kaiser, Uncle Herman, a soldier for the German Kaiser, now that was something very special. Lilli's chest filled with pride for him. But she also understood that these new responsibilities kept him very busy and he might not get a chance to come to America for a very long time. As Lilli hurried home, she said a little prayer that she would hear from him soon.

Immersed in thought she soon arrived at the front steps juggled and balanced the bundles in her arms as she rushed into the building. Climbing up the three flights of stairs to the third-floor landing Lilli was out of breath, standing at the door she thought, "Maybe Walter and I will have one of those lifts or new elevators in our apartment building." Now that would be really nice."

Entering the apartment, Lilli ran straight to her room, placing the heavy bundles onto the polished floor in front of her sewing machine. Lilli nodded, pleased to see that she had left her machine all set up and ready for her to add the final touches on her beautiful wedding dress.

She and her mother had designed her dress together with a lot of help from Emma. Emma and Wilhelmine had become dear friends. Lilli loved that her mother had such a loving friendship. Lilli always felt love from her mother, Wilhelmine was her best friend, and Lilli knew she could always count on her for all of the love and support a daughter would ever need. She recalled how it was her mother who sat by her bed day and night for weeks after Lilli's terrible accident in Stuttgart so many years ago. A shiver ran down her back and she gulped as she remembered how she had fallen beneath a speeding carriage and had been dragged down the street by a team of horses. There had been concerns about possible long-term effects of that frightening event but the cuts, bruises and scrapes were external and would heal over time with no long-lasting ill effects. The doctor had assured her of that, he said it was truly a miracle. Eventually Lilli's wounds healed and all was well.

Lilli knew that it was their combined determination, fortitude and inner strength that helped her get through it. They had certainly faced tough times before, and as she pulled the upholstered mahogany bench closer to her sewing machine, Lilli hoped the tough times were behind them. Calling hello to her mother she placed the pinned raw edges of her wedding gown on the sewing machine platform and quickly became absorbed in her sewing. Pushing her feet forward she pressed down on the treadle as the heavy metal grate moved forward then backward. Rhythmically the sewing needle began to slide up and down into the thick silk, creating perfect seams uniting the material where just minutes before rough edges had been.

Lilli loved to sew; it was a passion for her; she could imagine the completed piece before she even began making it. As she pushed down on the treadle feeling the ease of the pedal as it gently moved back and forth, she relaxed and the pinching tension left her body. She had become so absorbed in her task that she barely heard her mother's tapping on the door jamb behind her. Lilli jumped startled at her mother's voice, "Bitte, Lilli, bitte, a large crate has just arrived from Stuttgart, quick, bitte come and see."

Sitting up and placing her sewing to the side, Lilli rose and hurried to the hallway where indeed a very large crate stood. Excited Lilli was anxious to open it, but as she examined the massive delivery, she realized that this gift was not just for her. This large bulky crate stamped with markings from all the way across the Atlantic Ocean was addressed to her and to Walter. Leaning in to examine it more, Lilli said, "Maybe I can just begin to rip back this piece of covering." But with her fingers eagerly poking and prodding she stopped. Tilting her head to look around she examined it from all sides Lilli wondered, "What could possibly be inside this and who would have sent such a large gift?" Standing on her toes she craned her head back and asked her mother, "Do you know what this is and who sent it?" Wilhelmmine just as bewildered as Lilli shook her head, "Nein." She had no idea. Lilli smiled and stepped back, putting her arm around her mother she said, "I guess I'll just have to wait until Walter gets here so we can open it together."

"Wait?" questioned Wilhelmmine thinking that this large crate was taking up the entire entrance to their apartment's narrow hallway. If she had to wait to get it opened then at least she wanted to have it out of the way. "Let's try to get it against this wall, "she suggested. Together they pushed and rocked it inch by inch back and forth until finally they moved it as close to the wall as possible. "Phew." Wilhelmmine said, as she saw that now they could squeeze in to the entry way of their home. Looking over her shoulder Lilli reluctantly walked back to her sewing while her mother relieved returned to the kitchen to finish dinner preparations.

Streams of the late afternoon sun poured through the large

west facing windows in Lilli's room. They created a magical golden aura as they gently blanketed the yards of silk that were now being transformed into Lilli's wedding dress. Looking around her workspace Lilli thought, "I love this room, it always brings a sense of peace to me especially at this time of day." Lilli straightened, pushing away from her sewing, as she felt an inner warmth and sense of peace stronger than she had ever felt before. After several minutes allowing this feeling to embrace her, she returned to her stitching and softly began to hum Stille Nacht.

With her feet placed evenly on the treadle, she began working the machine, easily pedaling, pushing forward then backward, forward then backward as each seam came together with a binding strength that bound the two separate pieces of material into one. Her thoughts began to wander, she thought of Walter, and began dreaming of their marriage, visualizing the family they would have and the life they would make. Lilli saw a future as bright as the light filling her room and as peaceful as a Christmas Carol.

Wilhelmmine's call asking Lilli to help in the kitchen brought her back to the present, as she reminded her, to set an extra place for Walter remembering that they had invited him to join them.

Lilli smiled thinking of Walter joining them for dinner and since this was a special occasion, she chose the pink and white flowered pattern De Havilland china plates to set on the shining mahogany table. Excited with anticipation of both Walter and the gift Lilli's mind raced. Suddenly the Black Forest Cuckoo clock, a gift from Uncle Herman on his last visit, indicated 6 o'clock. At the same time Lilli heard the light quick steps on the back stairs announcing her future husband's arrival. Placing the last dish on the table, her hands flew up to pat down any loose hairs. Taking a quick glance in the mirror hanging on the wall she happily opened the door.

Walter stood before her, his hand in midair, ready to knock, "Walter, Walter, wait until you see what came for us today. It must have taken weeks to get here. Mother and I have no idea who sent it." Lilli exclaimed.

She grabbed his hand and pulled him hastily through the apartment to the front hall where the crate stood straight and tall as a wooden soldier. Immediately, Walter took a step backwards, his eyes widening as he took in the sight of the immense crate against the wall, his face a mix of curiosity and wonder. He couldn't imagine what was inside and he had no idea who would have sent such a very large gift.

He noted that the crate was also partially blocking the doorway to the parlor. "Hmm" thought Walter, "this is where I want to speak with Mrs. Von Holzapfel about where Lilli and I might live after we're married. Apparently we have to open the crate first."

Walter held Lilli's hand as for several moments, they starred in amazement, wondering what was inside a box of this size. No longer able to contain her curiosity, Lilli let go of Walter's hand, and ran to her room to get a pair of scissors. Taking them from her sewing machine, she approached the crate with determination. First, she tackled cutting the heavy binding, then she cut the strapping. Catching her enthusiasm Walter joined by pulling and loosening the side strapping which was wrapped tightly all around the crate.

Finally, the first layer of packaging was ripped open only to reveal a second more thicker layer of protection covering it fully. Letting out a groan of frustration Lilli was prepared to continue ripping but stopped quickly grabbing Walter's hands "Stop, wait." She instructed, noticing a large yellow envelope taped to one side of the crate. Walter watched as Lilli quickly ripped the envelope off the crate, tearing open the seal. Without looking up she pulled out several folded papers, unfolded them and began to read out loud.

"To Lilli, my dearest niece and to Walter," Glancing up from the note Lilli said, "It's from my Uncle Herman in Stuttgart." The letter was dated July 26, 1901. Lilli continued reading, "First and most importantly, I wish you and Walter all the happiness, joy and love this world can offer. It is with regret that I will not be able to attend your wedding celebration on September first. My heart is sad and heavy that I must decline due to commitments and responsibilities I have here in Berlin. Many important events have happened this year and the Kaiser plans to speak to the Reichstag this summer. It is critical that I remain here in the capital. As we have heard it said our place in the sun is coming and Germany will shine as brightly as the island of King Edward VII, our Kaiser's uncle. Even though I will be in Berlin, I will be thinking of you and Walter, on your very special day. Please accept my apology. I am sending a gift that I hope you will love. It is something I have been working on for several years, I always planned that you would receive it and I had planned to give it to you in person.

It is a special gift not only for your wedding day but a gift I hope you will treasure for the rest of your life. It is a rocking chair which I have made especially for you."

Continuing to read, Lilli's voice choked with emotion.

"Now Lilli my dear, this is not an ordinary chair but a chair made with love, care and I believe a soul. This chair is designed specifically to hold you snuggly as you sit with its arms surrounding you, soothing you in its movement and nurturing you in its rhythm. Let me tell you a little bit about this wonderful chair."

Lilli leaned against the crate continuing to read out loud she slid slowly down its side until she sat on the floor with her back against its base. Walter sat down next to her gently placing his arm across her shoulders and pulling her closer to him.

Wilhelmine wiped her hands on her apron as she leaned against the wall for support, her eyes closed as she heard her big brother's words. Herman went on to say, "As you know Lilli, ancient Egyptian history tells us that chairs must represent natural forms to keep balance in the universe and to keep chaos out. Your chair's natural form has not one but two Lions looking to the left and to the right both guarding your universe, balancing it and hopefully keeping chaos out. Their manes are carved long and curled, spreading across the upper back of your chair to support your head as it rests. The spindles of the back of the chair are contoured and curved to firmly and securely support your back. The arms on each side are wide and designed for your fingers to curl into the soft grooves at the end each representing the paws of the lions. The rockers are especially long for smooth rocking to help calm a crying baby on a long winters' night and to allow the rocking movement to fall forward and backward with the ease of a pendulum. The seat is wide and curved, large enough for more than one child to sit and rock comfortably, maybe several children giggling merrily.

Something else I want to share, meine Liebchen, is what I believe; I believe that an artist leaves a little piece of themself in everything they create, so please know that there is a part of me, maybe of my heart, my essence or my soul in your gift. No matter what happens I will always be with you Lilli. Whenever you are rocking in your chair Lilli I will be there.

"This chair sounds amazing!" Lilli thought. And as she looked at Walter tears were filling her eyes. "I can't imagine Uncle Herman not being here," she said.

Walter pulled Lilli closer to him, and held her tightly, telling her, "I have a feeling Lilli, that Uncle Herman will always be with us. Come let's take a look at our wedding gift."

Taking Lilli's hands, he lifted her to her feet. For a moment they stood face to face and looked tenderly into each other's eyes. Then without further hesitation simultaneously they began tearing off the brown wrapper that was covering the large box. Lilli, Walter and Wilhelmmine all stared in awe as the trappings of the box fell away and Lilli's stunning wooden rocking chair appeared

The first thing Lilli saw were the profiles of the two lions, one looking right, the other left, the lion's mouths were open in wide grins showing sharp pointed teeth. Uncle Herman had perfectly described the carved curly manes which covered the entire back of the chair Together, Lily and Walter lifted the chair up from the base of the packing crate and placed it gently down on the dark hardwood floor in the hallway.

Running her hands over the carved profiles Lilli felt the curls of the manes, the open eyes and the sharp points of the teeth. Lilli slid her hands down the back and placed them momentarily upon the wooden grooves and curves. Slowly she moved her hands across the spindled back and along the arms on each side marveling at the smooth wood, inhaling its rich oak scent. She felt the grooves that ended at each arm on the chair, where her fingers would rest comfortably. She rubbed the contoured seat of the chair feeling its slight uplifting curve on each side and took in a breath at the length of its long rockers securely beveled into the base of the chair. The shiny and polished wood was a blend of rich, and warm shades of brown.

Lilli stood back as she imagined rocking in this spectacular chair. Even though it was brand new it looked like it appeared already as if it was a very old chair. It possessed a welcoming and protective aura; she knew it definitely had a soul.

"This is a truly special chair." thought Lilli,

She understood that this chair would be a wonderful member of their new family and she was looking forward to rocking in it at every opportunity she had.

Walter gently took Lilli's hands and guided her to sit in its seat. Sliding back in the seat Lilli felt a peaceful sense of comfort, she rested against the spindles as her head leaned back on the curly wooden mane. Lilli placed her arms on each side of the chair, her hands automatically resting in the carved grooves of the lion's paws, and began to slowly rock back and forth. Releasing a breath and closing her eyes Lilli relaxed, its rhythm soothing her as she began to imagine the day when she would be holding her and Walter's babies and rocking just like this. Lilli believed that this chair would not only rock her and

Walter's babies but even a long time from now the many grandchildren that she planned on having too.

"There would never be another wedding gift such as this," Lily thought as she rocked, her thoughts flew back over the last several months and remembering her April 30th birthday when she turned 19. She couldn't believe how so many things had changed since that day.

Enjoying every moment celebrating the day with her mother, Lilli expressed concern later in the evening that being 19 and not married made her feel quite different from so many of her friends. Most of Lilli's friends were married and already having children.

Continuing to rock back and forth Lilli began to feel more confident about the future. Soon she was getting married and she would have a family too.

A smile spread over Lilli's face as she thought, "How foolish I was to be worried about those things."

After several minutes, Lilli's mother, suggested they move the chair out of the hallway and into the parlor. Lovingly, Walter lifted it as Lilli and Wilhelmine cleared away the wrappings from the hall floor. Finding the perfect location for their wedding gift he gently placed it down, as he inhaled the sumptuous aroma of dinner which was wafting throughout the apartment.

Feeling his stomach rumpling in anticipation of his favorite meal, Walter went to wash his hands happy to be having dining with his soon to be bride and mother in law.

Tightening the ties on her apron, Wilhelmine left the parlor heading for the kitchen. Lilli was the only one not in a hurry to leave the room. Left all alone, deliberately she slowed her pace, turning once more to gaze at this wonderful gift. Stealing a glance at her chair, Lilli mused that it seemed to be looking right back at her. The sheer, light curtains in the front windows blew slightly as a breeze from the east wrapped itself around them. It was then that the chair appeared to rock, very slightly forward then back. "Danke, Uncle Herman," she whispered softly, "Danke."

"Oh, bride and groom, for you my prayer; is not that every day be fair, for that could never be. I pray that love shall last, whate'er the day; through all that comes of grief and pain and hurt and care may love remain. " - Edgar A. Guest

7

WEDDING DAY

*O*pening her eyes, on the early summer morning, coming out of a deep sleep, Lilli stretched casually, gave a hearty yarn before suddenly realizing that today was the day! Sitting bolt upright she shouted,

"Oh my gosh, I'm getting married today!"

Springing from her bed Lilli's feet quickly hit the cool damp floor, the early September weather was warm and humid and after sleeping with the windows open all night her room felt it. The sheets, the spread and her nightgown were unusually moist and damp. Lilli thought," What was I thinking getting married in the hot summer weather?"

Her mother often said that the heat in Brooklyn during the summer was almost as bad as she remembered at home in Stuttgart. Lilli could tell by the mornings' heat that today's humidity would certainly not abate. Not knowing what to do first she stopped for a moment and gathered her thoughts, then she reached for her bathrobe from its nearby hook, her hair brush and combs from her vanity and rushed to the bathroom in the hallway which they shared with several other tenants on the third floor.

Lilli hoped she was ahead of the other tenants along with the relatives who were staying at their apartment but dreaded that she wasn't. Her brows furrowed as she thought, oh no today is Sunday so many of the other residents will be home too. Sharing the water closet floor Lilli worried that getting herself ready might take even longer this morning than usual.

There was already a line of people queuing up at the door. Lilli sighed realizing that it would have been better to get up so much earlier. "Too late now." she said aloud. Glancing at the line she smiled, went to end and waited her turn.

Normally she would be tuned in to every nuance of the building, on this day Lilli was oblivious to the typical Sunday morning sounds. Yes, babies were crying, people were shouting, and doors were banging, they barely registered to Lilli. Instead she was imagining the beautiful notes of Beethoven's "Ode to Joy" emanating from the organ of her church where she would soon be walking down the aisle to become Mrs. Walter von Vetterlein.

Lilli was ecstatic that they would be getting married at St John's church on Prospect Street. She and Walter felt at home there, she knew their families from Germany would too, as this church closely resembled the churches back in Germany. Its Gothic appearance, pointed entryways, and rounded arches with lines above the windows. Lilli smiled thinking that those lines made it seem like each window had a raised eyebrow above it.

On this special day Lilli wanted to cherish and remember

her home in Germany. Since she wasn't being married in the church she grew up in, then St. John's felt the closest to it. Life was definitely moving forward but it was also important to honor the past. Suddenly, Lilli was back in Germany, transported across the ocean to so many Sunday mornings at her family's church. It was only a short while ago that she was attending services with her cousins, aunts and uncles. Together they would sing the familiar hymns, greet friends and neighbors always admiring the carved spirals, the stained-glass windows and the extraordinarily high ceilings.

Lilli's breath caught as she remembered how it all changed, all of it ended when her father had been killed. From then on it was Lilli and her mother alone, everything was different. Oh, how Lilli wished her father was alive to meet Walter and to see how much he loved her and she loved him. Even though she knew Walter loved her deeply but since her father's death a feeling of emptiness sat in Lilli's heart and never went away.

She was jarred out of her thoughts by the opening of the bathroom door. Finally, it was her turn. Lilli smiled thankfully to the person who had been before her. As she closed the door and began to wash up, she wondered how she could feel so many emotions at once. She was excited, sad and nervous all at the same time.

When Lilli was finished, she gathered her toiletry items, and returned to the apartment, noticing that everyone had gathered in the kitchen. "Of course, they would, "Lilli smiled to herself "That's always where the family gathers." Wanting time to herself, Lilli tightened the pull on her robe and walked into the parlor, she headed towards the chair Uncle Herman had carved for her. She needed to be alone with her chair, with

Uncle Herman even though she knew that he wasn't with her in person she believed that his spirit was.

The quietness of the parlor was in stark contrast to the noise and chatter in the kitchen, the entire room itself felt like a cocoon, protected from everything and everyone else. Welcoming the uniqueness of the quietness of this moment Lilli walked over to the chair, actually it seemed to Lilli that the chair drew her in. As Lilli approached the chair her hands instinctively reached out to hold onto the arms of the rocker. She closed her eyes, inhaling a deep breath. Again, she smelled the rich oak wood. There was a warmth to the chair which permeated the air around it. "Yes," she said, "Uncle Herman will be at the wedding, I feel it." Sliding onto the seat Lilli felt the curve of the chair back offer support as she rested against its spindles. Lilli felt supported gently in its embrace as the chair began to slowly rock forward and backward. Allowing the rhythm to gently move her, Lilli knew that her life was moving forward too and she prayed that from this time on everything would be good.

"The duties of the average housekeeper who does her own work are so many and so varied that it is often hard for her to know just where to begin." - Josephine Morris

8

HOME

Since Walter's family was in Germany, he and Lilli decided to look for an apartment near Lilli's mother. They were thrilled when an apartment became available right on Prospect Ave. It was small with only three rooms and a bathroom that was shared with other renters on the floor, but Lilli adored it.

"This is perfect!" She said. "How much room do we need?"

Knowing that it was within walking distant to Lilli's mother and the church they attended made it even better.

Lilli loved Walter, she loved being courted, planning her wedding and getting married, but she hadn't thought much about actually being a married couple. This was new and different, Lilli found it very overwhelming. It seemed as if every day there was so much to learn and to do. Lilli spoke out loud asking herself rhetorically, "Will I ever be able to manage a home, to cook meals on time and to take care of children, too?"

Growing up it was always her mother who took care of everything. Of course, Lilli helped with chores but when it came to actually planning, shopping and scheduling meals, knowing how to keep the apartment clean and orderly, washing and hanging out the laundry, cooking delicious meals, well her mother always did this and somehow it looked as if she did it effortlessly.

"Did she always know how to do this, when did she learn?" Lilli wondered.

Lilli's mother told her that she would help her get started but Lilli really wanted to be able to do it on her own. She wanted Walter and her mother to be proud of her. Since she considered herself, "the woman of the house," keeping an orderly home was her responsibility inside and outside.

Lilli once again remembered how in Stuttgart it was common to see your neighbors sweeping the steps in front of their apartments, the sidewalks and right onto the street. Everything was neat, clean and orderly. "That was the German way," her mother told her. "Otherwise, what would people think"? Lilli wondered were there any other ways?

As Lilli glanced around, she noticed a wedding gift on the seat of her rocking chair. When she and Walter had opened it earlier, she told herself, "I'll look at this later." Lilli thought that perhaps now was a good time. Lifting it off the seat of the chair, Lilli snuggled comfortably into her rocker, holding the gift in her hands she thought, "Such a small book, I wonder what I can learn from it?" Becoming settled she placed the book in her lap, opened it, and began taking a thorough look through it.

The cover, a checkerboard pattern of cream tiles with small

blue diamond designs in the corners, gave no indication of what the book was about. Its design reminded Lilli of a bathroom floor she had seen in Germany as a girl. The pages were bound by three rings which opened allowing the owner to remove or add more information as necessary. Lilli grew more curious about this gift as she carefully opened the book, not sure what to expect inside.

The first page offered a simple dedication, to Miss Rosemary Reilly, for her interest and cooperation in the accomplishment of this work, and for her extraordinary skills as a teacher. "Well, what work is this?" Lilli uttered, turning to the next page, she read out loud, "Household Science and Arts" simply stated Lilli thought as she chuckled. "There you have it." She began to read, "Running a home is both a science and an art. No wonder I am overwhelmed. I was never really good in science, and as far as art is concerned, I'll leave that to the professionals." Lilli hoped the book offered specific instructions and grinned broadly when she found that it did. "From soup to nuts as it is said in America," she muttered.

Lilli ran her pointer finger down the table of contents noting that her new guide was divided into categories each with a section offering specific and detailed instructions on home management. Reading them out loud, she noted such specific categories as The Kitchen Fire, Home Furnishings, Composition and Cost of Menus and at the end of this lengthy list a section dedicated specifically to The Home Maker's Duty to Herself.

Not only did Lilli's book offer American recipes but also tips on how to clean and organize your home, everything from setting the table to cleaning kerosene lamps. It recommended which days of the week to do the wash, and how to hang it out, which days to sweep the floors and clean the bathroom. It gave instructions on how to accomplish each chore and how to keep a manageable schedule to do it. It even explained why keeping a clean and orderly home was important. "Not only does it look better, but it is also healthier." Lilli read, gasping as she pored over the section on dust. It stated that much dust is alive and contains germs and microbes, and these germs and microbes can actually be dangerous. Reading intently, Lilli appreciated how her new guide explained the ways of protecting yourself and your loved ones from the living germs found in dust. "Now I get it." Lilli nodded to herself.

Holding the book in her lap she slowly rocked, understanding that being a homemaker was truly a science and an art. With her new guide Lilli felt her fears and concerns subside knowing what the next steps would be, a sense of calmness washed over her. The late morning sun streamed into the room as Lilli looked out the window seeing the chaotic and busy street below. Leaning back, she snuggled into the seat of her rocking chair, and felt the chair as it comfortably supported her. Lilli smiled, she now had a plan, a process and a blueprint as Walter would say.

As Lilli rocked back and forth an old English nursery rhyme came to mind. "Wash on Monday, Iron on Tuesday; Bake on Wednesday, Brew on Thursday, Churn on Friday, Mend on Saturday, and Go to Meeting on Sunday." she recited out loud. "Now I even have a schedule."

These were the answers and the directions she needed. Her confidence returning Lilli relaxed. "I know it will take some time, but I can manage this."

Again, patience was becoming a part of Lilli's character and behavior. By becoming more patient she was becoming more confident in her ability to overcome challenges and obstacles. Her mother would help her but this apartment was ultimately Lilli's and Walter's home, along with the children they would have. Lilli realized that having a guide was just what she needed. Not knowing how or where to start was really the most difficult part and now she had guidance.

"I can do this." Lilli said aloud. She gave the chair a push rocking a bit faster, her head relaxed against the carved wood of the lion's manes. Gazing around the parlor of her new apartment she said, "I can do this, one step at a time."

As the sun began to climb higher in the sky Lilli enthralled with her gift, continued to read different passages. There was a section in the book she wanted to read, one that had nothing to do with cooking, cleaning, or washing clothes. The section was titled The Home Maker's Duty to Herself. In this chapter Lilli read about the importance of taking time to rest, of taking your work outside in order to enjoy pleasant weather and fresh air, and of sitting down to unwind several times a day. Lilli was intrigued to read that the use of labor-saving devices was not a luxury, but an investment in your home and your health, this made her smile, knowing that she would not feel guilty purchasing something she needed and wanted.

After a while she rose from her chair and set to work making the apartment feel and smell like their home. Lilli worked methodically beginning in one room first, bringing her duster, Bissell carpet sweeper, rags and bucket of hot water with a pine smelling cleaner. Entering a room she would work from left to right one step at a time and over the next several days everything began to come together. Nearing completion, she remembered the long-ago lesson learned while doing chores with her mother, when your job is done, stop, take a breath and admire the completed task. Smiling she did just that, feeling pride, accomplishment and satisfaction, she absolutely loved their new home and she loved how it looked.

What Lilli also enjoyed along with their close proximity to her mother and their church was the open market area nearby. Together she and Walter would shop on Saturday mornings. Since they lived in what was known as "Little Deutschland" the market area featured many of the German foods and ingredients they grew up with in Germany. They were thrilled to find sauerkraut, bratwurst, schnitzel, and spatzle as common ingredients to purchase.

She noticed too that in other Brooklyn neighborhoods, farther away from her own, the smells, the vegetables and the meats were quite different, the result of people from myriad ethnicities having made this part of America their home. Once when venturing out a couple of blocks to a different area Lilli asked a vendor about a particularly strong smell which she didn't recognize, "That'sa garlic!" the vendor replied proudly. Wrinkling her nose at its pungency, Lilli thought, I can't imagine ever using that ingredient in anything I cook." But then Lilli chuckled to herself remembering that she was now in America where the cuisine was different from her homeland. Even though the foods might smell different and would likely have unfamiliar flavors Lilli delighted in hearing all of the different languages and accents as she traveled further out of her small neighborhood. This was such a new experience;

back in Stuttgart she could travel for miles and it would all be the same since everyone spoke German. Here in New York, she could walk around a block and enter a new world.

Lilli smiled thinking how America reminded her of the patchwork quilt that lay across the large bed she shared with Walter. She had begun sewing it months before using pieces of cloths from fabric remnants, along with material from clothes they no longer used. Each segment was unique in color, shape and texture, yet together they became one large lovely blanket. Lilli noticed how each piece of fabric was made even more interesting when placed next to another than when it was alone and separate. Lilli adored her quilt, she appreciated how it looked, how it felt and what it meant to both her and Walter.

Thinking of her quilt and the thousands of immigrants who had, like Lilli and Walter come to New York, she wondered if perhaps it was the diversity that gave America its extraordinary uniqueness. Lilli recalled a recent event where people were reciting poetry. There was a young woman, whose name she couldn't remember, but the poem she read was about coming to America. This powerful piece described huddled masses yearning to breathe free.

Was she part of a huddled mass? Did she yearn to breathe free? In Germany they had a Kaiser, a king who inherited the throne. In America the people elected a president in America there was a choice, no one became president forever and the president represented the people. Lilli wasn't sure but it seemed as if each day she thought less and less about her homeland then she did about where she was now. She was an American and enjoyed the freedom to make her own choices, of meeting people who had different backgrounds, and who spoke different languages. Lilli had heard discussions about the possibility of women being allowed to vote for elected officials. "Wow," Lilli thought "that would really be something."

Lilli and Walter settled comfortably into the activities and routine of a young married couple. Months went by, quickly turning into years, and before they knew it, they were approaching their third wedding anniversary. They were happy together and took joy in being together and sharing a home. Lilli was always busy cleaning, sewing and cooking. It seemed as if there weren't enough hours in the day for all of the things she needed to do. Meanwhile Walter's assignments at the architectural firm of Moran, MacAleese, and Stampfl, kept him away from early in the morning to late in the evening. He was appreciated at work and had become an important part of the team there. Yet, he looked forward to coming home to his beautiful wife, to a wonderfully cooked meal, and to smoking his pipe while finally relaxing at the end of another day.

But lately sitting across the table from each other over dinner there would be a pause in the conversation. The silence was becoming deafening. They didn't need to say anything about it. They looked at the empty chairs around the table and they both felt it, the ache in their hearts, the fear in their bellies and the silence, the overwhelming silence in the room.

Walter understood that both he and Lilli knew what was missing. They wanted to have a family. They wanted children, they were ready, but it just wasn't happening. They couldn't understand it and they didn't know why. Several of their friends who were married after them already had one or two children and some like the Schwartz family had twins and were planning more.

Each time Lilli's hopes were raised that maybe this time she was pregnant; they were dashed just as quickly.

"Lilli my love, I just don't know what we can do anymore." Walter softly said, as he looked across the table at his wife and reached for her hand. Walter lowered his eyes because the pain and despair that he saw in Lilli's were too much for him to bear. As tears came to his eyes Lilli drew her hand away, pushing her chair back she rose from the table and began to clear their dishes. Walter's shoulders slumped, he kept his head lowered, he knew that there was nothing more to say.

"Gentle is that gentle does."

English Proverb

9

WILHELMMINE, GERMANY, 1864

Lilli's mother was born Wilhelmmine Alvine Herzele in Esslingen, Germany in the year 1864, the fourth daughter of Eduard and Alvine Herzele's family of three daughters and one son. When Wilhelmmine was born her brother, Herman was 4 years old. Gertrude the oldest, was already 14. No longer in school she was helping out on the family farm. Following close behind Gertrude by one year was Ingmar and Anna followed one year after her. Sadly, their mother had suffered several miscarriages before Herman was born, with more miscarriages occurring in the years following his birth. By the time Herman was 4 years old his parents believed that he would be their youngest and last child, but when beautiful little Wilhelmmine came along not only were they very happy, they were also very much surprised.

As the baby of this large family, Wilhelmmine enjoyed a childhood of being loved and cared for by everyone. She grew up with indulgent tolerance, and not given the same expectations that her older siblings had received. Her parents simply wanted to enjoy this beautiful little gift they had been blessed with. So Wilhelmmine was just a bit more spoiled and adored by not only her parents but her siblings as well. However, being the child on whom everyone doted didn't stop her from wanting to help out, to contribute and be an important part of her family.

Often, she would follow, watching the others, while chores were being completed. She loved tagging along with her siblings, straggling behind and copying everything they did. Even though she was so much younger she never let it stop her. In truth, she welcomed the challenges. When she wasn't with her sisters and brother, she missed them and felt left out.

Wilhelmmine learned quickly as she observed closely how things around the farm were done. She did her best to participate and pitch in by watching and mirroring their mannerisms and behaviors. Of course, her persistence and feistiness made her family laugh and love her even more.

Along with having a can-do attitude Wilhelmmine was also a natural nurturer. She delighted in playing with her dolls. Having three older sisters meant Wilhelmmine had quite a few, many of which were hand-me-downs from Gertrude, Ingmar and Anna. She spent hours pretending to be their mother, taking gentle care of each doll, always making certain they were all covered at night, ensuring that her dolls were regularly snuggled and held, for her there would be no favorites.

She was also dedicated to helping her family, and before long she knew how to mend clothes, plant in the garden, carefully collect the eggs from the hens and even milk the family's cow.

Wilhelmmine loved all of the farm animals, but of all the animals on the farm, her most cherished was a big yellow tabby cat Felix. Felix was great at catching mice and small creatures, frequently dropping them off as gifts on the front porch. He was a big barn cat and meant to stay outdoors. He was not to be allowed in the house, but, whenever Wilhelmmine was around, he would follow her everywhere she went. He followed her in the yard, the barn and if he could, even into the house. There were also times when Wilhelmmine would sneak Felix into the house to feed him warm milk and even bring him to snuggle with her at night in the bed she shared with Anna. When Anna spotted Felix, she would giggle and warn her younger sister not to let anyone else know or it would be Felix that got into trouble. As they fell asleep Felix would nestle between them purring contentedly all through the night as his wide paws massaged the sheets. The girls giggled and dubbed his gentle movements as "making muffins."

Even though Wilhelmmine was the youngest in the family, she was as smart as her sisters and her brother. She was also the most precocious. This is where having a loving, kind and fun big brother was very, very helpful. Herman would bring her along on his adventures outside of the farm and on trips to town to explore even further out in their village.

Since Herman loved to read, he would always be telling her stories from the many books he enjoyed. He was a particular fan of history, and mythology, not just that of Germany, but also of the world. He'd spend hours researching and reading about the Roman and Greek eras, the battles, the politics, the economy and the ancient lore of these amazing empires. He eagerly shared these stories with Wilhelmmine, and she would sit and listen, peppering him with questions. Even when he met with his friends Herman would let her hang out with them and be part of the gang.

When Wilhelmmine would look for Herman, she frequently found him in the barn or sitting on the back-stoop whittling with his knife on an old piece of wood or large branch. These were the times that Wilhelmmine liked the best, she would sit next to Herman and listen while he told her about an epic Roman battle or a mythological demon like Medusa. Often times he'd simply share his thoughts as he skillfully moved the blade of his knife turning it over and over carving something beautiful and useful from something that had been raw and rough. As he told tales of past empires he would work his knife, and soon without even much effort that rough piece of wood would magically be transformed into the beginning of a table or the leg of a chair. Sometimes he whittled entire battalions of wooden soldiers, each standing resolutely at attention on the ground beneath his knees.

All the while they were together, Herman spoke to Wilhelmmine as a friend, a confidante, listening thoughtfully to her queries and offering advice when asked. He never teased or taunted her. Wilhelmmine knew she was lucky because many of the brothers of her friends really enjoyed teasing, taunting and sometimes even terrorizing their sisters. The wonderful sibling bond between Wilhelmmine and Herman strengthened through the years, as they became each other's confidant and best friend.

Always enjoying her company Herman invited Wilhelmmine with him as they ventured through the hilly cobblestoned streets in their town. Wilhelmmine loved running down those streets feeling her feet hit the raised curve of each stone, careful not to turn an ankle while racing her brother to the end, Herman often letting his little sister win.

Through Herman's guidance Wilhelmmine learned of the world outside their farm and even beyond their town. She adored and admired him and she couldn't imagine a better big brother for any little girl. It was from her brother Herman that she learned, she gained confidence and was willing to take risks. He taught her to trust her instincts and to follow her gut feelings. With his encouragement Wilhelmmine quickly became far more daring and adventurous than her sisters had ever been or would ever dream of being.

The Herzele family was close knit and loving, they took pride in self-sufficiency even with the evolving mid nineteenth century standards. Both of Wilhelmmine's parents knew that times were changing and understood that the lives they had were not going to be the kind of lives their children would experience. The thriving city of Esslingen, a short distance from Stuttgart, which offered opportunities for employment at the many manufacturing and textile factories. When Herman and his older sisters came of age, they moved from the farm to the city, taking jobs in those factories. Eventually, Gertrude, Ingmar and Anna got married and started families of their own.

Wilhelmmine grew older too; Herman had already decided to enter the German military and become a soldier. Even Felix their beloved tabby cat was gone now, having passed away quietly in the barn one late summer evening at the ripe old age of 22. With only Wilhelmmine and her parents at home now, life was pretty quiet on the farm. Wilhelmmine kept herself busy traveling to visit her sisters and helping them with their families. But then one day Wilhelmmine's life changed too. She always remembered that day with startling clarity; it was December 24th 1880. She had been visiting her sister Gertrude, helping with her babies, when it came time to leave and head home. A light snow was just beginning to fall as Wilhelmmine's horse drawn carriage was headed back toward the farm. She heard the distant peal of bells as the sound of Christmas Carols rang throughout the town, it was Christmas Eve.

Wilhelmmine knew it was best to keep to her destination, it was cold, snowing, dark and getting late, but for some reason the sound of those bells beckoned to her. At first, she hesitated but only briefly before asking the driver to turn the horses around and to head to the church. Though she couldn't explain why, she had a feeling of being pulled towards that cozy building, its windows aglow in the snowy darkness. This strange feeling made her feel anxious but not afraid, knowing that the storm would only become stronger and fiercer but also knowing she needed to go to that church. It was the night before Christmas and Wilhelmmine was being pulled by a stronger power than she had ever felt or would ever be able to explain.

As the driver pulled up in front of the old stone Lutheran church, bells were ringing out merrily, and candles lit up every window, Wilhelmmine quickly jumped down from the carriage and hurried inside. She stopped only to brush off the snow from her coat, swipe at her hat and stamp her boots. The church was full, parishioners overflowed the pews, with many more standing in the vestibule. Though doubtful of finding one, Wilhelmmine quickly looked for an empty seat toward the back.

Craning her neck, she saw one, it seemed that it had been waiting for her, the last pew on the far left. Wilhelmmine rushed over and sat down just as the organ began the chords of the most beautiful Christmas hymn Wilhelmmine had ever heard: Stille Nacht. Of course, she recognized the tune, but it never sounded or felt like this before.

Wilhelmmine stood with the congregation and began to sing, but stopped so that she could listen to the sounds of voices in harmonious unison. As she stood there transfixed a rich tenor voice, as mellow and as smooth as melted chocolate resonated through her bones. Wondering who possessed such a powerful voice, Wilhelmmine closed her eyes immersing herself deeper in the experience and listened. She had never before heard, Stille Nacht sung so soulfully.

When the singing stopped and everyone sat back down, Wilhelmmine stole a glance to her left and there he was the source of the beautiful voice. He was a young man with curly dark brown hair, the straightest nose and the longest legs she had ever seen. Wilhelmmine was awestruck. As she stole glances out of the corner of her eye, she thought to herself "He actually is beautiful."

The rest of the service was a blur. As it ended and she slowly began filing out with the rest of the parishioners, there was a tap on her shoulder. Wilhelmmine turned and found herself face to chest with the tenor, who introduced himself as Willi von Holzapfel.

"Was this Divine intervention?" Wilhelmmine asked herself later, wondering what had drawn her to this particular church on Christmas Eve. It seemed she would quickly have her answer. Within 3 months she went from being Wilhelmmine Herzele to Frau Holzapfel.

Willi was a skilled carver, a sculptor, who had earned his trade certificate in his mid-teens. His parents had apprenticed him as a young boy to a gifted master craftsman and Willi was a quick and talented student. Becoming a Journeyman, he planned to become a master craftsman and have his own business employing apprentices for his own shop.

Wilhelmmine loved that her husband was a wood sculptor and so skilled that he was in demand throughout the city. She was proud of the attention he gave to each job. When he was finished with a project, he would bring Wilhelmmine to the site so he could show his work to her. She was awed and amazed each time at the intricacies and the beauty of each finished product, he shared with her that his work always bore his mark.

But there were times when Wilhelmmine would be fearful, when her breath would quicken and goose pimples would break out on her arms upon seeing how Willi often worked precariously perched on the edge of a building or the steeple of a church. She didn't tell Willi how she worried but she did worry and deeply.

Often times when her husband would leave for work in the wee hours of the mornings Wilhelmmine would wrap her arms around him, holding him tightly to her body as they kissed good bye. As she did, she would say a silent prayer for his safe return home that evening. If Willi knew how fearful Wilhelmmine sometimes felt, he never let on, but reassured her frequently that he was confident and careful, though maybe not always as cautious as he should be, he knew the risks and would always look out for himself and for others while at work.

The morning of April 30th, 1882 began as any other morning except that as Willi was leaving for work, he noticed a strained and painful expression on Wilhelmmine's face. Nine months pregnant, she was determined not to let him see her fear. She turned her face away from him and bit into her bottom lip so hard that she tasted blood. Curling her fisted hands into themselves her fingernails' dug deeply into the palms. Wilhelmmine forced a grim smile on her face as she wished her husband well that morning.

Wilhelmmine knew what to expect, she had been through this before with devastating tragic results, she knew what to prepare for and what could go wrong. When she was younger, she had listened to her older sisters regale each other with their explicit and frightening tales of painful labor and births, still there was no way to really know until it actually happened.

Having been raised on a farm, Wilhelmmine was no stranger to the delivery of calves, piglets and other farm animals. She knew it could be a long arduous process and one she did not want to bear alone. However, she was also vehemently opposed to having Willi witness this process, which had begun several hours ago, waking Wilhelmmine from slumber well before she usually arose to see her husband off.

As Wilhelmmine watched Willi prepare to leave for another day's work, her fear of being alone suddenly welled up inside her. She called out his name, her voice thick with emotion. He turned, knowing the voice and fearing the urgency it contained. Willi starred wide-eyes at his wife, seeing her face a pained mask. His mouth went dry and he felt his knees buckle.

"It's coming Willi. The baby is coming. Wilhelmmine gasped as her husband rushed to her side. "Go get the midwife, please hurry! "She cried.

Wilhelmmine felt sticky wet moisture flowing rapidly between her legs as she forced herself to fold her body forward and sit in the chair by their bed. As each pain intensified Wilhelmine gripped the arms of the chair and tried to focus on something, anything but the pain. Suddenly she saw it actually, she saw them. They were on the chest by their bedside, the gift her brother Herman had made for the new baby. As she looked at the carved small army of individual miniature soldiers all lined up in parade fashion she smiled. "And what if this little baby is not a boy?" Wilhelmmine had chided her big brother. "Then that little girl will need to learn to play with soldiers. "He replied as he looked lovingly at his beautiful baby sister. Looking at the soldiers all lined up on the chest Wilhelmmine was able to take a breath and smile as she remembered that conversation with her brother. "Well Herman, she thought we will soon know. Wilhelmmine's pains were coming faster and faster and still Willi had not returned. "Oh God, she cried, "Where is he?"

Alvine Lilli Holzapfel came into the world at 12:15pm on the 30th of April in 1882, weighing approximately 6 lbs. Her eyes were tiny slits as a full bushy head of dark brown hair stood out in all directions. Starring in disbelief, at her brand-new baby girl, Wilhelmmine stated, "This cannot be my child." the midwife holding a pink, slippery, screaming, bushy haired baby with the umbilical cord still attached, assured her, "Oh, Mrs. Holtzapfl she most certainly is." Wilhelmmine's head fell back on her wet bed pillow as her baby cried releasing her first breath. Tears came to her eyes as she thanked God for this gift, the sound of life from her new born daughter.

Willi, Wilhelmmine and Lilli were a family. Willi adored and cherished his daughter Lilli and laughed out loud as she played with her little wooden soldiers. Putting them in lines and chastising them as one after the other would topple and fall down. She was very patient though just like her mom, never really scolding her little soldiers, just picking them up and putting them next to each other again and again, as she babbled her baby language to them.

The years went by quickly; Wilhelmmine suffered several miscarriages, delivered two still born births and lost two infants Arthur and Almina, before they reached one years old. Shortly afterwards she and Willi accepted the fact that Lilli would be their only child.

Willi's business prospered and he was able to hire several apprentices to work with him. One day he brought home a young boy approximately 15 years of age to introduce to Wilhelmine and to Lilli. "This is the one." he told them," This is Fritz Speer, I will groom him to become a craftsman with me; he has the skill, the talent and the drive to be successful."

As they sat around the dinner table Willi spoke about his hopes and dreams for their future. Fritz ate heartily, boldly asking for seconds and even thirds. Lilli was only 9 years old but she remembered how her mother's eyes narrowed as she looked at this young man. He was tall and lanky, with sallow skin and dull brown hair which fell into his eyes, he looked like he could use several good hearty meals as he ate gluttonously, even though he appeared strong and agile.

Wilhelmmine didn't quite understand the connection which her husband felt towards this boy but she trusted his instincts even though every time she looked in Fritz's direction a shiver went down her spine and her heart skipped a beat, she didn't understand her concern but she felt it deep in her soul.

Later that evening Wilhelmmine spoke with Willi about her apprehension. As always Willi assured her that Fritz was a talented young carver, yes, he was impulsive but that was due to his youth and naiveté he said. As far as his youth, he would mature, as far as his naiveté he would learn. "I will teach him." Willi told her, "As I had been taught."

Several months passed and Willi and Fritz became a team, they would meet early in the morning, review the plans for the day and then begin their work. It seemed that as the buildings in Stuttgart were growing taller and more detailed Willi was in more and more demand.

Then one evening after dinner Willi mentioned that at the crack of dawn tomorrow, he and Fritz would be traveling far north to work on a church. He was excited because this would be the jewel in their portfolio. Yes, he said the building was extremely tall, the steeples were very pointed and sharp and the roof angle was perilously slanted. He assured Wilhelmine not to worry, he was prepared and would take all of the precautions necessary. He would make certain that Fritz did too. Wilhelmmine was not comforted; she felt a chill and a churning in the pit of her stomach, a feeling so powerful and ominous that she could do nothing to alleviate it. It came from the depths of her core; she had never felt anything like this before and it petrified her. She pleaded and begged Willi to change his plans, to choose another building that day, to let Fritz go with another apprentice; surely, he was now able to supervise on his own. Willi listened patiently but simply shook his head saying softly this was the plan, they would leave early in the morning and be home very, very late that evening, everything will be fine.

Wilhelmmine did not sleep well that night, tossing and turning, frequently reaching out to touch her husband as he slept soundly beside her. In the morning she pleaded again with Willi to reconsider his plans; he smiled at his wife, put his arms around her waist and pulled her so tightly that she felt the beat of his heart against hers'. He nuzzled his face into her neck as he told her, "No." he would not reconsider, that she was being overly anxious, this was his job and as always, he would be home for dinner. Before leaving, he stopped at the door, turned and asked if she would please make that beef stroganoff with noodles for dinner; "I really love the way you make it, it's my favorite."

Wilhelmmine felt her heart freeze in her chest, as a premonition of doom permeated the air around her, offering her no clarity as to why or what was about to happen.

Her eyes filled with tears as she smiled and tried to reassure herself that she was being too anxious, thinking that maybe she was over tired. She kissed her husband goodbye and as Willi shut the door, Wilhelmmine's felt her breathing almost halt, for most of the day she hypnotically walked around their home, she walked into rooms, looked around then left, touching nothing, adjusting nothing, wanting nothing. As the morning turned into afternoon, she did not begin the preparations for beef stroganoff, nor did she plan to. Somewhere far deep in her soul, in the bottomless depth of her heart where our primitive instincts still exist, Wilhelmmine knew what she felt, she knew that Willi would not be coming home tonight. Wilhelmmine did not make Willi's favorite dinner for that evening, she never would again.

As the evening approached Wilhelmmine became even more anxious, she looked up and down the street for Willi's horse and buggy, equipped with ladders, buckets and tools but the streets were empty. As the sun set deeply into the west with no sign of Willi or Fritz, Wilhelmmine's stomach filled with fear and apprehension. She knew the fear she felt was palpable, she tasted it. Then she heard it, the sounds of horses coming quickly to her door. Exhaling the breath, she had been holding all day she rushed to open the door chiding herself saying, "See you were being foolish, here they are; they are home just a little later than usual."

But as she flew the door open to greet her husband and his worker, her heart stopped, it wasn't them, a carriage slowed down and stopped at an angle in front of her door, it wasn't Willi's carriage and the two men approaching her, she didn't recognize. They walked to the door as if they were carrying a very heavy weight, too heavy for even the two of them to carry but their arms were empty. Getting closer they removed their hats respectfully and asked for Frau Holzapfel, Wilhelmmine nodded in response, then as their hands opened and closed in nervousness, they informed Wilhelmmine that Willi would not be coming home tonight, he wouldn't be coming home any night ever again.

Wilhelmmine felt the ground beneath her begin to give way as she swayed side to side. The men continued speaking as her ears began to buzz, she heard the words, fallen, hitting the ground, it wasn't his fault, they assured her, Willi had done everything correctly. He had the ladders secured; he had the safety straps on both him and Fritz, but for some reason Fritz had loosened and unsecured his strap while at the top of the steeple and as he reached for a tool, he began to slide down the side of the steep roof. Willi tried to reach him but couldn't, he loosened his belt to get a further stretch. That was when it happened; his footing failed him as his belt slipped off and he fell. Fritz was ok, he was able to hold onto the ledge until help came but Willi slipped through his strapping to an instant death.

Wilhelmmine's knees began to buckle as she grabbed onto the door jamb her fingers clawing into the wood for support. Staring straight ahead she stopped breathing, she felt the beat of her heart pulsing into her ears, her mouth went dry and everything around her spun. She could not speak, she could not cry, she could not move.

The year was 1891, he was 36 years old, Willi and Wilhelmmine had been married for 10 years; Lilli was 9 years old. "Oh, God, no, she thought, this is the worst, this can't be happening, this can't be real" Wilhelmmine's eyes stared straight ahead but she saw nothing. All noise ceased, as silence wrapped around her like a shroud. She felt weightless as though she was no longer tethered to the earth. The men's mouths were moving, they were opening and shutting but she heard no sound. She felt her body become rigid as she stood there frozen, not moving, not breathing, all of her oxygen locked inside her core. A voice in her head screamed, "You knew this was going to happen, you felt it in your bones." A cry uttered from her throat as Wilhelmmine screamed, "Oh God, why did you tell me, when I couldn't stop it!"

"Breath is the power behind all things...I breathe in and know that good things will happen." - Tao Porchon-Lynch

10

NOT BREATHING

It was all changed; in that instant she had changed, everything in her life was different from that moment on. The person she had been on the morning when Willi left for work for that very last time, no longer existed. Now her days were chronicled with thoughts of before Willi died and after Willi died. She would awaken and rise each morning, wake up Lilli, begin the chores of the day, go through the movements all without feeling, without thoughts, in a vacuum of time. It was as if she too had stopped breathing. She refused to allow herself the release of tears or the right to mourn, Oh, no, she thought… you do not rest; you will not cry you must be strong; you have a responsibility, to not only Lilli but to Willi. You will not show weakness.

She had to protect herself, because the pain was too hard to bear. She would not allow tears to open that wound, she knew that if she released and let her tears fall, they would never ever stop.

Lilli was only 9 years old but she understood by watching her mother what was expected. She understood that giving in to grief and despair or that forgetting one's responsibilities was not an option. She understood that keeping not only their home but themselves in proper form and order was expected from both of them. No one told her this, but she understood.

Before where there had been laughter, now there was sadness, where there had been joy now there was pain, and where their lives once had dreams now were only memories. It seemed as if their lives too had ended with Willi's. Lilli felt that with her father's death, she had also lost her mother.

"Is this how it was going to be from now on? How long will I carry this pain, this hurt in my heart? "Wilhelmmine asked herself. She felt a deep heaviness weighing in her bones, an ache which she had never felt before; she hurt everywhere.

Often Lilli's aunts would come to visit and bring their children to play with Lilli. She loved those days because her mother became more present, engaged more in conversations and sometimes even smiled a small smile but a smile. Time passed slowly and again routines took over. It was different, they were different, never again to be the same.

Then one day as Christmas was approaching Lilli heard something, she thought she'd never hear again, her mother's voice humming a tune, yes, she was humming that tune. It was that hymn which they all would sing together on Christmas Eve, Stille Nacht, yes, it was Stille Nacht.

Lilli listened as her heart swelled and then quietly holding her breath, she slowly and silently went over to her mother's side not wanting her to stop. Approaching her mother, she wrapped her thin slender arms around her mother's waist, hugging her as tightly as a child can. She clasped her small hands together, grasping and locking her fingers tightly behind her mother's back. "No, I am not letting go." Lilli thought.

As she held on tears flowed down her face, slowly Wilhelmmine's arms dropped and her hands too clasped together around Lilli's small back, and as they held onto each other tears which they had held in for so very, very long flowed from their eyes and down their cheeks. Their tears flowing together tasting not only of salt but of pain, loss, and sadness washed down and over that raw open wound which each of them had been holding inside so tightly, allowing no air, no light of day, to begin to heal. And now this deep, painful wound was being washed and cleansed by those tears; holding onto each other tightly, they cried as one.

Lilli couldn't remember how long they stood holding each other, crying together. Both of them feeling the pain and hurt which each of them had held in for so very, very long. This terrible loss that they shared together. At that moment, at that young age she knew their lives would go on. She understood that she and her mother would pull together to find the strength, purpose and joy to live again.

It was as if they had exhaled a breath which they had held in for a long, long time, yes, they were breathing again.

The days blended into weeks, weeks into months and months into years, Lilli was growing into a beautiful young lady. It became clear that as she grew, she inherited her father's dark hair and slow Mona Lisa like smile along with his height. And from her mother her delicate slenderness, grace and dark brown eyes which looked directly at you and at times even appeared to look through you.

But Lilli also inherited something far more important from both of them; she inherited character, that sense of responsibility, knowing that you are responsible for yourself and for your actions. Doing the right thing, even when it means unexpected pain or sacrifice on your part.

She remembered being told by her parents that "You are who you are when no one is watching." So often she had heard these words spoken at home that she never had to question an action, she knew that you just always did what was right.

This belief was her moral compass. She knew instinctively that regardless how menial the task you gave it your best, and when your assistance was needed you offered it. These were the lessons Lilli had been taught.

These virtuous traits were forged deep in her soul; they defined her, her daily thoughts, her everyday actions and her dreams for the future.

Afterward she only remembered that it all happened so quickly. It was a warm summer morning in Stuttgart. Lilli and her mother had many chores and much shopping to do that day. They decided to leave early for town knowing that as the day progressed it would only become hotter, so leaving after the sun rose and getting home before noon made sense to both of them.

It seemed to Wilhelmmine that everyone had similar thoughts since the streets were more crowded than usual for a weekday morning. After completing their chores, Lilli and Wilhelmmine tried walking side by side chatting, as they traveled down the busy street heading home. Both of them had their arms full and were juggling bags heavy with groceries and sewing materials. It was almost noon and the streets were bursting with shoppers and workers.

Several times, Lilli and her mother couldn't avoid being jostled and bumped. First, it was Lilli's right arm and shoulder that was bumped causing her to almost drop her packages, and then Wilhelmmine was jostled by someone rushing right into her almost knocking her down. Startled, Wilhelmmine exclaimed, "Ach du schreck! "With that the gentleman looked up, placed his hand on the brim of his hat, tipped it apologetically as he said, "Bitte," and continued hurrying down the crowded sidewalks.

Lilli noticed that the streets were becoming even more chaotic as children were running, darting in and out apparently chasing each other. Becoming concerned and annoyed, Lilli shouted loudly, to be heard by her mother but also to make a point to anyone else listening, "Is anyone watching these children?" She felt herself wince as many children were running right next to the carts and wagons being pulled by teams of large horses down the street.

She cringed noticing how many of the drivers were hurrying apparently oblivious to those on the crowded sidewalks and in the gutters. Frequently, the drivers needed to swerve their teams of horses to avoid hitting a running child yelling out angrily as the children ignored their commands.

Lilli felt a sense of responsibility finding herself compelled to pay more attention, keeping a keen eye on the number of children running haphazardly. She noticed how hard it was for the drivers to avoid so many children and how hard it was to maneuver their teams of horses. Leaning into her mother she said, "Watching them run so close to the street is making me nervous." Wilhelmmine nodded in agreement saying, "I agree, you're right, so many of these mothers with little children have their hands full."

But then it happened, she sensed it, without seeing it, the quick movement of a child rushing past her, running at full speed, head down and without looking as he ran directly into the path of a rapidly moving wagon being pulled by a team of horses at full gallop.

Instinctively, Lilli dropped her packages and rushed out after the child. Using all of her might she pushed his little body out of the pathway of the galloping horses' hooves. By Lilli's sheer force and strength alone, the child was catapulted out of the way of the kicking horses' feet, his life was saved. But by saving his life she almost lost hers, Lilli found herself trapped as the horses bore down on her. With nowhere to turn, she threw her arms across her face and shut her eyes against the impending stampede.

Wilhelmmine screamed as she saw her daughters' slim body flying under the wagon's axel being tossed up and kicked by the legs of the frightened horses as they reared up and back. The driver's voice was heard yelling and shouting as he pulled back with all of his might on the reins trying to halt the huge animals. Then suddenly Lilli was gone, she was nowhere to be seen.

Wilhelmmine's cries reverberated in the street as she ran with all of her might after the horse drawn wagon. Hearing the screams of this frantic running woman and seeing the driver as he tried desperately to pull his horses to a halt, many of the people who had been walking along the street, stopped and gaped at this grizzly scene. Their mouths open they stared and asked each other, "What just happened? What did you see? What did you hear?"

As the wagon slowly came to a halt people gathered around the sweating and frightened animals as Wilhelmmine looked frantically for her daughter. Lilli was nowhere to be seen. She wasn't there; Wilhelmmine didn't see her daughter on the street or under the wagon. Panic in her voice Wilhelmmine screamed out, "Where is she? Oh God, where is my daughter? No, please God, no!" she cried.

Lilli was gone. Where did she go, how could she have disappeared? This is what had happened, she had disappeared, "She isn't here, what is happening?" Wilhelmmine cried, "Oh, my God, where is she?"

Others too, spectators began looking up and down the street; they knew they had seen a young girl pushing that child out of the way. They knew what they had seen, but they couldn't believe what they were now seeing.

As a crowd gathered around the halted wagon and panting horses, people began looking everywhere for that brave young girl. Suddenly someone yelled, they had noticed a piece of cloth hanging from underneath the back of the wagon. "What is that?" a man yelled pointing at the printed material, "Is that her?"

As people pushed closer some looking away and some getting down on their bellies to look up and underneath the wagon, they saw her. Yes, there she was, Lilli's body was pressed firmly against the bottom of the wagon, held tightly against the floor, her long hair twisted around the axles and her long skirt wrapped tightly around her body like a cocoon.

She was pressed against the underneath bottom of the wagon. Lilli's long dark hair had whipped around the axles pulling and lifting her up away from the wheels and away from the horses' feet.

"Is she breathing? Is she breathing?" her mother screamed! "Oh, God, please breath, God help me, God, please help Lilli! "Please let her live, Not her too God, not her, I can't lose her too!" Wilhelmmine cried and prayed.

Strangers suddenly joined forces and became teammates, helpers, solace providers...people Wilhelmmine had never before known stopped what they had been doing to provide assistance, offer guidance and support to Wilhelmmine and to save Lilli. The team of horses was quickly unhitched and brought to the side, men, strong men, slight men, young and old men, boys of all ages and sizes, suddenly appeared to jack up the wagon and free Lilli from her bondage.

Lilli let out a soft whimper and then a painful moan as her body was gently and carefully removed from the base of the wagon and carried to a hastily created litter. "She's breathing! "They cried, "She's breathing, she's alive! "For a second time Wilhelmmine's entire body froze as she saw Lilli's slight form being removed from the wagon's underbelly and carried to the waiting litter.

Tears ran from Wilhelmmine's eyes and down her face as her lips moved softly whispering the words of the Lord's Prayer, "Our Father who art in heaven," she began softly.

Quickly running to Lilli's side, she thanked everyone around her. Wilhelmmine approached the litter and leaned into her daughter, kissing her bruised arms, neck, and torso, her tears flowing onto Lilli's face as thankfulness flowed from her heart.

Then, in front of all, as Lilli laid on that litter, Wilhelmmine bent down on her knees, her head bowed, she placed her palms together in front of her heart and thanked God the Father Almighty for giving her back her daughter.

Wilhelmmine now understood the worst. Now she knew exactly what it was, yes, she knew as her whole body shivered with that possibility, this was it! This was the worst that most painful loss of all. Wilhelmmine believed that before when a life needed to be spared, another had been taken. This time when a life needed to be spared another was also saved.

For the remainder of Wilhelmmine's life she thanked God for this decision each and every day.

Lilli's recovery was slow; amazingly she had no broken bones, but she would need time to heal from the bruising, cuts and scratches. Her entire body was in pain; she ached everywhere; at times just the act of breathing hurt. It appeared that she had pulled every muscle in her body and more so her entire abdominal area. But eventually Lilli did begin to heal and recover.

The only unusual symptom which Lilli and her mother later noticed wasn't until several months afterwards when they realized that she wasn't "coming around" as the older women in the town would say.

It was now more than 6 months since the accident, Lilli's body was getting stronger, the cuts and bruises had healed, even her hair was growing back but she was not menstruating as she had been since she was 12.

Maybe her body was still in shock, maybe she had bruised her lower abdomen, maybe it would just take time, no one knew, not even the doctor. When he was asked, he said that he believed she would be fine and not to worry. They heeded his sage advice and tried not to worry. "The doctor would know, wouldn't he?" Lilli asked her mother. Though Lilli and her mother continued to put up a brave front, as time went on each couldn't help feel concerned that there was something amiss.

"If there was no mud, how would a lotus grow?"
- Thich Nhat Hanh

11

HEARTBREAK

The days went by slowly but the years flew quickly and before long Lilli and Walter were celebrating their 10th wedding anniversary. It was 1911, so much had changed, not only in their world, but in them also. They were different than before, no longer believing that anything was possible. Lilli had matured, perhaps had become a bit more skeptical, definitely more cautious. Sitting and rocking in her chair, she thought back to her wedding day in 1901. She remembered how she'd believe that anything was possible, that your dreams come true, all that was needed was determination and faith.

Her life with Walter had fallen into a routine. It was quiet, orderly and comfortable but with no children to complete their family, they both felt a painful emptiness in their core. Eventually Lilli had begun to menstruate, even though it was infrequent and sporadic. She would often have awful cramping and pain the entire time, but Lilli knew that many young women suffered painful monthly cramps so she didn't believe that was the cause of her many miscarriages.

She wondered if somehow that accident many years before had something to do with her not being able to carry a child. Did saving the little boy's life, something she knew she would do again cause her body not to be able to carry a child of her own?

At the start of their marriage, Lilli and Walter would sit and talk about their plans for their future. Their eyes would glisten as they shared in soft and hopeful voices about the babies they dreamed of and wanted so badly. As the years went by there were multiple times that their hopes were raised, when several months would go by with Lilli not "coming around." She would notice a small curve in her otherwise flat stomach and even her breasts would begin to fill out. Waves of nausea would hit her for no apparent reason, though Lilli knew why.

She and Walter would try to keep their hopes at bay, try not to imagine a tiny baby in their arms. But they couldn't help it, each clinging to the hope that maybe this time it would be okay. Time and again, Wilhelmine would begin to knit little booties, sweaters hats, and blankets. Lilli would begin to think of various names. For a girl, maybe Almina after Wilhelmmine's mother, or even Frida after Walter's aunt, and for a boy either Willi or Walter after their father's or maybe Arthur or Wilhelm after the grandfathers. Sometimes Wilhelmmine would offer Herman after Lilli's beloved uncle.

But then those awful cramping pains would start, bright red clotted bleeding would appear. Lilli knew what was next. So many times, she would scream out at God, "Why, God, Why us? We're good, we're doing our best, we followed all your rules. This isn't fair God, it's just not fair."

Lilli, now almost thirty, was heartbroken, she found herself becoming distraught, even angry, very angry, angrier than she had ever been in her life. God didn't seem to hear her, not the God that her mother prayed to anyway. He didn't listen to her prayers. He certainly wasn't paying attention and Lilli found it difficult to believe that he cared. If he did, then why were they being denied the only thing they ever wanted, ever dreamed of? Where was that God she had worshipped her whole entire life? Why wasn't he there for them now? He'd taken her father, and now he wouldn't even give her a child.

"What kind of God are you?" She would scream. "Why, God? Why? How cruel you are, how cruel this is." Lilli raged as so many of their friends were now raising families, large families, she couldn't believe this was happening.

She knew they would be good parents; she knew they would love, nurture and cherish children, their children. She knew that she was meant to be a mother and Walter was meant to be a father. They wanted to be a family, to raise children to hold and love.

Lilli cried herself to sleep at night with growing frequency, she and Walter began to spend more time alone and see less of their friends. It wasn't that they no longer enjoyed their company, but it seemed that they didn't have as much in common with them anymore, not to mention the sharp sting of seeing their friends who were expecting or already with growing families. It happened slowly but eventually they found it easier not to engage and not to socialize.

Lilli found herself asking, "Why is this happening to us?

Where is my child, where are our children?" She had wanted nothing more than a happy home, a content life and to have children with Walter. She had worked hard to make their home the center of their interests, a warm and welcoming place, but lately she wasn't finding much happiness or interest in anything, including Walter. Lilli felt like a failure, she asked, "Is this it? Is this going to be our life together? Was it really just going to be Walter and me alone?"

Many evenings found Lilli in the parlor, sitting in her rocking chair. Slowly, like a ticking metronome, she would rock back and forth, finding solace in the movement. For some reason when she was feeling lost and heartbroken, she would find herself drawn to her chair and almost hypnotically walk over to it.

Standing next to it she would take hold of the top feeling the carved heads of the lions. Slowly, purposely she would bend down to sit sliding onto the seat, and pressing the small of her back into the curved spindles. Then her eyes would close as she placed her hands onto the chair's arms, curling her fingers into the deeply carved grooves, slowly exhaling. It was there rocking that she found solace. Perhaps, it was the memory of opening this beautiful gift, maybe it was her belief in the future she and Walter had before them, maybe it was the dream of the children that she would rock to sleep. Maybe it was simply the chair that offered comfort. Rocking in her chair Lilli found that she still believed, she still hoped and she still dreamed that someday, their dream would come true.

There were times when as she rocked, her head resting against the carved wood, she could almost catch the scent and feel the weight of a child held lovingly in her arms. She felt the beat of its heart against her chest, the weight of its body curved into hers, snuggled within soft knitted blankets as it rested on her chest. In these moments' tears would flow, but also a slight smile would cross her face. Then softly, she would begin to hum the song that meant so much to her. Stille Nacht, for Lilli, that song offered far more than seasonal melodic notes and peaceful harmony. Stille Nacht soothed her soul as she knew it would soothe her child too.

But there were times when Lilli couldn't find comfort, when pain cut deep and soothing herself wasn't so easy. There were times when Lilli would shout, her voice rising as she asked, "Where is our God, now? "At times even yelling out loud at God, telling him and letting him know, "I don't believe in you anymore. You're not so all powerful, not so omnipotent and not so loving. If this is how you bless, then I don't need your blessings."

During these times Lilli believed that God certainly wasn't with them, because he definitely wasn't on their side. She couldn't find words to express or explain her emotions, and she didn't like how she felt, she hurt all over, her pain was so deep. But one thing she did know, she knew she was angry at God, not only for herself but also for Walter. She couldn't understand how or why this was happening to them.

Walter, too, felt a hollow aching pain, but as he had in the past, he kept his feelings to himself, holding them deep inside of him. He never lashed out or demanded answers, not from his God and definitely not from Lilli. He knew how Lilli felt; he understood her pain and its depth. Still, when they sat down for dinner, he would press the palms of his hands together as he prepared to offer grace to God.

Looking across the table at Lilli he would wait patiently until her palms too were placed together. Then he would drop his eyes as his chin tucked and he bowed his head. Then for them both he thanked God for the meal in front of them. Lilli pressed her hands together tightly as she felt her back go rigid and she squared her shoulders. Then as Walter bowed his head Lilli would lift her chin and look defiantly straight ahead starring as if at nothing until Walter finished. Then they would eat together in a silence so loud it was deafening.

After years of trying, years of miscarriages and false hopes, Lilli told herself she didn't care anymore. "If God isn't going to give us the children, we want so badly well so be it." she thought. Her hands curling into fist and her chin sticking out in anger, Lilli thought, I'll show him, I'll show that God." as the muscles in her body tensed with hurt and outrage she spoke out loud," You know, you can't hurt me God, because I don't want any children either." she told herself. "Yes, I don't want any at all ever." As tears filled her eyes, she stamped her foot saying, "I never did God, really, I never did."

From this moment on Lilli felt different, she felt empty, as if she was hollow inside. There was a painful ache deep in her soul, almost as if her life had no real purpose. The hurt of living with this physical pain each and every day, holding onto so much anger and sadness slowly began to take its' toll on Lilli. She no longer had energy to do the daily activities required to maintain her home. She complained of headaches and stomach aches frequently. Often, she would simply not want to get out of bed in the morning. She didn't find joy or beauty or even love in anything around her. She was angry, not only with God, but also at Walter and at Wilhelmmine, but most of all she was angry at herself.

After several months, of evenings without words, of meals without laughter and rooms thick with the mist of emptiness, Lilli realized that she didn't like living like this. She didn't like the sadness this feeling created in her. She didn't want to live her life with the weight of these feelings. She didn't know how or where to turn to change but she knew if she didn't, she would break, just break.

She had recently heard about a program to help orphaned children so during dinner one evening Lilli mentioned to Walter about it. It was called Placing Out. Setting her fork down, she told him about a Reverend Brace, a prominent Methodist minister from a local church that was sponsoring a program of sending children to the Midwest in hopes of a better life. Both Lilli and Walter were familiar with the concerns the community had regarding so many of the orphaned waifs roaming the streets of the city.

Walter was pensive for a moment before replying, then placing his fork down, he replied, "Well, I suppose that it is better for these children to be raised on farms then in the slums and gutters of this city. I know that without my Aunt Frida I might have ended up in the streets. My father couldn't manage all of us boys. That was for sure." "You know, "he continued, "I have always been thankful for how Aunt Frida took all of us in Lilli."

She nodded because even though her father had died when she was young, she never knew the fear of being really alone, or felt the terror of not feeling safe or the hunger from not eating for days without end. Later that evening as she rocked in her chair, she thought of the lives these children experienced each day and night. She thought of how these children were trying to survive without anyone loving them, caring for them, or even protecting them.

She knew that many of these children suffered unimaginable and horrific experiences and her heart broke for their lost souls. Thinking of their plight she slowly became less angry with God and became more grateful for what she had. That night as Lilli rocked back and forth, she began to think that somehow, some way she could do something to help these orphans. She didn't know how or when but she knew she must do something. Unbeknownst to her, a seed had been planted in her heart; slowly it took root and was beginning to grow pushing through and opening her heart again.

Then slowly it began, before she would go to sleep at night, Lilli found herself thanking God. She thanked God as she had done for many years before, pressing her palms together she began, "Dear Lord, thank you for today, thank you for the food I received, the warmth and shelter I know and the love I have. Please send your love to all children in their homes or to those who are homeless so they will know the power of being loved each and every night. Amen God, Amen."

Through the simple act of nightly prayer, Lilli began to heal. She felt it too; this slow change soon became noticeable to others. Lilli was looking and feeling different again and she viewed her life through different eyes. Opening her heart had opened her eyes, Lilli found that she was grateful and hopeful again.

With this simple act of praying, this simple act of gratitude her outlook on life began to change and she felt a new energy, a new purpose. Though she still ached for a child, such thoughts no longer filled and crowded her mind. Lilli began to focus on her family, her home and her work. She joined other women at church activities where the focus and energy were on preparing meals and gathering clothes for several of the orphanages located in the city.

She was opening up again and because of her friendly personality along with her dressmaking skills, her following at Emma's dress Shoppe grew. She was introduced to women from different economic, social and educational backgrounds. Through their conversations she found herself becoming interested in not only the social but also the political events happening all around her.

Lilli and Wilhelmmine made friends easily and enjoyed learning new ideas, attending lectures, literary social teas and book readings.

At many of these events the conversations were beginning to turn to current events, and the importance of being involved in local activities. One movement in particular that fired the passion in both of them was the women's right to vote.

Both Lilli and her mother found themselves swept up in the burgeoning suffrage movement and in the opinions of the political candidates, especially following those who supported women's voting rights. The staunchest supporter of this burgeoning suffrage movement was no less than the former president himself Theodore Roosevelt.

Then on a late afternoon in April, with the rain falling hard against the window panes, Lilli noticed how the sound created was the rhythmic sound of thousands of marching feet. Warm, and cozy, she was alone in the dress shop enjoying the calm sensation this sound created. Lilli had always found pleasure in the rain; she wasn't sure why it gave her this feeling of relaxation and peace but it always did.

Lilli was content, as she focused on her stitches, admiring how even and straight they were, each stitch perfectly following the other, spaced evenly apart holding the seams of this beautiful dress together and creating a unified piece where once there had been many individual pieces. Putting the finishing stitches on this dress which would be worn for afternoon teas she smiled knowing it was for one of her favorite customers. She imagined how lovely her customer would look and how happy she would be. Just then Lilli heard the tinkle of the chimes from the front door as Mrs. Andrews entered the shop, she stood in the entryway shaking the rain from her umbrella. Mrs. Andrews was a frequent customer, and Lilli had liked her immediately. Smiling up at her Lilli enjoyed seeing her enter; there was just something about her that connected with Lilli.

When they had first met Lilli had noted how intelligent and well-spoken she was. Lilli knew she was an avid reader, up on current events and one who held strong beliefs on women's rights and was not afraid to state her mind, she admired her spirit.

Lilli placed her sewing on the side table and rose in greeting. Since, Mrs. Andrews was in no rush to venture back out in the rain, she lingered, telling Lilli about a march for Women's Suffrage that was coming up soon in New York City.

"We're all marching, Lilli. We will all be there," she said. "We will get the vote; they can't stop us. This tide is swelling and it will prevail. Will you join us Lilli? Please think about it, maybe your mother will join us too? If we all march together, they will see the strength we have in numbers and they will see how united we stand. They will have to pass the legislation Lilli. There is power in numbers and we are getting them."

Lilli listened feeling an excitement well up inside of her. Isn't this why they had come to America? She felt as if a purpose was truly returning to her life. Nodding in agreement, she thought, "I will march, I will take a stand and I will make a difference."

Lilli knew that by marching she would be helping create change to benefit all women's lives. When she left work that evening, she was inspired, an energy she had not felt in a long time was welling up inside of her. Heading to her mother's flat she remembered the Certificates of Citizenship hanging on the walls in her home. Initially, she had accepted that Walter could vote, his certificate stamped in the upper right-hand corner by the Board of Election Committee, hers' was not. She was not registered, she could not vote, her voice did not count. Entering her mother's flat, she quickly told her about the Women's March. "What do you think Mutter? I agree with them. We should have the right to vote, look at us." She went on, "We are working just as hard as any man, supporting ourselves, keeping our property in good form. We follow the news and events; we are impacted just like any man by these events but we can't vote. We should have this right; it is an inalienable right you know; women still can't even vote in Germany. If we don't march, don't raise our voices, don't demand and take a stand then nothing will change, nothing!"

Listening intently Wilhelmmine smiled at her daughter,

nodding her head in agreement. "Yes." as a tear came to her eye. In her heart she silently spoke to her husband long gone but never forgotten, "Willi mein Liebchen, you and I have raised an amazing young woman, I know you are as proud of her right now as you were when she was your little fraulein."

Wilhelmmine let that tear roll down her cheek as she squeezed Lilli's hand in agreement. "Yes, Lilli, we will do this together too."

On May 6, 1912, standing shoulder to shoulder Walter and Hank cheered proudly from the sidelines, as Lilli and Wilhelmmine joined 20,000 like-minded and courageous suffragettes as they marched in the first of many marches supporting women's suffrage. Like so many journeys before, Lilli and Wilhelmmine were together for this journey too. Lilli looked up ahead of her and spotted a baby carriage being pushed by a young mother.

Smiling she turned, looking at her mother they locked eyes, and arms as together they marched forward. Women from all walks of life linked arms as side by side they marched. They carried banners, shouted slogans, they were determined that they would not be stopped. You could see it in their faces, each one acknowledging the nervous butterflies fluttering in their stomachs, not sure what they faced and what they would encounter as they marched in unison through the streets of New York City.

Each woman marching knew what might happen, knew what had happened. They were afraid, apprehensive and worried. They all feared would they be attacked, would they be arrested, would they be hit by thrown objects? But each one of them, each woman marching was willing to take those risks to have the right to cast her vote.

In 1913 not many politicians supported the suffrage movement. Especially none of them, with the vigor and enthusiasm that Theodore Roosevelt did. Even though he never overcame his own speech impediment, no one spoke more eloquently and passionately as he did when it came to this cause. Lilli was in awe of this man, so vibrant, so much larger than life. Like her, he too had suffered tragic losses and didn't let them stop him. She recalled how he'd made positive changes as Police Commissioner of New York City many years before becoming Vice President and then President of the United States. Lilli believed that if Roosevelt was on their side they couldn't lose. Learning that he was scheduled to speak at the New York City's Metropolitan Opera House on behalf of the suffrage movement she vowed to be there.

Along with her mother, Lilli invited a new friend, Catisemma Bonnaceto, a young woman just recently arrived from Italy and hired by Emma at the Shoppe. Catisemma knew her craft well and was a quick study being partnered up with Lilli. She told the women in the shop that she was currently single but was betrothed to a young man from Italy; Arturo Giampa was his name, a skilled stone mason; "He is the head man on the job." Catisemma would say proudly raising her chin as her chest lifted swelling with pride.

Arturo was currently living in Boston with his brother Giuseppe a plumber; in a section called East Boston, but Catisemma always called it Eastabost. "Soon." she told them, Arturo would be coming to New York City to bring her to their home, back in Eastabost as soon as they had saved enough money for the train trip and the wedding.

Catisemma proudly told Lilli and her mother about a huge project Arturo was working on. He and Giuseppe traveled up to New Hampshire for weeks at a time with other stone mason, plumbers, carpenters, skilled craftsmen and tradesmen, many from Italy. There they were working for a Mr. Thomas Plant, a rich business man, who owned a shoe factory in Massachusetts. Thomas Plant was building a castle, "A real castle in America." Arturo told Catisemma in his letters, it's called The Castle in the Clouds. It would take quite a while to finish which meant that perhaps Catisemma's wedding with Arturo would be in maybe in a year or two.

Having been raised in a strict and disciplined convent Catisemma shared her hopes and dreams with Lilli about the family she and Arturo planned to have. Catisemma never mentioned how she was orphaned or what happened to her family and Lilli never asked. She would listen quietly remembering the dreams and plans she too once had. She would feel her heart begin to ache as tears came to her eyes, but she never stopped Catisemma from talking about her dreams, and never ever shared that they may not come true.

Giuseppe, Arturo' brother was betrothed to Catisemmas' cousin Maria. Since they were from the same village their parents had made these marriages many years before and these were promises to be honored and kept even in this new country far away from their homeland.

Lilli liked Catisemma, she had a quick sense of humor and an honest and open approach to life. Lilli admitted with a grin that sometimes between her German accent and Catisemmas'

Italian dialect they didn't always fully understand exactly what each other was saying, but there was an unspoken understanding. They had similar dreams and goals which made up for any small differences. Lilli listened, eventually learning about the hard childhood her new friend had experienced. She was sympathetic as she learned that Catisemma was not raised in a loving family but instead in a strict, rigid convent in northern Italy. She had been orphaned at a young age and grew up under the tutelage of martinet nuns and priests who ran the convent school with a quick hand and discipline that was impatient and stern.

So grateful was she for her friendship with Lilli that every morning as Catisemma entered the shop she would run over to Lilli embracing her, kissing both of her cheeks as she wrapped her arms around Lilli's shoulders. Initially Lilli was shocked by this gesture and emotional display. She would stiffen and pull back, uncomfortable with the obvious demonstration of affection from this woman, so different from Lilli's reserved and stoic manner.

But after a while Lilli began to relax and enjoy Catisemmas' enthusiasm for life and willingness to put herself out there emotionally, letting people know how much she cared. Lilli had found a friend in Catisemma, a dear friend and for this she was grateful. She cherished Catisemma and prayed that their friendship would last a lifetime.

"Everything Changes, everything is connected, pay attention."
- Jane Hirshfield

12

FAMILY

The year was 1914, sensing the revolution in transportation, Henry Ford doubled the wages for his workers. The United State Senate passed an anti-immigration bill prohibiting entrance to illiterate immigrants, along with excluding negroes from Africa. The British House of Lords rejected Women's Suffrage and Woodrow Wilson proclaimed May 9th as Mother's Day across America.

Change was in the air, but not for Lilli and Walter. Their life had settled into a predictable and comfortable routine. Quite often, Lilli would invite Walter's cousin Henry, now a writer for the New York Post to join them for dinner.

On one particular night, while Lilli was setting the table, he enthusiastically shared that he had applied for a job as a feature writer for McClure's Magazine. For many years McClure's was the magazine you read when you wanted the inside story, the truth about wealth, power, corruption and politics. Being a writer for Sam McClure, joining the staff where Ida Tarbell and Ray Stannard Baker were legends, was Henry's dream.

"I'll have my own byline, Lilli, it'll be Hank Schonfeld." He told her excitedly, "I love how it sounds, so American, listen to it Lilli," he repeated, "Hank Schonfeld."

Slowly backing into her chair, Lilli immediately gripped the arms and sank onto the seat, thinking "He's dropped the von." She didn't say anything but a chill ran down her spine, pressing her back securely into the chair and feeling its support, Lilli cast a quick glance to Walter. Their eyes met as they understood the impact of their cousin's name change.

Many other things were changing also, not only in New York but in all of America and across the ocean in Europe as well.

Unaware of Lilli and Walter's exchanged looks, Hank continued, "Do you remember hearing about that Reverend Brace? The one who was instrumental in those Orphan Trains which ran out of Boston and New York to the Midwest?" Lilli looked up at him with curiosity, "Well, I'm planning to work on that story. I mean, what is happening to those children? Where are they going? Who is taking them? What happens to the ones who are not taken? There is so much mystery, so much not known and so much to uncover."

Hank's cousin's watched him as he gestured animatedly, "Lilli, Walter, change is in the air, you know." he exclaimed, "Look, if you face east towards the ocean, and draw in a deep breath you not only smell the salty whiff of the Atlantic but also the pungent smell of gun powder. That smell my friends is coming from across the ocean."

Lilli reflected on those words. She knew that much of the

power of Hank's written word was his ability to be a barometer for his time. Often the poignancy of his stories stemmed from his sense of knowing what was in the air well before others. His fingers rested not only on the keys of his Royal typewriter but also on the beating pulse of his generation.

Lilli sensed the changes too, there was an unease to it which made her want to hold those she loved even closer. Feeling this need, she gathered her family and friends around her more often. She decided to host weekly dinners with her mother, Henry and now her dear friend Catisemma. This was her family, the family she and Walter had created.

Lilli spent hours reading her recipes, buying ingredients and then beaming in anticipation as she tied on her apron to prepare a sumptuous meal. She seemed to always create a delicious variation on a German favorite from the faded and smudged recipes she had lovingly packed away on their voyage across the Atlantic.

For Wilhelmmine, it was desserts that were her specialty. At each visit the aroma of a warm strudel or cobbler would announce her entrance. Catisemma would join introducing a new and special dish from Italy, blending ingredients and spices that Lilli had never even considered.

Inhaling deeply the delicious aromas wafting from Catisemmas hands Lilli would greet her friend with both arms embracing her tightly and smiling widely asking, "Now, what did you bring this time?" Catisemma was always coming in with a delicious and robust pasta dish or a thick soup, happily expanding their palates with onion, pasta, beans, garlic and tomatoes.

"Oh, my I remember that smell." Lilli exclaimed one

evening as Catisemma brought her contribution to their dinner. "I remember the first time I smelled that; it was so long ago." Raising her face and lifting her eyes to the heavens, she placed her fingers on her forehead, saying I remember, "It's a garlic," he had said," not able to hold back the smile as her eyes misted, "umm, it's garlic."

Catisemmas' dishes were so hearty that often everyone was full even before the meal was over. Yet, somehow everyone found room for more and they would linger at the table laughing at each other's stories or becoming embroiled in long and lengthy discussions about all that was happening not only right in their Brooklyn neighborhood, but also the rapidly changing events happening in Germany, with Catisemma filling them in on the goings on in Italy and Boston, too.

For Lilli and Walter, it was as if their legs widely straddled the ocean, one leg planted with tender and fragile roots in America and the other leg with thick branches and strong roots in their mother country often referred to as Deutschland.

Hearing from back home was important and Lilli looked forward to the letters and notes from Germany, but there were times when months would go by without a word. Then the post would arrive bulky with letters and packages full with gossip from Walter's Aunt Frida or news and clippings from Lilli's beloved Uncle Herman.

Reading Uncle Herman's letters was always a special time for Lilli. She wanted to savor each word and enjoy each story. She tried to be patient, waiting until her chores were done before opening the letters. Then she would boil water for a cup of tea as her heart quickened in anticipation. Her practice was to sit in her rocking chair by the window and begin to rock slowly backward and forward sorting the day's mail.

Her pulse beating quickly Lilli wanted to rush through this task, thankfully, her chair calmed her with its gentle rocking as Lilli carefully sorted and divided the letters into piles. Walter's letters mostly from Aunt Frida were piled on the table next to the rocking chair, and each letter addressed for Lilli was gently placed in her lap to be read in order by the postdate stamped, Uncle Herman's letters were always placed on the top of the pile.

Once the mail was sorted, she carefully opened her uncles' letters, marveling at his perfect penmanship with its strong and clear script. All of his letters were perfectly formed, evenly and clearly scribed, each I precisely dotted and every T crossed straight. Lilli noticed that even the letters j, p, y, and z all were perfect in length not extending their loops lower than the other. There was no mistake here, this man knew his p's and q's, as he meticulously kept everything neat and in order, even his letters.

Lilli's heart would leap and a smile would cross her face as she began to read, hearing his voice in her head, "Lilli, meine Liebste; I must tell you of everything that is happening and happening so quickly." His letters were full of the many political and social events of their motherland. He wrote of how vastly their country was changing. He knew that Lilli and her mother remembered a quiet rural country as did Uncle Herman. But that memory was now a distant one for so many of their relatives in Germany.

Lilli's uncle was a soldier, high in rank, patriotic and proud of the power of the newly created German Army, but he was also proud of their Navy as well. "Lilli, meine Liebste, we now have a strong and powerful navy. For the last 12 years we have been working hard to make it bigger, greater and stronger. Soon it will be us, who will rule the seas. I believe that in the near future the only rival our navy will have will be England and that meine Liebchen, will not be for long. But along with a strong army and navy, my eyes have been looking upwards at the sky. I have been reading a lot about those two brothers in America, the Wright brothers and what they have been doing with their flying machines. I find them very interesting. From what I have read your government is not interested in these young men, but Lilli, my government is, our military sees an opportunity in these flying machines. Our countrymen, Lilli, are proud of how Germany has grown. I see it in the eyes of our soldiers, in our workers and I even see it in how we walk and talk. Lilli, we, the German people, are being taken seriously. We are being respected, and this is all good. This is very good; it is being said that we too will have our place in the sun.

Lilli understood that Germany, once a farming country, had lagged behind its neighbors, as the industrial revolution rapidly spread throughout Europe and America. Eventually though, once it came to Germany, the change was rapid. Germany's industrial production grew so quickly that by the turn of the century it was out producing Britain in steel and had become the world leader in the chemical industries.

Feeling its new strength and might the Kaiser planned to reach outside of Germany's borders to expands its influence internationally vying for power and prestige with his cousins on thrones throughout the continent and in England.

Uncle Herman was excited about these changes, he felt

pride in being German along with being a soldier in the Kaiser's army. In a previous letter, he had written telling her about the passage of a new law. "Lilli, meine Liebste, recently a law was passed whose sole intent was to increase the size and strength of the German army to nearly one million soldiers. With this law our Kaiser will have one of the strongest and largest armies on the continent."

Uncle Herman's excitement was sincere but also tempered by his knowledge of history. He was concerned that with all of Germany's new found pride and power it might fall into what he had read about long ago known as "Thucydides Trap."

It was this knowledge that gave him pause, because even though he was a very important soldier in a powerful and strong army, he was well aware of the delicate balance of power which had developed throughout Europe.

Studying history gave him insight to the direction he believed Europe was heading. He knew that there could not be two strong and powerful countries as leaders of the world. He understood that there was room at the top for only one, but this fear he kept to himself

Lilli's Uncle was not only a soldier, there was also another side to Herman, Lilli knew this and she knew that her Uncle's heart was breaking. This side was apparent as her Uncle continued, "Lilli, regretfully, I will no longer have the time to continue with my carvings and woodworking's. I will not be building or designing any more furniture for a long time. So, my dear Lilli, please cherish your rocking chair, it will most likely be the last one I build for a very long time. I have a wish Lilli and I am compelled to share it with you. I wish that someday your beloved chair, your wedding gift, will be shared for generations to come and that it will continue to rock long after I am gone."

As Lilli read these words she noticed that the chair's gentle rocking slowed down, its' flow of back and forth became almost unnoticeable. Like the gentle ebb and flow of a tide licking the shoreline on a windless day Lilli's chair resisted the gravitational forces pulling it forward and gently stopped.

In her heart Lilli knew that this rocking chair, her most treasured wedding gift would be the very last gift of its kind from Uncle Herman. Their lives had changed; outside forces had changed their lives. They were being pulled in many different directions with new and different demands being made and expectations being set. Uncle Herman would no longer have time to create, to design and to build; he was a soldier, he had orders to follow and commands to obey.

As Lilli pondered the impact of Uncle Herman's words, she felt a great sadness overcome her. Her chair was motionless, the room had become silent and a sense of stillness permeated the air; nothing moved. She wondered, had she stopped rocking, or had the chair just stopped by itself? The light of the midday sun poured in through the window bathing Lilli in its rays but she didn't feel any warmth. Looking down into her lap she realized that Uncle Herman's letter was clutched tightly in her hands. Suddenly, she felt a cold tremble race through her as an icy chill ran down her spine and goose pimples broke out on her skin; shivering Lilli felt a gripping coldness from deep down in her bones settle in.

There were other letters too, those from Aunt Frida came with news of cousins and brothers. Aunt Frida wrote proudly telling Walter and Lilli that many of his cousins, and nephews were entering into the service of the Kaiser. Like Uncle Herman there was pride in Aunt Frida's words as she described her sons and grandsons serving as soldiers for their country.

Lilli enjoyed receiving those letters often carrying good news as Walter's aunt wrote about marriages, births, and celebrations but sometimes her letters became difficult to read as they told of sicknesses and deaths. These letters brought tears and an aching heart from Frida.

Sometimes Lilli would read aloud to Walter, other times Lilli wanted to listen and so Walter would read them to her as she rocked. These letters were their only lifelines to those they loved who were so far away. They couldn't help but feel their kinfolk's connection as they read them. This was family, a family they sorely missed and they were brought right back to them, their homeland; both Lilli and Walter believed in the importance of holding tightly onto their families across the ocean. They loved them dearly, this love went beyond the shared ancestry, the history and the memories; it was the lineage that connected them even across the ocean. They were kinfolk no matter how far apart they were, they were blood.

Often there was more information revealed in those letters than just news and stories. Lilli and Walter both noticed that their beloved Aunt Frida was getting older; her writing revealing her oncoming frailty as her handwriting frequently became illegible with her letters becoming more difficult to read. Often stories were repeated from one letter to the next, and sometimes they simply trailed off with no salutation, as if she forgot that she was writing a letter at all. Still Lilli and Walter cherished each letter, reading and rereading them to savor each word like a delicious morsel from a treasured family feast.

Also, at the same time Lilli and Walter were beginning to feel a shift in their own neighborhood. Even though they had a deep love of their kinfolk and of their homeland across the ocean they were becoming aware that these feelings were not what they felt in their community. They were beginning to notice an obvious shift in attitude , a hostility that seemed to have happened overnight. It began by them hearing angry, disparaging and hostile words spoken about their old country, and about German people. They began to notice looks of contempt and to hear snide comments coming from people they had once considered friends and neighbors. Sometimes people would look at them then quickly look away avoiding their eyes and ignoring their greetings.

Then early one Saturday morning, Lilli was outside washing down her front stoop, when an older man walked past her. At first Lilli didn't even notice him lost in her chore, until he abruptly stopped and loudly spat on the sidewalk nearby. Turning sharply, he looked straight at Lilli with fire in his eyes and shouted, "You people, you people! All of you think you're better than the rest of us!"

Stunned, Lilli looked up trying to see who it was he was yelling at and about what he was yelling. Aghast, she realized it was she, he was yelling at her.

Forcefully, he leaned forward getting closer to her as his eyes bulged with rage, both of his hands clenched into fist, violently he shook them at her. His face was flushed bright red with venomous anger, his voice becoming louder, his words spitting out like flames from his mouth, as he hissed, "Why don't you all go back where you came from? Get out of here! You don't belong here. You, you people, you're nothing but a bunch of lousy, dirty, stinking Huns!"

Suddenly he pulled his head back, raising his chin and then with all of his force he let out a volley of sputum this time aimed directly at her. Lilli gasped and jumped back, nearly tripping over her bucket and brush. Without another word he turned abruptly spinning on his heels with the intent of continuing on his way, but not before turning to spit again on the clean steps in front of Lilli's home. He proudly marched down the street, his arms swinging wildly as he mumbled curses under his breath about the lousy, dirty stinking krauts in his neighborhood. Reaching the corner of the street, he turned towards Lilli once more and shouted hatefully, "Huns, stinking barbaric Huns!"

Lilli watched in shock as he stalked away, appearing smaller as the distance between them grew until he and his venom faded into the distance. Only then did Lilli realize she had stopped breathing as she burst into tears. Her heart sank like her brush into the hot dirty water as she slowly and cautiously bent to pick up her bucket. Then rushing inside, she quickly slammed and locked her front door behind her. Leaning her back against the heavy wooden door, she doubled over, her arms wrapping protectively around her body as she shook all over.

Lilli was filled with despair, hurt and disbelief. She felt her heart and her breath coming in short spurts, as she cried," Where did that come from? Why did he say such things to me? What did he mean? Why did he do that, why us?"

She stood for a long while, her back against her locked

door, bewildered and shocked until her breathing finally began to slow. At that moment she decided not to mention the event to Walter, not wanting to cause him to worry. Lilli wasn't aware, but, Walter had also begun to notice an icy coolness from his coworkers, who were now keeping their distance from him, he too wondered why.

Then the unthinkable happened. The incident happened so far away that at first it appeared that nothing had changed and life would continue on as before, but everything had changed. Those responsible called themselves The Black Hand. Founded in 1911, they were terrorists and their chief purpose was to create agitation against Austria on behalf of disgruntled Serbian extremists. On June 28th, 1914, the 14th wedding anniversary, of the Archduke Franz Ferdinand and his wife Sophie, the Duchess of Hohenberg, the Black Hand struck. The 28th of June had represented a very special occasion, and the Archduke and Duchess were traveling together in their motorcade on official business visiting the city of Sarajevo, in Bosnia. Suddenly, seemingly from nowhere a single assassin approached their open car, he shot both of them at point blank range.

From that moment on chaos was everywhere, as death was invited to join the motorcade and enter the world's stage. The assassinations of the Archduke and the Duchess marked the beginning of worldwide horrific violence, bloodshed and terror that was to last for years. This single gunshot set in motion the domino effect that became World War 1.

The summer of 1914 echoed with Declarations of War sweeping feverishly across Europe, which began one month to the day after the vicious assassinations. On July 28, 1914

Austria declared war on Serbia. On August 1, Germany declared war on Russia, then France on August 3 and Belgium on August 4. England followed suit on August 4, declaring war on Germany, and on August 12, France and England declared war on Austria. On August 23, Japan joined the fray, declaring war on Germany, adding Austria two days later. The declarations sounded like the beating of a dirge in staccato rhythm, one following the next even into the next year when Italy entered with its declaration of war against Austria in May of 1915.

From that time forward death boldly and proudly marched across almost every country around the globe. As one after the other declared war on each other sending its' young men to fight and die in the world's most horrific First World War.

As war savagely tore and ripped Europe apart, hostile anti German sentiment had taken root and was spreading like a rapacious poisonous vine across America. In Brooklyn, Lilli and Walter's once peaceful and happy world was beginning to splinter apart.

It was Lilli who initially became the recipient of the blatant hostility, making her aware of the subtle changes. They seemed to begin as small insults and verbal assaults so snide that it almost made her question whether she actually heard those words, imagined those looks or really felt the hostility as she traveled throughout her familiar routine in her neighborhood.

Then all too quickly, these subtle insults became more blatant and too obvious to ignore as she was again attacked personally.

On a cool autumn morning Lilli had, as usual, begun her

daily routine in her beloved Brooklyn neighborhood. Preparing for her chores, she made a list of tasks for herself speaking aloud in her bright, cozy home. "First I'll get my ingredients for a Salisbury steak dinner tonight." Smiling she continued. "Walter loves this dinner. I'll get the meat at the butcher shop, and then I'll go to Dominic's for the sauerkraut, where I can also pick up some potatoes, apples and onions too." Lilli thought this was a good start, collecting her things and heading out after finishing her household duties.

This section of Brooklyn had been her home for more than 15 years. She knew most of the families, and almost all of the shop keepers in her neighborhood. On many occasions through the years when a neighbor had fallen ill, it was Lilli who rushed over with a homemade soup or a hearty meal for them and their family. When a new baby came into the world Lilli presented the parents with a hand-knitted sacque, bonnet and booties for the newborn to be warm and snug, and sometimes even a matching carriage cover with a knitted blanket for swaddling.

Knitting such items brought Lilli immense joy, she always kept her knitting basket next to her rocking chair. Lilli looked forward to her afternoons when her work was completed and she could rock and knit the precious baby outfits, using only the best Bernat yarn.

Though they were for her neighbors' babies and would never be for her own child, she could dream. She loved the calming flow of the movement of the needles, the click, click, clicking sound as patterns begin to emerge and take shape becoming warm cozy outfits. Sometimes she let herself imagine how it would feel to place small chubby arms into the sleeves, to tie the bonnet under a delicately dimpled chin as she kissed pink cheeks and looked into adoring baby blue or maybe deep brown eyes. Knitting allowed her to imagine, to dream and for a brief moment she felt the soft, pliable feeling of warmly swaddling her tiny baby into a beautiful soft blanket and holding it tightly against her chest, feeling its' warm breath as she rocked back and forth on a cold winter's night.

This was her routine on many afternoons and often late in the evenings she would sit in her chair, rocking as she meticulously counted and knitted each stitch. Like the tick, tick, ticking of a metronome, she knew that the time had passed for her to ever knit anything for a baby of her own.

Still when she had completed another set, she would smile and proudly show them to Walter, and he too would smile and tell her how beautiful they were, and how this new little baby was going to feel so warm, cozy and loved. "Lucky baby." he would always say to Lilli as he held her hand in his, lucky parents Lilli would think.

But times were changing, Lilli's neighborhood was changing, people were changing, even though Lilli hadn't changed, always pleasant and cheerful. She had begun to notice a difference, in those around her. Some of the store clerks were no longer friendly, didn't smile at her as they once had, and sometimes stopped talking when she approached them as they ignored her completely. Lilli noticed too that many even stopped engaging her in conversations as they had in the past.

Lilli felt the pain and hurt of this new behavior deeply, she sensed the hostility and was confused by it. She hoped that whatever it was that was causing this would end and her old friends would return to their warm ways. But that didn't happen, instead the frosty behavior was actually becoming more and more common, not only for Lilli but for other American Germans just like her.

Then it happened, the one experience that nearly shattered Lilli's world, the one that shocked her so much she felt compelled to share it with Walter. They had both almost finished the Salisbury steak dinner Lilli had lovingly prepared for their meal, when no longer able to keep it to herself, Lilli slowly shared with Walter what she had encountered while shopping that day.

"Walter," she began, "I really don't know how to tell you this, and I really don't want to even talk about it… I am so sorry, but I have to let you know what happened to me today at the market. It was awful. You won't be able to even imagine it."

She paused to take a breath and stifle a sniffle, delicately dabbing her nose with her napkin, she explained, "I was doing our shopping for tonight's dinner at Dominic's Market. I had picked up the apples and onions and I was looking for the sauerkraut. When I didn't see it, labeled anywhere, I asked Dominic where it was, since I planned to have it with our meal tonight. At first it seemed that no one heard me, so I spoke up a bit louder, "Dominic, can someone please tell me where the sauerkraut is, it's not where you usually keep it. Again, there was no response and I felt people just staring at me. All of a sudden, well, I don't know who it was, but from someone behind me I heard a nasty, voice telling me, "You don't see it? Well we don't sell sauer**KRAUT** here anymore, **Mrs. von VETTERLEIN**! And if you don't see it here maybe you should leave and shop somewhere else for your **German** food!" We sell Liberty Cabbage to our customers not **SAUERKRAUT, Mrs. von Vetterlein!** We sell Liberty Cabbage to our **American** customers! We don't sell sauer**KRAUT**!" Taking a breath, Lilli continued, "Walter, I just froze, I couldn't move, I couldn't breathe. I almost dropped the apples and onions I was so startled. My heart started beating fast and then I felt sick, literally sick to my stomach."

Pausing for a moment Lilli wiped the tears that fell from her eyes, then taking a deep breath, she continued. "Walter, I didn't dare turn around." She said her voice full of emotion. "I was afraid to look at anyone. I was so scared, Walter, I was so frightened. I couldn't believe it. I had no idea what to do, I had no idea what I had done wrong, I wanted to run, to just get out of that store but where could I go? At first it felt like my feet were nailed to the floor… I don't get this, Walter. Why do they hate us so much? What have we done? What have **WE** done? I just threw the money on the counter and left as quickly as I could and came right home. I ran home Walter, I ran Walter, I was just so afraid. Lately, I haven't felt at home here, I just don't feel safe here, Walter, I am afraid, I don't feel safe in my home anymore."

Lilli's eyes overflowed with tears as her quivering chin dropped to her chest and her head shook in dismay. No longer being able to hold the hurt and pain that she had held in all day, her whole body began to shake and she sobbed uncontrollably.

Walter's heart was breaking for his wife. Reaching across the table he took her hands in his holding them gently. This simple act of love brought him back to that evening when Lilli, sat across the table, with tears in her eyes and a broken heart after the loss of their baby, Willi, being so small he only lived a few days. The baby they had so desperately yearned for many years before Lilli had asked those same aching questions. "Why us Walter, what did we do wrong?" And as before, this time too, he felt the hurt, that deep intense aching pain. He had no answers either, but he knew that all he could offer was his love, unconditional and undivided love, for this beautiful, gentle and caring woman who was his wife.

The hostilities in Europe intensified as the darkness of the summer of 1914 stealthily encroached enveloping America in its evil and hatred. Lilli and Walter's peaceful life was now shattered. On a daily basis they felt the uneasiness of the ever-increasing resentment, suspicion and hatred from their neighbors and former friends. Lilli changed her shopping and traveling patterns. Rising early in the morning she would leave her home at dawn to avoid the whispers, stares and outright glares from the shopkeepers and passersby, her head down and her eyes focused only on the sidewalk beneath her feet. She traveled farther from her neighborhood, sometimes taking the streetcar to different neighborhoods where no one knew her or her name.

Even more painful was that the letters and news from their family in Germany were arriving far less frequently, and when those letters did arrive, they were often short and held little information, even friendly gossip was absent. Lilli's eyes filled with tears at the memory of the joy she once felt holding those letters to her heart.

Like many of the neighbors, Lilli and Walter did not have a mailbox on the front of their home, the postman was required to stop and knock to hand deliver their post. This had always been a welcome interlude as the postman and Lilli exchanged pleasantries. But lately his animosity had been so blatant that now Lilli's hands shook visibly and her heart pounded loudly as she avoided his angry glare. He would stare at the post the markings on the envelopes from her homeland. Sometimes, emboldened he would comment saying, "I see that you have mail again from Germany Mrs. von Vetterlein!" as a sneer crossed his face and Lilli reached out to grab her post.

Now when those letters came Lilli would quickly stop her chores; untie the strings of her apron and head for her chair. "Oh, yes," she thought, "not everything has changed, I still have my chair, and I still have my Uncle Herman." It seemed to Lilli that when the post arrived and she stopped whatever she was doing, time stopped too. Heading to her chair, Lilli's breath slowed and as she slid her back to rest it securely against the rungs, she would close her eyes and only then did she feel at peace again.

"Silent Night, Stille Nacht"
- Franz Xaver Gruber, Joseph Mohr

13

CHRISTMAS EVE, 1914

*A*s December 1914 approached Lilli made a decision that she planned to announce at dinner. As Wilhelmine helped to set the table Lilli stated, "I know that recently we have all experienced hostile behavior from people in our neighborhood and we have become aware of the change towards us and our German ways since this horrible war has broken out in Europe. So much of our culture, our language and our heritage have been forbidden, outlawed and denied to us and I know we all feel afraid and, in some ways, have tried to hide our Germanness and not to attract attention to ourselves."

Wilhelmmine's eyes filled with tears, her lips pressed tightly together as she simply nodded her head in agreement. Walter looked up from the paper he was reading and taking his pipe from his lips, his eyes focused on Lilli with a questioning look. Hank, who had just arrived, stopped abruptly in the doorway his eyes twinkling and a slight smile crossing his lips, as he wondered what Lilli was up to.

Lilli continued, "I've decided that I'm not going to let it change how we spend our Christmas holidays," she said, matter-of-factly. "I want to celebrate as we have always done, as our families for centuries have done and are celebrating it in Germany right now. This truly is our holiday. If I remember correctly the first Christmas tree was introduced in Germany almost 400 years ago, and it was our Prince Albert who not too long ago, introduced it to England. Ever since I was a little girl Christmas has been the most important time of the year, and it's not going to change now."

They all stared at Lilli as she stood next to the head of the table with her hands on her hips and head held high. Walter couldn't help but laugh out loud. Somehow seeing his wife standing there so resolute and so determined reminded him of his relatives the Hufnagles and particularly his Uncle Paulus.

"Well, I guess then it will be so." he said as he placed his pipe down, rose from his chair and went to his wife's side. Taking her hands in his he asked, "So tell me my liebchen, when are we getting our German Christmas Tree?"

"Well," smiled Lilli, with a guilty look on her face, "It's already here, it's out back, we will just have to bring it in on Christmas Eve, for that I need you and Henry."

With Lilli's announcement, a breath of fresh air blew into the room as her family's traditional Christmas decorating began. Candles were carefully placed on window sills, boxes of delicately wrapped glass Christmas ornaments brought lovingly so long ago from their home in Stuttgart, were now being carried into the parlor ready to be opened once again on Christmas Eve and adorn Lilli's Christmas tree.

December 24, 1914, was an exceptionally cold and dark day, temperatures had been below freezing for several days, and ice storms had coated the area in glittering frozen glass. In the afternoon the sky had become an even darker shade of grey as just before dusk soft fluffy snowflakes began gently falling to the ground. Everything quickly became covered with a blanket of sparkling white.

Lilli helped Henry and Walter as she brushed the chunks of ice and flakes of snow from the branches, inhaling the strong scent of pine as it permeated the air around them. Together Henry and Walter noisily struggled carrying Lilli's Christmas tree up several flights of stairs to their home. Under Lilli's direction it was placed in the front parlor. standing proudly as it waited to be decorated with freshly made strings of popcorn, cranberries, nuts, glass ornaments, ribbons, candles and pieces of tin artfully cut in myriad shapes. Her twinkling eyes matched her smile, as Wilhelmmine entered the room carrying a large box that Lilli knew was full of as many memories as it was with dozens of beautiful wax angels with spun glass for wings. Looking at Lilli, Wilhelmmine's eyes softened as she reminisced asking, "Remember when you were little and the tree was decorated on Christmas Eve while you slept? That was always part of the magic for your father and me." Lilli smiled at her mother feeling a lump in her throat thinking of that long-ago time and the magical memory it evoked.

As a little girl she had always believed that it was Weihnachtsmann, Father Christmas, who brought and decorated her Christmas tree. Just at that moment Walter carried in the tray of marzipan cookies most of which would be eaten long before they were placed on the branches of the tree. "Look out!" Lilli called to him as he almost tripped over a basket of red apples that had been placed on the floor waiting for specific adornment under Lilli's direction.

Standing back to ooh and ahh as each item was strategically placed, they heard the distant ring of church bells. Without needing to look at one other, their voices rose as they began to sing O Tannenbaum, Kinderlein Kimment and the song that meant the most to everyone, Stille Nacht. With moist eyes and lumps in their throats they knew their voices were not the only ones singing Stille Nacht on that night.

Even as those words were being sung in their home, in Brooklyn, on Christmas Eve of 1914, they imagined those same words were being sung in the homes and churches of their loved ones across the ocean and maybe even on the battlefields, as well.

As this holy evening drew to an end and all the gifts had been opened, Lilli stood back to gaze upon her beautiful Christmas tree. Her heart almost burst, it was so full of love, contentment and peace. Looking at her family gathered together in her home that evening Lilli's eyes filled, as the flickering window candles bathed the room in a golden warm glow. Quietly she whispered "Frohe Weihnachten, Frohe Weihnachten, to all of us near and far."

Hearing her whisper Hank replied, "Yes, Merry Christmas to us all."

Lilli cherished the memory of that special Christmas Eve 1914 for the rest of her life, for after that night everything changed. The war in Europe intensified on the land, in the air and even more horrifically on the sea. In its rush to achieve naval supremacy, Germany had developed a stealthy new weapon, the submarine. As 1914 warily became 1915, talk of the war reaching America was everywhere, fanning the flames of increasing hatred and malevolence toward Germans and anyone who called themselves a German-American.

Then their letters arrived early in February of 1915. On that day the sky was a steel grey as snow fell heavily outside. Lilli was chilled finding it difficult to keep warm with the wind blowing icy blasts through the thin window panes in their flat. Wrapped in a shawl and sitting in her rocking chair sewing, she was not expecting anyone this wintry morning. BANG! BANG! BANG, went the knock on their door. BANG! BANG! BANG, even harder this time. Startled, Lilli quickly rose from her chair to open the door. "Who can this be? "she wondered. Having become fearful, she bent forward and opened the door only a crack as she carefully peeked out. She found herself looking directly into the hard glare of the cold eyes of a U. S. Postal employee.

Startled Lilli's left hand flew to her chest as her shoulders stiffened; though she quickly drew in a breath and composed herself. In spite of the adrenaline coursing through her veins, Lilli pulled herself up to her full five-feet-six and – one –half inches, which allowed her to look down at the five-foot five-inch postman standing only inches away from her.

Thrusting her right hand out to quickly take the envelope addressed to her, he scowled staring directly at her. For a moment too long, he kept a tight hold on the thick envelope as he looked down at the markings and stamps from Germany. Then shaking his head and grunting in disgust he begrudgingly released his grip, but not without firing off a nasty remark. Narrowing his eyes, he met her's, snickered and said, "For you *Frau* Vetterlein, this is for you." placing emphasis on the word FRAU.

Lilli had all she could do to hold her sometimes quick, sharp tongue as she looked directly into his eyes and replied clearly and distinctly "Thank you, sir."

Pulling her hand in she stepped back, and slammed the door shut, quickly locking it securely as she turned her back on the world outside; she felt her heart beating rapidly as she hurried to her rocking chair and placed the mail down.

Immediately she recognized the writing on the exceptionally bulky envelope even before she read the return address. It was from the Herzele's her mothers' family in Stuttgart. Only then did Lilli's breathing deepen and her heart begin to slow its heavy pounding.

In trying to keep with her routine upon receiving mail, she entered the kitchen, neatly folded the wash cloth, placing it on the edge of her black soap stone kitchen sink. Then she untied the strings of her apron and hung it on the high hook on the wall by the sink, struck a match to light the gas jet on her black cast iron kitchen stove and put on a kettle to boil for tea. Taking out one of her prettiest Theodore Haviland Limoges China tea cups and matching saucer, the one with the delicate pink roses, Lilli set it on the table, placed a tea strainer over her cup and shook loose tea into it. These were the steps she followed each time. This was her routine, she hoped and prayed that by maintaining this practice the news she read from overseas would be tolerable. After her tea had brewed, Lilli carried the cup carefully into the parlor where Uncle

Herman's gift waited for her with its wide arms welcoming and protective. Sinking into it, Lilli's shoulders softened. She set the sewing basket to the side and wrapped her shawl securely, tying it in front of her as she settled down to read her family's letters.

This time however a slight hesitation came over her as her fingers began to carefully rip open the tightly sealed envelope and withdraw the soiled and stained papers. As several pages fell into her lap Lilli felt a chill come over her whole body, maybe it was a draft, maybe the temperature in the room had dropped or maybe this time the news wasn't going to be good.

Deciding to wait a few minutes before lifting and unfolding the pages, Lilli opted instead to rock slowly back forth. As much as she wanted to read the words on the lined papers that had fallen onto her lap, she was hesitant. She asked herself, what am I going to learn? What news is going to be so painful that I feel so reluctant to open the letter?" She didn't know, she only knew that her hands did not want to lift these papers, that this news was not going to make her smile or even want to share it with Walter, and she also knew she couldn't change a thing the letters contained.

After several minutes Lilli slowly picked up the papers and began to read. She learned from the Herzele's that times were very, very hard in the old country. Coal for heating their home was scarce, firewood was hard to find, food was rationed and so many of the young men who had gone off to war by choice or conscripted into the army were dead or severely injured.

"What is this fighting all about?" Lilli asked herself, "Why are we fighting each other? Why is there so much anger and hatred? Where did it begin and where oh God will it end?"

Then as Lilli held her grandmother Herzele's letters gently in her fingers a sheet of paper slipped from between the pages onto her lap. Immediately, she recognized the writing. It was his writing, the perfectly formed words, the perfect slanting of every letter to the right, the greeting, always the same, "Lilli, meine Liebste;" Lilli's heart hammered as tears sprang to her eyes. Unable to read any further, she placed the letter down and pushed her back further into the chair. She closed her eyes as a long-forgotten memory appeared.

She was back at home in Stuttgart and she was smiling, no, she was laughing and Uncle Herman was with her and he too was laughing. They were laughing out loud as he was pushing her on a swing, one that hung from a wide thick branch of the biggest tree Lilli had ever seen. The rocking of her chair had always reminded her of the motion of that swing.

Lilli couldn't help but close her fingers around the arms of the chair gripping them tightly as she rocked. Smiling, she felt the freedom of that forward push, but also the strength of Uncle Herman's hands supporting her as the chair rocked in sync with the swing in her memory. She could see the tree; see its branches spreading out as they created a wide expanse of mottled shade and sunlight on the grass below. Looking up she saw splotches of blue as the heavens above peeked through the openings between branches and leaves. Glancing to her left she smiled seeing the large, bumpy and gnarled trunk of this sturdy tree, so wide neither she nor Uncle Herman could touch fingertips as together they spread their arms around its girth.

Uncle Herman had told her that this was a Beech tree. She remembered how awed he was as he proudly explained that some of these trees were almost 400 years old. This tree was magnificent, tall with a broad thick trunk, its strong sinewy branches opening far and wide. Often, when Uncle Herman visited, they would sit underneath its broad, protective leafy crown and talk for hours at a time. Lilli loved this tree, she always had and when Uncle Herman put a swing in it for her, it became their tree.

Often, she would look at other trees in other yards in her town and think, "My tree, is so much more beautiful." She remembered fancying herself a bit of a tree snob even, taking pride that this amazing tree was in her family's yard. Gazing at its magnificence, Lilli would think, I truly love this tree. She remembered how she once told Uncle Herman that if she were a squirrel and were looking for a tree to live in this would be it.

They laughed and laughed at that idea, imagining a squirrel casually crossing the yard, and then stopping, spotting this tree, standing on his hind quarters, his bushy tail twitching left and right, his little paw scratching his chin, as he hemmed and hawed, tilting his head one way and then the other, contemplating his decision. They giggled, each telling their story and laughing about the furry grey squirrel. They each created a whole narrative about how this little grey squirrel went back to his family and told them in a deep squirrel voice, "By the way, we are moving, and we are moving tonight. Quickly gather up all of our acorns and nuts. I saw the best tree in this whole world and we are making it our home." Then she and Uncle Herman would laugh and laugh even more about how this tree became the squirrel family's home and how they all lived there happily ever after, for squirrel generations to come.

As this sweet memory of so very long ago lingered in Lilli's thoughts, she sniffled even though a smile crossed her lips. "Smiling and tears at the same time." She said, blinking away a tear drop falling from her eyes. But she couldn't stop tears from forming and she couldn't stop them from dropping onto the pages that she cradled gently in her lap. "I can't stop the smiles either," she thought gratefully. With a heavy sigh she pulled her shawl tighter around her arms, wiped her eyes, and leaned her head back into the chair. She continued to rock gently back and forth, the echo of Uncle Herman's laughter softly ringing in her ears. For a while, Lilli was comforted, the temperature in the room had not changed, but the memories of those days had sent a soothing warmth deep into her soul.

Opening her eyes, Lilli now looked at the pages in her lap again. Holding them gently in her hands, her breath slow and even, she picked them up and began to read the last letter she would ever receive from Uncle Herman.

The letter was dated December 24th, 1914; Uncle Herman was stationed on a battlefield at the Western Front. He explained that he had begun writing Lilli's letter from the trenches during what appeared to be a lull in the fighting. As Lilli read his words, she couldn't believe what he had written. Strange and unusual images came to her and she asked herself, how did this happen? Who began this? Why did it stop? Who stopped it?"

Uncle Herman had begun his letter in the usual manner, "Lilli, meine Liebste, it is Christmas Eve and my thoughts are with you and my dear sister Wilhelmine. As I picture you tonight on this Eve of Christmas, I can see you, your mother, Walter and of course, Henry, all busily decorating your beautiful Christmas tree, just like we always did at home. As it happens sometimes in battle, that there are times when it becomes eerily quiet, well it has here tonight. I believe that if I close my eyes, I can truly hear your voices singing those hymns which we always sang at home.

As you can imagine Lilli, Christmas Eve on a battlefield doesn't seem like Christmas Eve. Yet, for some reason, the guns have stopped firing. It has been a while now without gunfire and I am grateful for this peaceful time. I can think of home, I can remember times past and I can write to you. But Lilli, I am suddenly noticing that along with the quiet, there is a sense of calmness in the air which I have not felt before. No rifles firing, no bullets whizzing by, no grenades being tossed. Lilli, right now at this moment, no one is shooting, no one is screaming, there are no blasts of bombs and there are no calls for help. It is very silent this night almost a still night if you will, meine Liebste.

So, with this peaceful silence I too am trying to forget where I am right now; I am trying to feel warm, thinking about the Christmas Eves so many years before when we would all be together. I can imagine that your mother is opening that big box of wax angels which she loved and brought all the way to America, so long ago now. Closing my eyes, I can see them hanging on your tree. I imagine that you taking out each cherished ornament and considering, "Now where does this little beauty belong." I know you have candles burning in your windows; we always had burning candles in our windows, a tradition that I know you continue there in America. Lilli, as I look down through the trench line, I can see that some of the soldiers have placed lit candles in the trenches, Lilli, they too are remembering.

You know Lilli, I have just noticed that I cannot even smell gun powder and without that pungent smell I believe that I am sniffing the cool, clean scent of an evergreen. Maybe it is my imagination, or maybe it is a long-carried memory. Whatever it is I want to keep this moment and make it last forever. Lilli, I believe that I am hearing voices, they sound far away but they are not yelling they sound as if they are singing. It is not in German but in English... Lilli, they are singing English and they are singing Stille Nacht, mein Gott, these voices are singing.

I think I am going crazy, the soldiers near me are singing too, they are singing back but they Lilli, are singing in German. These men, my soldiers they are singing Stille Nacht back to the Tommy's.

This is unbelievable, I am sitting in mud in a trench, it is Christmas Eve, we are at war but we are singing to each other. Has the world abandoned its' senses? Have we all gone mad? There is no more shooting Lilli. I don't understand what is happening. This is not making any sense. It's unreal, but there is no more shooting. Singing instead of shooting. I must look, I have to raise my head out over the trench, I do not believe what I am hearing so I must look.

Herman folded his half-written letter to Lilli and placed it in his breast pocket. Stretching up he looked out over the battlefield as his eyes widened in disbelief. Gasping he saw what appeared to be hundreds of soldiers from both sides of the barbed wired battlefields approaching each other, shaking hands, talking and even laughing together.

Suddenly, someone took a ball of sorts and tossed it in the air. Herman climbed out of the muddy trench; his hands shaking as he quickly lit a cigarette. Inhaling deeply, he watched in disbelief and shock as soldiers that only hours before had been shooting and killing each other were now playing kick ball.

He stared in disbelief, as enemy combatants greeted each other laughing out loud. Steadying himself, he folded his arms across his chest and watched as if it was long ago and he was back home calmly watching the neighborhood boys play ball on the streets of Stuttgart.

Then he remembered Lilli's letter and pulled it out of his pocket. With his lit cigarette dangling from the corner of his mouth, he began to write exactly what his eyes were seeing but what his mind could not comprehend.

Her fingers gripped his letter, as she held her breath and continued to read, "I am standing outside of my trench. I see the barrier of barbed wire stretching into the distance, they are cutting it Lilli, they are crossing over and greeting each other. In front of me are soldiers, British and German soldiers, they are talking, sharing cigarettes, showing pictures of loved ones, exchanging chocolates. They are kicking a ball. I cannot believe what I am seeing. Lilli, something miraculous has happened, no guns are firing, it is only the sound of voices singing, talking and laughing.

I am hearing that we may even have a Christmas Eve service, maybe a joint service. I don't know what is happening Lilli but maybe just maybe this is over. Maybe this whole war is over."

"Man must know the spiritual at some point."
  - BKS Iyengar

14

THE KNOCK, WINTER 1915

*N*othing was the same anymore. Lilli and Wilhelmmine were often fearful and dreaded the moments when they had to leave the safety of their homes. Neither of them wanted to be on the streets or in the shops alone any longer. They didn't really discuss it; they just started doing things differently. Where they used to live somewhat independently, they began spending their days and evenings together more often. It felt safer, and at least they could protect each other, they believed.

Walking together to work in the morning they kept their heads down, not making eye contact or responding to any comments. The walk wasn't far and they were relieved that they still had their jobs and still worked together. The shop was quieter now; the easy conversations they had enjoyed with the other seamstresses were no longer so easy. Now when they entered the shop the others kept busy with their work, not looking up, not greeting them and not offering a chair or spot at the table for them to join.

Lilli remembered how surprised and hurt she felt when the atmosphere changed, how it seemed to begin with the new girl Bridgette, "Bridgette, what was it we did to make you so unkind?" Lilli asked herself, trying to recall the girl's full name, Bridgette something. "I know it began with an M," Lilli thought to herself. She remembered when Emma asked her to work alongside Bridgette and check her work, that Bridgette became annoyed and angry. She truly resented that it was Lilli who was checking her work, or perhaps she was appalled that anyone dared to check her work.

It was at that time that Bridgette began to mock Lilli's handwork and question the quality of her stitching. Surprised and baffled, Lilli said nothing, but the pain of the insults was real. She physically felt it and she didn't understand it. She tried to ignore Bridgette's behavior and comments. But soon she noticed that Bridgette was recruiting the other girls. They were beginning to follow her lead, smirking, whispering and even mocking her German accent which she was trying harder to stifle. Lilli, who had not a single bone of unkindness in her, struggled to understand this cruelty, and meanness. Lilli admitted that she was hurt, more hurt than she realized, and the deep pain of it would stay with her for a very long time.

But there was someone for whom Lilli was grateful someone that she knew she could depend on. Her friend, Catisemma, she was the one who would look up, smile and greet Lilli and her mother as they entered. When Catisemma joined Lilli and Wilhelmmine the others with lips squeezed tightly and shoulders hunched together would glare with narrowed eyes and whisper between themselves. Lilli, Wilhelmmine and now Catisemma would sit at a table in the far corner of the shop and work together. They shielded and protected each other, ostracizing themselves as they were being ostracized at work, on the streets and in their country. Catisemma would often mutter something in her native language closing the fingers of her left hand and pointing in the direction of the bullies.

Even though Wilhelmmine lived nearby, Lilli and Walter often invited her to stay and spend the night with them. They were becoming more and more fearful thinking of her living alone. At first Wilhelmmine insisted on going to her home but then more often she acquiesced. On those nights, Lilli would sleep more soundly knowing her mother was close, safe and protected.

Their fears were not unreasonable or unfounded, Lilli and Walter were hearing terrible stories, unbelievable and chilling tales about lynchings, beatings and even arrests of German Americans. These were unimaginable times. "Not in America," Lilli thought, "Not in a country where the promise of freedom for all was its founding principle."

Across the ocean the war continued, while in the United States a war of propaganda against all things German grew. The harvest it brought was violent intolerance and hostility to a population of more than a million American Germans, many whose ancestors had been American citizens for generations.

Mirroring the world outside, the tension at Emma's Dress Shop also became more openly vitriolic and eventually unbearable for Lilli and Wilhelmmine. Working together in the back of the small shop they felt the sting of constant insults and animosity which so many Germans were feeling daily. It was becoming more and more difficult to ignore the ongoing attacks, the constant slights and mocking jibes.

Emma watched with a broken heart as her once harmonious shop was itself turned into a battlefield. These women, who once were as close as sisters, were now pitted against each other based solely on their ethnicity. She didn't know how much longer either Lilli or Wilhelmmine or even she, would be able to take this behavior of intolerance and viciousness, the cruelty of it being more than she could bear.

Sadly, this was not something new to Emma She remembered well all of the pogroms that both she and Saul had experienced. Those memories were seared into her memory, alive each day still in her soul. "Here it is again." she said to herself, as she felt once more the pain she knew only too well. She understood deep in her core how this vile cancerous hatred consumed and fed upon itself, creating its own sense of self-righteousness, justifying its own punishing hatred and then feeding gluttonously on its feast of cruelty, intolerance and injustice.

Working alongside her seamstresses Emma often spoke to them about the need to see each other as the friends they had been, to remember what had united them before and not what now divided them. She knew there would be no good coming out of this hatred and she implored them to see the common humanity in each other, to listen before lashing out and to remember that first and foremost they were Americans or Americans to be.

But, the desire to believe the worst, to see others as less than and to relish in the false power of bigotry was just too strong for some. The truth, the power and meaning of her words fell on deaf ears.

She began to wonder if closing her shop would be the only answer, for she knew only too well, how it felt to be abused by others, to be treated with hostility, hatred and violence. But closing her shop was not a viable option; her shop was her life, and her financial living. Saul was ill and unable to work her shop had become the only income that they had.

The solution came one morning as she opened the back door and the sun shone through, lighting an interior where darkness had reigned only minutes before. Emma stood at the entrance, shaking her head in disbelief. She had never believed that she would experience such conflict between cultures in America. It was just too hard for her to witness this intolerance again; she knew she could not experience it again. "Not in America!" she said out loud. As Emma's frightening yesterdays seemed on the verge of being repeated, she looked up to the heavens. "Hashem this is why we left; it's not supposed to happen here."

Discrimination and the violent behavior it created was why she'd risked her life, leaving everything and everyone she loved behind in order to live in a country where you were not judged by your place of worship, your land of birth or even from where your ancestors hailed. As her chin fell to her chest, tears filled her eyes. She knew this animosity in her shop could not continue, it was intolerable. The time to do something had come. "There is only one thing to do." she advised herself.

Along with being an immigrant, Emma was also a business woman who knew that losing the skilled work of Lilli and Wilhelmmine was not an option, so she made a decision. It was in the middle of April 1915. The weather was beginning to show signs of spring. The sun was warmer, the daylight becoming longer and happily business was picking up. Emma had made up her mind then and there.

Walking together to the shop early that morning Lilli and Wilhelmmine were enjoying the spring air. Approaching the front door, their gait slowed as they steeled themselves against the hostility and resentment they would meet inside. Sadly, this was something they now had become accustomed to on a daily basis.

But that day, it was not to be. That day Emma greeted them, appearing calm and very much at peace, almost serene.

She sat in her solid old chair by the desk, smiling at them as they entered asking them to sit by her at the first sewing table.

Pulling up their chairs, Lilli and Wilhelmmine glanced surreptitiously at each other with questioning looks. But before they were even seated Emma began, "Lilli, Wilhelmmine, today, I believe I am doing a good deed, some may even call it a Mitzvah, maybe. Who knows? For me, I am not so sure. I have made a decision though and it will involve you and your work."

Lilli and Wilhelmmine turned towards each other with eyebrows raised in concern and apprehension as Emma continued, "The tension and intolerance cannot continue in this shop any longer." She paused looking at both of them, her face glowing and her eyes filled with tenderness, compassion and deep understanding. Leaning towards them, she placed her aged gnarled hands over both Wilhelmmine's and Lilli's. Taking a breath, she paused before she spoke again. Emma's eyes were strong and direct, as she looked into theirs, conveying an intensity, strength and vitality that they had never before noticed, with her voice strong and resolute she began.

"Hatred is vile! It is evil! It is contagious! It is the bane of a civilized society. Emma's words came from a place deep in her soul. "It destroys both the hater and the hated, I have seen it up close, I have experienced it, and I have lived it. The chill it has put in my body can never be warmed; it will live in me forever… I have seen what you both have been experiencing and exposed to here in my shop. It is unacceptable to me and I will not have it, hatred will not survive here. It will not grow and it will not continue and I will stop it right now.

Pausing, Emma closed her eyes and exhaled, then continued, "I have made a decision. I have an idea and I know it will work."

Immediately Lilli leaned closer to Emma as she spoke to be sure she caught every word. Wilhelmmine straightened her back, lifting her chin just slightly. Keeping her gaze fixed on Emma's face she looked straight ahead directly into Emma's eyes.

"This is what will happen." Emma went on, "Since both of you are my best, most experienced and most skilled seamstresses, I do not want to lose you. As you know business has picked up, so I need all of the skilled seamstresses I can employ. Also, but very importantly, I cannot have my customers become involved in any of this intolerance. This is my shop and this is my hallowed ground."

Not sure where this conversation was going, Lilli tilted her head to the side questioningly. Wilhelmmine did not move an inch; she simply continued to sit her back straight and head held high as she listened quietly.

Noticing their demeanor, Emma continued to speak, squeezing Lilli and Wilhelmmine hands tightly. They felt her strength, her resolve and her soul in those weathered, hardworking, loving but strong and powerful hands.

"So, this here is my plan or maybe it is a Mitzvah, again I am not so sure. Starting tomorrow both of you will work from home; there is no need for you to try to work here each and every day under these circumstances. I trust you, I know you will do the work and you don't need supervision. You never did. Your pay will remain the same, all of your supplies here can be brought to your homes and if your own sewing machines need repair, I will take care of that for you. So there, it is done, so be it."

Emma exhaled deeply, realizing that she had been holding her breath. Looking directly at her friends, a gentle smile crossed her weary face. Still holding tightly onto their hands, her wise blue eyes filled with tears that spilled down her winkled cheeks. Emma's voice softened as she struggled with the catch in her throat. "Maybe who knows, with a bit of luck this will all end very soon."

The tension that Emma had felt between her shoulders released as she pressed her back into her solid, sturdy and heavy old oak chair. "This chair," she thought, remembering how their hearts had broken with so many of the decisions, she and Saul had to make. Asking themselves again and again, "What can we bring? What can we put in our box? What must we leave behind?" In that moment Emma felt the pain and sadness of all they had left behind, so much more than mere personal possessions.

This chair was one of the few family possessions that had survived their long journey from Russia to America, and when she pushed further back into its solid backrest, she felt its strength and support. "So much, Hashem, we left behind so much." She whispered, closing her eyes. Then Emma's gaze lifted as she looked beyond the walls of her shop into the unseen distance.

Lilli leaned forward and for luck she knocked three times on the thick wooden arm of Emma's chair, "Thank you," she said. "This is a great idea, let's hope it brings us all peace and a bit of luck." Lilli's eyes were pensive as she looked at Emma, quietly almost in a whisper, she asked, "You brought this chair over from Russia, didn't you?"

Emma smiled replying, "Yes, we did."

"Emma, what did you and Saul leave behind?"

As her eyes filled with tears, Emma gazed downwards, inhaled deeply then quietly answered, "Everything, Lilli, we left everything."

Reaching toward her friend, Wilhelmmine squeezed Emma's hand as tears fell from her eyes, smiling through them she said, "Danke, Emma, Thank you!"

Emma nodded, unable to speak. She bowed her head slightly and released their hands, then whispered more to herself than to anyone else, "Mazel Tov."

Walter and Lilli had recently asked Wilhelmmine about

moving in with them. They loved her company and they were convinced that she too would enjoy staying with them. Wilhelmmine gave it a lot of thought and finally decided. "Yes," she told them, "I'll do it. "

With the help of her daughter and son-in-law, the pieces of furniture she needed were easily moved from her home to theirs, but because of limited space there was one particular piece that Wilhelmmine felt was too big for the small space the three of them would be sharing. As Wilhelmmine stood in the middle of her room, realizing that this piece, the bed she had shared for so many years with her cherished husband, would no longer be part of her life anymore, she swallowed the lump that rose in her throat and pressed an open palm across her chest holding back an ache she thought had healed long ago.

On so many nights for so many years alone in the bed they had shared, Wilhelmmine would run her fingers over the circular carvings, along the top and sides, as she felt the grooves, the depth and the warmth of this wood. It was then that she imagined again holding Willi's hands in hers. Their fingers entwined as they created and captured every movement, every shape and every memory that now rested above her head only, his side of the bed having been empty for far too long now.

So often she would dream of Willi, of him being with her again, of them just sitting together, maybe talking even touching. When she would awaken, the gentle memory of her dream brought her solace.

But then one night her dream was different. Somehow in this dream she felt that he truly was with her again. It was a cold winter's night. It was dark, and snow was softly falling.

They were outside walking together. Wilhelmmine noticed their footprints as the light snow melted beneath their boots. Around them everything was blanketed in a soft glimmer of sparkling white. She marveled at how the snowflakes seem to shimmer like diamonds as they swirled around in the light of the gas lamps along the street.

At first, they were walking at a brisk pace but suddenly their pace slowed, Willi paused as they stood side by side their shoulders close but not touching. Turning, he faced her, as the wet white flakes melted on their cheeks. To the left was a church, it was the one where they had met, so many years before. Wilhelmmine noticed that they weren't alone, there were others around. She observed two nuns in full habits walking past them. She was curious as to what they were doing, where they were going, and why they were out on such a cold, wintry night.

In her dream state she understood that Willi was dead. Even in her subconsciousness she knew and accepted that he was dead. She also understood he had returned.

Looking back, it had all made sense, it was natural for him to be with her again.

Without a word, they began to walk slowly past the church, Wilhelmmine sensed that time was running out and her breathing became shallow with anxiety.

Her breath rapidly leaving her mouth in heavy puffs of smoke. She tried reaching out to Willi, to touch him, his arms, his back, his hair and then his face. At first, she couldn't, he was just beyond her outstretched fingertips, just slightly too far from her. Then finally, she felt him. "Yes. "She thought. He was real. She felt his solidness, his strength, his skin and his energy. Grabbing frantically, she tried to hold onto his hands but they kept slipping away.

Then he stopped, turning he faced her, their eyes met as the lightly falling flakes of snow caught onto his eyelashes. Locking his gaze with hers, he said, "I have to leave." Begging him to stay she cried, "No, not again Willi, not again."

Straining to clearly see him, she locked her eyes into his, she saw his lips moving, heard his voice but she saw no breath escaping from his mouth. "I have to go, I can't stay," he replied. Tears fell on her cold, wet cheeks as she pleaded, "Please, Willi, please don't go, not again, please." The snow had become more intense, it swirled around them creating between them a filmy invisible barrier. Lilli knew that she would never be this close to her husband again. In despair Willi shook his head from side to side and repeated, "Wilhelmmine, I must, I have to go, I can't stay. Please remember this, I love you with all my heart, I always have and I always will."

Willi had never denied her before, had never said no to her wishes, and never had he made her cry, but this time Wilhelmmine knew he was leaving her again. As she reached out trying to hold onto him, tears flowed from her eyes. Her heart beat faster and it was becoming harder to breath, as desperation enveloped her body. "No!" she cried, "I am not letting go."

Her wet fingers slipped as she tried to grab tightly onto his hands, his coat, his arms, as she begged and pleaded. Her face was cold and soaked with tears that blurred her vision, they spilled over her cheeks and down her face to her chin where they fell onto the snow. Her body wrenched with sobs, shaking and gasping for breath, Wilhelmmine slowly blinked open her soaked, heavy eyelids, becoming aware that she was awake.

Her face was wet with the tears she'd been crying in her sleep. Her throat sore and raw from her sobs. She realized at once, that it had just been a dream, and she buried her fists into her face. Once again, she was back in their bed, and again she was alone.

In the muted darkness of her room, Wilhelmmine continued to cry, choking on sobs that violently escaped from her throat, as her body shook uncontrollably. Ever so slowly she began to calm herself, suddenly she became aware that her hands were clenched firmly into fists so tightly that her fingernails were digging into her palms creating deep red welts. Gently, she opened her fingers, releasing their grip, and felt the wet ice-cold water that lay in her palms like melting snowflakes.

As the last of her tears subsided, she remained motionless in bed listening to the silence around her that might have been comforting to another but to her, roared like a storm that would not relent.

Wilhelmine lay still as the memory of her dream played out again in her head and in her heart. "Was it really a dream?" She asked herself. "I can remember every detail, every feeling and every word. Why were my hands so cold and wet? Maybe," she thought, "Maybe he was here with me, maybe he never left."

At that moment in the silent, stark darkness of the seemingly endless night, she knew then that she really had been holding onto Willi, and that she would never let go.

Since then, on the long dark nights Wilhelmmine would close her eyes, returning to that time and place when she felt once again Willi's passion, and heard his focused breathing as he worked late into the evening carving the headboard that would eventually become part of their bed. She saw clearly the intensity in his face as he created the seraphim and cherubim who guarded them as they slept in each other's arms at night. She knew it wasn't just his skill, his talent or his artistry that he had carved above her head, it was also his soul.

Wilhelmmine's breath stopped and her heart skipped a beat when she knew then, with certainty, that even though Willie had died, his soul had never left hers. Along with the grooves in the wood, along with the intricate carvings, along with the angels, he too had stayed with her. He had never ever left her, and after all of these years he continued to sleep by her side, holding her in his arms each night.

Knowing he would hear her, Wilhelmmine gazed through the thin veil of the gossamer curtains which covered her windows to the world beyond and whispered, "I love you Willi, I always have, I always will."

Wilhelmmine remembered every detail of that dream for the rest of her life, as if she had just awoken from it. She never told anybody about it, never shared that night with anyone else. She knew that it was much more than a dream. It was their time, he had come back on that cold winter night to be with her once more, walking with her, offering her one last gift: a love that even death could not end. She understood now that he had to leave, but was eternally grateful that he had returned to say a final, "Good bye." With that parting message, he left to go to a place where Wilhelmmine knew he would wait for her to come to him.

Meanwhile, a solution regarding Wilhelmmine's cherished headboard presented itself during the move. Both Lilli and Walter had insisted that Willi's headboard belonged in their home with Wilhelmmine. Lilli discovered that by leaning the headboard against the wall and placing the chaise in front of it she could create a comfortable sitting area, which truly made her home complete.

It was late on an April evening when Lilli and Wilhelmmine, their legs curled underneath them, sat next to each other on the long chaise in Lilli's parlor, sipping tea and reminiscing. Their backs comfortably against the soft pillows, which had been placed in front of the beautiful carved head board.

With tears of gratitude in her eyes Lilli told Walter, "Now I have both my mother and my father with me again."

As Lilli and Wilhelmmine sat together that evening hearing the hard rain and rushing wind outside they felt shielded and protected. It was a wind and rain-soaked nor'easter, a typical April weather event had buffeted the entire east coast throughout the day and appeared to be keeping up during the night. Outside it was black as pitch and at times the rain was so heavy that the pelting drops against the glass panes echoed the rhythmic sound of marching feet. Sitting snugly under a heavy wool blanket that Wilhelmmine had knitted many years ago, she and Lilli were grateful to be warm and dry.

Walter had gone to bed earlier and now Wilhelmmine began to feel her eyelids drop as she stifled a yawn. In the quiet of the apartment she heard the old Gilbert mahogany mantel clock chime 11 times. "Oh gosh, Lilli." she said, "I had no idea it was that late." As she was beginning to get up, she stopped abruptly. Turning towards Lilli, she asked, "What was that, did you hear it? I think it was a knock."

Lilli, startled, replied with a worried look on her face. "Yes,

I heard that too. It was definitely a knock. But it wasn't on the door. It sounded like it came from outside somewhere."

Looking towards the door with raised eyebrows, they tiptoed quickly to the front vestibule of the flat, opening the heavy wooden door slowly and cautiously. Holding tightly onto each for courage, they peered into the hall landing. Seeing nothing they quickly closed and locked the door. Not satisfied though, they went to the windows facing the front of the apartment building. In the moonless murky darkness, with the rain falling forcefully, it was impossible to see anything except the liquid reflections of their own ghostly images.

Wilhelmmine thought for a moment then looked at Lilli her eyes questioning. "You did hear the knock, right?" She asked.

"Yes." Lilli responded.

"So, we both heard a knock?" Wilhelmmine said. Lilli nodded in response.

"It's strange," Wilhelmmine told her daughter, "But I don't feel afraid. Are you Lilli? I don't believe that it was an intruder, has this made you nervous?" Wilhelmmine felt an unusual sense of peace as she noticed how quiet it had become. There were no sounds at all, not even the sound of the rain on the windows or the sound of the ticking clock.

Checking in with herself, Lilli was surprised to note that she, too, felt no anxiousness or concern. "For some reason it didn't make me nervous at all. "she replied, "Should we be?"

"Not at all." answered her mother confidently, it hadn't unsettled Wilhelmmine. Actually, it was quite to the contrary. She noticed that she felt very calm, unusually calm in spite of the odd circumstances. Somehow, she knew in her heart that this knock was not the knock of an intruder.

With a faraway look in her eyes, Wilhelmmine said, "Lilli, sit down, bitte, I want to share with you what your grandmother shared with me." After the two women had returned to their seats on the chaise, Wilhelmmine continued. "Lilli, meine Liebchen, there definitely was a knock. We both heard it. But it was not a knock on the door; it was not a knock on the window pane. This was not a knock of someone wanting to come in. It was a knock of someone saying good bye. It was the knock of a soul as they passed through to the other side, they were telling us Lilli, that all was well.

I believe that what we heard tonight was a knock on that thin veil that separates our world from the next. It was a message Lilli, a message from someone we know and love. They have left this earth and their soul was simply saying good bye, all is well, good bye."

Lilli nodded; she knew her mother was right. She knew that if you listened carefully you could always hear the good bye somehow.

The next morning Lilli and Wilhelmmine rose to see the sun shining brightly, the air sweet with the smell of spring and filled with the gentle sounds of birds twittering back and forth. While they ate their breakfast yet another knock was heard, but this time it was on the front door. Pushing back her chair, Lilli rose and went to unlatch the door, recognizing the uniform of a telegram delivery boy who looked up at her and asked, "Does a Mrs. Willi Holtzapfl live here?"

"Yes," replied Lilli, curious about what he was delivering to her mother. Quickly, thrusting his hand towards her he said, "Then this telegram here is for her."

Her hand began to shake as Lilli took the envelope. Closing the door, without so much as a nod towards the uniformed boy, she turned and quickly walked back into the kitchen and handed the telegram to her mother. Wilhelmmine gasped and her eyes widened when she saw the return address. Her hand rose to cover her mouth and her heart sank. She knew this would not be news she wanted to hear. When she looked up at Lilli, tears were already brimming in her eyes. She tore open the envelope and read the first of the large block letters:

REGRETstop, BROTHER HERMAN KIL...

Reading no further, Wilhelmmine dropped the telegram onto the floor and looked up at Lilli. "I know who knocked last night," she told her daughter through silent tears. "It was him Lilli. It was my brother, your Uncle Herman...He knocked as he passed by.

He loved us so much, that his soul had to say good bye."

Even though Wilhelmmine already knew, deep in her soul that she had already sensed her brother's death, her grief was nearly unbearable. With the telegram on the floor at her feet, she began to sob. Shaking her head left to right, she laid her forearms on the table, pillowing her head as her body was wracked with tears.

Lilli rushed to her mother's side, wrapping her arms tightly around her, holding on as she had done so many years before and sobbed uncontrollably along with her. This time their tears weren't cleansing. This time their tears were suffused with pain, disbelief and heartbreak. This time the tears washed away everything that might have been, all of the possibilities, and all of what could be, but never would again. This time their tears fell as if they, like the war waging on across the world, would never stop.

"I'm a Yankee Doodle Dandy, a Yankee Doodle do or die!"
- George M. Cohan

15

THE PATRIOT

The month of April, 1915 seemed to rain tears from heaven, none of the news was good. Newspaper stories and propaganda posters, intent on fanning the flames of anti-German sentiment with hostile and inflammatory rhetoric continued to polarize the country. It was reported that the German military was using a hideous new weapon, it was not one involving guns, torpedoes or bombs dropped from planes, but an almost unseen weapon. The German government had introduced chemical warfare, a toxic yellowish green and extremely poisonous gas had become the unseen weapon of choice against the Allied forces. This hideous gas killed slowly and painfully, burning eyes, throats, skin and lungs, making breathing impossible violently choking soldiers to death. With the advent of submarines and airplanes World War 1 also introduced chemical warfare across Europe.

German people and the German military were now being

portrayed as barbaric and inhumane. It had been many years earlier that the Kaiser himself compared the strength and might of the Germans to the conquering warriors under Attila the Hun. Now that description was being used to describe the German people and soldiers as vicious, murderous barbarians. Whether the reports were true or not were irrelevant, to be a true American patriot meant to despise anything that was German.

Trying desperately to remain neutral and out of the war the United States was being drawn into it with every passing day. Then the crushing blow came that brought America even closer to entering the war. Early on the morning of May 8th Lilli and Wilhelmmine were heading outside to enjoy the spring weather. Standing on the steps of their apartment building, they heard a young boy of maybe 11 or 12 years old hawking The New York Herald. Hearing the headline that he was shouting sent an icy cold shiver down Lilli's spine.

She recognized his voice as it shrilled in her ears, "Extra, extra, read all about it!" Germans torpedo and sink the Lusitania! Innocent civilians' slaughtered! Women and children drowned! More than 1000 dead, bodies floating in the cold Celtic Sea. Read all about it in today's Herald!"

Stopping abruptly, Lilli grabbed her mother's arm. "Wait." she cautioned, "We need a paper. I'll get it, wait here Mutter, bitte."

The boy continued shouting as he walked up and down the sidewalk, but it felt to Lilli that he was just standing still, shouting his terrifying news directly in front of their home.

Not believing what she had heard, Lilli walked gingerly

down the front stairs, holding tightly onto the cast iron railing for support. Speaking as calmly as possible she beckoned to the newsboy, "I'll take a paper, please." Staring at her, recognizing her and remembering her name, his eyes narrowed with hate and suspicion. He held onto the paper until she handed him the coins, then jabbed it toward her, spitting on the sidewalk in front of her shoes before venturing to the corner of the street to hawk more papers, he spat again a second time straight at Lilli before he continued on his way.

Tucking, the paper hastily under one arm, she turned running up the stairs to her mother's side. Her hands trembling, she spread the paper open, the headlines boldly proclaiming, "**THE LUSITANIA IS SUNK; 1,000 ARE PROBABLY LOST!**" The report continued, "On Friday, May 7, 1915 a German U-Boat torpedoed the luxury passenger liner The Lusitania. This act of aggression is being dubbed, "the most infamous event of this War to date." Of the total 1,198passengers and crew that were lost at sea 128 were American citizens! "

Even though numerous notices had been posted regarding the dangers that the war had brought to ship travel, many did not believe that the Germans would actually sink a passenger liner.

Lilli's whole body went cold as goose pimples broke out on her flesh causing her to shake in spite of the warm May air. Wilhelmmine's chin dropped to her chest, she shook her head, saying simply, "Mein Gott, mein Gott. Nein, nein, nein."

Lilli knew that from then on, they were not safe anywhere, taking her mother's hand they began climbing the stairs returning to the front door of their building. "We need to go inside, right now, bitte Mutter, bitte. Wilhelmmine didn't have the will to resist, as she followed her daughter back into their home.

Feeling safer inside, with the doors securely locked Lilli tried to rationalize her feelings. Lately, everywhere she had gone, whoever she saw, she felt scorn, anger and even outright hostility. She had never felt this way before but now it was as if she was an enemy in her own country, a country that once had welcomed her and her mother. For reasons beyond their control, the land she now called home had become a frightening place to live. Lilli asked herself, "Do other's feel like this? Is it only those of German heritage who feel this scorn? This is too hard to bear. I too am an American, and I am an American citizen." Lilli reminded herself, her face brightening as the memory of how proud they all were on the day when she, Walter, Henry and Wilhelmmine had become citizens of The United States of America. Even now in spite of growing hostilities, Lilli smiled as she recalled the ear to ear grin on Henry's face. How he beamed looking at her, holding his certificate proudly in his hands, "Lilli," he said. "We are truly Americans now, Americans!" His pride showed in his squared shoulders and puffed out chest, of all of them he boldly wore his love of America for all to see.

She laughed out loud thinking of that day and how they were so excited and happy, as they celebrated with their favorite meal of sauerkraut, and weiner schnitzels, raising cold glasses of beer, heartily toasting each other as the white foam sloshed and splashed on the table.

LILLI'S CHAIR

She and Walter had proudly hung their framed U. S. Citizen Certificates on the wall of their home. They wanted everyone who entered to see them. Reflecting on that incredible day Lilli read out loud the words inscribed on her own certificate, hanging on the wall above her chair.

"United States of America. Circuit Court, U. S. NEW YORK DIST. SS. To all People to whom these Presents shall come...Greeting.

On the fifteenth day of May, in the year of our Lord one thousand nine hundred and"...Lilli paused for here the words were hand written and harder to read " *...two* **To Wit:** on the *Tenth* day of *November,* **A.D. 1902** *Lilli Alvine Von Vetterlein of Brooklyn* in said district, *Seamstress,* born at *Stuttgart, Germany* having produced the evidence and taken the oath required by law, was admitted to become a citizen of the said United States according to the Acts of Congress in such case made and provided."

It went on, indicating this was the 127th year of Independence of the United States of America, and was sealed and witnessed by the Deputy Clerk of the Circuit Court of the United States for the District of New York. Both Walter and Lilli's certificates appeared identical, they were stamped on the lower left with a seal of the Circuit Court of the state of New York but Lilli noticed something different about hers, something she missed when looking at it before. Her certificate was missing another stamp, one in black ink on the upper left corner. Walter's Certificate had a stamp confirming that it had been duly "inspected by the Registrars of Voters, Brooklyn, New York." Her certificate did not. No Registrar of Voters had inspected it, and no Registrar of Voters had stamped it. They didn't need to because Lilli, a woman, wasn't legally allowed to vote.

She'd gone years without noticing that detail, but at that moment she understood well its deeper meaning. Back in 1902 she wasn't aware of the impact of not having the right to vote. At that time, she was thrilled and honored to be a citizen of the United States of America. But now, she realized the inequality and injustice of such a situation.

Shaking her head, Lilli's spoke out, her voice determined. "No, we don't have the vote right now, we will, we most certainly will."

Lilli knew she was no less a citizen than any other American in the United States, man, woman or child. This was her country too, and she didn't need any further confirmation or black ink stamp to tell her she was qualified. Straightening her spine and squaring her shoulders Lilli told her mother, "We will vote and we will vote soon." she continued, "Me, my mother, my sisters, my daughters, and my granddaughters, we will vote in our lifetime."

But with that statement Lilli felt a twinge in her heart, as her breath caught in her throat. She and Walter didn't have children. There were no sons or daughters, no grandchildren, this was something Lilli tried not to focus on too much. Although her quiet, orderly home was a constant reminder. Approaching their 14th wedding anniversary, Lilli felt more deeply each day that having a child of their own wasn't a possibility.

Pulling herself out of her melancholy thoughts, Lilli turned to read her certificate again. "I am a citizen of the United States of America, I belong here, none of us are more entitled than another. Yes, my history is German, I was born in Germany, and I speak German, but I came here to be an American. I left my country of birth for this place and the freedoms it promised. I am an American, this is my country too."

Reaching behind her, she pulled up her rocker and slid onto the seat. Taking in a deep breath she felt the comforting support of the hand carved spindles on her back. Instinctively her fingers found their way into the deeply carved grooves at the ends of each arm, she closed her eyes and rocked. Lilli hadn't realized how tightly she'd been holding everything in until she looked down at her knuckles, white with tension. "Calm down," she told herself.

Immediately, the chair's rocking motion began to sooth Lilli, each forward movement bringing her closer to her future, while each backward movement brought peace as she remembered the solid foundation of her past. Stopping abruptly, Lilli realized that the rocking was symbolic of how she was feeling within. "I chose to come to America, to become an American, to move my life forward," she thought. My German heritage is still with me, but it is behind me. It will always be a part of me, something I will honor and cherish. But I am an American, that is how I see myself and that is how I want others to see me too.

Loud knocking on her door startled Lilli from her thoughts as she stood up and went to answer it. Opening it only a crack she saw Henry, he was standing holding the newspaper in his hands, his head low and his eyes heavy with sadness and disbelief. "Lilli." he stated as he rushed in, and wrapped his arms around her. They held each other tightly sharing the sorrow, shock and dismay at what they had each read about their homeland's unfathomable actions.

"Johnny get your gun!"

- George M. Cohan

16

AMERICAN DOUGHBOY

The sinking of the Lusitania became a rallying cry for America to enter the war against Germany, but that wasn't enough. President Woodrow Wilson campaigned under the slogan, "He kept us out of war!" and the American people breathing a collective sigh of relief elected him for a second term on November 7th 1916.

As the conflict raged in Europe, many Americans believed that like so many other conflicts over there this one too would not affect them, Europe and European problems seemed a comfortable distance away.

But this time that distance was narrowing. Events overseas, on our border in Mexico and on our Atlantic Ocean shoreline were creating an atmosphere that brought Europe's war frighteningly closer to America.

In late January 1917, Germany made a belligerent and bold declaration stating that from now on it would wage unrestricted warfare on all ships in the Atlantic Ocean. Flying the

Stars and Stripes on Merchant ships no longer kept Americans safe, unrestricted warfare meant, every ship whether enemy or neutral was now a target for the German navy.

On February 3rd 1917 all diplomatic relations between Germany and the United States were severed. Shortly afterwards the State department released the Zimmermann Telegram exposing the German Government's attempt to enlist Mexico's support with a planned invasion into the southwestern region of the United States. These actions created an atmosphere of anger, fear, and patriotism in America. Being patriotic meant looking for spies and enemies everywhere, in homes, schools and churches. Lilli noticed that not only were her neighbors more distant many of them wore badges indicating they were members of the newly organized volunteer vigilante group, The American Protective League – Secret Service. To be patriotic meant to surreptitiously watch your neighbors, to eavesdrop on their conversations and to guarantee that spies were not living in your community. For Lilli and her family, not only were they living in constant fear but the daily abuse of intolerance and trauma of suspicion everywhere they went was taking its toll. Lilli and Wilhelmmine were grateful that they worked from home and only left their apartment when absolutely necessary always together.

Once again, one by one the dominoes fell, like the crimson red of an early morning sunrise foretelling the coming of a storm, a rallying cry began to swell, sweeping across the country, reaching a fever pitch the war in Europe came crashing down on America's shores.

Sensing the tone and sway of the American population, both

American propagandist and the English government stoked the fires of German hatred and intolerance. England fervently, hoped America would join the war, sending American money, American munitions and most importantly American soldiers and sailors.

On April 2, 1917, contradicting his campaign slogan, President Wilson, went before Congress requesting that a state of war between the United States and Germany be declared. On Friday, April 6, 1917, Congress declared that from that day forward a state of war existed between Germany and the United States of America, the War to End All Wars was now worldwide.

Being an American meant being a Patriot; it meant fighting for your country, and it meant enlisting into the newly established National Army. Recruitment stations and posters were everywhere with a stern-looking Uncle Sam pointing a finger, beckoning young, patriotic, American men to join up and defend their country against the Germans, the barbarians, the HUNS!

The fledgling Broadway Theatre District in New York City echoed with patriotic themes. George M. Cohan, dubbed "The Man Who Owns Broadway," composed the inspirational battle cry, "*Over There,*" with the explicit lyrics, *"Johnnie, get your gun, get your gun, get your gun, Johnnie show the Hun who's a son of a gun."*

The repetitive verse from this song *"The Yanks are coming!"* became the rallying cry across the nation.

Everywhere men and boys who only days earlier were working in shops, selling papers, shelving groceries were queuing up in lines at quickly established recruitment storefronts responding to Uncle Sam's command and enlisting to fight for their country.

It was late in the afternoon when Lilli and Wilhelmmine were in the kitchen preparing dinner, the room was warm from their cooking. Thankfully the late day breezes brought relief through the opened windows. Every now and then the whiff of a cool east wind gave the indication of a change in the weather and even a coming storm. They were expecting both Henry and Walter soon, Lilli smiled at Wilhelmmine as she heard their quick footsteps coming up the stairs.

Setting aside their spoons and ladles they went to greet the men. Lilli tucked her dishcloth into the waistline of her apron so she could open the door, but before she could, Henry excitedly flung it wide, rushing inside. He quickly embraced a surprised Wilhelmmine. Then smiling widely, he turned to Lilli saying, "Lilli, I did it, I did it!" his face flushed with pride. "You did what?" Lilli and Wilhelmmine asked in unison.

"I joined the Army, the infantry, to be exact."

Lilli and Wilhelmmine looked at each other in shock and trepidation. Swallowing a surge of fear, Lilli paused, then asked him haltingly, "Henry, wha, what have you done?"

Mustering more pride that he knew he had Henry straightened his shoulders and pulled himself up to his full height of 6 feet explaining, "Today, I joined the 165th Infantry Regiment. You might know it as "The Fighting 69th" if you've read your American Civil War History."

"I have and I specifically remember that its' mostly an Irish regiment with many of the enlistees just from Ireland themselves, isn't it?" Lilli asked, recalling with distaste her experience with Bridgette at Emma's Dress Shoppe.

"It could be, I guess, "he replied, but as far as they're concerned, Hank Schonfeld is as American as all the rest of the boys. You can officially call me a Dough Boy now sweet cousin."

Standing in the entry way he laughed out loud as he looked at his stunned relatives. "Since it is as you say, an Irish Regiment then you had better learn to cook with a lot more cabbage and potatoes than you've been doing lately and from what the boys tell me there is a Catholic Chaplain named Father Duffy. He claims that, anyone who isn't Irish when they join the 69th becomes Irish by adoption, Irish by association or Irish by conviction. So, from now on I'll be sporting the green and humming the, "Garry Owen in Glory tune."

Lilli stared at her cousin in bewilderment, "How do you know so much already?" She asked. Looking at Lilli with mock impatience he replied, "I'm a journalist Lilli, remember? I did my research before I joined. I know what I'm doing. As far as I could see, if you want to demonstrate patriotism, grit and guts, then you can't go wrong joining a regiment known as The Fighting Irish. You know how the Irish are don't you Lilli? You know."

Standing completely still, Lilli met Hank's gaze and said coolly, "Oh, yes I do. I sure do Henry."

Turning on her heel, her eyes flashed as she shot a quick look at her mother. Then she stormed into the kitchen where she balled up her wet dishtowel and hurled it through the open kitchen window.

"Your life is a journey, it is about change, growth, discovery, movement, transformation; continuously expanding your vision of what is possible, stretching your soul, learning to see clearly and deeply, listening to your intuition, taking courageous challenges."
- Caroline Adams

17

BOSTON, MASSACHUSETTS, 1917

With Henry's departure, it had become quieter around Lilli's home. The silence made her realize once more how much one person impacts an entire household. Again, there was a hole in their family, this time created by Henry's absence. With their cousin preparing to fight for his country, she thought of her Uncle Herman and his death fighting for Germany. Lilli prayed that Henry would return, safe and sound, to sit with them again at dinner, regaling them with stories of his adventures in France. Lilli felt some reassurance knowing that he was still in the U.S. training with his regiment to be sent overseas. Missing him terribly, she prayed that maybe this awful war would end before they shipped out.

Life had taught Lilli that it was important to remain optimistic and to be grateful, so as she thought of her many blessings, her friend Catisemma was one of them. Often, she would join Wilhelmmine, Walter and Lilli for dinner. Over dinner

Catisemma would bring news of the daily events at Emma's shop, lengthy stories, of how Emma was doing, as well as gossip about the clients, the workers and of course, Bridgette.

Lilli always knew when a story would include Bridgette, because before Catisemma began she would turn up her nose, and look sideways away from her friends. Then she would make a strange gesture, extending her right arm to the side, folding the center fingers of that hand inward, her two outside fingers pointing outward. This was something Lilli had seen Catisemma do before, but never asked its meaning. While in that position Catisemma would say something under her breath, nod, and unfold her fingers, then she'd continue with her story.

Upon hearing that Bridgette continued to maintain her vitriol, talking about everyone and everything, Lilli would shake her head. She still didn't understand that kind of hostility, why someone was capable of such meanness. Lilli and Wilhelmmine would meet with Emma early in the mornings to deliver their completed work and to take new assignments. Emma did not gossip or tell any tales, Lilli missed the camaraderie of the shop and was glad that she still had Catisemma as a friend. Along with her friendship Lilli looked forward to her contributions to their shared dinners, always something with a sauce, tomatoes and wide pasta, things that Lilli would never think of putting together but which made her mouth water.

As the long shadows of the summer of 1917 shortened, the sky turned a deeper blue and the leaves turned to crimson, gold and orange. Lilli noticed Catisemma was withdrawing, appearing anxious and concerned about her betrothed Arturo.

"My man, I have not heard from him lately," she confessed one evening after dinner. "I am afraid for him; I hope he is ok. He the head man, you know." her eyes misting, she would say, "Maybe he just too busy." She'd admit, trying to conceal her worries.

Catisemma didn't know if Arturo was in New Hampshire, Boston or even still in America. She wondered whether he would have left and not told her, maybe joined the army. Sometimes Lilli and Wilhelmmine would talk about leaving their neighborhood but they were afraid that they would find the same hostility no matter where they went. Germany and Germans, whether American citizens or not, were the enemies. Though she once felt so proud of her heritage, Lilli no longer shared it with others, often offering only her first name when asked and taking care to shop in stores where the clerks didn't know her or her ethnicity.

Lilli looked forward now to hearing from Henry, even though the letters he'd sent had taken on a solemn tone. He wrote saying how they were expecting to be shipped any day but of course he couldn't and wouldn't disclose the date. He didn't quite know where they would end up, but he knew wherever it was the enemy, the powerful German Army, would be ready.

In one of his letters he had written, "Lilli, you can't imagine how proud I am to be an American, to be able to fight for this country, to fight alongside boys not only born in America but from Italy, Ireland, Scotland all fighting for the United States. I never thought I'd be a soldier, and experience being an American Doughboy. I can't wait to write about this when this war is over. By the way Lilli, I've met Father Duffy the chaplain of the 69th Fighting Irish and I've begun attending mass regularly with the other boys."

"He always knew how to fit in," Lilli thought.

She read on, hearing Hank's voice in her head as he described the living conditions in his barracks." Lilli, imagine a long horse barn from the old country, rough wood on the inside and outside, windows stretching the length of the walls, covered by thin panes of glass. There are no screens so when we open them to let a breeze in or simply clear out the smells, then anything and everything flying outside joins our regiment inside.

"There are two dozen cots lined up next to each other running down both sides of the walls each covered with a rough sheet, a flat pillow and a thin blanket. So far, the weather hasn't been too cold, but I can only imagine the shivering that will be going on in here during the winter."

"We try to keep everything as neat as a bunch of boys can, hanging up our uniforms on poles and hooks. When we get bored luckily, we can always find a deck of cards to get a game going, a cigarette or two to share, even some writing paper to send letters to the folks back home.

By the way that's how I met a bloke, a real nice guy. He was sitting in the corner of the barracks, real quiet and pensive, with a pencil and paper in his lap, I walked over to him and asked if he had an extra cigarette. Looking up he smiled and said, "Sure buddy, here help yourself." "He tossed me several, real generous guy, I thought. So, I seated myself next to him on the edge of his bunk and asked him, "You writing home?" He looked up at me, grinned and then rather shyly said, "Well no, I'm actually writing a poem, I write poetry."

"I didn't know he was a writer, not to never mention a poet of sorts. I guess he didn't share that with everyone so I felt really honored, being a writer myself. It was then that I told him that I, too, am a writer, and that I had written for McClure's. I told him my byline was Hank Schonfeld, asked him if he had ever read anything I had written. I mentioned that I had done some work on those trains taking orphans and street kids out of New York, Boston and other major cities and bringing them to the west, Minnesota, Wisconsin, even the Dakotas and all. I thought maybe he had read an article or two. To be honest he said that he had read McClure's but couldn't remember if he had read anything I had written. He told me that when we get back, when this war is over, The Great War as they call it, he'll look up my writings then."

"Then the call for mess came and as I was getting up to leave, he called me over. Sticking out his hand to shake mine, he said, "By the way Hank, call me Joyce, my name is Joyce Kilmer." Lilli, I was floored, of course I had heard of Joyce Kilmer; of course, I knew his work. Here I was puffing out my chest and brazenly saying how I write for McClure's and I'm talking with *the* Joyce Kilmer! He's a swell guy Lilli, really swell.

Well just so you know Joyce and I have become good friends and we've decided that when this war is over, when we are back at home, we plan to write about it. Not sure yet how it will go but maybe a story about how a bunch of American Doughboys, from different backgrounds, from different countries and different faiths came together to make this world safe for democracy. I might even become a sergeant Lilli, you never know. We're hearing rumors that Joyce might become one. Good for him Lilli, good for him."

Sitting in her chair, rocking back and forth Lilli could hear Henry's voice in her ears. Of course, he would find a friend, of course that friend would be a writer and of course that friend would just have to be the poet Joyce Kilmer. "Leave it to Henry," Lilli thought, as a smile spread across her face, and her heart swelled. "Just leave it to him, gosh I miss him."

Lilli's quiet reverie was broken by the sound of footsteps on the stairs and the excited voice of her friend Catisemma echoing through the outside hall. Seconds later she was banging on Lilli's door, shouting, "Lilli, Open door! Quick open door! It's- a from my man, he's- a okay. I'm-a going to East- a -Bost, he's- a comin for me. We go to Boston Lilli, I got-a his letta, we getting' married, I'm a gonna be Signora Arturo Giampa, grazie Dio!"

"Rock-a-bye baby, on the treetops."
    - Mother Goose

18

MARION, OCTOBER 1916

She tried but it was hard to open her eyes, her eyelids were stuck together. She was cold, her body was shivering, and her face was soaking wet. She had never felt this cold before. Why was she so wet? Why was her bed feeling so hard and scratchy? Where was her blankie? Her blond curls were plastered to her forehead and cheeks, and her arm was stuck, bent up behind her head. She couldn't pull her hand down, or move it from behind her head. Each time she tried to bring her arm down it hurt and pulled her hair. Her chubby fingers were stuck, entwined in her short, thick blond curls.

She must have twirled her curls tightly around her fingers. How would she get her fingers out of her hair? Mama always did that, Mama knew how to unwind the hair, releasing her fingers, kissing and rubbing them softly, as she gently brought Marion's little arm down. Mama would kiss her face, her dimpled elbows and dimpled knees. Holding her tightly on her lap, pulling her in close and snuggling her in her arms, tickling her and telling her she loved her, and that she was a good girl.

But lately Marion had been twirling her fingers into her hair more often, especially since the man had arrived. She would wake up hearing loud noises, yelling, banging, it was scary, he was scary. She would become afraid and whimper quietly holding her blankie to her face. Sometimes her Mama heard the cries and she would come, lift her up and wrap her in her arms holding her close. Her lips would gently tickle her ear as she softly whispered, "Hush little baby, don't you cry, mama's here, mama's right here."

She needed her mama now, "Mama! Mama!" she cried out. But no one came. Where was she? Why wasn't she coming?

Sticking out her little pink tongue, she licked at the mucous running from her nose, and tasted its salty wetness on her lips. With her free hand she reached out for the railing slats on the side of her crib, her small, chubby pink fingers feeling the coldness, the rough sharp wood and the dirty stickiness of the slats. This wasn't her bed. Where was she? She wasn't home, where was blankie and where was mama?

It was so dark. From somewhere far away she heard voices, then she heard cries. This wasn't her home, it couldn't be. Sniffling, Marion thought that even the air smelled different. It was damp and the acrid smell hurt her nose, it smelled of poo and pee, pee. Those words she heard her mother saying as she cleaned and dressed her every morning.

Her mother sang to her, and talked to her, in a voice that was soft and soothing. Marion would giggle as she crawled into her mother's arms, feeling warm, safe and loved. "Mama," she softly cried, she loved her mother with her whole heart.

Rolling her little body over and pressing down on the hard mattress with her one free hand she pushed her round bottom back as she drew herself up onto her knees. Rocking back and forth for several minutes she reached out with her free hand, grabbing onto the grimy, sticky crib railing. Using all of her strength she pulled herself up. Looking over the rough railing she gazed around the room trying to recognize anything familiar. Not being able to, her little knees buckled as she despondently lowered her little forehead onto the cold hard railing and screamed, and screamed and screamed.

Before long she heard quick footsteps, someone was coming. Mama! It was Mama! Lifting her head and blinking her eyes, she swallowed her sobs, and choked back her tears, everything would be ok. Mama was here. Suddenly, from somewhere in the darkness, rough, icy hands gripped her little arms, squeezing them tightly, painfully. A voice uttered harsh sharp words that hurt her ears. "Shut up! Shut up you brat, you bad, bad little girl, you little bastard shut up!"

She was thrown roughly upon the hard mattress, the back of her head bounced off its unyielding surface. All the air rushed out of her lungs; she couldn't breathe, she couldn't speak, and her hand was still stuck in her hair, but she didn't dare move.

Too afraid to do anything, afraid to cry, afraid to call for Mama, she just lay there. No one came to help her. Marion was alone cold and wet. She was a baby only 2 ½ years old. "What did I do?" Marion thought. "Me bad…Me berry bad."

She began whimpering softly. She needed to be held, to be embraced and to be told she was a good little girl, but there was no one here to do that, she was all alone. Forming a small fist with her hand, Marion stuck her pointer finger and her middle finger into her mouth, sucking on them as she cried herself to sleep. All through the night her little body shivered, wet and cold. Her heart was broken as she longed for the loving arms of her mother.

"Practice gratitude daily, and your life will change in ways you can hardly imagine."
- Rev. Ruth Wallace

19

THE TRAIN STATION

Wanting to surprise Lilli with flowers, Walter quietly climbed their back stairs. On tip toes he stealthily walked to their door, turned the knob, carefully opening it he poked his head in to see where she was. He spotted her in her beloved chair, rocking slowly gazing out the window. "Good, there she is." he said to himself, a playful grin on his face.

"Lilli has been doing that a lot lately," he thought, "Just sitting, rocking, and staring out the window." But when he would ask her what she was thinking, she always said, "Nothing, really, nothing." Walter knew that couldn't be true. In all of the years he had known his wife, she had never been thinking of nothing. Her mind was one of the quickest, sharpest and insightful minds he knew. Even without her telling him, he knew her thoughts, her heartaches and her dreams. He loved her more than she would ever know or could even imagine.

Realizing he might startle her with his sudden appearance, he stepped back into the hallway, slowly shutting the door behind him. Before opening it again, he loudly shook the wet snow off his head and wiped the heavy flakes from the shoulders of his wet woolen top coat. Then he paused, coughed out loud, and stamped the slush off his shoes before he turned the doorknob, this time opening it widely.

Lilli was standing when he walked in, immediately she caught sight of the big, beautiful bouquet he was holding in his hands and rushed to him. "Walter, what have you done?" She asked, "This is so sweet, but why? It's not my birthday, or our anniversary, what's the occasion?"

"Let's just say Lilli, beautiful flowers for a beautiful lady." He replied, kissing her gently on the cheek. "It's the holidays and they're for our dinner table tonight. Hopefully they'll last long enough for our Christmas Eve dinner on Monday. They will, won't they? It's only Saturday." Taking in the bouquet, she smiled and nodded noticing Rosa Piano Freiland, Dahlias, green millets, wild rose hips, and chrysanthemums along with cut sprigs of fresh smelling winter pine boughs.

Lilli looked up at her husband, tears filling her eyes, as she unbuttoned his wet coat and folded herself into the welcoming embrace of his open arms. But, like an uninvited visitor, the damp, cold, night lingered in the wet wool of his coat, making Lilli shiver as its chill penetrated the cotton housedress she had worn for cooking. Feeling her quiver, Walter pulled her closer into his embrace as their arms encircled each other. Standing motionless, they held on tightly, the heat from their bodies dispersing the outside chill, as it filled the air around them with comforting warmth. Lilli exhaled as she rested her head on Walter's shoulder tears fell from her eyes, seeping into his damp collar. She wasn't sure whether the tears were of joy for the unexpected gift of flowers, sadness for Catisemma's nearing departure, or pain for all that they had endured. All she knew was that she couldn't hold them back, they had spontaneously released, and there was no stopping them.

Time stood still as they held each other, no words were needed, their embrace spoke a language far more powerful. The smell of pine needles, aromatic flowers and wet wool permeated the air around them as they breathed in each other's oxygen.

After several minutes, Walter slowly and reluctantly released Lilli from his hold. "Let me give you these, so I can take off my wet coat," he said, handing her the bouquet. Smiling Lilli inhaled their heady scent as she went to get a cut crystal vase from the China cabinet.

"So Catisemma and Arturo are coming to dinner tonight?" Walter asked.

"Yes." Lilli replied. "We will have five people here, you, Mother, Catisemma, Arturo and me. It's been a long time since it's been more than the three of us Walter." Seems too long doesn't it?"

"Yes." Walter said, a shadow of sadness spreading over his face. "Yes, it does."

After hanging up his coat and closing the closet door, Walter walked over to the empty rocking chair, Uncle Herman's wedding gift, given more than 16 years ago. Slowly, he ran his fingers along the curved back, feeling the carved flowing grooves of the lions' manes. He traced the deep concentric circles of the eyes and the diagonal points of the teeth, marveling at the preciseness and perfection of Herman's work.

"It feels almost real," he thought. "No wonder Lilli finds this chair so comforting, there's an energy in this wood, a feeling of timelessness.

As Walter's hand moved over the carvings, the chair moved gently back and forth. Instantly, he felt a wave of peace wash over him. Turning his gaze toward Lilli, he watched as she approached the dinner table, smiling happily she placed the bouquet of flowers in the center and took a step back to admire them, unaware of her husband's watchful eyes. "It'll be okay, Lilli," he said softly. "Everything will be fine."

Later that night, Lilli looked around her table, she felt the steely strength of the glow in Catisemma's eyes and marveled at the wide grin on Arturo's face. Her eyes welled up with happiness for them both. "Gosh, they are so in love," she thought, "They are so full of hope and anticipation."

Lilli caught Wilhelmmine's eyes as she was looking at them, too, and saw the hint of a sparkle in her mother's eyes but quickly she recognized the shadow of all of the yesterdays at the same time. "Life," Lilli thought, "is like a running river, always changing, always moving. Sometimes flowing smoothly, and sometimes hitting rough water and churning over rocks you never saw coming, but it continues to flow always hopeful that the ocean is ahead. Even if you try, you can't stop it, the next turn will come, I don't know how but I guess you just might try to embrace it, each and every day." Catching Catisemma and Arturo's eyes Lilli smiled at the two young lovers soon to be wed.

"I guess that we really should enjoy the day in front of us," she told everyone, "That's all we really have, this moment, right now."

Her husband, mother and dear friends nodded in agreement. Seizing the moment, Lilli raised her glass of wine, offering a toast to her friends, for the beauty of the moment, to their happiness, and to their life together. Then clinking their glasses everyone drank to their future, they drank to a wedding, to a new family, to their friendship and most importantly, they drank to peace.

Later in the evening as the women were clearing the dishes, Catisemma turned to Lilli and said, "Lilli, I don't know where to begin this time, it's not like before, this time is different. Could you help me this time? I have so much to pack into our box, so much to bring back to Boston. I don't know what to leave and what to keep." A brief look of remembrance came to Catisemma's eyes, for it was not so long ago that she, like Lilli, Walter and Wilhelmmine, had left so much behind. Glancing away so Lilli couldn't see her tears, she pleaded, "What do I leave behind this time, Lilli?"

Lilli smiled at her dear friend and placed a hand on her shoulder, saying, "I'll help you," Looking over to her mother she nodded, adding "We'll both come over this week. We know what you are asking, and we can help Catisemma. You've been through this before, you can do it again, and this time we'll be with you. We'll even go to the train station with you and Arturo. Why, you'll get a grand send off, as if you were royalty, Queen Catisemma and King Arturo, that's how we'll send you off."

Cheered, Catisemma lifted her chin up, pulled her shoulders back as she puffed out her chest and began gliding around the kitchen in a circular dancing motion, as she hummed the popular tune of, "Pack Up Your Troubles in an Old Kit Bag." She spread her arms wide as her pale blue cotton dress swirled around her ankles and her eyes sparkled merrily. Swept up in the moment, Lilli and Wilhelmmine each took one of Catisemma's hands as together they too twirled around the kitchen. Catisemma laughed joyfully as she circled the room with her friends. Then releasing their hands, she twisted and turned her arms, her palms facing backwards she exclaimed, "Look at me, I a double joint." Neither Lilli or Wilhelmmine understood what she meant but they smiled in agreement as the three women danced merrily around Lilli's kitchen. Giggling out loud, Catisemma exclaimed, "Mama Mia, look at us, we are doing the kitchen dance."

Lilli and Wilhelmmine couldn't stop laughing. They laughed until tears of joy blurred their eyes. "I love you Catisemma," Lilli told her dear friend. "I love you my dear friend. You have taught me so much, to laugh, to share and most importantly when you feel joy, let it out and dance. Thank you, grazie and danke, Catisemma you are my sister." Wilhelmmine watched as her daughter and dear friend circled the room a second time and clapped her hands at their joy.

Soon the day came for Catisemma and Arturo's departure. Everything they needed and wanted to bring to their new home now in East Boston was tightly packed away in their boxes. The sky was steel grey that frosty Saturday morning in late January when Lilli, Walter, and Wilhelmmine helped the newly married couple carry their belongings to the train depot. Walking together to the station Lilli felt the icy cold wind as it whipped around them finding any uncovered spot on their bodies to bite. Pulling her heavy wool coat tighter didn't seem to help, it still felt like the bitter winter wind cut right through it. Wilhelmmine had crocheted colorful cloches for them to wear and they were grateful to have their heads covered, keeping their warmth within.

Inside, the station was crowded with people hurrying to and fro, they didn't meet each other's gazes but looked down avoiding each other's eyes. Lilli noticed how much this scene reminded her of that summer day in Brooklyn so many years ago when she was rushing around getting ready for her wedding. She remembered how the sidewalks were so crowded and how difficult it was to find a place to rest. The memory of how overwhelmed she felt at being in America, but feeling excitement and pride that she was an American immediately came to her. Lilli thought how that was 17 years ago, it was now 1918, and so much had happened; so much had changed, they all had changed.

Standing in the center platform with the train tracks on both sides, Lilli looked around at the people in the station. Seeing groups of older individuals, warm in their winter coats and hats, she couldn't help but notice a group of about 50 or 60 children, off to the side, huddled close together, appearing to be different ages. Though many were barely toddlers, a few of the older children were holding babies in their arms.

Lilli didn't mean to stare, but somehow the children looked out of place. Their clothes seemed soiled, unkempt and ill fitting. Some wore winter coats, while others didn't, and most of the children appeared pale and thin. Many of them wrapped their arms around themselves as their bodies shivered and they tried to keep warm, stamping their feet on the platform of the station hoping to create heat in their frail little bodies.

She noticed, too that none of the children looked at anyone. Instead, they kept their eyes averted, staring vacantly off into space or focusing on the concrete beneath their feet. When they did look at you it was as if they looked right through you. There was no connection, no acknowledgment of another human being, again she was remined of a memory from so long ago.

Walter saw Lilli looking at the forlorn children. Taking her arm, he drew her closer and whispered in her ear, "Lilli, these children are orphans, they are going on one of those trains heading out west. These are the children that Henry wrote about."

She stared at him in disbelief. "Walter, oh God, orphans, they have no families?"

"No, no families, Lilli." he said flatly, trying to hold in his emotions.

Her warmly gloved hand fluttered to her throat as she whispered, "I can't even imagine Walter. Reading about them is one thing, but actually seeing them, looking at their desperation, oh God, that's another thing all together. This is awful Walter, really awful. I wish we could do something. Feed them, clothe them, maybe just make them warm."

He shook his head sadly, "I know, if only we could, but these children are being sent out west to farmlands away from the dirty streets and pollution of the city. Maybe it will be better for them out there than here."

Lilli shook her head, "I don't know Walter, look at them. We have failed these children; society has failed them. I know we can't help that many but maybe one or two? Even just one would be better than none."

Walter nodded and began to speak again, but the simultaneous rumbling of two massive steam trains pulling into the station drowned his response out. One of the trains was heading east to take Catisemma and Arturo to their new home. The other was heading west to bring the children to unknown futures. The train doors opened and in the frenzied hurry to get their friends safely on board, Lilli momentarily forgot about the children as kisses, hugs, and promises to keep in touch blended together, then they were gone. It all happened so fast, Lilli barely had time to wave as the train horn blared and the engine loudly pulled away, its steam creating an impenetrable thick barrier of mist.

Walter took Wilhelmmine's arm as they turned to leave the station, but Lilli lingered behind, remembering the children she turned to take a last look at them, but they too were gone. Lilli sent up a silent prayer that their new lives would be far better than the lives she had just witnessed.

As the trio headed home, Lilli couldn't erase the image of the orphaned children from her mind. She kept thinking of what she had seen, all of those children, babies holding babies. She couldn't stop seeing their faces, their pallid skin and thin bodies, their soiled clothing and the haunted look in their eyes. She knew those eyes would stay with her for a very long time.

Walking along the busy streets of New York, Lilli looked over at her mother and for the first time noticed the silver hairs peeking out from beneath her crocheted black cloche. She noticed the soft lines and wrinkles marking the years on her face, taking her mother's hand in hers, she felt the slightness of her fingers, the frailty, the knuckles that sometimes swelled and ached from those early years on the farm and many years of sewing dresses.

All of a sudden, Lilli felt a surge of immense gratitude for all her mother had been to her, for everything she had given to her. She believed in that moment that if angels dwelled upon the earth, then her mother was one of them. Lifting her eyes heavenward, Lilli smiled as she hooked her other arm in Walter's. For the first time in a very long while, Lilli felt a feeling of peace come over her. "Thank you, God!" she thought. "Thank you for my family."

"The life and passion of a person leave an imprint on the ether of a place. Love does not remain within the heart; it flows out to build secret tabernacles in a landscape."
- John O'Donohue

20

LETTERS

They piled up on the table, all of them, opened, read and reread; sometimes they spilled over and onto the floor. Tenderly and gently she would pick them up; pile them together and place them neatly back on the table, one on top of the other. They didn't need to be in any order, it didn't matter if the dates were intermingled, they just needed to be there for her to see.

She kept them there, simply adding new ones as she received them. Sometimes Lilli found herself pausing, gently placing her hand over them and holding it there just for a moment, believing that she felt the pulse of his presence as she passed by them.

She didn't understand why she couldn't put them away, out of sight, but she couldn't. Even thinking of doing that caused her to catch her breath, and resolutely shake her head no.

His letters must stay there, on the table; she had to see

them, touch them, and feel their presence, all of them. She told herself that having Henry's letters nearby was important, it felt good to see them, to feel them, to know they were there, right there. Looking at them meant he was alive. Yes, somehow, she believed that having them there, where she could see them, actually kept Henry alive.

If she couldn't have him with them, she believed that these letters kept his spirit near them. Sitting in her chair, by the window, gently rocking, Lilli tenderly held the pages of his latest letter in her hands. Reading his words, she heard his voice speaking to her through his pen.

No matter what she was doing; no matter what time it was, or who she was with, when she heard the heavy footsteps of the postman in the outside hall, she stopped everything. Without moving, she would listen for his knock, then she waited until she heard the scuffle of his footsteps drift away, echoing down the hallway and hear the stairs creak as he descended. Not until she heard the outside door slam shut, only then did she slowly open her door a crack, peak out and quickly retrieve her mail.

If there was a letter from Henry her heart would skip, she would exhale and a smile would cross her face. These letters were read before anything else, Lilli believed that if she received a letter it meant that he was alive, he had written. As she began to open the envelope, Lilli would automatically walk over to her chair. This was her sacred place, slowly rocking in the chair that Uncle Herman made for her, she was able to find the courage to open Henry's letters from the battlefields across the ocean.

His descriptions were graphic, he wrote in vivid detail the horrors of this Great War, of the long days, and longer nights. He wrote of aching, blistered feet from exhaustive marching, sunburns and blistered skin caused by scorching sun and frostbitten toes and fingers from the frigid cold. His letters told of days and nights of absolutely nothing but total boredom, as hollow emptiness filled their spaces.

He spoke of living underground in tunnels dug deep below the surface of the earth. These tunnels were their homes now, here they tried to create a sense of what they once had. But even underground was not safe, he explained how being there could be even be more dangerous than being up and outside where the guns and bombs were firing.

He wrote of rescues, of pulling fellows from underneath tons of rock, wood and dirt from a caved in trench. His words spoke of hearing the cries of trapped fellow soldiers knowing they would never be found alive. He wrote of how a single sound of tapping or the whistling of a missile would cause everyone to freeze. The quiet emptiness broken violently by hours and days of gun fire, of gas attacks, and bloodcurdling screams. He wrote about the palpable fear that lived in the trenches, fear that you could taste and smell, as everyone held their breaths in the deadly quiet knowing there would be another attack. Stopping everything, they would wait for it to hit, not knowing if this time it would be them.

But he also spoke of times when they played cards, or sang old songs, even drew pictures, on the walls of the tunnels beneath the earth. He described how many of the pictures were scenes of farms and homes, religious symbols, pictures of the women they loved, maybe even pictures of the American Flag or Uncle Sam. He described the pictures drawn of the enemy, his cousins, and what they would like to do to them if they were captured.

At times reading Henry's letters became too much to bear and Lilli would stop, close her eyes, and lay the pages in her lap. It was these times that the only comfort she found was rocking. She thought of all the young men fighting, and found herself in complete awe of the formidable strength of the human spirit. These boys, these soldiers, trying to survive amidst unfathomable brutality, destruction and death, were still able to think of love, see beauty and keep their faith. Lilli prayed that they would survive, she prayed that Henry would survive.

Upon finishing his letter, she would close her eyes and rest her head against the solid back of her chair. Then she would rock slowly, back and forth, the completed pages now gently spread across her chest and over her heart. Lilli believed that this was Henry, right here, she was holding him, holding onto all that she had left of their cousin, their dear, dear friend. Lilli knew she couldn't throw these letters away, she couldn't let them go, she would never be able to let them go. These letters were Henry; they were him, reading his words she heard his voice, she felt that he was there with them and for one brief moment she almost believed that he was back. Lilli could see his face, his smile, the mischievous wink of his eye, the laughter always just below the surface in his voice. She felt his presence, his energy, and it surrounded her.

Damn this war, she thought, damn this, "Great War "as they call it, what is so great about it? What is all the killing for?

Why should so many have died? Where is the glory in this insane slaughter? There would be no winners, the only victor would be death, blood and tears. Rocking back and forth, Lilli closed her eyes tightly, feeling comforted by long ago and fading memories.

Lately, Lilli had developed a practice that became her habit, before going back to do her chores. Finishing Henry's letters and before placing them with the others on the hall table, she would bow her head and pray. These words began Lilli's prayer, "Dear God, please keep Henry safe, please bring him home to us, please protect him for us." Then before ending Lilli would pray, The Lord's Prayer, saying the words she learned as a child, praying from her heart as her lips moved and her voice softly spoke the language she spoke first, "Vater unser im Himmel, geheiligt werde dein Name; dein Reich komme; dein Wille geschehe, wie im Himmel so auf Erden. Unser tägliches Brot gib uns heute. Und vergib uns unsere Schuld, wie auch wir vergeben unsern Schuldigern; und führe uns nicht in Versuchung, sondern erlöse uns von dem Bösen. Yes, thine is the kingdom, and the power and the glory forever and ever. Amen."

Late on this rainy and cold afternoon, after praying, Lilli remained rocking back and forth in the quiet, dark room, as she thought, " I am praying in German, for my German cousin who is now an American fighting against his German cousins in Europe. Does God know my German language is really for my German cousin, now an American? Does God translate from German to English, to Italian, to Polish, to Russian? How does that work? Who does God hear?" Lilli pondered, "Who does God listen to? Who does God answer and how does God know who the enemy is? Who is the enemy?" This thought remained with Lilli as she questioned, "Who really is the enemy?"

There would be other letters too now, letters from Catisemma; those letters Lilli would hold onto, waiting to be read later when chores were done, when tea was brewed and when she and her mother were together. But there were no longer any letters from Germany, no longer did they receive news from home in Stuttgart, no one was writing letters to families in America.

In the evenings Wilhelmmine would rest, as Lilli shared the latest letters from Catisemma with her. A broad smile would cross Lilli's face even before opening the envelope to read Catisemma's message. She missed her dear friend so much and just holding the letter in her hands she felt the energy, the optimism, the spunk and the joy carried in each word.

Always, just before unsealing the envelope she lifted it close to her nose believing that she was drawing in a whiff of those wonderful scents from Catisemma's kitchen. Her mouth watered as she believed that she smelled the aromas and could taste those savory dishes.

Lilli would think of Catisemma, her mischievousness, delicious cooking and zest of life filled Lilli's heart.

Catisemma wrote that all was going well, she and Arturo were happily married, they were living in East Boston, and they were trying to begin their family. Catisemma's cousin was already pregnant as she wrote, "My cousin, she got the belly." Lilli closed her eyes and silently prayed that soon Catisemma would have the belly too.

Reading Catisemma's words, Lilli glanced over to her

mother, swallowing the lump in her throat she said, "Well, since Walter and I aren't having a family, we can certainly love, enjoy, and maybe even help Catisemma out. I can always make clothes, knit sweaters and bonnets; maybe even we could visit once in a while. I guess since I am not going to be a mutter and Walter is not going to be a vater, I could actually be an aunt you know and well you, Mutter, you could be Oma, you could be a grandmother.

Catisemma is like a sister to me, her mother is not here and certainly her children will need a grandmother, I can think of no one better than you Mutter, absolutely no one."

Nodding her head in agreement, Wilhelmmine's eyes glistened as she forced a slight smile, but inside her heart was breaking for she knew that the words Lilli had said were true. By now, after several miscarriages and the losses of two babies, born prematurely, a girl and a boy, it was apparent that Walter and Lilli were never going to have children. She would never see her daughter carrying full term with child, a child that would have been her grandchild. Never hear the words Oma calling out to her. She would never hold the soft delicate hand of her grandchild or inhale the heavenly baby scent of Lilli and Walter's newborn.

Sitting in her daughter's chair, the chair her brother had made for Lilli and Walter, Wilhelmmine rocked slowly back and forth, not wanting them to see the tears filling her eyes, she closed them and pretended to be snoozing. Leaning back into the firmness of the chair she felt comforted, the hand carved rungs encircled her back securely holding and supporting her. Herman had made this chair, and tonight she felt his presence near her. Rocking slowly a sense of stillness came over her, she slowly dropped her chin to her chest letting her thoughts travel inward. Wilhelmmine worried for Lilli; she knew the heartbreak that Lilli and Walter were experiencing, the loneliness they felt without a family. She understood the emptiness of the void created when there were no children to complete them.

For her whole life Wilhelmmine felt the strong but gentle tethered hold that generations of a family gave you. This anchor, a link from the past, guided each generation by creating the foundation for the next to build upon. Wilhelmmine's heart broke knowing that for Lilli and Walter there was no future generation, no matter how strong their foundation.

Swallowing hard to hold back her tears, Wilhelmmine felt truly helpless, there was nothing she could do to stop, heal or change events for Lilli. In the beginning she had been hopeful but as time passed her hope became more of a cautious optimism then as the years turned into decades Wilhelmmine felt anger at the apparent unfairness of it all, "Why God?" she questioned and sometimes demanded.

For so many years she had been there to catch her daughter, to nurse her and pick her up when she had fallen, to be her support when she couldn't stand alone and to share all that she knew, to give her all that she had. But this time, this hurt, this intense pain, she could not ease, she could not stop what had been horribly stolen from Lilli and she could not protect her from its wrath.

In the background Wilhelmmine could hear Lilli and Walter speaking, their voices soft, sounding far away, but she was not listening. Lost in her own thoughts, her own guilt and her own pain she stopped hearing the voices outside as she listened for the answers from inside.

She asked, "Am I responsible for their heartbreak? Was it that accident with the horses? Had I not been paying enough attention that day? Should I have run out after that child pulling Lilli back? What did I do wrong?"

She knew she wouldn't find the responses to those questions for she had searched for them for so very long. Then from within she heard another voice, "Let it go." Exhaling a sigh, she listened more intensely, she began to hear answers, "Yes, they needed to be a family. Yes, they needed to love a child and yes, somewhere there was a child who needed them."

Right then in her heart she understood, she believed they would become a family, there was a child. She didn't know where, she didn't know when and she didn't know how, but somehow at that moment a sense of peace, an inner calm filled her with warmth, told her to have faith, to believe and to trust, for it will come.

This message was stronger and more powerful than anything she had experienced in a long time. But this was not the first time, she had experienced a message before and again this time she knew it was true.

Lilli might never carry her child in her womb, she might never give birth to her child, never nurse her baby at her breasts but Lilli and Walter would become a family, and Wilhelmmine would become an Oma.

If not on earth then truly in heaven. Feeling the power of these words wash over her, Wilhelmmine felt a burning intense joy in her heart. Rocking slowly back and forth, she blinked open her eyes. A knowing smile crossed her face, as she lifted her gaze and looked straight ahead, for now once more, she saw the future.

Suddenly both Lilli and Walter noticed that Wilhelmmine had awakened and was smiling, a beautiful radiant smile. But she wasn't looking at them, she appeared to be looking further, to someplace far off. Wilhelmmine understood that the power of love was the only absolute force in life. By honoring that love it gave you purpose, roots and hope. Your grandparents, your parents, they are your grounding holding you secure and firmly to the foundation they have built, honoring those deep roots you learn from them, and then you grow, sharing your journey with those who walk beside you and then finally, you teach, giving it all back, everything and more; all that was given to you, you give to those who come after you, knowing that they are the future you leave behind.

This love keeps you tethered, it gives you purpose and validates the life you have been given. This is how you are loved and how you love back. Wilhelmmine knew this, she believed it, understood and she shared it. She was grateful for Lilli and Walter; for the life they had, she knew that there would come a day when she was no longer with them. She believed wholeheartedly that they would continue to build their life together as a family. She sensed that the time was coming when she would hear Willi's voice and taking her last breath, she would answer his call. Wilhelmmine's hands rested comfortably in the grooves of the arms on Lilli's chair, gently she rocked back and forth, in peaceful silence.

Seeing that her mother had awakened Lilli once more picked up the pages of Catisemma's letter that laid in her lap.

She continued reading out loud about the life Catisemma was creating and living in East Boston.

She read about all of the building Arturo was doing as he worked for many of the wealthy Brahmins on the busy and luxurious Commonwealth Avenue in Boston. She read about all the friends Catisemma was making, and the job she had in a local seamstress shop on Maverick Street not far from her home in East Boston.

Lilli wondered if maybe living in a smaller city, living near dear friends and living in a quieter location was something to think about. "Who knows, we left our home in Germany, crossed an ocean, came to a new country where we didn't even speak the language and we knew no one. This would be like crossing the street. And if Catisemma and Arturo had babies." Well this thought brought tears to her eyes and a lump to her throat.

Later that night as she and Walter lay in their bed, she rolled onto her side turning to him, resting her hand gently on his shoulder she said, "Walter, darling, have you ever thought about leaving New York, moving to a smaller location, another city, maybe even another state?" In the darkness, Walter turned facing his wife, reaching for her he wrapped his arm around her pulling her closer, he held her tightly, then he quietly answered, "No, Lilli, no, I never have."

Not willing to let this conversation end here, but not wanting to discuss it further at this hour in the middle of the night Lilli nodded her head and said, "Ok, we'll talk about this later. I'm not saying we need to make drastic changes immediately but maybe someday we won't want to call New York our home." With that said she kissed Walter's cheek, turned her back to him, closed her eyes, and fell into a deep sleep.

Turning onto his back, Walter lay there, wide awake, staring at the ceiling, sleepless well into the early hours of the morning, wondering if he could truly explain to Lilli his concerns about leaving this place, their neighborhood, their home. How could he tell her what he knew, what was happening and what he feared.

"We have found the enemy and it is us."
- Pogo by Walt Kelly

21

THE FRONT, 1918

*E*very day Walter read the morning papers, every day he hoped that the news would be better than the day before, that this war would come to an abrupt end and their life, everyone's lives, would return to the peace and security they had once felt. But the news wasn't getting better, the life they had known wasn't returning, it seemed as if it was never coming back and everything was getting worse. Walter believed that the life he and Lilli had built together was gone forever.

Many of the friends that they once knew no longer socialized with them, many of their kinsman, people with positions in the community, no longer held those positions. Some had voluntarily resigned but others had been forced out. As he had once feared names were now being changed so as not to reflect any German heritage. He noticed too that many had even dropped the title von. This pained Walter, he wondered, "Were they that frightened and that ashamed?" But he too had become fearful, fearful for Lilli, for Wilhelmmine and for himself. It was easy to get into trouble, easy to be accused of being anti American and easy to be suspected of being a spy or pro German.

Reading the daily papers, he was aware of how tenuous their safety had become, not only in Brooklyn, but everywhere. Lilli was thinking that Boston might be safer but he knew it wasn't. He recently had read of the eminent conductor of the Boston Symphony Orchestra, Dr. Karl Muck. Accused of being anti American, he had been arrested, placed in jail and then sent to an internment camp in Georgia joining approximately 4,000 German-American and Austrian-American inmates because he was considered a dangerous enemy alien. He had been a conductor of the BSO and now he was a military prisoner of war. Walter also read, that among the prisoners of war with Muck was another symphony conductor, Ernst Kunwald, from the Cincinnati Symphony Orchestra.

"How many more would be arrested; how do you defend yourself when a finger is pointed at you accusing you of being dangerous? How is it possible to protect yourself and those you love when the enemy is everywhere?" he asked.

Walter was feeling isolated and very alone, fewer and fewer relatives lived nearby, Henry's family, fearing the big city, had moved further away joining the Hufnagles in Schenectady.

He feared for Henry too, fighting on the Western Front, letters from him had become increasingly scarce, and now the Triple Entente, Russia, Britain and France, was breaking up. Russia, the ally on the eastern front had just signed a peace treaty with Germany. On March 3rd 1918, the new Soviet Russian government under Vladimir Lenin agreed to The

Brest-Litovsk Treaty taking their country out of the war. With the Russians out, Germany no longer needed to keep forces on the eastern front, all of their military strength would now be brought to the western front. The days of boredom that Henry had once written about were ending. Walter, knew now that the powerful German military would be able to focus everything, all of its strength, all of its guns, all of its toxic gases and bombs would now be aimed at the Americans, the British and the French.

Walter, tried to calm his fears by telling himself that this war was far away across the ocean, but in his heart, he knew that it was truly not so very far away. He understood that this war was much closer than anyone wanted to believe. He couldn't tell anyone what he thought, but to Walter it seemed as if there actually were two fronts in this war, the Western Front in France and the eastern one right here in America.

Somehow the enemy in France was far more identifiable, far more recognizable and far less stealthy than the one right here; my enemy in America is the one standing right next to me, he thought. This one doesn't wear a uniform, doesn't speak a foreign language and doesn't carry a gun. This one sometimes wears a badge, but sometimes doesn't, this one listens, makes assumptions and then accuses. Walter was aware of how easy it was to be identified as an enemy and that knowledge sent a chill down his back keeping him awake at night.

For the first time in Walter's life he feared for his family, where can we go; he asked himself, where is it safe? Where will we be safe? If you are an American- German you are now considered an enemy in both America and in Germany.

Even though German immigrants had been part of American culture since the revolution and large pockets of German-Americans lived throughout the United States, being of German heritage, practicing German culture and speaking the German language now made you suspect.

Over the last decade propaganda from both the United States and Great Britain had created a historical sense of kinship. This resulted in the creation of strong financial ties resulting in Americans becoming increasingly pro-British and through extraordinary British efforts created an increasingly strong anti-German sentiment.

Recently, Walter had read a Hollywood film producer Robert Goldstein, the son of German Jewish immigrants, arrested because of his 1917 silent film, *The Spirit of '76*. The claim being that his film which included graphic but truly accurate scenes of wartime atrocities during the American Revolution by the British Redcoats. For telling the true narrative of the Revolutionary War, Goldstein was accused of inciting hatred of our allies and found guilty of subverting the United States military.

Walter was heart sick knowing that this hatred permeated everywhere. Only recently he had read that in Illinois, a mob lynched a German immigrant, Robert Prager on the accusation that he was a spy, there was no proof of the validity of their accusation.

In the daily papers he read horrific tales about German Americans being tarred and feathered. Shaking his head in despair Walter worried, "Now Boston is where Lilli wants to go. But Boston, how can that be safe? Especially now that I have read about what is happening there too with the BSO?"

He understood why Henry's family, moved away, trying to create a distance for themselves and the daily hostility they encountered. Even with their son, joining the Fighting 69th and fighting in France, they felt the need to move, no longer living in the city. Walter felt truly alone on a drifting boat without a Lode Star. He didn't know where to turn, who to trust or even where to go. Placing his palms together and dropping his head, he murmured softly, "There really is no place; there is no place that is safe anymore. "Then doing what he had always done, he bowed his head in prayer, his words were simple, "Please God, help us, please help us all. Amen."

Walter had not meant to pray, but he had, raising his eyes skyward he smiled, "Yes, there is one place, where I find peace, comfort and even safety." Affirmingly, he gave his head a nod, as he remembered, it is at our church, it is at St. John's where I finally relax and find peace, sitting in the pew next to Lilli and Wilhelmmine. Even though the sermons were no longer in German, now having been mandated to be in English. Even though he often saw strangers, men whom, he had never seen before, sometimes he saw the badge they tried to hide, but he knew who they were, The American Protective League identification was pinned underneath their coat lapel. He knew they were listening; they were watching, taking notes and they were suspecting. Even though he no longer heard the powerful and melodic sounds of his favorite German composers since they had been banned also, nor did many of the names sound like the old country, Walter still felt like he was home, he was welcomed and where he belonged. Remembering, he realized that it was on every Sunday morning, that he felt a sense of calm wash over his body. His shoulders relaxed, as the pinching tension which covered him daily like a tightly wrapped shroud eased, recalling that cleansing peace, Walter exhaled.

The constant barrage of news, stories of raging battles won and lost kept coming as the warm spring of 1918 turned into the long hot summer of 1918. But Lilli, Walter and Wilhelmmine found solace every Sunday morning. It would begin as together they walked to their place of worship. They found kindred spirits as they joined fellow German Lutherans, greeting each other, sitting together in the same section, the same row, the same hard wooden pew with the cushioned seat in their church, St. John's Lutheran Church. The church where they took their marriage vows almost a score ago.

As had become the practice at St John's on Sunday mornings, after the greetings had been exchanged, after the congregation was seated, and after the voices had been prayerfully raised singing the opening hymn, the minister requested any news that could be shared in the congregation and any petitions offered for all to hear.

Frequently, a request was made for prayers for an ailing parent or a brother or son who was fighting overseas. As the congregants listened heads nodded, names written down to be repeated in prayer, and sympathetic murmurs were echoed throughout the sanctuary.

This Sunday which had begun like all the rest suddenly and irreversibly changed. Walter, Lilli and Wilhelmmine had not expected this, nor were they prepared for it.

It was late August, the heat on this particular morning was oppressive; Sitting in the pew, listening to the congregants and the minister, Walter felt the sweat beading on his brow and ripples of moisture soaking his back. Looking over at Lilli and Wilhelmmine he smiled as they desperately fanned themselves trying to find relief in moving the hot air around them. Lilli's face glistened as the collar of her high-necked dress caught the perspiration sliding down her cheeks and onto her chin.

The sanctuary appeared to darken as the minister's voice began to drone, sounding distant to Wilhelmmine, she felt nauseous, and thought, please God don't let me faint, not here God, not here. Turning she looked at Lilli, noticing that in this heat her eyes had closed and her chin had dropped to her chest, she appeared to be dozing. Reaching over to nudge her, she squeezed her daughter's hand; Lilli blinked her eyes open and smiled at her mother in gratitude.

At that moment, their minister's voice seemed to become louder and far more somber, his face taking on a pained expression announced, "I am sorry to inform the members of our congregation but I have some very sad news. I was recently informed by a family that attended this church some time ago, but has moved out of the city that we have lost a young man, a former parishioner, killed in action. He was killed in France at the battle of Chateau Thierry, back in late July with many others in his regiment of the Fighting 69th. Please say a prayer for the family and for the soul of our brother Henry von Schonfeld killed fighting for our country."

Lilli and Wilhelmmine gasp as they squeezed each other's hand holding on as tightly as possible. Lilli, only moments earlier sweating from the oppressive heat suddenly felt a cold shiver run down her back. Her breath caught in her throat and her hands became cold as ice, she violently shivered as goose pimples broke out and covered her entire body. Walter's mouth dropped open, as he curled forward, covering his mouth with both of his hands, holding in the vomit he felt rising in his chest.

Wilhelmmine alone, did not move, she remained sitting frozen in place, her eyes stared straight ahead they were locked on the cross which hung above the altar and now only loosely holding onto her daughter's cold fingers. She had seen too much death for one person; had felt too many losses for one person and now she refused to believe that Henry Schonfeld was dead. "No!" Wilhelmmine said firmly but softly to herself, "No, Henry is not dead; death will have no victory here!"

In the oppressive heat and heartbreak, the minister's voice droned on but Wilhelmmine did not hear his words, she was not listening to his voice, she was listening to words much louder and far clearer, words that were coming directly from her heart. The sermon that she heard, was for her ears only, it was her sermon.

"So, tell me," she asked, "Was it a cousin, who shot you Henry, was it an uncle who fired that gun? Was it a neighbor from our village, where we once lived, maybe even shared a meal with, who took your life or maybe was it someone with the same last name? "With dry eyes she lifted her chin as she swallowed the lump in her throat and breathed in a deep inhale, sitting taller, straighter, and drawing strength from a well filled with faith, love and courage she listened to her heart's reply, "Oh no, it was hate, ignorance, greed and avarice that took your mortal life. The finger pulling that trigger was being controlled by forces more powerful, more vengeful and far more malicious than a young man wearing a different uniform from yours. You have been taken from us here on this earth but nothing Henry, nothing can take your soul. You will always be with me; I will carry your spirit, your humor and your love of life with me until we meet again... your heart no longer beats, your eyes no longer see and your body no longer feels, no longer are you fighting, no longer are you in pain, we can no longer see you, we can no longer touch you, but you will live on. Your soul has risen, Henry, you have been released, you are with our Lord and you are waiting for us. We will meet again Henry von Schonfeld, we will meet again, and this I know.

On the eleventh day of the eleventh month at the eleventh hour in the year 1918 peace broke out and Armistice was declared, Great Britain, France, Japan, Italy and the United States claimed victory and were prepared to take their revenge.

"May the nourishment of the earth be yours; may the clarity of light be yours; may the fluency of the ocean be yours; may the protection of the ancestors be yours."
- John O'Donohue

22

BURNING UP

*L*illi had been working from the early morning on a heavy winter coat for one of Emma's most particular customers. It was important that everything on this piece be perfect. Bending forward over her machine she was focused on attaching the intricate style Frog Fasteners made up of a braid and a loop securely onto the garment. Having difficulty Lilli called out to her mother, "Mother can you come and help me with these frogs, this wool coat is so heavy and I'm having trouble with them, they just don't seem to want to lay straight. Taking a heavy breath before rising slowly from her chair, Wilhelmmine started to walk over, as she moved Lilli noticed that her mother's breathing was labored and she was reaching out cautiously, holding onto each piece of furniture on the way as she appeared to sway and her steps dragged. Frightened and concerned Lilli asked, "Are you all right Mutter? Mutter, what's the matter?"

Letting out a heavy sigh Wilhelmmine collapsed back onto

the chair next to Lilli and replied, "I don't know Lilli, lately I've been feeling really tired, I just don't seem to have any strength and I can't even seem to get my breath." Reaching over to take her mother's hand Lilli gasped, "Mutter, you are freezing, your hands are blue, come on let's get you into bed now." Dropping the heavy woolen coat onto the floor, Lilli jumped up to help Wilhelmmine to her bed.

Trying to follow her daughter's order, Wilhelmmine gripped the arms of her chair as she tried to rise. Suddenly, she gasped as drops of bright red blood fell from her nose and dropped onto the floor. Turning and looking in horror at her mother, Lilli cried out "Walter, come quick, kommen sie hier-her, bitte!"

It was December 31^{st,} and it appeared that the rest of the world was crowded into Times Square to celebrate the dropping of the iron and wood ball welcoming in the New Year of 1919. Outside their home, as the world celebrated, Wilhelmmine tossed and turned in her bed, she was burning up with fever. For the next several days, all through the long nights Lilli and Walter kept vigil at Wilhelmmine's bed side. Alternating, they placed cold, wet towels on her hot forehead, covered her with blankets and then quickly removed them as she burned up with fever and a cold soaking perspiration covered her body. Then without warning she would violently begin to shiver from a deep bone chill. There seemed to be nothing they could do, at times they were hopeful, it appeared she was improving and then suddenly the burning fever and violent chills would begin again. "No," cried Lilli, "I can't lose her, not her too." Lilli and Walter tried to remain hopeful as Lilli kept telling herself that her mother was strong, and healthy. "She'll be fine, she'll get better. I know she's 55 years old, but that's still not that old." Repeating the mantra to not only Walter but to herself as well.

For almost a week over the long days and sleepless nights Lilli and Walter took turns sitting on a hard chair close by the Wilhelmmine's bedside, nursing every need, applying wet cloths, offering tea, broth, even dry toasted bread but nothing helped.

In desperation, Lilli sought out medical guidance, she reached out to doctors but was told to go to the American Red Cross. When she was finally able to reach them, she was told that the pandemic, the Spanish Flu, was everywhere and with the volume of people sick and dying there was nothing that could be done to help them or her mother. Soon Wilhelmmine became too weak to swallow, too tired to chew, simply moving her body was too great an effort, even her eyelids had become too heavy to lift. They were on their own, there was nothing they could do but wait it out, hoping Wilhelmmine would recover.

At times she tried to speak but the words were incoherent coming out only as grunts as her lips moved slightly in incomprehensible whispers. Then finally after several weeks, late one night it appeared that it was over, the battle had ended as Wilhelmmine's fever broke. Her cracked and parched lips parted as a thin smile crossed her face. Wilhelmmine's eyes blinked open, and in them Lilli saw time melt away as her mother appeared ageless before her. Wilhelmmine's clear gaze however was not at Lilli, she was looking beyond her daughter. On that night Wilhelmmine's eyes were looking farther than her daughter would be able to see.

Her lips opened as she began to speak, her voice now clear and strong. Slowly she lifted her arms, her hands reached forward extending her long slender fingers as she spoke words not intended for her daughter's ears.

Lilli raised her hand to her lips as she watched in amazement. Suddenly, she felt a tap, it was a gentle but strong pressure tapping her on her shoulder, quickly she turned thinking Walter had entered the room, but no one was behind her. At the same time Wilhelmmine's voice grew even stronger and more confident as she continued to speak to someone that she saw standing right behind Lilli. "Willi, Willi, yes my darling yes."

Lilli felt herself quiver as the room became deadly silent, devoid of any noise, empty of any air, it felt as if it had become tightly cocooned, sealed with a thick heavy shroud. It seemed as if all of the oxygen had been sucked from it.

Turning back to look at her mother, Lilli noticed that she was no longer wheezing, the perspiration on her skin had evaporated, her chest no long lifted with labored breath; there was no sound, there was no movement, Wilhelmmine had died, finally she was at peace and in her husband's arms once more.

Lilli screamed out loud, as tears poured from her eyes, jumping up she reached out lifting and holding onto her mother's lifeless body. Lilli's mouth opened as a sound that came from a depth deeper than her soul, deeper than her bones; a sound that was primordial came from where her life, where all life had once begun. "No, no, no, no, not mutter, not mein mutter, no, no, no!" Tears of despair, loss and pain poured down her face.

Falling onto her knees at her mother's bedside her body shook as she sobbed, feeling as though her heart had truly cracked open. Again, as she had so long ago, Lilli tightly wrapped her arms around her mother's body but this time, it was for the last time.

Bending over the motionless body of her mother, Lilli wasn't aware of a gauzy haze filling the room. Wilhelmmine's spirit had risen, releasing itself from the lifeless shell of her body, it expanded until it engulfed both Lilli and her mother wrapping them in its fog as one. Holding her mother in her arms Lilli felt herself powerfully drawn to her mother, as their bodies cleaved into each other. At this moment Lilli understood that they had never been separated, they had always been one, never untethered and never would be.

Even though she had called out to him she didn't hear Walter as he ran into the room, and swung open the door. Startled by his presence she was shaken as if she had just awoken from a deep sleep as Walter appeared beside her.

Looking straight at her husband and with resolve she never knew she had, she told him, quietly and clearly, "She's gone Walter, she is with my father. They are together again."

Pulling her into his embrace Walter gathered his wife into his arms and held her tightly. He lowered his head resting his cheek onto Lilli's soft hair saying simply, "Oh God no, oh my God." This time Walter couldn't find the strength, not for Lilli nor himself. As he held onto Lilli, his body was wracked with sobs. Lifting her head and looking at Walter with eyes full of tears, she said, "It's just us now; no one's left, Walter we are all alone."

Yea, though I walk through the valley of the shadow of death, I will fear no evil: for thou art with me; thy rod and thy staff they comfort me." - Psalm 23

23

EVERYTHING CHANGES

She thought that it was the middle of the night, the room was pitch dark, lying in her bed Marion reached out, stretching her small hand, her fingers straining to find her one and only doll, Big Red. Sliding her hand over the rough bed sheet she couldn't find her. Then awakening more, she noticed that somehow tonight, everything seemed different. There were noises, strange sounds that she had never heard before. Then she felt it, the hand, as it reached furtively under her blanket, its fingers extended, stretching to touch her. "No." she pleaded, holding her breath, she stopped breathing, as she pushed herself protectively against the wall. Instinctively, she clasped her little knees together tightly closing them, curling them into her body. But the hand kept reaching, she began to shake, as she softly whimpered, "Please don't hurt me again, please don't hurt me this time, not again." Still half asleep she didn't want to wake up, she wanted to find her baby, Big Red, hug her to her body, and she wanted to go back to sleep. Slowly, stealthily trying not to move or make a noise, Marion stretched her fingers trying to find Big Red. She felt terrified and confused, she wanted to open her eyes but was afraid to look, no she thought, I don't want to see you. She felt the hand reaching, grabbing, but this time the hand wasn't traveling up between her legs, forcing her knees apart. The rough fingers weren't probing or pushing, nor had they tried to tug at her panties yanking them down. Suddenly Marion realized that this time was different, this time the hand wasn't spreading her legs, this time it was grabbing her arms, reaching for her and yanking her entire body from the bed. Afraid, confused and sleepy she pushed back against the hand with all of her strength. She had been squeezing her eyes tightly shut but now she was trying to open them. The room was dark, it felt burning hot and her eyes were beginning to sting. She heard crackling sounds, she heard screams, voices yelled, "Get out, fire, run!" Her heart was beating faster, it was becoming harder to breath. Disoriented she didn't know what to do, or where to go. Yelling she screamed, "I can't see, I want Big Red." All of a sudden she felt the hand again, this time it grabbed her roughly pulling her off the bed; dragging her half asleep and tired body across the floor, screaming at her, yelling, "Run, Marion, run, it's on fire, Marion, we have to get out." The hand was now wrapped tightly around her arms and was pulling her down the wooden flights of stairs. The hand was yelling, ordering her as it pulled her down, "Run faster, jump over here." The hand wouldn't let go, it held on tightly as it dragged her down 3 flights of wooden stair. She slipped banging into another child, together they almost fell, tumbling onto others running also trying to escape.

Marion didn't want to leave, she wanted to go back, she tried to break loose from the hand, she tried to pull free. She knows that she had to go back; she'd left her baby, she'd left Big Red. "I've got to get Big Red!" she yelled. She started to cry, pulling back trying harder and harder to break loose, screaming, she tried pulling herself back into the burning building, but the hand was squeezing harder, it wouldn't let go.

Fully awake now and determined to go back, Marion was angry. She twisted her fingers trying to release her hand, forcefully she yelled, "Let me go, let go!" Suddenly a second hand slaps her hard across the face screaming, "Do you want to die Marion? It's burning up! It's on fire!" Marion feels her cheek turning red from the slap, burning heat is all around her, red and orange flames are shooting up the walls, black scary towering shadows loom over them everywhere. The smoke is suffocating, she can't breathe, she is choking, people are screaming, everyone is coughing, crying, yelling. People are shoving each other; they are pushing at each other. Then suddenly she was outside, the hand stopped pulling her, they were no longer running, as she gulped, breathing in the cold, damp air, she's standing barefoot on the frozen, wet ground. She began to shiver, suddenly she's shaking all over, she's cold, so very cold, and she's afraid.

Outside, standing away from the burning building, she is alone as she watches the fire fighters rush into the building spraying water everywhere. No one is beside her; the hand was gone, Marion stood all alone in front of a building that she had shared with so many other children, watching it burn. This was the only home she knew, now it was burning to the ground. She stood watching it burn down, all by herself in a crowd of people.

Looking around in the early morning light, she doesn't know the hand that slapped her, pulled her down the stairs and brought her outside, the hand that made her leave Big Red inside. Solemnly she stood, as if rooted in place, her feet felt frozen to the icy ground, tears were flowing down her face. Her baby, her only doll, Big Red was inside. Looking around she told herself, I have to get Big Red, no one will see me; I'll go back in, it will only take a minute.

This building has been Marion's home for almost three years now; she knows how to get around, she knows how to get upstairs, into the large room where all of the children slept. She knows where her bed is, where Big Red is lying, snug under the warm covers, this was where she wanted to be too. Without uttering a sound, slowly she began to walk right back in. As she approached the building the crowd quickly jumped back in unison as one side of the roof collapsed into the building with a loud woosh and flames shot out from the windows on all floors, Marion continued to walk forward.

With all the noise she didn't hear a strong, deep voice shout, "Whoa, little girl, tell me lass now where do you think yer going? "a large muscular arm, like a slinking cobra quickly wrapped itself around her waist, and easily lifted her off the ground. This arm was much bigger, thicker and stronger than the hand which dragged her out. Struggling, she twisted and turned trying to release herself, but she couldn't. The cobra arm holds her even tighter; she can't move, she tried to look at the face belonging to this strong arm but she can't turn her head around. She tried to cry out, to yell, to scream too, but no sound came out. This thick arm was too strong, it's holding her up, squeezing her tightly; she can't get down. Then suddenly there's a loud explosion as flames jump out of every window, every door and through the rooftop. People scream and run farther away from the building as sparks fly, bricks and timbers fall as every wall collapsed, she hears voices yelling, "Oh My God, it's going, it's gone, get out, get away, get back!"

Marion's mouth opens to let out a scream, but she hears no sound. Big Red is in that building and now is gone. Lowering her head, she whimpered softly, her heart breaking because whenever she loved someone they eventually left her, gone forever.

Daylight was breaking; as the early morning sun glowed fiery orange and red. Everywhere, everything was bathed in an eerie sickening greenish light created by the smoke, steam and haze. Marion looked around, she recognized many of the children standing outside, looking dazed and shivering. The early morning was cold and damp, some of the children are stomping their bare feet up and down, trying to get warm, some are huddled in groups and some are just standing by themselves like Marion had been, all alone. People who lived on the streets nearby had seen the fire engines, and heard the screams, they had come running. Many were opening their hearts and their doors offering warmth, food and a place to rest for the children and the staff.

In the gathering crowd Marion recognized two people, she remembered them, they had a chicken farm. Often, she had seen them as they brought eggs to the orphanage, from their farm down the street. They were coming closer towards her, walking over to the arm; they were speaking with the strong arm which was still holding her tightly. Their voices sounded different, they were speaking a language she understood, but their voices had a soft musical sound, she realized that she liked it and found it comforting.

The couple smiled at the arm as it suddenly uncoiled and released her from its grip. She was being lifted again, wrapped in a blanket and carried across the street down to the home of the egg people and their chicken farm. Marion noticed that the smell, noise and chaos of the burning building had begun to sound distant, she could still taste it in her mouth, it was on her tongue and teeth. She still felt the chaos in her body as her muscles ached and her stomach hurt. Nobody could see it but Marion felt it.

The chicken farmers brought her into their home, they spoke softly to her as they gently laid her down on a bed, and covered her with a clean, warm blanket. Then standing over her they prayed, Marion squinted her eyes open, peeking out from underneath her lashes, as she saw the woman make a sign of the cross above her, then without a sound, they tiptoed from the room. She recognized this gesture made with the hands, having seen several of the children at the orphanage make the same movements with their hands before meals and at bedtime. It wasn't a gesture she made and she wasn't sure what it meant or why people did it. Shrugging, she turned, rolled onto her back, and looked around the room. It was a small broom, but since she was the only one there it felt large. She was used to sleeping in a room with lots of other children, their beds nearly touching each other. She liked this room, it had two windows with clean white curtains hanging neatly, a straight wooden chair and a chest of drawers, but it didn't have Big Red, rolling onto her side she faced the wall. This time she drew her knees up to her chest, stuck her two little fingers into her mouth, which now had little bumps near the knuckles from years of sucking them and began drawing her breath in comforting herself like so many nights before. Instantly her eyes closed, her other hand rested on the back of her head as it traveled into her hair. Her fingers knew where they needed to go, hypnotically, they began to wrap themselves around the curly, blond strands. Laying there sobbing Marion's little body shook in quiet spasms.

Later that morning, even with the windows closed Marion could smell the stench, the pungent odor of burnt wood, charred furniture and other noxious smells she didn't recognize. Pushing her face into the pillow beneath her head she sniffed trying to connect with the sweet, familiar smell of Big Red, inhaling as deeply as she could she didn't find it, it wasn't there.

They heard her moving around and knowing she had awoken the chicken farmers came in to greet her. They smiled and asked her questions. Again, she found their voices comforting, "How are you feeling little one? Tell us now are you hungry? Is there anything you need or want?" they inquired. Marion lay still, staring up at the ceiling, she was afraid to respond, she didn't know how to reply, no one had ever asked her if she was hungry, or what she wanted or needed. She didn't know how to tell anyone about her wants or needs, she didn't know she had any or even what they were. She remained quiet, she had no energy to open her mouth, it felt easier to just lay still and not say a word. She didn't know these people, nor did she understand why they brought her to their house, but she did know something — that she was alone and afraid all over again.

Exchanging a glance, they left the room and quietly closed the door behind them. Once again Marion lifted her hand into her hair and slowly began to twist her fingers into her thick blond curls making tight little knots. Each time she completed a knot, she made another. She knew it would hurt to get them out but she didn't care, lately pain was the only feeling she understood. Blinking tears away she stuck her two fingers in her mouth again and cried herself back to sleep like so many times before.

"For everything there is a season and a time for every purpose under heaven." - Ecclesiastes

24

A TIME TO HEAL

Walter climbed the stairs, trying to ignore the smells of dinner meals being cooked as the aromas filled the stairwells and floated down into the vestibule. In the past these smells had put a smile on his face and added an extra lift to his steps, now they no longer did. Slowly he stepped up to their landing, he paused, standing there for several minutes deciding whether or not he really wanted to go in. He noticed that there was no aroma of dinner cooking, no sounds of preparations being made. He could turn, head back down the stairs but why, where would he go? He knew that other men went to taverns, had drinks before they headed home. That wasn't him, he had always wanted to be with Lilli more than anyone else. Walter took in a breath for resolve, and reached for the door knob. Grabbing the knob his fingers recognized the familiar shape, and wrapped themselves around the shiny round ball, slowly turning it, he opened the door. Making no greeting he quietly walked in. He wasn't acknowledged, she hadn't noticed his entry, and if she had she ignored it. There were no lights on, all the rooms were dark except the kitchen, and everything was silent, not devoid of sound but devoid of life itself.

She didn't know how to tell him, but she knew they couldn't stay. She was exhausted with bearing the heavy weight of grief every day. Too much sadness had crawled into their walls; too many tears streaked the clear glass panes of their windows, too much hurt seeped out of every polished wooden crack and crevice. It was as if death itself had moved in, was alive and living with them.

She didn't know how she could let him know her plans, thoughts and wishes. She was afraid he wouldn't understand. How could he? He doesn't know how her heart is breaking. He's never experienced losing a mother he loved; he couldn't know how she felt.

Unseen in the shadows, Walter leaned against the kitchen door frame quietly watching Lilli as she worked at their black cast iron stove. He noticed how shiny the chrome handles gleamed, how the kitchen was spotless from her attention. But lately she's not paying attention to anything or anyone, she was lost in her private thoughts. Methodically stirring the bland potato soup, she didn't know he was home, didn't know he was watching, she didn't know that she was not alone.

Holding the hot ladle, slowly and carefully she continued to stir the pot, lost in her thoughts she asked, "Am I being selfish? He never knew his mother, never heard her voice, felt her touch, or listened to her laughter. How can he miss what he never knew? I had all of that, and I want it back. Oh, God, I must be incredibly selfish. But it hurts; I want back what I had.

Why is this pain so hard to bear? Is this wrong, mourning for what I had for so much longer than he can even imagine? How can this be? Will I have to live the rest of my life hurting so much? Feeling this ache, feeling this pain in my heart. Sometimes it hurts so hard I can't breathe. Will I ever be able to look at another mother laughing and talking with her daughter, without bursting into tears and without feeling so angry? I don't believe that I'll ever smile again, it's too hard. I don't have the energy to do anything. I don't want to talk, I don't want to read, I don't want to sew, I don't care about anything, I don't even want to breathe anymore, it's all just become too hard."

Turning Lilli wiped her eyes as she noisily dropped the soup ladle into the deep black and white speckled soapstone sink. From the corner of her eyes she spied a form and suddenly she saw Walter, screaming she jumped in fright, "Holy Mary, when did you come in?" Smiling slightly but not moving Walter continued to lean against the door frame, "Only a few minutes ago." He replied, "But long enough to know how much you are hurting, how much pain you are in, how much you have tried to keep this from me and how much I love you."

Stepping forward he walked over to his wife. Reaching for her he gently took her hand in his and said, "Let's turn off the gas, I want to talk with you and this might take a while."

As Walter led his wife into their parlor, he guided her over to her beloved chair. This amazing wedding gift, this solid link to her mother, her uncle and the life they shared. He understood that so many times it was this chair that offered them solace, comfort and guidance. Walter believed that Lilli's chair, Uncle Herman's gift had become the very foundation of their marriage, many times it was in this chair where they found the strength upon which they built their life. It was in this rocking chair where Lilli found peace, gathered memories and built her dreams. Holding onto the arms Lilli easily slid onto the seat, then slowly the chair began to rock. Walter pulled up one of the hard kitchen chairs, placing it directly in front of her.

Sitting face to face, knees touching, he leaned into her, reaching out he took both her hands into his, holding them tightly. Knowing that the words he planned to tell Lilli would bring back pain and heartache, quietly he asked God to give him strength. Then he looked directly into her eyes and spoke, "Lilli, when I was little, I tried to imagine my mother, I tried so hard to know what it was like to be touched by her, how it sounded to hear her voice, how it felt to have her hold me, how it felt to know she loved me.

At night in bed, as I laid there squished in between my brothers, under the heavy blankets, I would close my eyes as tightly as possible and try to see her face. Sometimes in school when the teacher was talking, I would look out the window and imagine I saw my mother outside looking in, watching me. Sometimes even in the privy I would sit, staying longer than humanly bearable, trying to hear her voice speak out to me.

For so long I heard nothing, felt nothing, saw nothing. I was beginning to think it was useless, that I would never know my mother. Lilli, I was angry, I was hurt and I was in pain for a very long time. This affected me so much, often as I listened to others I chose not to speak or share because I truly felt that no one really cared to hear me or even about me.

Then one night, somewhere deep in my soul, I heard an

answer, it came to me, I was trying too hard, I was pushing her away, all I had to do was let her in. She was already with me; she was already there; she always had been. Her presence was all around me, Lilli, she had never left me, but I, Lilli, I had kept her out.

It was me Lilli, my grief, my anger, my pain that's what was keeping her out. By opening up my heart I let her come in; it was me Lilli, I had to open up, to let go, to let her in.

It was then that I embraced my mother. She had always been embracing me, she had never stopped. From that night on Lilli I felt her love, I sensed her touch, I heard her voice. Lilli, I inhale her presence every day now; she's all around me. She had never left me; she was always with me; she always will be.

Exhaling deeply, Walter's head dropped as tears fell from his eyes, looking down at their enfolded hands, he saw that it was now Lilli holding onto his.

"Is there a place where our vanished days secretly gather? I believe that there is a place where our vanished days secretly gather. The name of that place is memory."
- John O'Donohue

25

BOXES, SUMMER OF 1919

Crouching on the floor Lilli called, "Walter, can you come here, I don't really know if you want to pack all of these draftsman tools with us. I remember how they were important when you began working, but do you still use them?" Walter walked into the large nearly empty living room, unable to keep the smile from appearing, he surveyed the various boxes scattered about the room. Shaking his head, he placed his hands on his hips and looked down at Lilli, "I don't know, you're right, I really don't use them anymore, but at one time I really needed them. They were with me from the beginning. I, I can't explain it, but I guess I have an emotional attachment, a connection with them. Gosh, it's hard to understand, I don't get it; we really could throw them away or give them away. I suppose that if I needed them again, I could purchase new ones or borrow some, but these were with me right from the beginning, they came with me from Germany. They were the first tools I used in my career. When I hold them there's a familiarity I feel, I know their weight, I know how they perform, I trust them, they're like an old friend." Pausing he let out a chuckle, as he stated, "And as you know Lilli, you just can't get old friends at our age, either you have them or you don't." Lilli smiled as her head nodded in agreement.

Walter went on, "Lilli, it's like they've become a part of me." Looking down at the shiny gleaming tools of his trade a twinkle appeared in his eyes as he decided, "I want to keep them, I have to keep them; actually, I can't part with them Lilli, I'll pack them away now." Bending down, he carefully placed his tools in the old weathered black leather container. Lilli watched as he placed each tool one after the other carefully on the dark blue velvet liner, he skillfully surveyed each one for scratches or nicks before gently laying it next to the other. Satisfied that he had placed each one in its' appropriate holder he straightened up and smiled at Lilli, saying, "There're fine now, they're coming with us."

A slight smile crossed Lilli's face as she remembered a conversation from long ago with her father. She could see him still, even after a long hard day working, he would come home with his cart loaded full with the tools of his trade. She remembered standing at the door, jumping from one foot to the other, impatiently watching him, waiting for him to come in, wanting his greeting, knowing he would lift her in the air making her belly jump as she laughed with joy. But first he would survey his cart, painstakingly removing his tools, placing them on the ground one by one as he assured himself that he had left nothing behind. Then picking up an old rag, he would wipe each one of his tools clean, carefully checking for breaks and nicks. Only when he was satisfied that all was in good order and form would he carefully and orderly place the tools back on his cart ready for tomorrow and his next job.

Her father had told her that his tools were his partner; they were his friends on the job. If they were broken, rusty or dull his job would not reflect the care, professionalism or the quality his work deserved. Lilli remembered his words, "No matter how small a job is, no matter who the job is for, you give it your best, because the job and your customer deserve no less, you always give it your best, nothing less."

So Lilli watched as Walter carefully placed his tools in the box, she realized that her husband and father were kindred spirits. They didn't look alike, they had different personalities, but they shared a far more important trait, they shared a common bond in how they lived. It was at the core of their character; an honorable quality born within them which grew and became part of who they were and what they gave to everyone and everything. Both always gave their best, never wavering, never faltering.

Knowing that he listened and that he would hear her voice, Lilli quietly whispered, "Danke, Papa, thank you for teaching me what was truly important."

Quickly her eyes misted, but a smile remained on her face as she busied herself with wrapping her own kitchen tools and placing them in the box too. Then without turning to look Lilli reached behind her, knowing right where it would sit, she felt her fingers fall on a book, smiling she twisted to look over her shoulder, she knew exactly what it was, that old wedding gift. She hadn't opened that book in years but when she was a new bride and homemaker, this book offered guidance and instructions. It had been her household bible, one she needed and followed religiously a very long time ago.

She began to flip the pages, "I remember each of these instructions, oh gosh, I remember first following this recipe. I loved this book, I still love it, I can't give this up, it's coming with me." A wide grin lit up her face as Lilli carefully wrapped and placed her blue and white checked book, "Household Science and Arts "almost 20 years old and now a bit frayed on the edges, into the box. Side by side Walter's dependable draftsman tools and Lilli's beloved homemaker's instruction book lay next to each other.

Finally, looking around the room now filled with boxes, Lilli slowly stood up, stretched her tired, cramped legs and walked over to her chair. Automatically her fingers slipped into the grooved arms as she relaxed onto the seat and began to slowly rock. Glancing over her shoulder she saw that she was alone, Walter had left the room, she easily spoke out loud, in an affectionate teasing tone, to her intimate friend of many years. "So, should I bring you too my dear friend, do you belong with us as we leave Brooklyn, New York? Or would you prefer to remain here in the great metropolis?"

Lilli's smile vanished as her heart became heavy and a wave of nostalgia washed over her. Pensively she confided, "My friend, I always thought I'd be rocking and holding my children here in this seat. As you know that hasn't happened, I guess it never will. Who was I so long ago, as I confidently ran up the stairs and saw that large box from across the ocean which contained you? You were the most amazing gift from an amazing man. I believed that you were an omen, that it truly meant Walter and I would have a family, maybe even a large family. I didn't doubt it then but now, well, we know that it won't happen, there is no doubt about that. Well, my old friend, just like in the beginning, it's you and me rocking here, no one else. Will I bring you with us? Will you once again be packed in a large box to travel a great distance?" Lilli continued to rock back and forth; releasing a deep breath her head rested against the back of the chair as her eyes closed. She knows the answer; there is no doubt, for no matter wherever Lilli goes this chair will always be part of her life.

As the chair rocked gently, Lilli prayed, "Dear God, thank you, you knew that Uncle Herman's gift was so much more than a simple rocking chair. When I realized that I would never have a family, this chair comforted me as I rocked. When hate and intolerance threatened us, rocking in this chair gave me comfort, and when those I loved were gone, it was rocking in this chair that brought them back to me. Uncle Herman your gift, was my foundation, I guess you could call it my lodestar. I pray that it always remains part of my life and hopefully the lives of others for a long time to come. Thank you, but I know you knew that already."

A sense of peace crossed Lilli's face for she knew that she would pack this chair in a box just like she had already packed Henry's letters, bringing everything and everyone with her, this time nothing and no one was left behind.

"It's not about how much you do, but how much love you put into what you do that counts."
- Mother Teresa

26

RIPPLE EFFECTS

*C*atisemma's heart was breaking, those poor little children had so little, now they had nothing. Everywhere she went she heard fragments of their story, but it was from the women in her neighborhood that she heard the lurid details.

It was a story she knew only too well, as she listened, it wasn't the orphanage she saw in flames, it was a grove of burning olive trees. Her breath caught in her throat and a deep pounding ache exploded in her heart. Once more she saw orange, red and yellow flames bursting high into the sky, again she heard the agonizing screams and from the back of her throat she tasted that thick lung filling black smoke, as pain engulfed her body once more, all the horror of that long ago day returned, the passage of time had not diminished it. Its memory remained in her body, living in her very cells, surviving just below the surface. This was the time she had lost everything, her father, her mother, her baby twin sisters, all of them gone. Catisemma listened as she nodded her head, she was speechless, she understood the horrific fear the children had experienced that night and the nightmarish dreams that would keep them up for many more. She had never forgotten, she remembered it all, the fear, the hurt and the poverty of her childhood in the old country, this time she was determined to do something.

Working in her kitchen, she made a decision, standing erect, shoulders back and head held high she resolved boldly and confidently, "I can sew; I can crochet, I can knit, I can make anything they need."

With steely determination, she walked into her small sewing room off the parlor of her apartment. Moving as if in a reverie, she lifted the lid, on the scratched wooden top of her sewing table. She reached in and lifted up the heavy steel and cast-iron body of the second hand Singer Sewing Machine and secured it in place. Her quick actions increased only by her intense desire to begin moving forward even before she had decided where to begin. Grabbing her stool, she pulled it over, sitting down on its edge. Remnants of material filled the large basket beside her, she leaned into it and picked out several pieces from the top of the pile. Examining them she stated out loud, "We'll start with a jumper," threading the needle she squinted as she focused her eyes and placed her feet on the treadle, pressing down hard she pushed it into action and began to sew.

Knowing that she would need far more material and supplies than she alone could provide she asked for help, requesting contributions from everyone she knew.

First, she collected remnants and pieces of fabric from the

local dressmaking shops. Then, she went door to door and flat to flat in her neighborhood of triple decker homes collecting leftover material and remnants of any type. She took everything no matter how small, no matter the material, she took it all. From square pieces of fabric, she made blouses and shirts. From nylon and silk material she designed skirts with sparkles. From thick heavy material she fashioned warm coats with matching hats. She made dresses with smocking and knickers with buttons. With any remaining scraps she made soft dolls and stuffed animals for the children to carry, hold and hug. Nothing was wasted, everything had a purpose.

Still knowing that she could do more, she took the remaining empty boxes and walked everywhere in her neighborhood. She carried them to shops, up flights of stairs to apartments and to the church asking everyone to help fill them up.

Finally, her tasks completed, the boxes were filled, the tops sealed and categories were assigned. Now, she needed help and this time she recruited her husband, Arturo, again the head man on his crew. Not asking, she told him that she needed him to bring the boxes where the children were staying. Immediately he resisted, saying, "Catisemma, they don't know me, I can't do that, I don' aspeak good English like you. Look at me, I'm a big man, they won't open their doors. I can't do this alone; I will do it, but you must come with me."

Standing toe to toe with him she looked up and shook her head no, "I am too busy, Arturo, I need to stay here, to keep sewing. It will take too long to deliver the boxes; you must do it." He persisted, and refused to listen to her excuses, repeating his reasons. But Catisemma insisted that she must remain home to sew. She was determined and would not back down. For hours their long, loud discussion went on. Even with the windows closed everyone heard them, finally their neighbors knew it was over when they heard Catisemma loudly give in, agreeing to go. Cheers erupted throughout the neighborhood as grateful neighbors enjoyed peace and quiet once again.

On a Friday evening, Arturo borrowed his boss's Model T and with everyone's help, they filled the car with boxes planning to leave early on Saturday morning. Waving good bye they drove off in the frigid cold. Only Father Dominic, the parish priest, remained standing outside the church. Catisemma's hand waved out of the car window, as she waved back. Father Dominic raised his arm and extended God's blessing as misty clouds escaped from his breath and filled the cold air around him. His moist eyes following them as the car driving in the distance, grew smaller. Wrapping his arms around his body he stamped his cold feet on the stone steps of the church and watched until Arturo, Catisemma and their boxes could no long be seen.

Catisemma tightly clutched the list of addresses, names, and an introductory letter from Father Dominic in her hands. Both the front seat and the rumble seat were jammed packed, full with boxes separated for boys and girls, the clothes all neatly arranged by sizes, small, medium and large, leaving only room for Arturo behind the wheel and Catisemma squeezed tightly next to him.

Along with the desire to clothe the orphaned children, Arturo and Catisemma's parish had become concerned about the many children who had already lost parents and family due to the deadly pandemic which had spread across the country after the war. Recently, Father Domenic along with many members of his church had met with several other parishes in the city and discussed plans to build a home, a place of refuge for all children. Some of the parishioners wanted to name it The Home for Children, but others thought A Home for Orphaned Children, or maybe even just Our Home might do.

He knew that many hundreds of children were homeless or living in temporary housing which couldn't be sustained. He feared that soon many of these children would be placed on orphan trains and sent out west. The current situation for these children was dangerous and hopeless. Father Dominic knew that a safe, secure, place for the children to call home was desperately needed. He knew that Catisemma's project was only the beginning of a much-needed change for children, and he blessed her for that.

Their day had passed quickly and a pale-yellow sun was lowering in the western sky. They had delivered over 30 boxes of clothing to homes throughout the greater Boston neighborhoods, they were tired but pleased with the results of their efforts. With hungry bellies and thirsty throats, they began to head back to East Boston. Catisemma held tightly onto the papers from Father Dominic, which now were stained, wrinkled and had many cross outs as she looked down reading the remaining list of names and addresses.

They had covered almost a hundred miles, introduced themselves to welcoming and not so welcoming people, they had seen countless children, many of whom they just wanted to take home with them, but knew they couldn't. It had been a day of difficult emotions, some good, some worrisome and some downright frightening.

The setting sun brought a colder chill in the air as she shivered and looked over at her husband, she saw his fatigue, she felt his hunger. They were over an hour away from home and tomorrow they would be busy again, they will have little rest. But there was one last address that pulled at her; it was a farm in Tewksbury, not far from the awful fire several months ago. She considered it but then thought maybe we'll just go home, looking into the back of the vehicle she saw several boxes remaining for delivery on another day. Feeling torn between her exhaustion, their hunger and memories of her own childhood she decided just one more. She assured herself that this would be the last one. Her decision made, she gently placed her hand on Arturo's strong, muscular arm and looked at him, "We have one more, it's the last then we go home." Buoyed by winning their last discussion, Arturo turned and looked at his wife in amazement, "No whatsa matta for you? It's late, we've done enough for today, this is not my car, we go home now." Tears immediately filled Catisemma's sky-blue eyes, she knows he's tired, hungry and she knows he is right. Looking at the address she wondered how they missed this one, it's on the way they took, she began to agree, maybe they should just go home. Then she read the name on the list and she recognized it, it rang a bell.

Turning to Arturo she said, "I think I know these people. I think that this is the farmer who comes to our street, he is the chicken farmer, his name is Teuthorn. He comes to our neighborhood with eggs and the live chickens in the coop. Arturo, remember, we get our chickens from him, we pick out the ones we want, sometimes he kills them right there and you know sometimes I do it, by snapping the necks." Arturo's eyes widened as he looked over at his wife and remembered the chickens and the ease with which she twisted their scrawny necks and chopped off their heads. Reconsidering quickly, he thought, I should probably agree. Looking straight ahead at the road in front of him, he stated, "Ok, I remember that guy, now this is the last one tonight." Smiling he turned the car around, confident that this was the right decision.

Turning down a long tree covered dirt road, passing corn fields and large vegetable gardens, they eventually approached the farm house. Instantly they smelled a lingering whiff of burnt wood and damp ash hanging in the air. As Arturo pulled the car up to the front of the house Catisemma noticed the small face of a young girl peeking out from a front porch window, the white curtain pulled to the side. Knowing that this child like herself had experienced far too much in her young life, her eyes softened and a smile crossed her face as she quickly jumped down from her seat. Not waiting for Arturo, she rushed up the steps and knocked on the closed front door. Suddenly she felt a sense of peace wash over her, she was content and very glad that they had made this their last and final stop, this was the right decision she told herself, and she was glad that she remembered about the chickens.

Getting out of the car, Arturo followed close behind carrying a box marked "girl." As he approached the front porch Catisemma turned towards him, her face beaming as she smiled at him. Standing there in the cold and dampness of the early evening she rapidly knocked on the door for a second time. Patiently they waited and after several minutes a thin woman cracked open the door, as a tall thin man stood protectively right behind her. Not saying a word, they peered out at the strangers on their front porch and waited for an explanation.

Catisemma quickly offered their introduction as the farmer slowly took in both her and Arturo's measure. Then continuing to remain there not saying a word, neither he nor his wife appeared to move or intended to open the door further until suddenly he recognized Catisemma. As his face brightened with recognition it was only then that the door opened and they were invited to enter. But still both the farmer and his wife were cautiously concerned about their new guests.

Catisemma quickly shoved Father Domenic's introductory letter to the farmer. Hesitantly, he took it in hands, quickly looked it over then turning he gave it to his wife, saying, "Here Blathnaid, read this."

Anxious and not waiting for her to finish reading it, Catisemma began, "Gracias from Father Domenic and all of us at the church, gracias, for opening your home after that horrible fire." His wife having quickly read the letter had placed it precariously on her knees.

She looked up at her new guests and told them, "In Ireland they call me Blathnaid, my husband Fred, uses the Gaelic, but here in America I am called Florence."

They sat closely together on the couch, in their sparse but clean front room. The neatness of it giving the appearance it was used only when guests arrived. "Tank you, fer your words." Florence said as she looked at her guests with gratitude.

Picking up the lilt in her voice Catisemma remembered that same accent from Emma's shop and was reminded of Bridgette. Knowing that Florence's country of origin was not America, for she too had left her home in search of the promise of an opportunity and a better life. Catisemma immediately felt as if they were kindred spirits as an ease and a sense of friendship began to fill the room.

Conversation became easy and as the adults were discussing the purpose of their visit, the fire, the children, the orphan trains and the possibility of what might happen next, the box sat in the center of the room.

Tired and feeling himself relax Arturo reached into his shirt pocket and removed two Italian stogies. He stretched his arm offering one to Fred, and as the women talked a match was struck. The two men lit up their slim cigars, each relaxing as they inhaled. The scent of aromatic tobacco quickly filled the room as voices rose in friendly conversation. As they talked, they were unaware of the child, standing quietly behind the door, she listened, not wanting to enter the room, breathing slowly, afraid to make any noise and wary about what she was hearing.

She had heard them say orphan trains, hearing those words her breath caught and her heart beat faster. She felt a chill on her skin as she found it harder to breathe. "Are these people bringing me to an orphan train?" she wondered and felt fear engulf her all over again.

She knows about those trains, she's heard about them, she knows what orphans are, and that she is one. She had heard the stories, late at night the bigger kids would talk quietly about the trains, often the older boys and girls spoke of them, telling the younger ones to be careful. But, no one knew how to be careful, how to protect yourself from the trains and from being taken. She remembered hearing about waking up in the morning and the person who had been next to you the night before would be gone. She remembered that this was exactly what happened to Geraldine, the girl who used to sleep in the cot next to her. She had liked Geraldine; she would read stories to her and she had long, curly red hair that was always in her face which she would push out of her eyes. Sometimes Geraldine helped Marion with her hair too, untwisting her fingers and combing the snarls from her curls. Marion liked it when Geraldine giggled, it always made Marion giggle too even if she didn't know why. Geraldine had told her too, to be careful and try not to let anyone touch her or hurt her. But Geraldine got into trouble, she would get yelled at for wetting the bed. She remembered one time that the head matron, Mrs. Adams, made Geraldine sit in the play yard with the urine-soaked bed sheet wrapped around her head as punishment. Geraldine was so embarrassed, for a long time she didn't talk to anyone. She wasn't sure if that was why Geraldine had been taken or maybe it was the time when she got sick and threw up all over the floor between their beds. Marion remembered how she tried to hide under her covers that night as she heard Mrs. Adams screaming at Geraldine making her clean the throw up by wiping it up with her thick, curly red hair. It was not long after that Geraldine was gone. That was how Big Red became her baby, she saw him lying under the empty bed, the thin blanket twisted and fallen off the side, Big Red was lying on his back on the floor. She wondered if Geraldine meant to leave Big Red for her or if she was missing Big Red now too.

She also remembered that if you asked where they were or if they were coming back you were told to shut up and to mind your own business, Marion never asked anyone about Geraldine.

At the orphanage you learned quickly to keep your mouth shut. The older kids told the younger ones don't draw attention to yourself, pretend nothing is the matter, pretend you're fine. She remembered wondering, had they done something bad, had they said something wrong, and if she got sick would she disappear too.

She was afraid, because she didn't know what to do or how to hide. She wanted to know who drove the trains? Why were they called Orphan Trains? Did the orphans drive the trains? Where do they go, did the trains come back and what happened when you were taken? She had begun to shake. Standing there she believed that this was now going to happen to her too and she didn't know what to do.

She was afraid to ask them; fearful those questions were the exact ones that got you taken and placed on a train and sent somewhere far away. It was scary; she was always so fearful, she wanted to stay here with the nice farm people. She didn't know why she was at this house; she wondered if they would keep her, she hoped they would, but she missed her friends too. She wanted to ask where they were, would she see them again?

She didn't really know how to explain what she was feeling or what she wanted and needed to know. Tears filled her eyes as these thoughts rushed in , placing her hands on her face Marion thought, my head hurts.

Feeling powerless and tired she closed her eyes and leaned

her back flat against the wall, suddenly she slid down with a thump to the floor.

Startled by the noise Florence jumped up and went into the next room, she saw Marion sitting there, quiet and saying nothing, her eyes red from crying, she bent down and scooped her up in her thin but strong arms. Her voice soft she said, "Come on out here Marion; let's wipe those tears and let me introduce you to some very nice people."

Startled to see the little girl from the window being carried into the room Catisemma jumped up and walked over to her. As Florence placed Marion down, she introduced them to each other. "Marion this is Catisemma and Arturo they have brought some things for you." Relieved they were not taking her away Marion looked up at Catisemma's face and smiled the biggest smile she had smiled in a very long time. Looking back at her were the kindest most loving blue eyes she had ever seen. "Marion." Catisemma repeated softly and then she tilted her head and told her, "Marion, hmmm, you look like a beautiful little Mary to me, not a Marion. Come take my hand and let's see what's in this box that is just for you."

Together they opened the top of the box, Marion let out a squeal of joy, for on top was the most beautiful cuddly and soft doll she had ever seen. Without hesitation she reached in to lift it off the pile of clothes and hugged it tightly in her arms. The doll's body felt warm and cuddly, the arms, face and legs were made of a soft flannel, the long full-length dress was made of a red and green plaid with a small pleated ruffle around the front and back and on its feet were tiny white booties. Marion looked at this beautiful baby doll and thought, "You're not Big Red but I can love you like I loved Big Red." She then looked up at Florence and Catisemma her eyes wide and said, "Thank you, thank you, I love babies, I just love babies. I missed my baby so much!" Catisemma's eyes clouded with tears, she knows the desire to hold a baby of your very own and she misses that too. She understood Marion's words, "I just love babies," for she does too. Immediately Catisemma realized, "We are kindred spirits this little Mary and me." Marion looked at her new baby and told her, "You will be Baboo, you are my baby Baboo."

By now Arturo's stomach was growling loudly, flicking the ash of his stogie into the large ash tray on the end table, he stood up and looked over at his wife, this was his signal to tell he was ready to leave, Catisemma nodded at him and stood also.

Marion shyly gave her new friend, a gentle hug saying good bye. She watched as the adults gathered at the door. Feeling a bit more confident, she told herself that this woman, this woman with blue eyes, a kind smile, and a nice voice, she won't put me on any train, I know that she won't.

Florence and Catisemma smiled at each other as they said good bye, both of them felt as though they had met a new friend and hoped that they would see each other again.

*"Much I've done and much I've seen, to many a place I have been.
But to me there's no delight like the lights of home at night."*
- Edgar A. Guest

27

FOREST STREET, BOSTON, MA

"I can't believe that we're here. Did you think it was going to be this hard? It was worse than I thought to leave New York; It was so much work; I think it was easier to leave Germany than Brooklyn. Do you believe we have really done it? The questions flew from Lilli as they sat together, exhausted, on the hard wood floor of their new home.

Both of them weary with sore muscles, they rested their backs against the paneled wainscoted wall of their dining room. Walter stared straight ahead, he had one arm resting over his bent knee, while the other wrapped itself across her shoulders. His answer was short and without hesitation, "No, Lilli, nope, I don't believe it."

"Neither do I." she replied her eyes glistened with tears. "This was hard Walter, here we are starting out all over again and at our ages. What were we thinking? We're not kids anymore Walter. I'm 38 now and next April I'll be 39 yikes, that's almost 40. I've already lived most of my life. I hadn't realized how difficult this would be. This is it for me Walter, no more changes, I'm done."

Without looking at his wife, Walter nodded in agreement and was about to speak, but having taken a breath, Lilli went on, "Before, I always had my mother beside me, now without her it's just so different. Everything is so different. I don't know how she did it all. But, when I think about her, I feel as if she just kept blowing life into me again and again. There were so many times I wanted to give up, when I was a little girl and my father died, when I had that terrible accident back in Germany, I remember wanting to just let go then, I hurt so badly.

Then when we came to America, just the two of us. We were a team starting out together at Emma's Dress Shoppe. Then marching together demanding the vote for women. Even after you and I got married and I had miscarriage after miscarriage. She was always right there, never wavering lifting me up again and again.

Now I feel so alone, I know I have you Walter but you don't need me, if something happened, you'd be fine. But my mother, Walter, I feel as if a part of me is missing. I don't know, maybe what's really bothering me Walter, is that there will be no memories of her here with me. Maybe it's just that I can't sense her here or feel her presence like I did back at the old place. I can't get another mother, Walter." She wiped her eyes apologizing saying "I'm sorry, to be babbling on and on, maybe I'm just too tired. It's been a long journey and I'm exhausted. Thank God I have you Walter, but if something happened to me, I hope you'd remarry right away and not wait too long I really wouldn't want you to be alone."

Turning his head to look at her, he squeezed her shoulders and pulled her closer to him. Smiling he said, "No one Lilli, could ever replace my love for you, never, ever. I love you Lilli, I always have and I always will. But" ...he paused as a twinkle appeared in his tired eyes, "If there was a nice fraulein who could cook as well as you, well maybe we could be friends." Pushing him away she laughed out loud saying, "Well, at least you wouldn't starve. That's certainly encouraging." "I know," he said smiling, "I still remember those early meals when we were courting Lilli; thankfully at that time your mother did do most of the cooking." Looking off into the distance the two of them sat quietly for several minutes both lost in warm and loving memories of years ago.

Then he turned to Lilli and said, "You know Lilli; I'll be 43 this February, who hires men at 43? They'll laugh at me when I walk in. I don't think they realized my age. I hope Arturo was right that they were really interested in my ideas and designs. Well Lilli if this doesn't work, we'll just have to rent out some of the rooms in this big house to cover the mortgage. But seriously, Liebchen, I believe we'll be ok, we've come this far, we still have a lot of life in us. We can't give up Lilli, we come from good stock, there are so many who came before us, they are depending on us to carry on. Who knows Lilli, there may be many after us who are depending too and glad, we did?"

Shaking her head at his optimism Lilli leaned against her husband of 19 years. She inhaled his familiar scent and felt the comfort of his wide broad chest and strong arms as they wrapped around her. He held her tightly in an embrace she never wanted to end. But after several minutes he gently released her and stood up, then taking her hands in his he helped her up too. Holding hands, the two of them headed to their bedroom grateful for a fully made bed to sleep in and hoping for a well-deserved night's sleep.

Without shades or curtains on the windows the morning sun poured into their east facing bedroom, the brightness waking the tired couple as dawn broke into their room.

Hearing church bells in the distance Lilli slowly stretched before getting up and suggested that they take a short walk down the street to the church she had seen earlier. "Is it a Lutheran Church?" Walter asked, "I don't think so, but it doesn't matter to me, does it matter to you? "Lilli replied. "Not really." he answered, "I doubt anyone will be greeting us in German or even doing a "hell fire and brimstone sermon" in German, so it really doesn't matter. However, I could use with a good "hell fire and brimstone sermon" every once in a while, it keeps me honest." He chuckled.

They ate a quick breakfast of scones and coffee, pulled their Sunday best out of the trunks and found appropriate shoes for walking. Holding hands, Lilli and Walter headed out for the first of many Sunday mornings at their new church.

Walking into the vestibule they were surprised by how diverse the congregation appeared. Before at their church in Brooklyn so many of the congregants were from Germany but here it appeared that the pews were filled with people from all over the world. This difference made Lilli realize that she was glad to see so many different parishioners. As she thought, how American, what a truly diverse blending of those faithful to their belief. Looking around Lilli couldn't help but smile; there was a feeling of joy and welcoming here that she hadn't felt in a long time. Walter felt it too; however, he attributed it to hearing the gentle strains of Mendelssohn being played on the large church organ and bellowing out of the pipes which surrounded the altar.

Taking Walter's hand Lilli slowly walked down the center aisle and chose a pew in the middle of the sanctuary next to what appeared to be a very large family. Raising his eyebrows, Walter gave Lilli a look that easily translated to, "Do you really want to sit here, next to this big family with all of these children?" Looking directly back at him she raised her eyebrows in a mocking response and shook her head yes. Sliding into the pew and sitting down she smiled at the family. She noticed that the parents immediately smiled back, while many of the children, sitting straight, with hands tightly folded in their laps looked straight ahead.

Throughout the service, the sermon, the prayers, the singing and the collection Lilli was awed and impressed by the polite, courteous and excellent behavior of these children. She looked at Walter with a look of smugness, smiled and winked. Then Lilli slightly inclined her head forward, she took in the family and surreptitiously counted, one, two, three, four, five, six, seven. Looking at the young mother, she mouthed questioningly, "Twins?" At which the mother smiled shaking her head no. Smiling back and giving her a nod, Lilli turned to the front and defiantly looked up at the altar. Lifting her eyes, she petitioned God directly, "Seven God, seven, really. Couldn't you have just given me one God, just one?" Then sitting back, she resigned herself to enjoy others people's children accepting God's wishes and saying, "Ok God, you win, then that's what I'll have to do."

As the church service came to an end, Lilli had already decided that she would introduce herself and speak with the parents. She wanted to let them know what lovely, well behaved children they had, that they were very blessed and must be very good parents.

Listening to the musical strains of the recessional play loudly, Lilli stood up and faced the young mother and father. Smiling she reached out her hand introducing herself and Walter. She told them this was the first time they had attended this welcoming church and she was so glad she chose to sit down next to their lovely family.

The two young adults smiled shyly, introduced themselves and expressed gratitude for her kind words. Then the wife looked at her husband and gave him a questioning look, he nodded his head and said, "It's ok." Blushing, she swallowed and began, "Well, I know you must think we've been very busy bringing all of these children into the world, and I truly appreciate your complements. But I have to tell you that of the 7 children sitting with us actually only two belong to us, only two are ours. And those two were the ones we kept poking to sit still and keep quiet; all of the others aren't ours; they don't belong to us. They are state wards. Orphans. My husband and I opened up our home when they recently became homeless. I hesitate to say it, but I think we probably saved a couple of them from being put on one of those horrible orphan trains. I don't know if you heard about the fire at the orphanage several months ago, but these children were from there."

Lilli shook her head, indicating that she hadn't heard about it, she didn't bother to explain that they had recently moved into the area and often events that happened out of New York City, where they had lived, frequently were not reported in their local papers. Lilli realized how her perceptions of what she saw had impacted her thoughts, her emotions and her beliefs throughout the entire service. "Why did I jump to that conclusion?" she asked herself, "Why did I assume that this was one complete family? Why did I take it out on God? Instead of being upset and hurt, God was sending me a message this morning."

Reconsidering this awareness Lilli was overwhelmed with the opportunity she had just discovered. State wards, she pondered, of course, orphans. Yes, they would certainly need a place to live. Lilli was impressed by the behavior of the children who were wards of the state. She started to think about possibilities, the large home which she and Walter had just purchased. She began imagining the changes and the possibilities, which only the night before she had determined no intention of making.

As Walter and Lilli left the church, she felt energized and filled with a new sense of purpose. Turning to look at her husband, she tightly squeezed his hand and said, "I think we made the right move, Walter, I have a feeling that everything will be fine."

Walking side by side, with his wife of almost 20 years, he nodded his head in agreement, he knew that she was absolutely right because he felt it too. Suddenly everything they had been through over the last several years, flashed through his mind. He saw the good times, the celebrations, the heartbreaks and the frightening moments, they all played out before his eyes like a quickly turning kaleidoscope. Slowing down he turned to her saying, "You're right, this was a good move, I agree everything will work out."

Overcome with emotions, he abruptly stopped and looking at Lilli in a way that he hadn't in a long time, he wrapped his arms around her and kissed her right on the lips. Lilli laughed out loud, blushed and pushed him away as his mustache tickled her face, bringing back the most wonderful of memories.

For several moments they stood with their arms wrapped around each other staring into each other's eyes. Then smiling, they turned and with the sun in their faces, arm in arm they hurried to their new home talking nonstop, making plans, each of them knowing that they couldn't wait to get there, to begin all of the changes they were planning.

"One word frees us of all the weight and pain of life; that word is love." - Sophocles

28

PERCEPTIONS

The late afternoon sun shone, spreading wide beams of warmth through the panes of the three west facing bays as it washed the parlor in its 'golden warm hue. Lilli and Walter had spent the afternoon arranging furniture, emptying boxes and putting dishes into cabinets, they both needed a break. Lilli put a kettle on to boil, making preparations for a pot of tea. She wanted to make this moment special so she located her mother's silver tray, unwrapped her best china tea pot, placed her de Haviland tea cups down and opened a second box of scones. Pouring the boiling water over the tea leaves she headed for their new parlor.

Handing the tray over to Walter she pulled her rocking chair, moving it closer to him as he sat on the floor. She was bursting with thoughts and ideas about this new possibility which seemed to have dropped out of the sky at their feet this morning and she had thought of little else since.

As Walter poured the tea into their cups she asked, "So, my

darling, have you had a chance to think about what we discussed on the way home?" Looking up at Lilli, Walter smiled as his eyes twinkled. "Do you mean whether or not I need to shave off my mustache to keep you from giggling like a school girl on the sidewalk?" he asked.

Laughing out loud Lilli leaned against the back of her chair and rocked, as she remembered the joy, she felt earlier just from his one kiss. "How do you do that?" she asked him. "How do I do what?" he replied smiling back at her, his eyes laughing mischievously looking at her. "How do you make my heart skip a beat just by holding my hand, looking into my eyes or simply softly brushing my lips with yours? Seriously how do you do that?"

Pausing before answering, his eyes softened as he looked at his bride and smiled. Coughing slightly just to clear his throat he began to recite the romantic lines of Elizabeth Barrett Browning's sonnet 43 "How Do I Love Thee. Let me count the ways. Leaning back in her chair, Lilli slowly rocked listening, when he finished, Lilli's eyes were moist with tears.

Walter's eyes glistened too, yet he was smiling as he explained, "When I was a young boy Lilli, I truly believed that I would never love anyone as much as I loved my dear departed mother. In my mind, in my heart and in my soul, I loved her, even though I didn't know her on this earth, I still loved her. Then on one beautiful spring day in May you came into my life. You showed me that love is not something you keep to yourself; it is not something of which you have a limited quantity. Love is meant to be shared, and that is its' sole purpose. Had I feared loving anyone else, if I was covetous with my love for my mother and if I held back thinking I didn't deserve you then I would have missed so much.

I love you more today than the day we were married; I will love you more tomorrow than today. I truly believe Lilli that the greatest gift we can give each other is love, but also, to be open to receive love, to love others and to let them know they are loved. I believe that when you know you are loved, I mean loved unconditionally, when you can bask in the warm radiant glow of that love, feel its comfort, its security and its validation, then you have been given the greatest gift of all.

We all deserve to be loved Lilli. So, my darling, when I look at you, when I hold you in my arms and when our lips meet, all of my love the essence of my life itself is yours always forever and ever."

This was not the answer Lilli expected but as she listened to her husband's words, she understood how important the gift of love was. She thought of the love shown by that young family, opening their doors to those children, opening their arms and their family to children who desperately needed love. Sipping her tea Lilli looked over the top of the flowered cup and thought, we can do this, we can fill our home with love too and that's what we'll do.

Placing her cup in its saucer, she asked, "Walter, remember the love and joy we felt back in Brooklyn when Henry, Catisemma and my mother would come over? Remember the laughs we would have, the meals we shared and the warmth that we felt surrounding us? That was love Walter, it was real, it was palpable, we felt it for each other, and it was always there. It has never left us, even now our love for Henry, for my mother it hasn't diminished; it's still here, with us."

Nodding his head in agreement, Walter replied, "Lilli, I know we will fill this house with love too, I agree, it's already here, it's in this house, we brought it here with us like a beautifully wrapped gift we just need to unwrap it!"

"Well, then my husband, where do we begin, how do we fill our home with love, where do we start?" she asked. Looking around the room Walter exhaled a deep breath and suggested they finish unpacking first, then get some ideas, maybe talk to the minister at the church, and maybe later they could speak with the family they met today.

Feeling as if they had the beginnings of a plan in place and filled with renewed energy Lilli focused on making her new house a home.

The next day was Monday and Walter left early to begin working in the office at the construction firm where Arturo was the crew superintendent. Kissing her husband good bye and wishing him luck Lilli immediately started creating a home where before empty rooms had existed.

Across Boston in another home, Catisemma kissed her husband good bye, and rushed back into her kitchen to clean the breakfast dishes. She had plans for today, she planned to leave her house early that morning and visit a dear friend. Hurrying to complete her morning chores, she couldn't wait to finish putting the breakfast dishes in the kitchen strainer to dry. It was hard for her to keep her excitement under control because today she was taking the city trolley cars across Boston to surprise Lilli. She hadn't let Lilli know that she had planned to visit. She figured, "I will just show up and knock on the door, that's what I did in Brooklyn, that's what I'll do here too. She'll be home, she's unpacking; of course, she'll be there."

Arriving well before noon time Catisemma stood on the sidewalk admiring Lilli and Walter's new home. A smile crossed her face as she climbed the wide wooden steps of the veranda. Before knocking on the door Catisemma gazed with pleasure at the craftsmanship of this beautiful Victorian style home. She appreciated its long parlor windows, the ginger bread trim and the full wrapping veranda. Nodding her head, she softly whispered, "This isa very nice home." Then with a grin that spread across her face she lifted the heavy brass door knocker and gave the solid oak door a very loud bang. Hearing the knock Lilli turned from her chores, with a surprised and questioning look she untied her apron strings and hurried to answer the door not knowing who or what she would find.

Calling out, "I'm coming," she arrived within seconds of the knock and opened the door partially to see who it was. A squeal of joy escaped from her as she saw her friend, and flung the door wide open. With arms outstretched she embraced Catisemma gathering her up in a tight embrace and pulling her close. "I don't believe you are here." she said. "And I don't believe you are here." Catisemma replied.

Then the two of them just stood there, holding hands and smiling at each other. Her eyes filling with tears Lilli shook her head in disbelief. Then without further ado she pulled her old friend into the entry hall.

Words immediately poured from Lilli's mouth as she said, "Before we go any further Catisemma, I want to thank you for suggesting we come here, for recommending that Walter reach out to Arturo and most importantly for being my friend, my beloved dear friend. I am so happy to be here, so glad to be close to you again and so excited about the possibilities Walter and I believe we have here in Boston."

Catisemma smiled back and nodded her head, "I know this was a huge move, I know it wasn't easy and I know you've been through a lot. I know too, how hard it was for you to lose your mother. You must miss her so much Lilli." Looking at the floor, Lilli's head nodded affirmatively as she tried to swallow the lump that had formed in her throat. Seeing her friends' pain Catisemma quickly changed the subject and said, "So show me your house Lilli, show me everything, I want to see it all."

Together they began to walk through the house. Both of them admired the bright light which shone in through the large windows. Lilli pointed out the wooden built-ins in the dining room for her de Haviland china. Standing in the middle of the dining room, Catisemma pointed to an opening in the wall that separated the dining room from the kitchen, and asked, "What is that for Lilli?" Turning to look where she was pointing Lilli looked at the opening and replied, "I believe that is what they call a butler's pantry. That's where food can be passed through from the kitchen to the dining room when dinner is being served." Catisemma laughed out loud, "I don't believe you have a butler Lilli, do you? Well I am looking forward to seeing my gravy, meatballs and pasta being passed right through that little window." Shaking her head too Lilli answered, "Oh no, Catisemma, no butler for me, not in this lifetime."

Arms locked they headed into the parlor, Lilli pointed out the wide bookshelves and the black onyx marble fireplace framed in dark cherry wood. Catisemma complimented everything she saw; telling Lilli how beautiful it all was. Then it was upstairs to the second floor, they climbed the curving staircase leading to the large airy bedrooms all waiting to be furnished. Catisemma let out a gasp, when she saw that Lilli had her very own large room devoted only to her sewing. "You are a lucky woman Lilli Vetterlein, I think I need to call you Lady Vetterlein maybe. I know you will love having this room, I have one, much smaller but it is good for me." she said smiling. "Now you will have no excuse not to make everything you need and maybe things others need too. I think you could get yourself a nice little business here my friend. Hmm, I definitely could have recruited you recently for some sewing."

Lilli laughed out loud, as she reminded Catisemma, "Now that's really a great idea, sure Emma started her dress shop in New York by herself. Who knows maybe I will do that? I remember that my mother and I considered it." Exhaling, she shook her head realizing the possibilities and how much could be done. Looking at her friend she replied, "I never thought it would be like this again, it really is in how you look at it. Life throws opportunities or hurdles in your way, it just doesn't tell you which is which. I guess it's up to you to decide, it's truly up to your perception." Catisemma smiled back in agreement. Walking down the stairs together their laughter was laced with their happy voices, sharing all that had happened since the last time they saw each other.

Once in the kitchen, Lilli filled the kettle and placed it on the stove. She lit a match for the gas and turned the flame high, for it to boil and took out her china cups again, the second time in two days. As lunch was being prepared and dishes placed on the table Catisemma began to tell Lilli about her life in East Boston. She spoke about her struggle with becoming pregnant, her heartbreak with each miscarriage and finally the infection which resulted in an emergency hysterectomy. Looking at her friend, her eyes sympathetic and misty, Lilli nodded her head. She understood, she knew the pain in these losses, she knew how much they both loved children, and how much they both wanted to have families. The room became silent for several minutes as each of them allowed these painful feelings to wash over them. It was Catisemma, who spoke first, wiping her eyes with her handkerchief, she sniffed and began to tell Lilli about events in the city.

She told her about the recent fire at the orphanage and the many children who were now homeless, with no one to watch or protect them. She talked about the placing of so many children in various homes and the tragic deaths from the fire. Hearing this Lilli nodded her head and told Catisemma about the family she met at church just the day before. Catisemma smiled glad to hear that not only were the children being fed and clothed but they were being brought to church too. Catisemma thought of the remaining boxes and planned to get the address of that family also.

Then Catisemma began to talk about the boxes, Lilli listened in awe at how her friend had been able to gather material, make dresses, shirts, pants and coats and then ask for help in making even more. With deepening admiration, she listened as Catisemma talked about Arturo's help in filling up the borrowed Model T and driving all over delivering boxes with only a list of names, addresses and an introductory letter from Father Domenic.

Coming to the end of this amazing odyssey Catisemma

paused, she exhaled a deep breath, as she pushed her back against the firmness of the chair and smiled. She felt good about what she had accomplished but she wanted to do more.

"So, Lilli when I mentioned sewing earlier, I wasn't kidding. You could help me Lilli, please say you will." Nodding, Lilli replied, "Give me some time first, let me get unpacked then we will talk." Lilli was overwhelmed at her friend's efforts and skill in mastering this entire process. Reaching across the table to take her friends' hands in her own, she said, "First, tell me about the children, what do you remember about any of them, was there anyone in particular that stood out or did you just fall in love with them all?"

Pausing before she spoke, because there were so many, Catisemma needed a moment to recall each and every one. Suddenly a smile crossed her face, as it lit up with the memory of one particular child. "You know Lilli; there was one little face that I can't forget, one little face that still lingers in my heart." Lilli leaned forward to listen as Catisemma continued, "Lilli, there was something about her; I remember her, blond curls, beautiful almond shaped eyes, she was pretty, very pretty but she was shy and at first very quiet. That was until we opened the box for her. Once we opened it her eyes lit up. She saw the stuffed doll right on the top of the pile. Her little hand reached in and quickly took it out of the box, she hugged its little body right to her heart.

But what really touched me Lilli, was when she looked at me and said, I just love babies, I just love them. I was so touched by that comment; all I could do was look back at her and say, Me to. Lilli, there were so many though, but she stood out to me and still does. I don't remember her name, it was a different name, and actually I really hadn't heard it before. I remember calling her something else, now what was that? I can't remember now." Shaking her head, Catisemma suddenly noticed the time on the banjo wall clock, realizing that she needed to leave to begin dinner preparations for Arturo, " I gotta get back to my shack, my man, he works so hard and he is always hungry when he gets home." She explained.

Giving each other a hug, Lilli locked her arm in Catisemma's as they headed for the front door. Then reaching out to her friend, Catisemma gave Lilli a second hug. Before releasing her, Lilli paused saying, "You know Catisemma, you are a younger woman than I, you're still young enough to adopt a baby and to raise a family. Walter and I are older and I'm not sure if I have the energy or stamina any more for babies, I mean really little ones. But my dear friend if there is ever any child or children that come into my home; well, they would be yours too. I hope you know that, because I mean this from the bottom of my heart. I never had a sister Catisemma, but somehow, I feel as if you and I were always meant to be sisters. You have taught me so much, I love you, I always did right from the beginning."

Catisemma's eyes moistened as she looked at her friend, "Never worry, Lilli, never worry, if Arturo and I were to adopt a baby, or maybe twin babies," her voice added wistfully, "then you and Walter would certainly be the zio e zia." Catisemma then turned quickly so Lilli wouldn't see the tears which had filled her eyes. Stopping at the bottom of the porch steps, she paused and looked over her shoulder up at her friend, telling her, "I'll be back. Next time I'll bring pasta, ciao, Lilli."

"For he satisfies the thirsty and fills the hungry with good things."
- Psalm 107:9

29

EGGS, CHICKENS, AND CHURCH

The following Sunday morning Lilli couldn't wait to attend the service at their new church, she was hoping to see that young family again. Walking beside Walter, she beckoned him to walk faster, "Please hurry Walter; I want to try to sit next to that family again, come on please." Smiling Walter's stride became longer and quicker as he matched his steps with his anxious wife.

Suddenly he pulled back slowing down as his fingertips brushed her arm as he hesitantly asked, "Lilli, what if they're not here today? What if some of the children have been placed elsewhere?" Abruptly, stopping and turning she looked at him, her eyes widened as her face registered shock and surprise, "What do you mean not here today? Where would they go? What are you talking about?" Now it was his turn to stop, he turned and looked directly at her, "Lilli, these placements are only temporary you know. People can't be expected to feed and house these orphans forever. From what I understand many of these children will be sent to other orphanages, some may be old enough to be on their own or maybe even sent out west on those trains. You can't expect people to suddenly change their lives or take on such a burden especially for strangers. You just can't do it; it just doesn't work that way."

Looking at him, listening to his words, Lilli had never contemplated the circumstances he had just described. Drawing in a deep inhale and pulling herself up, Lilli replied defensively, "Walter, didn't your Aunt Frida take you in, didn't she take in all of your brothers and your father too? She took everyone Walter; she didn't say times up, she didn't kick you out or let anyone else take you? What are you saying?"

Knowing how upset she was, how concerned she had become and how disappointed she might be, he took her hands in his and said, "Yes, Lilli, my amazing aunt Frida, did take us all in, but we were family Lilli, she was my father's sister, that's what we did in the old country Lilli, families took care of each other. There was no system for orphans, there were no programs, or orphan trains and for many Lilli if they didn't have families they were on the streets, they were on their own Lilli. We were lucky, my father was lucky to have the sister he did, my brothers were lucky Lilli, I was lucky."

Listening to his words, Lilli sighed understanding his comments, she resolved, "Well, let's just go there then, maybe the family will be there, I hope they are but if they aren't, we can speak with the minister or someone else at the church."

Taking his hand, they turned walking side by side hurrying to get to the church on time.

Upon entering Lilli looked everywhere for the large family that she had met last week. The pews were filling up but she was not recognizing them anywhere. She tried to remember what they looked like, what did the mother look like, what color hair did she have, what did the husband look like? It was all a blur; she couldn't remember, and looked for any family with a gaggle of children.

Feeling discouraged and disappointed she pressed her hand to her abdomen as her shoulders dropped and she lowered her head in despair. Walter's heart broke for her; he understood how much she had counted on talking with the unknown family. Taking her arm, he led her into an empty pew. Sitting down she folded her hands in her lap, and kept her eyes downcast. Walter looked around as the opening chords of He Leadeth Me rang throughout the church.

Turning slightly to watch as the choir proceeded down the center aisle of the sanctuary in unison the congregation stood and sang this familiar hymn.

Suddenly Walter saw them, a large family entering the rear of the sanctuary as they frantically hurried in trying not to make a disturbance they walked behind the choir. Everyone saw them and everyone was watching, it was hard not to smile as the parents tried to coral the children. He gave Lilli a gentle poke, and directed her to look over her shoulder behind her. As Lilli stretched her neck to see beyond the choir, she spotted the familiar family. Not wanting to cause a distraction they anxiously looked for the first available pew, seeing it they ushered the children in one at a time not far from Lilli and Walter.

Feeling relieved Lilli exhaled releasing the tension and the breath she had been holding. A smile crossed her face as she sang the remaining line of the refrain, "For by his hand he leadeth me."

Sitting back down she leaned into Walter and whispered, "How will I get to them before they leave?" Knowing how difficult it can be to politely exit the church or even your own pew, after the service, as people remain standing in the pews or gather in the aisles to exchange greetings. Walter pondered different strategies for a quick exit to the pew behind them. Well he thought, as he stifled a chuckle, I'm not sure catapulting over these pews is an option anymore, not at my age now."

As the service continued, Lilli and Walter barely heard the minister's message until the beginnings of the 23rd Psalm, "The Lord is my shepherd, I shall not want." With heads bowed Lilli and Walter in unison with the rest of the congregation recited these words. As Lilli softly said, "Amen." She felt a sense of calm wash over her, the anxiety she had been feeling was gone, she felt at peace. Realizing the power of the words she had just recited; Lilli's faith was restored. She believed, yes, the Lord is my shepherd and I shall not want, these inspiring words from this beautiful Psalm of the Old Testament assured her that whatever happened, it would be all right.

Reaching over she took Walter's hand as she smiled at him locking her eyes into his, he knows that she will be fine. He doesn't need to worry; everything will be fine. The hymn In the Garden played.

As the service came to an end and the congregation stood to leave the church, Lilli gratefully noticed that the family was not exiting the pew, but were walking down the center aisle to the front of the church. Waiting in the pew to let them pass

Lilli and Walter noticed the differences in the children's faces. The two youngsters that had been identified as the children of the parents seemed so very confident. They walked down the aisle with their parents holding their hands and looking straight ahead their heads held high, their shoulders back. She noticed that their step was quick and buoyant, not hesitant or shy. She also noticed that they are looking around, smiling at the other congregants, nodding their heads as they are greeted.

Lilli noticed too the stark difference to the other children was profound. The other children, the orphans were far more reticent, they kept their heads lowered, crowding together as they slowly followed the others walking down the church aisle. They neither smiled nor looked up; they were not greeting anyone. Lilli thought it was as if they didn't want to be noticed, and they didn't want to make eye contact or respond to a greeting. They were being protective of each other and of themselves.

Observing this behavior Lilli turned to look at Walter, she saw the tears which filled his eyes. She knows that he is thinking of the life he was given when his mother was taken away, and now she knows how it could have been so different. At that moment both Lilli and Walter see the vivid effects of the profound power of love.

They understand that it takes far more than providing clothing and a home for a child, far more than providing sustenance for a child to thrive. It takes love, the kind of love that is never questioned and never removed. This is how a child thrives, feels protected, wanted and accepted. This is how a child learns to love.

The young couple were providing everything they could

and these children understood that. But for most of their lives these children had not known love, not the kind of love that was always there surrounding you, the love that never diminished and never ever left you.

As the young couple came closer Lilli reached her hand out to greet them. The mother quickly recognized Lilli. She smiled back as she stopped and extended her hand in greeting also. Lilli and Walter introduced themselves again and asked if they may have a moment with them. Both of the parents looked back at their large brood and told the children to take a seat in the pew next to them so the adults might talk.

Knowing how difficult it was to keep children sitting and quiet for an extended period of time Lilli and Walter got right to the point. The questions come pouring out of Lilli's mouth, "Where did these children come from? How can we open our house to an orphan? Who do we need to speak with? How long are you having these children? When will they leave and where will they go?" Standing next to Lilli, Walter waits for the answers before he too begins asking questions.

Finally, they have all of the information they need, they know what to do and they know how to do it. Feeling uplifted and grateful Lilli asks what she can do to help with this large family. The young mother is overwhelmed with Lilli's graciousness telling her she is grateful but not to worry, just knowing that Lilli and Walter plan to open their home too is all she needs.

Looking around they see that everyone has left; they are the only ones standing in the now empty sanctuary. One of the children walked forward to place a coin in the collection dish at the front of the church. Then turning, they all begin to walk out together.

Lilli overhears the young mother remind her husband that they will need some more eggs this week from the farmer since the children have been enjoying bacon and eggs for breakfast every morning. Smiling a fond memory came to Lilli as she thought, I remember fresh eggs from the farm when Mutter and I lived in Germany that was a long time ago, and they were delicious.

Turning she asked, "Where do you get these eggs and how do you get them?" Now it is the husband's turn to offer information as he speaks about, the farmer who brings his horse driven cart to the center of their town twice a week. Smiling as his eyes widen describing the tall thin man, he continues to explain that if you simply want eggs well these are the best but if you want chickens and fresh vegetables this farmer is the only one you want. That's all Lilli needed to hear, she quickly asked, "How do I reach him, and when do you expect to see him again?" She is already thinking of the wonderful breakfasts with fresh farm eggs and maybe a delicious chicken dinner or two with wide noodles and a butter cream sauce.

Saying their good byes Lilli has one more question she is curious to ask, looking at the young mother she says, "May I ask where you are from? I notice you have a bit of an accent but I can't quite determine its origin." The young mother smiled replying, "Well it's a blend, we are the Norton's from Northern Ireland, near the top eastern coast at the North Channel, next to Scotland, some people call us Ulster Scots, you know. Also, many people refer to us as Orange, the protestant section of Ireland. Going back to the reign of

William and Mary of Orange" Nodding her head, Lilli understands now why she was confused hearing the lilt of an Irish accent in a Baptist church. She also thought of Bridgette and how Lilli was so quick to judge the people from Ireland based on her one experience. I was wrong she thinks, I was too quick to judge. I'm grateful my eyes and my heart were opened. "Thank you, God. Thank you."

Taking Walter's arm, a smile crossed Lilli's face as she acknowledged the common bond connecting all people. Yes, she pondered, we come from different countries, we have different religious beliefs and we celebrate different customs but we are all members of the same family, we are all members of one family, one amazing, beautiful big family.

Turning to look at this kind and generous young couple caring for so many different children, holding hands as they head back to their home, Lilli called out waving, "So glad we have met and thank you for everything today, yes thank you for everything."

As they wave back Lilli noticed that not only are the two little children, the Norton children waving, but several of the orphan children are waving too. Then just before she turned away to take Walter's hand she smiled, as she saw several of the children holding hands, all of them skipping home, following the lead of the adults.

"Our very cells respond to the thoughts we think. With every word, silent or spoken, we participate in the body's functioning. We participate in the functioning of the Universe itself. If our consciousness grows lighter, then so does everything within and around us. This means that with every thought, we can start to recreate our lives. In saying yes to new beginnings, we bring them forth." - Marianne Williamson

30

BUTTERFLIES

*L*illi was ecstatic, now she had a plan, Walter was ecstatic too, now Lilli had a plan.

Walking home they chattered incessantly discussing and agreeing on just what their next steps would be. As the Norton's had recommended their first step was to contact the State of Massachusetts, Department of Public Welfare to inform them that they wanted to open up their home for one or two orphans in need. Lifting her pointer finger in the air as if counting off the steps, Lilli asks Walter, "Did she say we had to petition the Department of Public Welfare? I'm not really sure that I know what that means do you?" Shaking his head that he didn't know either, Lilli was undaunted. "Well, we will find out and just do whatever we have to."

Secondly, and most important, they would need to prepare two bedrooms upstairs on the second floor for any quick arrivals. Knowing that this was her area of expertise, Lilli began thinking of the boxes with the quilts, the curtains, the pillows and dresser scarves she would need to take out for washing or pressing.

"Phew." she said excitedly to Walter, "Getting everything ready is going to keep me very busy for the next week or so." Looking at his wife, her face flush with excitement and beaming with joy he smiled, "This is what we call good busy Lilli, very good busy, I have a feeling that you are going to enjoy every minute of this."

Nodding her head in agreement she smiled, "You know, I'll have to get my sewing room all set up too, I can't imagine that any children we get will have a large wardrobe. Can you? Thankfully I also brought all of the patterns that my mother and I had made together over the years." Immediately a memory of the times she and her mother would sit together and cut patterns for dresses, coats, and hats came to her as her face beamed remembering this warm and heartfelt image. Looking at Walter she replied, "I loved my mother so much Walter and I miss her, but you know what? Even though she's gone I still feel the love, her love for me which I never doubted, it keeps me going. I always knew she loved me; I just knew it. And that's all that matters isn't it my darling?"

Looking at his wife, he couldn't help but be awed by this change; it was only hours before that he had seen her in such a state of deep despair and sadness. But after meeting and talking with the Norton family, knowing what to do next and thinking about the future possibilities she had morphed into a radiant vision of joy, excitement and happiness.

Purpose, Walter thinks, it is purpose that gives life meaning as his heart bursts with gratitude and thankfulness.

Walking side by side, heads bowed together they discuss their plans, Lilli wraps her arm around her husband's as they hurry home. Walter can't hide his smile too, he is excited and happy knowing that now their house will be a home, a home with children, bursting with noise, excitement, laughter and love.

Suddenly his heart burst full, as a memory of his aunt Frida, his father, his cousins and brothers appear before him filling his vision. He sees them, they are all together, clearly, he sees all of them, yet this vision doesn't bring him sadness. No on the contrary, it brings him joy, for they are all smiling, they are all smiling at him, it is as if they are looking right at him, he is in their vision, as they are in his and as their eyes meet he knows that they are truly seeing him as he is seeing them, he feels it and he believes it.

From that moment on he has faith that Lilli and he will have a family. From that moment on he has no doubt that all he needs to do now is wait and get prepared to become a father.

Approaching their home on Forest Street Lilli quickly bounded up the front steps and onto the veranda. Tilting her head from side to side, lifting her hand to her chin she astutely appraises everything as she looks around the entire front porch. Standing back Walter quietly watches as she points to a corner saying, "I think we should get a wicker rocking chair and put it there, children love to rock and maybe a chaise for over here to sit and read, and definitely I think a table here would be good for lemonade and cookies. Guffawing, as he bent forward his palms falling onto his knees Walter laughs out loud saying, "So just tell me my little Dutch Schultz, which bank did you rob on the way back?"

Turning to look at her husband Lilli smiled too, "I'll just have to sew more that's all, maybe I can ask Catisemma in helping out too. She loves to sew and she loves children, I know she'll want to help, she will, I know that."

As Walter opened the door to their home, Lilli suddenly remembered about the farmer with the eggs and chickens that the Norton's had mentioned. Heading for the kitchen Lilli turns saying, "Tomorrow I'll see if I can find out how we get in touch with that farmer, I want to try his eggs and chickens. They're supposed to be the best you know. Who knows he might be just the person we need?"

Folding the Sunday paper under his arm Walter headed for his favorite upholstered chair in the parlor to read. Walking to the parlor he warmly clucked out loud like a chicken, he knows that that is exactly what Lilli will be hearing tomorrow. Chuckling he thought, well we'll be having a lot more eggs and chickens, I guess. Heading into the kitchen Lilli hears his clucking as she too laughed out loud.

Settling down he heard the sound of dishes being set on the table, pots and pans placed on the stove as Lilli prepared their Sunday dinner. Lighting his pipe and inhaling he relaxed as he opened the newspaper and began to read the headlines.

But then his ears perked up, he heard something unusual, something he hasn't heard in a long time. Slowly lowering the newspaper onto his lap and removing his pipe from his mouth he quietly listened intently.

The weather outside is cool, not yet cold though the sky is a deep blue and the suns angle has lowered creating darker and longer shadows on the ground. It is autumn, the leaves on the trees outside have turned from dark green to yellow, gold and reds, yet he is hearing his wife's voice singing a song, a song usually heard in the winter, a seasonal winter song. He has heard this song before; he has sung this song before. As he quietly listens his eyes mist over as the gentle soft notes of Silent Night resonate throughout his home. She was singing Silent Night. Yes, he thinks, Lilli was singing Silent Night as she made their dinner. Resting his head back he closed his eyes letting the sound of Lilli's voice and the words from her heart wash over him as he breathed in deeply knowing that right now in their home, right at this very moment, all was calm and all was bright.

Early the next morning Lilli couldn't wait to rise. Full of energy and ready to clean the bedrooms from top to bottom, she quickly gets dressed in her oldest house dress. Choosing an apron with deep pockets she pulls the bib over her head and then reaches behind to grab the strings and ties a double knot in them, saying silently, "I do not plan on retying this all day."

Because of her mother's lessons, and how Lilli remembered learning them, she always enjoyed housework. However, today was different she was truly happy and excited to get her home in order for her potential new guests.

Quickly she gathered up her tools for cleaning making several trips up and down the stairs carrying an assortment of wet and dry mops, cheese cloth rags, buckets for water and cleaning solutions, a pine smelling detergent for the woodwork and floors, vinegar to mix with water for glass cleaning and soft flannel rags for furniture polishing with butcher's wax and Borax for scrubbing. With each step up the flight of stairs she thanked her mother for teaching her this process and for teaching her to take pride in the tasks ahead.

She knew that when all was done the rooms would sparkle and shine, they would smell clean and be dust free and of that she would be proud. Lilli already felt good about the job she had done and the home that reflected her efforts.

Heading into the first bedroom she quickly looked around and did a mental inventory of the steps before her. Then she began, taking her long-handled duster she automatically turned to the left and working around the room circling to the right, top to bottom she wiped down the corners, the walls and the woodwork. Secondly Lilli squeezed out a wet cloth from her bucket of pine smelling detergent and wiped every piece of woodwork in the room. Next, she cleaned the glass windows, polished the furniture, mopped the floor and worked her way right out of the room. Turning to look back at her efforts, she smiled. It felt good to do this and to see the amazing results.

Then she was off to the next room, as the tried and true process began all over again.

Before long Lilli's stomach growled, as the sun shone brightly into this beautiful sparkling clean and shining bedroom. Looking up at the windows Lilli noted, "Well, since my stomach is growling and the sun is shining right in here it must be almost noon, it's time for lunch."

Running down the flight of stairs to the kitchen she heard the front door knocker banging on the door, wiping her hands on her apron she headed to answer it wondering who was calling.

As Lilli opened the door her face brightened in a huge

smile for standing there with a large dish of cooked pasta and gravy was Catisemma, she too was smiling and wearing her apron. Throwing the door wide open Lilli almost knocked her friend over trying to hug her and take the proffered meal at the same time.

"Thank you, Thank you so much! This is perfect, I have been so busy this morning cleaning that I hadn't even thought of dinner tonight, Walter will love this.

Catisemma walked in and inhaled, "It smells like a hospital in here, so antiseptic." "I know," Lilli replies, "Don't you love it?" Catisemma laughed out loud as she grabbed Lilli's arm saying, "I need a cup of coffee do you have some brewed?" Together they walked to the kitchen arms around each other talking and laughing like the dear old friends they had become.

As the coffee was brewed Lilli told Catisemma about the church, about meeting the Norton's, the family with so many children, about the chicken farmer and his eggs. Catisemma listened intently and thoughtfully, when Lilli was through, she looked at her intently as her eyes became pensive, "Lilli, "she said, "I think we might be talking about the same farmer."

Remember, when I told you that Arturo and I delivered the boxes of clothes and dolls to the families sheltering the orphans? Remember I said we went to the house of a chicken farmer? Remember the one who comes to East a Bost with the eggs and chickens?" Lilli's face scrounges up as she tries to remember, but shaking her head she said, "Oh gosh, Catisemma, there has been so much going on, I don't really remember. Why? Is that important or something?"

Shaking her head, no, Catisemma replies, "No, not at all,

just curious, I don't know how many chicken farmers there are that come to this area, probably a few anyway. Well, I guess if you want chickens and eggs, I can ask the one that I know if he covers this area the next time, I see him in a week or so."

Finishing her coffee, Catisemma looked around the kitchen smiling, and then she said, "So show me what you have done so far. You have turned this house into a beautiful home Lilli; it looks so different from just last week."

Jumping up from her chair Lilli couldn't wait to show her friend the bedrooms she has just recreated from drab empty rooms into darling little suites. Climbing the stairs Lilli began to let Catisemma in on the plans she and Walter had for opening up their home to orphans.

Looking at the first beautifully appointed bedroom, with the perfectly starched lace curtains on the windows, the iron and pressed hand crochet doilies on the dresser and night stand, and the beautiful quilt pattern of pink, yellow and green butterflies on a black background spread across the twin four poster bed. Catisemma nodded her head approvingly as she looked around. Not wanting to upset or disappoint Lilli, Catisemma carefully weighed her thoughts before asking, "Um, Lilli, this is perfect for a girl, it's just beautiful and so feminine! But tell me what if you take in boys?" Without missing a beat, turning she opened the steamer trunk located at the foot of the bed, reached in and pulled out a large blue and black plaid quilt. Holding it up for Catisemma to see she proudly stated, my mother made this one many years ago, so if we get boys well, we are all set, I actually have two. We just change the pinks to blues and voila. Catisemma looked at Lilli and laughed saying, "Talented woman, I didn't know you spoke French too. But you know Lilli, somehow, I see a little girl in this room, I don't know why, maybe it's the sunshine, maybe it's the air. I just sense it, that's just what I see." Then turning to exit the room, Lilli takes Catisemma's hand saying, "Now wait till you see what I've done to my sewing room too." Leaving the bedroom, she looked at her friend, as a smile appeared on her lips she said, "Catisemma, I have a mirror, it was my grandmother's and maybe her mother's too. I am so grateful that it wasn't broken when Uncle Herman sent it to my mother from Germany or when we moved. There is something about this mirror, just wait until you see it."

"People may not remember exactly what you did, or what you said, but they will always remember how you made them feel."
- Maya Angelou

31

COMMITMENTS

*T*he bright October sun gave the allusion of warm temperatures outside, but she knew better, grabbing a heavy sweater Catisemma quickly wrapped it over her shoulders, shoved her arms into the sleeves and buttoned it up. Mother Nature had played this trick many times before, pretending to treat with a warm bright sun but trick with a cold blast of wind from the northeast. In the summer though, when the sun was bright and the temperatures high, the winds soft breeze brought the earthy smell of molasses from the North End. Even though the pungent smell might be comforting the memory it brought was tragic and heartbreaking.

Opening the back door from her kitchen, Catisemma was startled by the darkness of the stairwell, with no light from the outside and the bulb at the top of the landing broken the back stairs were dangerously curvy, dark and steep. Catisemma was careful cautiously holding the railing with her left hand, as she walked down from her second-floor apartment. In her right hand she carried a heavy swill pail full of peelings and food scraps from last night's dinner and this mornings' breakfast.

Reaching the landing she opened the heavy door and stepped outside, the contrasting brightness of the sun startled her eyes causing her to momentarily close them tight. Opening her eyes and not looking forward to this task, she inhaled a deep breath and held it as she stepped onto the lever lifting the lid off the in-ground garbage can sunk in a hole just outside the back door.

"Yuk!" she uttered noticing that the garbage can was almost spilling over the top. She was determined that she was not going to put her hand or foot into this swill to push it down. Trying not to look into the swill she dumped her pail of scraps right on the top, then, she saw them, thousands of tiny white maggots crawling all over everything, the leftovers, the scraps, the sides and even outside of the garbage can, it was full with them. She was prepared for this, but it always wrenched her stomach and made her gag. Lifting her foot and checking her shoes she quickly slammed the lid down hard. Stepping far away from the crawling, slithering maggots, she looked up through the bare branches of the trees in the narrow alley which separated her house from her neighbor's before letting herself exhale, then she took in a deep breath, glad this chore was done for today.

Looking through the leafless branches she noticed that she saw all the way through to the clear cloudless deep blue sky. Even in the bright sun she shivered drawing her shoulders up and shaking her head she predicted a forecast, "winter she's a comin, she's a comin soon!"

Then taking a second glance down at the bursting garbage pail she turned looking down the street as she stretched her neck hoping to see the garbage man's horse driven wagon at any moment coming around the corner.

Yes, she reminded herself, today was Wednesday, this was his scheduled day. Checking out her swill pail's interior and making sure she has completely emptied its contents into the larger full garbage can in the ground she thought, Ok, garbage and rag men today then farmer tomorrow.

Musing she paused, tomorrow that's right, I've got to remember to ask him if he goes to the Forest Street neighborhood in Boston. Crossing her fingers, she quietly prays "Please don't let me forget this, Lilli would be so disappointed; she's really looking forward to getting a delivery of eggs and chickens from this farmer. I probably shouldn't have said he was the best; why do I do that? I don't want her to be disappointed. I know how particular she can be. It must be the German in her. Catisemma chuckled, at this thought, for she knows her dear friend very well.

Then she turned heading back in and climbs up the dark wooden flight of back stairs to her apartment on the second floor. Today she will be working on a very special velvet and satin holiday dress for one of her wealthy customers from the north shore of Boston. As she reached out in the dark feeling for the railing, she chuckled thinking of her friend Lilli and of the chore she just completed she uttered, "Das Gut. So, I guess I speak German too."

Entering her small but immaculate apartment she was

pleased with what she saw. Reminding herself that this was a long way from where she once was. " I know, I call it my shack, but it's not, it's not a shack, I know a shack. This is not a shack. I know that. I'm a lucky woman, this is a nice home. I make a nice home for my man; I like it here. I like it in America." Nodding her head, she thinks, this is good. Again, her thoughts go to her friend, Lilli as she smiled and repeated, "Das Gut."

Entering her kitchen, she walked over to the large black and white soapstone sink, deposited her pail and thoroughly washed her hands. Grateful for this habit, taught to her long ago, at another time, in another land. Next to Godliness, Catisemma was taught cleanliness and she practiced both, each in her own way. She quickly walked through the entire second floor, three and a half rooms. Heading to the front of her apartment she turned right and entered a small but neat sewing room just off the brightly lit parlor with its three front facing bays. Stopping for a second to enjoy the brightness and light these windows offered she smiled. "Light," she said out loud, "I love these windows; they bring in so much light, a home needs as much light as possible."

Entering her sewing room, she pulled up her chair and sat down in front of her trusted old sewing machine. Immediately picking up where she had left off, she placed the side seams of the heavy blue velvet dress under the threaded needle. Then she pushed the treadle back and forth binding together the two separate pieces with a strong even stitch.

Engrossed in her work, Catisemma hadn't noticed that the bright sun had moved from the east to the west high in the sky as her room was bright with sunshine. Looking up she was distracted from her sewing hearing the familiar call of the local rag man. As usual he was sitting atop his wagon, driving his horse through the streets calling out, letting everyone know of his arrival. She smiled recognizing his sing song call, "Rags, rags, any old rags. Rags to buy, rags to sell. Any old rags." Noticing the sun was at noon she thought, well, at least he's on time today.

She was glad that she chose this room for her sewing; it wasn't too big nor was it too small. At one time she had thought that it would be perfect for a nursery, but now she understood it will always be her sewing room. Catisemma particularly liked this room because of its one large window on the front of the house, which faced southwest and received sunlight from late morning to early afternoon.

But even more important than the sunlight, was that the front porch was directly under the large window, so whether the window was open or shut it allowed any conversations or discussions to be easily heard from her vantage point above. Equally important, if there was any noise, disturbances, or announcements, on the street below, such as the rag man today, even a disagreement among neighbors, or a problem of any type, she wouldn't miss it. Only recently, Catisemma had heard her neighbors speaking of the case of two Italian immigrants, a Nicola Sacco and Bartolomeo Vanzetti, both had been arrested, charged with armed robbery and murder. This was frightening because she and Arturo had noticed an escalation of hostility and suspicion against Italian immigrants in their city. Confidently, she did not anticipate trouble for her or Arturo and all of the neighbors tried to watch out for each other, protect each other and didn't want any problems in their neighborhood. From Catisemma's vantage point in her sewing room along with sewing, she kept her eyes and ears on anyone and anything unusual that happened on her street. Being aware of what was going on in her neighborhood was serious business, for both her, her neighbors and her man.

Florence had needed him this morning, but he was running very late from his deliveries today. He didn't know what to do, he couldn't change his route. He hated to leave with her crying the way she had, but he had to go, his route was waiting, his customers expected him, if he didn't leave when he did, he wouldn't get home until late and he wanted to be home before dark.

The hastily written letter she had received from her family back home had changed everything. They had written that they needed to leave their village in Northern Ireland. There were serious troubles, describing a potentially life-threatening situation. They needed a sponsor in America, a place to stay, a family, a house to live in until they got situated, they expected Florence and Fred to sponsor them. They had to leave as soon as possible. There was no question, they needed help and they were dependent on their relatives in America to help them; there was no doubt, there were no questions, this is what family does. This was their obligation, their commitment, they were blood.

Marion had heard them talking, she was holding her breath, watching them now, they didn't see her but she was standing in the doorway of her little room. This was her room; she even had a baby, her baby doll on the bed just like before, she had named her Baboo. Could all of this be taken away again from her? She stood sucking her two fingers and curling her hair with the other hand, trying to hold in the tears which were welling in her eyes.

She didn't want to leave, not again, she liked them; they were nice to her, she was warm and not hungry anymore. Yes, she missed the other children but she was afraid, she didn't know where they were. She didn't know where they had gone. Where would she go, she was afraid of the trains, oh no, please don't put me on those trains she thought, I don't want to go on a train, the older kids said that you never came back.

Her heart started beating faster, it was becoming harder to breath, what happened to you when you left, what happened? How come no one knew? Maybe she should just leave, run away. She could do that," I 've heard of other kids running away. But how do I run away? Where do I go? Where do I run? What does it mean to run a way?" all of these thoughts and questions ran through her head.

She remembered hearing about some of the kids that had left the orphanage; she remembered hearing stories about them running away. But they seemed older; they seemed smarter and tougher than she felt. They had what she had heard were street smarts but she didn't know how you got street smarts or where you got them. She was afraid all over again, her tummy started to hurt, she began to shake all over just like before.

After Fred had left that morning, Florence began walking towards the bedroom door and Marion stepped back so she wouldn't think she was listening. But she saw her; she saw her face, saw the tears and the trembling lips. She bent down reaching out to hold her, to take her in her arms and hold her tightly. No one had ever held Marion that tenderly before, not that she remembered.

As Florence's arms wrapped securely around Marion's small body, she heard sobs, deep wrenching sobs, sobs which came from the deepest recesses of Marion's soul. Marion looked up at Florence, thinking were these sounds coming from you and then no, she knew, they weren't coming from Florence, they were coming from her. These heart wrenching sobs, sobs of abandon, sobs of fear, sobs from the pain of hunger, of long cold nights, of hands touching her, hurting her and of despair, they were all coming from her. They were always there, now they were escaping from the deepest pit in her soul. She thought she had locked them up many years ago; but the lock was not strong enough, they were always at bay waiting, just waiting until they could escape.

Now they were flooding, pouring out, released, they had escaped and she would never be able to lock them back in again. She trusted Florence and Fred when they said that they would take care of her, she believed they would. Laying her head on Florence's shoulder now wet from her tears, Marion thought, I believed you; I really, really believed you.

Sobbing Marion snuggled her wet tear stained face deep into Florence's neck, soaking her shoulder and dress with her tears. Her small fingers weaved a path into Florence's auburn curls cradling the nape of her neck, as she began curling her own hair and Florence's strands together binding the auburn and blond hairs into one. Holding Marion tighter than she had ever held anyone, she heard the child's soft voice whispering, as she pleaded in her ear, "Please don't leave me, please don't send me away again, please keep me, let me stay!"

Florence held Marion in her arms for what seemed like hours, soothing her, wiping her eyes and nose, rubbing her back, holding her tightly, rocking her back and forth, and telling her that everything would be all right. They would not abandon her, she was not going on a train, and she was not going back to the orphanage. Florence didn't know how, but she knew that she would not betray this child and that somehow, someway everything would be fine.

Torn between her loyalty to her family, her commitment to family expectations and her devotion to this beautiful little girl that she loved she forced herself to believe that a solution was possible.

She knew that their home wouldn't be big enough for everyone, not with her family coming over from Ulster; they needed to be sponsored, to have a residence, a family to take them in, and a place to stay. They were family, they were blood. There were no other options, there were no other choices, it had to be her and Fred, she couldn't say no. If she said no where would they go? What would happen to them? She knew too that when they came it meant that the state would take Marion back, they wouldn't let her stay too. They had rules and one of the stipulations was that she needed her own room, and she couldn't share with other people. They just show up, they checked on her regularly, they would know and they would take her away. Looking up to the heavens above, Florence's mouth moved as she silently prayed saying, Please God, help us, help little Marion. She needs a home God, she needs love. Please help us."

The bright sun of Wednesday had given way to clouds and drizzle on Thursday. Having spent most of the day in her sewing room Catisemma stretched as she looked outside surprised at seeing how quickly it was becoming dusk. He hadn't come yet; she wondered if the farmer had forgotten his route, maybe he wasn't coming after all. She would have to go into Hay Market Square on Friday to the push cart vendors for her chickens and eggs.

She had done that before, the eggs were fresh, but sometimes they tried to sell you the cracked ones. She always checked her eggs even though the vendors tried to hurry her along. She noticed that often those cracked eggs were pushed off onto the younger women, it especially happened to the ones who might not know better. But when she saw the cracked eggs she would say, "Don't buy those, they're not good. "Of course, the vendors would glare at her, telling her to mind her own business, repeating her message she ignored them.

Arturo had told her what to say in their native language, he told her that these words would shut their mouths but she didn't; she knew what the words meant. She knew that their prices were fair and if you were careful you could get good deals. But it was just more work, you had to be more diligent watching the vendors. She knew with the farmer that everything was fresh and she didn't have to second guess what was being put in the bags, especially on the bottom.

Then she heard him, she heard the cart and his voice with the soft Irish lilt, as he called out, "Get yer fresh eggs and chickens here, get yer winter squash, tomatoes and late corn here. "

Jumping up from her sewing machine she looked out the window and there he was coming down her street. She saw several children running out to meet him followed by their mother's calling out for him to stop.

Catisemma laid the velvet dress carefully across her machine and ran down the front flight of stairs from her apartment and onto the front porch. All the while crossing her fingers as she kept reminding herself to remember to ask him, remember to ask him about Forest Street.

"Becoming requires equal parts patience and rigor. Becoming is never giving up on the idea that there's more growing to be done."
- Michelle Obama

32

BOSTON, MASSACHUSETTS, 1921, HAIRPIN TURNS

The cold, pelting rain, blew hard from the northeast hitting the window panes like the sound of a thousand small pebbles. Lilli slowly rocked back and forth in her chair. Her fingers were wrapped around the steaming, hot cup of tea, holding it snugly in her hands as she took sips and listened to the sound of the strong staccato beat. It's early in the morning, she and Walter have made a plan, today she would take the El into Boston, to State Street and file the papers they have completed.

But this morning she is having doubts, she is unsure of their decision, of this decision. Yes, she knows, they've talked about this for a long time. They've thought about this for years, but really, she wonders are we ready for this, what experience do we have? Do we even know how to care for, or how to raise and support children or even a child?

She's no kid anymore, she tells herself. She will be 40 years old in a few months. She has been married for over 20 years, Walter isn't young anymore either, he is 43.

She wonders is this is too much for us to take on at this time in our lives. When my mother was 40, I was 22 years old she reminds herself. I was a grown woman, I was married. "What are we thinking?"

Leaning her head back and lowering her hands into her lap she rocked, slowly moving forward then slowly moving backward. For several minutes she just rocked back and forth, back and forth. Then she asked herself, "Why am I so afraid? Why am I hesitating. What is it that is stopping me? I've changed things in my life before. I've made choices before and was never this hesitant. Why this time?"

Closing her eyes, she continued to rock letting her breathing and the motion of the chair come together until the rocking and the breathing were one. As Lilli slowly inhaled, she rocked backward and as she slowly exhaled, she rocked forward. In tandem, she and the chair rocking and breathing, slowly inhaling and slowly exhaling together they rocked.

Moving together new questions come to her, what if we do nothing? What will change? What if we wait? What if something happens to Walter or to me? What if I stay home today, I can drop off this paperwork another day, it doesn't have to be today. The what ifs continue piling up one on top of the other, there are so many of them, she is feeling overwhelmed and becoming paralyzed by all of the what ifs.

Then as if from deep in her soul new questions arise, ones which she hadn't expected and wasn't prepared to answer. She heard the questions in her head yet they were coming from her heart. "What if Lilli, what if you had stayed in Germany and had never left? What if you had remained in the old country and never left the security, the safety or your past? What if nothing had changed Lilli? What if?

Suddenly, the chair stopped rocking, as Lilli gazed outside at the pelting rain, she heard the wind rattling the windows, as a cold draft blew through the fragile glass panes causing her to shiver with goose pimples. Looking through the rain streaked window at the blurred view outside, she saw clearly, she had her answer.

All of a sudden, her doubts and worries were lifted, like rays of sun breaking through a cloudy sky Lilli was confident, she was sure and she was determined. Yes, they will go forward, this was a decision they had made, it was the right decision. They had already taken the first step, they completed the paperwork, the ink had dried, and the next step begins today.

Getting up Lilli looked at the mantel clock, and placed her cup in the sink; she then quickly put on her rain coat, grabbed her umbrella and headed outside. Opening the umbrella, she turned down Forest Street, heading to the Dudley Street Station to catch the elevated train to State Street.

Buffeting the wind, she quickly reached the station. Running up the rain-soaked stairs she waits standing on the station platform, as blasts of cold wet wind swirl around her legs and hard driven rain slams pelts of icy cold wet drops onto her stockings and shoes.

Glancing around Lilli observed the morning commuters, many with their shoulders hunched against the weather, some facing the interior wall were reading their newspapers, some leaning against the center poles had their eyes closed, and some stretching precariously over the edge of the platform as if by watching they could will the train to arrive sooner.

She noticed the large glass store window of Ferdinand's Furniture Store facing the platform, it displayed a wide assortment of top end home furnishings, looking at the display she thought, I just might come back later to this store, I like what I see.

Feeling the cold wind and rain hitting her legs she thought of how fashions had changed. Remembering that twenty years ago, her dress and coat, would have covered her legs all the way to her ankles and her shoes would have been laced tight up to her calves. I like the new fashions, she thought, there was a certain freedom to them but there was obviously some benefit to being all covered up too, certainly, a lot warmer and dryer she lamented. Who knows, she pondered, maybe that style will come back some day? Fashion, it comes in and goes out, I guess everything does she thinks, that's good, it keeps me in business.

Then she heard it, the loud ear piercing shrill of the elevated train's wheels screeching and squealing as the inbound train took a sharp hair pin curve as it entered the Dudley Street Station.

Hearing the loud sound of the squealing wheels, Lilli can only imagine the dangerous curve and sharpness of this turn, which required the engineer to take it very slowly and carefully as the engine pulled the line of coupled elevated cars into the station.

Seeing the train slowing down to a stop, the commuters rushed forward pushing Lilli along with them, but she hesitated, pausing to look back at the row of connected cars and wondered, had a train ever fallen off of these tracks, had the speed ever been too fast or the rails too wet, that a car might slip off the tracks hanging and maybe falling onto Washing Street below? She hadn't heard that it had happened, but she wondered could it? What would she do if it did, what could you do? What would they all do? But before she could ponder this thought any further, she was pushed forward again through the open doors and into the car itself.

Standing in the center of the car looking around she was quickly offered a seat by a young man as he folded his paper and politely stood up. Lilli thanked him as she sat down taking his seat, she crossed her ankles and placed her hands on her lap and observed the busy morning ritual of the city's many commuters. As the train lurched, pulling forward in starts and stops, she sat patiently, trying not to bump or bang into her fellow passengers. Traveling through the series of stations the conductor announced the approach of each and every one until her ears picked up and she heard his voice announcing that the next stop was State Street.

Quickly getting up, Lilli excused herself, as she moved through the crowd of standing commuters and headed out onto the platform. Not being familiar with the location she stood in the darkened, damp and smelly, underground subway station looking around before finding the sign above a stairway marking State Street, the way to her destination. With a smile on her face and her heart beating, she approached the stairway and using her umbrella as a cane she climbed them two at a time.

Reaching the sidewalk, she blinked, the brightness of the light outside causing her to squint. Realizing that she hadn't noticed the extreme darkness of the underground subway until she had reached the light at the top of the stairs, and headed out.

The rain had let up but the wind was still blowing cold as it appeared that the clouds were breaking up. Looking up at the sky Lilli thought, well maybe this was a good sign. You just never know she told herself; I'll take any good omen offered.

Getting her bearings, she noticed that the walk wasn't far and before she realized it, she was standing in front of a black wrought iron fence, a long stairway, and looking at the bright gold dome of the Boston, Massachusetts, State House.

Holding some of the most important papers she had ever held in her hands, Lilli took a deep breath and said, "Well, here goes everything family, I hope you're with me, I need you beside me right now." As tears filled her eyes, she blinked them away knowing that she was not alone and that she had the courage, the strength and the support to do this.

She knows that her parents are walking with her right now; that Henry is beside her and Uncle Herman is at the top of those stairs, she was not alone. She reminded herself that she and Walter could do this. They came from a long line of ancestors who had taken chances, had altered their lives by making changes and broken barriers. It takes courage to change, to go off the beaten track and to begin anew again, but she wasn't the first one in her family to do this and she knows that she won't be the last one either. We can do this she encouraged herself. We can change, even better our lives and by doing this maybe better the life of someone else too.

She knows that this is a good change; this is an opportunity to change a life not only for them, but for a child who might otherwise not have a chance. This is a chance for them all, a chance for everyone. Maybe we'll start with one child; we can do that, one child at a time.

Lilli drew in a deep breath clutched the papers to her chest, and starts to climb the steep stairway heading into the building with the bright golden dome. All of a sudden, she noticed a shadow beside her on the stairs, the sun was coming out, the blasts of cold wind had abated and the clouds had parted, it looked like today was going to be beautiful after all. Well Lilli thought, I've heard this about New England, if you don't like the weather, just wait a minute. I guess that change is truly a natural occurrence, she thought.

A smile crossed her face as she opened the heavy doors and entered one of the most historic and oldest building on Beacon Hill, the Massachusetts State House. Abruptly, she stopped as she looked around, taking it all in. Standing on the marble floor she slowly twirled looking at the panorama of the pictures, murals and statues of political leaders and events. 'This is magnificent," she says, "truly magnificent." Lilli was awed, thinking of the history in this building, so much had happened under this dome, so many changes, right from the beginning of this country. Yes, I'm at the right place at the right time she told herself. Walking from door to door she read the various office signs looking for the Department of Public Welfare, Division of Child Guardianship. Then she saw it, it was at the end of the long corridor of closed doors. Lilli approached the thick, heavy wooden door, and read the sign printed in bold black lettering on the glass out loud, for a second time, hearing her voice quiver.

Gathering her courage, she stood still for a moment, then

slowly inhaled as she drew her shoulders back and reached for the shiny brass doorknob. Her fingers tightly gripped the solid, circular doorknob, as she began to turn it.

Easily, the thick, heavy door opened, for a moment Lilli was taken aback. The door, now ajar, Lilli glanced at it with a raised eyebrow, as a small smile spread across her face, much like her father's; without further hesitation, she confidently stepped forward and entered.

"To live is to change, and to be perfect is to change often."
- John Henry Newman

33

THE ART OF CONVERSATION

"This is too hard!" she complained to Walter as they ate dinner, "It's been over a week and we haven't heard anything. Should I go back in there tomorrow? I'm really nervous, what if they didn't like us? What if we didn't answer the questions correctly? Oh God, what were we thinking?" Pushing her chair away from the table Lilli exclaimed, "This is stupid; we should never have even considered doing this. Why did we even do this? I wish we had never begun this process; I can't take the wait." Lilli grabbed her napkin from her lap and wiped her eyes as tears fell onto her face.

Looking up from his dinner plate of delicious beef stew Walter purposely and calmly placed his fork down before responding. Seeing how distressed she was he patiently replied, "Lilli, we are probably not the only people applying, they probably have quite a few applicants like us and they are doing the best they can. We wouldn't want it to be rushed; we want them to be deliberate and cautious, we want it to be right too. Let's give it another week, ok? The holidays are coming and maybe nothing will happen until after the first of the year. We have to be patient Lilli. Please try to calm yourself down; we know it won't do any good to get all upset. It will only make you a wreck and neither you nor I want that to happen. Please my Liebchen trust me. It'll be ok, everything will be ok."

Sniffing and trying to gain control of her emotions Lilli agreed with Walter. Looking across the table at her devoted husband she smiled letting him know that yes, she will try to be patient, yes, she will try to calm down and yes, she will try to let this process play itself out. However, still looking across the table directly at him, Lilli knows that this is going to be hard as she reminded herself, I'm not always the most patient person; patience had never been one of my strong characteristics like Walter. "Darn, why didn't I learn that one from my mother." she muttered under her breath. Now it is Walter's turn to look across the table, but this time he turns his head to the side as he picks up his napkin and tries to cover his mouth. Trying not to laugh out loud he holds it to his face as he stifles a chuckle. "I heard you!" he tells her smiling, "Trust me; I've often wondered that exact thought myself." Now they are both laughing as the tension which only shortly before had filled the room faded.

The following morning Lilli is working in her sewing room on the second floor of her home as she heard a voice calling out. Placing the winter coat, she was sewing across the top of her machine she got up and looked out of the window. "Who is this?" she asked herself, "What is he saying." Opening her window to hear clearer Lilli noticed that the wagon was being pulled by a horse and it was filled to the top with vegetables along with cages holding live chickens. "What and who in heaven's name was this?" she asks rhetorically as she turned to go down the stairs and opened the front door.

Once outside on the veranda Lilli called out, "Hello, um, excuse me, who are you and what are you selling there?" Calling out, "Whoa" and pulling the reins back telling his horse to stop, the man in overall jeans, a plaid shirt and a soiled wide brimmed straw hat looked over at Lilli. Speaking loudly he told her, "I'm a farmer, about a week or so ago one of my customers in East Boston suggested that I take my wagon down here in this neighborhood, but especially Forest Street, she said that I might find some customers who were interested in fresh killed chickens and fresh picked vegetables. I don't know any names but if you are interested, I can show you what's in the wagon."

Lilli remembered that Catisemma had mentioned a farmer and that his vegetables and chickens were excellent. "Yes, I am, I am interested. Just wait a minute, I have to run inside and get my money but I'll be right back out."

Climbing down from his seat Fred walked to the side of the wagon to straighten out the tomatoes, onions and potatoes, beets and cabbages. As Lilli walked forward, he turned smiling and he offered his hand saying, "Hi, my name is Fred." Taking it, Lilli noticed not only the many hard calluses but the strength in his handshake. My name is Lilli Vetterlein she offered back shaking his hand.

Looking directly at her he asked, "So tell me Mrs. Vetterlein, what are you thinking about serving to your family tonight or tomorrow night for that matter. I can kill the chickens fresh for you right here or you can kill them yourself.

Just so you know that when you chop off their heads the body will continue to run around the yard for several minutes, headless." Lilli's mouth opened as he continued in a matter of fact manner, "It all depends on what you want and what you want to see. Also, the vegetables are freshly picked probably the last of the season though. We'll be having a frost before long maybe even this week, but we have some in cold storage that I can bring during the winter if you like. We also have fresh eggs and I've got a pig which I will be slaughtering this winter. Many of my customers are giving me orders for the holidays, so I can take that too if you want, the holidays are right around the corner."

Lilli instantly liked this man; she liked his easy way and his willingness to find out what she wanted today and what she might need in a couple of weeks or even a month from now. She could tell he was paying attention and listening. He reminded her of her father, an honest businessman, offering the best for his customers and knowing that by doing just that he was keeping his business going too. She also noticed a bit of a brogue; it was different than what she had heard before but definitely Irish or Scottish, her memory quickly went back to Emma's shop, and to her experience with Bridgette. But she reminded herself to keep an open mind, remembering I know what it's like to be judged, I know what can happen when someone makes a quick judgment based on one experience. "Well," she replied, "It's just my husband and myself, so I won't need a lot but I do like to serve fresh chickens and fresh vegetables." Pointing to some tomatoes, beets and potatoes she tells him, "Let's begin with these and yes, definitely a chicken. If you don't mind, I would prefer that you kill it."

"Yes, of course." He said and turning to his wagon he opened the chicken cage and taking the chicken by its neck he quickly cut its head off and placed the body back into the cage as the blood oozed from the headless bird. Then he wiped his hands on his overalls, wrapped the chicken in newspaper and offered Lilli the bagged vegetables and the dead chicken.

Lilli reached into her pocket to pay him as she noticed that he was looking up at her house. Pausing she asked, "Is something wrong?" "Well", he replied, "If you don't mind me asking, you mentioned that it was just you and your husband, right? "Lilli nodded her head. "Well that's a big house for only two people, do you rent rooms out or something?" Stepping back and taking in his full measure Lilli wondered, do I tell him what we are planning to do? It's none of his business, but he just seems so open and it is an honest question. "Fred," she began, my husband Walter and I were hoping to offer some rooms in our home to orphans, I mean wards of the state. You know some of those children who lost everything during that fire a while back at the orphanage. We've heard from other people that some may be sent on the orphan trains and that some may be placed in other orphanages. We don't have children, we always wanted them but it just didn't happen for us. We want to help and are looking for a way to make it happen. We've just moved here and our friends Catisemma and Arturo they live in East Boston suggested...as Lilli continued, he is no longer hearing her words, as his eyes widened and his hand went to his mouth. Lilli stopped talking, quickly asking him, "Are you all right?"

"I am, I am, but you are not going to believe this. I mean my wife and I know your friends, she's from Italy, she is Italian, she's the reason I came to Forest Street. She told me that there was someone here who would be interested in what I sell, but I thought it would be an Italian person, like she is, but I guess not, it must be you. I shouldn't have assumed, should I?"

Nodding her head Lilli replied, "Oh, my gosh, yes, that's me. Catisemma and I have been friends for many years, too many to count. She and I met when we both lived in Brooklyn, New York. We worked together and now here we are again practically neighbors."

Fred looked at Lilli and then back at her house, too many thoughts and questions were running rapidly through his head. He paused, taking a breath before he resumed speaking. "Well, then you know that Catisemma and Arturo were at my farm. They met me and my wife Florence. They were giving out boxes of clothes to the folks who took in the orphans after that fire. They brought in clothes and a doll for a little girl who's staying with us. She was one of the orphans that lost everything."

Now Lilli too takes a deep inhale, pausing before speaking as she recalled the conversation with Catisemma a while back about just that little girl. "Yes." She says, "I remember that she said there was a little girl at one of the homes, Catisemma was quite taken by her and really enjoyed meeting her. I think she mentioned a doll or something that she gave the little girl. She couldn't remember the little girl's name though, she said it was different not a common name.

This time a wide smile appeared on Fred's lined face and his eyes sparkled as he told Lilli all about Marion. Lilli couldn't help but notice how his facial lines and weather worn features softened as he shared about how he and Florence knew of Marion long before the fire.

Marion didn't know him or his wife, but she would always wave at him when he brought the eggs and vegetables to the orphanage. He told her that according to one of the staff members she had been left there many years ago, abandoned at the orphanage door on a cold wet night, when she was a baby, maybe just two years old or so. Shaking his head, he repeated softly, almost to himself, "Left on the cold, wet stone steps, with no note, no explanation, no information, nothing." Pausing, he continued as he puffed out his chest like a proud father, "Well, she's about 7 years old now, has a very sweet disposition, blond curly hair which she likes to tangle in her fingers and the prettiest green eyes. I have to admit but I am very fond of her but it's Florence, my wife, she's in love with her, totally enraptured. Every day she tells me that she had never met such a sweet child."

His eyes moistened as he went on to say, "We were hoping to adopt her, we don't have any children ourselves so we've been hoping to have her stay with us. "But then his countenance darkened, as his head shakes, he continues telling Lilli about his wife's family in Northern Ireland and the dilemma they are having. "I don't know what to do or how we will do it. We never counted on this happening." Dropping his head down. Lilli had listened in amazement, how did this happen, I was just buying vegetables and a chicken when now I've heard all of this. Looking up she wondered, was this Divine Providence?

Lilli realized that suddenly the atmosphere around them had become silent, that she and Fred had finished talking and the two of them were standing there staring at each other with their mouths opened. Fred begins saying, "I don't know I'm not sure if anything can come of this but I have never experienced anything like this before. Maybe this can all work out. If you would like to meet Marion or if you think it's best to go to the State House and request a meeting first? I don't know, but maybe we can make everything work out so that Marion is safe, happy and secure. That she lives with a wonderful family, and my wife's' family can come over from Ulster and finally, you may be able to have the family you always wanted. Taking off his hat, Fred scratched his head adding, "I know this is crazy but sometimes things just work out, the universe moves in mysterious ways, my mother always told me that and now I know that she was right. Actually, Mrs. Vetterlein, she was very smart, my mother I mean, she told me to marry Florence. I'm glad I did, she's a much better reader than I am and definitely a better cook." he says rubbing his hungry stomach. "I'm good at math and farming, but she can read really good."

Lilli suggested that she take his full name and address along with Marion's full name. She couldn't wait for Walter to get home from work, she couldn't wait to tell him about this amazing and wonderful conversation that had just happened.

Shaking hands again and this time it was much more than a perfunctory hand shake it was a handshake that held friendship, trust and hope for both of them. As Fred jumped up back into his wagon he turned to wave and smiled again at Lilli. Then looking up the street he saw several other "women of the houses," waiting patiently for him, giving a shake to his horse's reins he ordered, "Ok, Tippy, let's go, I think this is going to turn out to be a very good street, I'll have to bring more apples to keep you going, Tippy my girl, let's go."

Watching him as she stood on her front steps she waved back calling out, "See you soon, yes, we will definitely see you soon."

Turning, she ran up the steps and headed for the kitchen, placing the bag of groceries and headless chicken in the sink, before she entered her parlor and dropped into her rocking chair, feeling it's support all around her. Lilli's heart was beating so hard she thought, "My heart is going to burst right out of my chest." Smiling, she began slowly rocking, back and forth, back and forth.

Don't be afraid to delve into the big picture. Think big thoughts. Do not just embrace Beauty. Be embraced. Let the whole grasp you in its mystery and hold you spellbound with divine possibilities.
  - Patricia Adams Farmer

34

PUTTING THE PIECES TOGETHER

*L*ooking back at the day's events he reflected, today had been a long one at work, it was one of those days when 6:00pm couldn't come soon enough.

Standing at the train's door as it opened, he threw his trench coat over his shoulder as he quickly walked down the stairs from Dudley Station and headed home to Forest Street. His leather brief case was heavier than usual tonight crammed full with blueprints and plans, along with the evening newspaper. From early in the morning he had spent the day working on the new and unique features of his building project.

It is the building that Arturo had mentioned to him. It was his ideas and the building designs which brought Lilli and him to Boston.

This will be a state-of-the-art building, a place that will function as a school, a recreational facility, an infirmary, along with supporting administrative services and providing the comfort of home, safety and shelter for the youngest and most vulnerable in this society, children.

This will be the new orphanage, a new type of orphanage; it will not be a place where children are warehoused like many other facilities but a place where these children will want to call home. Here they will be nurtured, they will learn, grow and thrive.

This was an idea which came from tragedy and began in the local communities; it began as a quick conversation in the churches and the synagogues with the members, the parishioners and the congregants all wanting to do something. Then it grew, as it took form and an idea became a reality with everyone wanting to do something and to do it together.

Everyone was committed, everyone wanted to help, so through fund raising, through pledges and through philanthropic gifting the money was raised. They did it, they did it all and as they had planned, they did it together.

The financing was unique, there would be no mortgage, the funds had already been pledged, everything had been budgeted according to precise specifications. The plans for this building were state of the art and the future was bright.

Walter was working with cutting edge ideas, new products and designs along with innovative caring partners. On most days he found the work exciting, energizing and intense. But tonight, he was tired; all he wanted to do was get home, to sit down, put his feet up and relax but as he turned the corner, approaching his home, he began to fear that these plans might go awry.

Looking up, he saw his house, he realized that something was different, usually the front porch light was turned on illuminating the stairs and the front door but tonight all the windows were bright as every light in the house was lit.

Stopping abruptly, he questioned, what's happening, it's not Christmas time unless I'm Rip Van Winkle and have just slept 100 years. Picking up speed, he bolted up the front stairs and called out, "Lilli, I'm home, where are you?" There was no response, then he called out again, "Lilli, where are you? "Wrinkling his nose, he inhaled, sniffing for an aroma to determine what's for dinner as he walked into the kitchen. Standing there he stopped short, there was no aroma, nothing was for dinner, nothing had been prepared, there was not even a plate set on the table.

First, he was disappointed, then concerned and finally curiosity registered on his face as his stomach growled expressing its distress. Now, this is crazy he thought, leaving the kitchen he walked back out to the entry hall, standing there quietly he looked around and then he heard it, the rumble of the sound of Lilli's feet rapidly moving the treadle petal on her sewing machine back and forth over his head.

Bounding up the flight of stairs to her sewing room in the front of the house he saw her, her back was to him and her head was bent down, her shoulders were hunched over her machine. Her feet were moving quickly, pumping rapidly, back and forth, back and forth focusing on one thing only, a child's red velvet dress with eyelet lace hanging from the cuffs and yoke. She was leaning into the material, squinting as she sewed the button holes along the back with the precision of a surgeon.

Quietly, standing there in the doorway, he took a long slow look around his wife's sewing room, her personal inner sanctum. This was the place where she found solace and this was the room, which he knows, she still shared with her mother.

He looked at the many boxes, the baskets and the accessories which came from their home in Brooklyn. He also saw many of the items which had come from her mother's home in Germany then too in Brooklyn.

Looking over to the corner he spotted Lilli's reflection in the six-foot-tall, large gilt-edged framed mirror which leaned against the wall. It was standing straight and tall, guarding this room as if it were a sentry, just like it did in Brooklyn at her mother's apartment, and before that in her grandmother's home in Germany, almost a hundred years ago. Now, it reflected Lilli, watching over her in this room, as it had done for so many years before, in other rooms, thousands of miles away.

Even though Lilli's sewing room was large, he felt as if the room was full, but not with boxes, thread and material, it was something much different. Then it came to him, he understood that this room was indeed full, but not only with sewing items. Lilli was sharing this room with her mother, her grandmother, her great grandmother and so forth. She was sharing it with all of the generations before her, no one had ever left.

They were all here, together in every stitch, in every seam, each time the scissors were lifted or a needle was placed, each time a button was chosen or smocking designed. It was their guidance, their teachings, their nurturing love which held and guided her hands. And now he knew, he understood, as again he looked deeper at Lilli's reflection in the mirror and this time, he knew far many more reflections were looking back.

Not wanting to disturb her he quietly stepped aside but

continued to watch, looking around he saw the room differently now, yes he saw the several large sewing baskets each brimming with spools of thread, pin cushions, silver thimbles, and scissors of all kinds not only for cutting but also for the most unique and decorative trimming.

He saw the remnants of material folded neatly on top of the chest and he knows that the drawers below contain even more cherished pieces of linen, silks, corduroys and plush velvets.

Nothing was discarded, because everything was valuable, from the smallest piece of a triangle cloth to a large bulky ream; everything had a purpose and a destination.

So many times, when a piece was nearly finished Lilli would remember one item, one type of lace, one type of ribbon or one package of buttons which would be the piece de resistance for her finished project.

Finding it she would remember where it came from, when she last used it, why it was important then and why now again it was needed. And when she found it, she was satisfied, she knew her masterpiece would be complete and she was finished.

Looking around he realized how in this room everything had a purpose, everything was valuable and everything was important. Just like the orphanage he was building everything and everyone, was important, slowly he nodded his head. Suddenly he was less tired, no longer fatigued or hungry, he felt energized. Leaning against the door jamb he smiled as he continued to watch Lilli.

Standing there for several minutes he started to wonder how long it would be before she realized he was there. Not wanting to startle her he softly coughed, no response, then more loudly he coughed, again, no response, now not knowing how to interrupt her, he then gently knocked on the door jamb. "Yikes!" Lilli screamed, turning as she jumped back and placed her hands over her heart.

Lifting her feet from the treadle she looked up at her husband and smiled with a rather sheepish grin on her face. "Gosh you're home already? What time is it anyway? What day is it? I guess I lost track of time here in my room."

Walter was slightly confused and concerned now, not knowing how to approach her as he remained standing in the door way, then he simply asked, "Um, Lilli are you ok? You look different? Do you have something to tell me? Is there something I should know? You are ok, right? You're not pregnant right, are you? Lilli, are you pregnant or something like that?"

Not saying a word, she pushed her chair back, and just kept smiling. Then placing the dress on the side of her machine she stood up, walking over to her husband he noticed there were tears in her eyes.

Reaching out he took her hands in his as he locked his eyes with hers and pleaded, "Lilli, please tell me, you look different, are you ok? Is everything ok? Has something happened? Please tell me now. You're not pregnant, are you?"

Standing there with that Mona Lisa smile on her face she nodded saying, "Yes, Walter, everything was fine. Actually, everything was amazing! I will tell it all to you, please come down stairs with me while I put together something for us to eat tonight and I will tell you all about today."

As Lilli headed down the stairs Walter took her hand,

drawing her back closer to him, he looked directly at her and asked, "Tell me now Lilli, are you pregnant?"

Not responding right away, her eyes moistened, she tilted her head to the side and replied, "Not quite, Walter, I'm not pregnant not really pregnant. Now come on down to the kitchen with me and you can help by pulling the feathers off the chicken while I begin to make dinner."

His mouth dropped open as he tightly gripped onto the banister for support and balance as he followed his wife down the stairs and into their kitchen. Just before he entered the kitchen he stopped, "Lilli, I need to know how you can be not really pregnant? I need to know now." Turning to look at her husband she replied, "Then you had better sit down."

"The other side of anger, if we experience its emptiness and go through it, is compassion." - Charlotte Joko Beck

35

CHOICES

Sitting and pulling the feathers from the chicken's cold lifeless body Walter felt grateful for this job he had been given. Having plenty of practice he knew from past experience that to do this task completely and efficiently one needed to focus, have a plan, a direction and a process. This is good he thinks, he is tired and knowing that to sit idle as Lilli explained in minute detail the events of the day would have been difficult. Focusing on the chicken, the feathers and the plucking he was able to not only listen but also to hear everything as he tried to digest it all.

When she was finished the chicken was completely plucked too. Feeling as if she had explained the events of the afternoon sufficiently, wiping her hands on her apron. Lilli crossed the kitchen floor. Anxiously she waited for his response, she pulled up a chair next to Walter, sat down and waited. After several seconds, she began to become impatient, she placed her hands in her lap and asked, "So are you thinking what I'm thinking? Do you think it would be possible for us to meet this little girl? We have the bedroom already you know. We can do this right away; we have to do this right away."

Before he could answer Lilli continued, "Walter, you understand especially if she is going to be taken away from the farmer and his wife and placed again in an orphanage or even put on a train and sent out west. We might never get to meet her. She might be gone. It could be happening right away. "

He opened his mouth to reply but, as her heart beat faster, she continued talking, "So, do you think we should contact the authorities before any of that is put into place? How do you feel about this? Are you ready? I can go tomorrow morning Walter; I can hop on at Dudley and take the El into the city.

This time Walter reached out, raising his hand, gesturing for her to pause. Nodding her head, she stopped talking inhaled and closed her eyes as tears dropped onto her cheeks.

Now it was Walter's turn to speak, "Lilli, I know you've been thinking about this all afternoon, but this is the first time I've heard of any of this. I hadn't even known we were having a farmer drive his wagon down Forest Street. Let's pause for a few minutes before we decide to do anything. Who is this farmer anyway? We don't know anything about him and we don't know this little girl or anything about her. I wasn't sure we wanted only one child and I think it is really up to the authorities to decide who goes where and with whom.

Lilli, I'm really not sure, I didn't think it would be happening this quickly. Don't you think we are rushing it a bit; maybe he just wants to pawn this kid off, maybe she's difficult or a problem or even trouble. We don't know anything about her Lilli. You don't know what you could be getting us into."

Lilli stared at him, her mouth wide open, her hand had risen to her mouth and she is was staring at him. Now she wasn't breathing at all, she felt the beat of her heart pounding hard in her chest. Her other hand lay still in her lap frozen in time as she just stared at her husband, shocked, she had never expected this response.

As Lilli's breath came back her face began to redden and her eyes narrowed, replying she said, "Walter, are you serious, are you telling me that you do not intend to open our home to children who are in need? Are you telling me that you expect me to wait any longer before I can offer my home to a child? Are you saying that if an opportunity like this was in front of us, if we could work with this farmer and his wife and shortcut the process, you still plan to go to some stinking bureaucrats and let them handle it? That Walter will take years and by God I'm not waiting any longer!"

Angrily, Lilli abruptly jumped up from her chair, as she violently pushed it back into the table and turned to walk out of the kitchen to the front porch. Walter heard the front door shut with a slam and for several minutes he just sat there. He didn't move, he didn't respond, he just sat there and felt his heart beat rapidly in his chest as he heard his own heavy breathing and felt it pulse in his ears. The kitchen was devoid of all sound, except for his breathing.

This was how he always responded; this was how he always reacted. This was how he had always handled conflict, when he was a young boy living with Aunt Frida and their combined families, when he came to America and lived with his Uncle Paul and his large family and always with Lilli. He always paused before responding, giving time for his emotions to slow down and letting his words be measured and even. This was the lesson he had learned from his father, who learned it from his.

He knew that by reacting quickly to your emotions, by letting anger take control, raising your voice, allowing your heart to race and your breath to become short, that slamming doors and letting hurt feelings or harsh words lead your actions then most likely words will be said that are not meant, hearts will be broken that may never mend and people who trusted you may never be able to trust you again.

Shaking his head, his voice soft and low, "I've seen much too much anger in my life to have it here, I won't have it here in this house, not in my home, not here." Walter knows that he had upset Lilli. He understands how hurt and disappointed she was. "I'll talk with her." Nodding his head, he told himself, "I know what I have to do."

Taking in a deep inhale he slowly stood up and walked out of the kitchen, heading for the front porch. Just as he was reaching for the door knob, it turned as the door slowly opened in front of him. She was there on the outside; he was on the inside; they were standing directly in front of each other. At this moment, both of them know that they had choices, the choices were in between them, a formidable wall separating them from each other. It could remain there or they could take it down, this very minute. It was their choice. It was standing right there in between them, this can end right here, right now, or it can continue for as long as the anger, the hurt and the disappointment chooses, planting itself and growing in this fertile sacred space.

But they understood how both of them have been through too much in their lives to want this to continue. Lilli looked up at Walter and saw that his eyes too were moist. She sees the pain in his face and the hurt reflecting from his eyes back into hers.

Shaking his head, he looks down replying, "Oh God, Lilli I must have disappointed you so much, I hurt you tonight, I am so sorry. I didn't realize, but now I know that all day you had been anticipating me to come home, to tell me about this opportunity this possibility, which you had been thinking about and when you did, all I could offer you were obstacles.

I am so sorry, please forgive me. Yes, we need to talk about this and yes, there is most likely a process but let's go forward with this together.

We'll start with a meeting, a meeting with the farmer and his wife, and we'll meet with this little girl. Then we'll go to the State House and get this process started. Maybe she can be a ward of the state, at our house, maybe we can give her a home until we decide what we want to do next. I don't know what I was thinking or afraid of, I'm not sure why I hesitated, but we are one on this Lilli, we will do this together, I know that we are ready. Please forgive me, Lilli."

Reaching out to place her hand on his face Lilli can't stop the flow of tears falling from her eyes as she tells him something he already knew, "Walter, all I ever wanted us to be was a family, a real family Walter, that's all I have ever wanted for us.

Walter, as adults we have choices, we make decisions that impact our lives every day, that little girl doesn't get the chance to make choices; her life will be impacted by the decisions we make. Let's make the choice to give her a chance, if it doesn't work out then it doesn't work out. But we deserve this opportunity too, maybe with one child or more, Walter and you know she deserves it."

Smiling at his wife, Walter tells her, "You're right but right now I'm really tired Lilli, it's getting late, do you think that chicken can sit on the ice in the ice box until tomorrow? Let's have some oatmeal and go to bed, it really has been a long day for both of us. We'll get all of this ironed out tomorrow, ok?"

Looking at her husband and wondering how only minutes earlier she was so angry at him, Lilli exhaled and agreed. Taking hold of her hand, together they head to the kitchen.

Lilli and Walter get it, they understand the want, the desire and the need that they have harbored for so long to have a family. This desire is bigger than both of them, this need has become their mission and they will accomplish their mission, they will have a family.

Then Lilli turned and looking directly at her husband she smiled as she told him, "By the way Walter, I really was ready to go to the mat for this with you, you know that don't you? I was ready!"

Standing in the open doorway to the kitchen, Walter looked at his wife of over 20 years and nodded his head, "Oh Lilli, yes, I got that, I saw that, and that's what made me change my thinking. I understood how important this was for you and I know how you were prepared to fight anyone, anywhere, to make this happen not only for a little girl who doesn't even know us but for us, Lilli. I just want you to know my Liebchen, whenever I am down, whenever I am out and whenever I need someone at my back…I want you, for there is no one better and no one I would trust more than you! So, umm, how long is this oatmeal going to take?"

Lilli was up early the next morning, she had a plan; first she would go into Boston to see if anyone had already looked at their paperwork, secondly, she would speak to them about Marion's situation. Heading out she checked her pocketbook one more time to make sure she had all of the information she needed; satisfied she locked the door behind her and headed to Dudley Station for the El. This time she was prepared for the screeching and squealing of the train as it rounded the precarious corner entering the station. She was becoming a professional subway commuter when it came to entering and exiting a crowded El. Holding her head up, clutching her pocketbook in her arms, she moved forward onto the crowded car her heart beating full of hope, anticipation and optimism.

Later that day, as Lilli walked down the flight of stairs into the subway, heading home, she thought, "Well that wasn't as bad as I had feared." Her pocketbook, stuffed full of new papers, which she and Walter needed to complete was securely tucked under her arm. Appearing like a professional commuter, Lilli stood on the subway platform, waiting for the outbound El, she felt a sense of confidence wash over her. Tonight, she would reiterate everything to Walter, as they ate the wonderful chicken dinner, she had planned for them. Lilli thought that Walter deserved a good dinner, since he hadn't eaten a full meal in two days, he would definitely be hungry. Boarding the crowded train, she held on to the overhead bar, half listening as the conductor's voice announced the station's stops. Her fingers gripped the bar tightly as her body balanced and swayed with the train's rhythm. Staring out the window, her reflection looked back at her. Hypnotically, she watched as blurred images sped by. Then suddenly, but for only an instant, she saw him, her father's image smiling back at her.

"So, Fred you have to explain this to me again," Florence requested as she put three dinner plates on the table. "When you came home from work last night you were exhausted, so I figured we could go over this tonight, after you had a good night's sleep."

Shaking his head and drawing in a deep breath, he slumped in his chair, as he began for the second time. "Ok, I'll start way back, at the beginning. Remember, several weeks ago, when the Italian woman and her husband came by with the box and the doll for Marion?" Florence nodded, as she pulled out the kitchen chair and sat down at the table. Looking over at the stove she told Fred, "The spuds will take in only a few more minutes, hurry up, I'll just sit down here." Nodding back in agreement, Fred continued, "Well, she lives in East Boston, and is one of my customers on my route." Florence nodded again, glancing over at the boiling spuds and the burner flame shooting up. "Ok, so I am delivering the chickens and vegetables and she asked me, if I also took the wagon over to the Dudley Street area. I told her that I had some customers on Cottage Street, and Wendover Street, but if no one else had laid claim to that route than I would give it a try, to see if it was worth the distance to cover more areas."

Again, his wife nodded, got up and walked over to the boiling spuds, to turn the gas jet off. She then walked back to her chair and sat down, saying "Ok, go on." Drawing in another deep breath, he continued, "Okay, here is where it gets a bit confusing and even harder to follow. So, as you know, I went over to the Dudley Street area and went down several streets. I got a good bit of business and plan to include that area in my route now, weekly." 'That's it?" Florence asked. "No!" he laughed, "Let me continue, so as I went down Forest Street I'm yelling out that I have chickens, spuds, tomatoes and that stuff, when a window opened up on a really big house and the "woman of the house," poked her head out asking what I'm selling. So, I yell up, that I'm a farmer and I have vegetables and chickens, if she is interested. She says she is and rushed out." "So that's it?" Florence asked again, getting up to drain the spuds and began to put pieces of chicken on their plates. "No," he says again, "Let me finish!"

Looking at her husband, with a twinkle in her eyes and a sly grin on her face Florence responded, "Fred, is this going to take all night? It seems like a very long story." He glanced up at his wife and nodding his head he replied, "Bláthnaid, you know, it just might, so sit yer arse down." She sat down, and began to listen intently. When Fred had completed his story, his wife blessed herself then quietly stood up heading for the stove.

After several minutes, she nodded at her husband and called Marion to the table. All three of them held hands as they bow their heads to offer grace. Florence's soft voice with her Northern Irish lilt began in Gaelic saying "A Dhia," thanking God for the food on the table, as Marion looked over she quietly mimics but in English "Dear God, thank you for the meal we have tonight."

Once the prayers were offered Florence smiled at Marion and gave Fred a look of expectation as he repeated, "So her name was Mrs. Vetterlein, she seemed very nice and she bought a chicken and some vegetables, she mentioned that it was just her husband and herself that lived in that big house, but they are applying with the state to open their home to orphans and wards of the state. Pointing to Marion with his fork he explained, "So I told her about Marion here and about your family coming over from the old country."

At that point Marion dropped her fork and looked from Florence to Fred and back again. Her mouth dropped open as she can't believe what she is hearing, tears come to her eyes and she begins sniffing to draw them back but she is finding it hard to breath. With a look of shock on her face Florence stares at Fred and asks him, "Tell me again how you found out she wanted to take in orphans. "Reaching over to console Marion he begins again, "Well, the house is very big and when she was telling me what she needed for dinner she mentioned that it was only herself and her husband but that they planned to open it up for children who needed a place to stay especially because of the fire at the orphanage a while back."

Now she is beginning to understand the direction that the conversation was headed.

Feeling compelled now to get to the point; he placed his fork down as he looked directly at Marion, "I had to tell her, this Mrs. Vetterlein, she seemed like a really nice woman, I had to tell her about you, Marion, I had to let her know. I told her that we had a wonderful little girl staying with us but that we knew she couldn't stay with us forever." Florence was looking at Fred as tears filled her eyes; she sees that his eyes too are becoming moist.

Marion stoically placed her fork on the table, breathing in deeply she drew herself up straight in her chair, expressionless she looked directly at Fred. It's happening again, I have no control, she told herself, I have no choice; it will be whatever they say. Looking from Fred to Florence she wondered how long this would go on, how long must I do whatever anyone else tells me, when will I be able to make my own choices, my own decisions? I'll wait, but when I grow up no one will tell me what to do, no one! I'll decide what I want and no one will make my decisions for me; I won't be ordered and pushed around. No one will tell me what to do, ever again, no one."

Florence, gently placed her hand on Marion's shoulder and looked directly into her eyes saying, "Marion, I love you, we love you, I want you to know this, Fred and I love you very much. We will never leave you; you will always be part of us. Things are changing here at our house; my family, my relatives from Ulster are coming to America, they need a place to stay, our home is not big and they need your room to stay in. My family needs to stay here for a while, we have to let them live with us. They have to stay Marion, but before they get here, we will find a place for you, a place for you to stay, to be safe, we will not let them send you away, and we will not let you be far from us.

Believe me, Marion, we love you, we always have; we want the best for you, you deserve that Marion, please trust us."

Knowing, that trusting them is all she can do; she has to believe in what they have told her. Marion's lips are closed together tightly as she looked from Florence to Fred, then looking down, she nods her head.

What choices do I have she thinks? Quietly she picks up her fork to finish dinner but notices that now she isn't hungry, she has lost her appetite and simply wants to go to bed, go to her bed, in her room with baby Baboo. Baboo is waiting for her, she had told her that she was coming right back and she was, Baboo trusts her and she won't let Baboo down.

"Blithe little song-sparrow, friendly cheery, Fearlessly, sociably caroling near me, varying ever the song that you sing, Yet always a run in it, Always the sun in it. Always good news in the greeting you bring." - Anonymous

36

THE VISIT

They knocked on her door early that morning, there had been no call, no letter had been sent; there was no notice, they just showed up.

It's early; she's in the kitchen, washing bed linens, her hairs pulled back tied behind her ears, her sleeves are rolled up to her elbows and she is perspiring.

"Let them wait." She told herself, the wash tub was full of hot sudsy water and she had just begun pushing a heavy, thick bed sheet through the rollers, slowly squeezing the soapy water out. Startled by the knock she turned as her fingers moved precariously closer to the rotating, thick, tight rollers, they nearly became squished. Looking down she yelled "Yikes!" as she quickly yanked her hands back. Hearing the knock for a second time, she shook her head as her lips pinched together. "It's Monday, wash day. Who is this now? Frowning she let out a heavy sigh questioning, "Who could be knocking on my door now"?

Not only was she startled, but she was also now annoyed, she will have to pull the sheet all of the way out, turn off the machine, the water will cool and then she will have to begin the process all over again.

Shutting the machine down she shook her head and exhaled as she muttered, "This is very annoying, it better be important." Wiping her hands on her apron she headed out of the kitchen, down the hallway and into the front foyer.

Seeing 3 shadows through the amber glass panels she stiffened as she reached out with a damp hand to grab the door knob. Turning the knob quickly she opened the door. Startled at what confronted her Lilli straightened up to her full height, wiped both hands on her apron and without a smile, looked at her intruders coolly asking, "Yes, how can I help you so early on this Monday morning?"

The two men and one woman, stand on her veranda, looking directly back at her; there was no apology, nor do they offer a greeting or an explanation. One man, the tallest one, removed his hat, exposing his bald head and introduced himself as Mr. James Fee; the second man wore round spectacles which made his large round face appear as round as the harvest moon or maybe a Halloween pumpkin. He immediately brought the tips of his fingers to his hat's brim feigning a polite greeting, then offered his moist, soft thick hand for her to shake. He identified himself as Mr. Davenport with the Commonwealth of Massachusetts. Standing back, a step or two behind the men is a female, she was a small woman, with dark hair pulled tightly back in a bun at the nape of her neck, she was the only one who smiled, it was a slight smile but it brightened her whole face and when Lilli saw it she let out a long slow exhale.

Mr. Fee appeared to feel satisfied that Lilli had enough information as without saying a word, he slowly reached into his coat pocket and withdrew several papers. Reaching out his arm, he handed them over to Lilli. She took the papers in her damp hands, which were shaking slightly and read them quickly; looking up she handed them back as she opened the door wider, gesturing for them to enter.

Anxious and feeling compelled to remove her apron Lilli showed them to the parlor and requested that they take a seat. Turning to head back into the foyer she reached behind to her back and untied the apron strings, quickly entering the kitchen to hang it on the pantry door.

Walking back into the parlor, her heart pounding so fast, she's certain they can hear it. Too nervous to sit, Lilli stood next to the mantle by her fireplace, folded her arms across her chest and looked at them, then waited patiently for someone to speak. After several seconds of uncomfortable silence, seeing that they too are looking back at her, she wet her dry lips, swallowed and asked, "How can I help you this morning, what do you want to know and what do you want to see?"

It was Mr. Fee again who began, "Well, Mrs. Vetterlein, you and your husband Walter, have petitioned the Commonwealth of Massachusetts to open your home to wards of the state, is this true?" So many thoughts are swirling around in Lilli's head, before answering she thinks darn; I wish my mother were here. Why didn't they tell us they were coming? Why didn't they let us know? What if I wasn't home? Why are there three of them? Walter needs to be here too; he should be here. This isn't fair I feel outnumbered. Why am I so nervous?

Knowing that they are waiting for her reply, Lilli drew in a breath, glancing at all three of them before responding, she replied, "Yes, my husband and I wish to open our home to wards of the state, particularly children who are indigent or have been made homeless by the recent fire at the orphanage. As you can see this is a large house and we have several rooms available. "

Having responded articulately, Lilli exhaled, relaxed her shoulders and smiled, her father's smile. All of a sudden, she didn't feel alone, she knew, she was no longer outnumbered, her smile widened and they too are smiling back at her. Her heart's rapid beat slowed down, as she unfolded her arms and leaned back against the wooden mantle. Then, looking to her left she saw her chair, her rocking chair and moved to sit down in it. Immediately, she noticed how calm she felt, how confident and comfortable, as her chair imperceptibly rocked back and forth.

The next question was from the female, she identified herself as Miss Sparrow, an assistant; she took notes as Lilli responded to the questions. But as Lilli was responding she was thinking, what a curious name, sparrow. Why you even look like a little sparrow, bobbing your head up and down with each question. Your little eyes darting up, staring at me, then quickly back down to the papers. Then she realized that Miss Sparrow had repeated a question, shaking her head slightly, Lilli brought herself back, telling herself to focus and answer.

Yes, she and Walter have been married since 1901; it is the

first and only marriage for both of them. Yes, they tried for many years to have children. Yes, she will take them to look at the rooms available. Yes, she will show them the entire house. Yes, her husband is gainfully employed as an architect. There are more questions, they want to know what brought them from Brooklyn, New York then to Boston. Are they American citizens and for how long? What country were they born in? When did they come to America?

Lilli became aware that some of their questions became perilously close to asking about their patriotism during the war, but not quite. They also asked about the church they attended and noted that it was a Baptist church. They asked about friends and associates and took notes asking for the spelling of Catisemma and Arturo's last name and where they lived. Then they asked to see the house. Lilli guided them as they walked through the rooms. Miss Sparrow furtively continued to take notes but Lilli observed that she is nodding; a smile crossed her face as she looked into the room that Lilli indicated was for a little girl. Lilli thinks, her eyes are small and dark but they hold a sensitivity that penetrates right through her. She was beginning to like Miss Sparrow.

Finally, it was over; they told her that they had all the information they needed. Standing at the front door Lilli asked, "How soon will it be before we hear from you?" Again, Mr. Fee, responded, "Well, Mrs. Vetterlein, you have given us a lot of information, we need to go back to the office, review you and your husband's profiles, check out with the church and look into your associates and friends, then a judgement is made."

Lilli nodded, understanding that he had not quite answered

her question, but before she let them leave, she needed to give them some information and then to ask them one more question.

Quickly she requested, "I have another question for you, do you have a moment?" Stopping they stood on the veranda, nodded and wait, patiently. "Well, recently my husband and I have become aware of a certain situation. We know of a little girl one who was in the orphanage where the fire occurred. She's currently staying with a family, they are a good family, but they may have to let her go due to responsibilities and commitments, out of their control. As you see, we have rooms here; we can take her in right away. She's been through so much, I can take her in here, I mean Walter and I, we can open our home now. It's ready now, we can welcome her here so she doesn't get moved around to another orphanage or even something else." Lilli let the something else hang in the air between them; she knew, what she meant and looking straight into their eyes, she believed they did too.

Without making a commitment, Mr. Fee nodded his head slightly and turned, to leave. Lilli reached into her dress pocket and pulled out a paper, "Here is her name, and the people's names where she is staying." She handed it to the only person who reached out a hand, Miss Sparrow. Lilli waited by the open door, again her heart was racing, beating loudly in her chest. She noticed how the men squared their shoulders and held their heads high, as they walked down the front stairs.

She noticed too, that Miss Sparrow was hanging back slightly; then she turned looking back at Lilli with her small sharp dark eyes. Conspiratorially, she raised her left hand connecting her thumb and pointer finger together making the universal symbol "ok" offering a small smile back. Then she quickly turned and ran down the stairs, to catch up with the departing men.

Lilli's heart burst, "Oh God, my heart hurts, pounding so hard, I'm afraid it's going to jump right out of my chest." Her hands were shaking with nervousness as she quickly turned, and headed back into her house.

Shutting and locking the door behind her, Lilli almost ran towards the parlor, her whole body was quivering. She was trying to control so many emotions, that were rushing through her. She felt as if she had been hit by lightning, her skin tingled, and the hairs on her arms stood up.

Grabbing her rocking chair, she collapsed into it, and closed her eyes, but she could not stop the tears as they flowed, she began to cry.

Lowering her head onto folded arms, her entire body shook, as she sobbed, she couldn't stop. She couldn't stop the tears, as they rushed out, they broke through the dam which had held everything back. This powerful, solid, dam, which Lilli, had been building all of her life, was breaking down. It was crumbling, right this very moment, she couldn't hold anything back. The tears, the sobs, the shaking, the cracking of her dam it was all pouring through. She had held everything in, so much, for so long, now, she wasn't even trying to stop it, she let it go, releasing everything, all of it.

Her tears, sobs and shaking unleashed, everything that had been held in, all that had been held back, for so very long. She couldn't hold back, she couldn't stop it, Lilli let it all out, releasing, everything, as it poured from her body and soul.

"I have arrived, I am home." - *Thich Nhat Hanh*

37

THE GATHERING, NOVEMBER, 1921

The buttery delicious aroma of a Thanksgiving dinner filled their home. Early in the morning Lilli had put the Turkey and stuffing in the oven as a warm heavenly scent filled the air. Turning the gas jet on the stove top, Lilli placed a pan of Farmer Fred's winter squash on the burner, she added pinch of salt to the water and struck a match to light the flame. She then adjusted the flame on high, setting the water to boil. Lifting up the lid of a smaller pot on the stove, she reached for her wooden spoon, and gently stirred the mixture of tiny red berries, orange slices, sugar and water as her delicious cranberry sauce simmered. Confident that everything was cooking to perfection, she turned and walked out of the kitchen, to the dining room doorway and stopped. Lilli stood there, taking it all in as her eyes softened. She looked nostalgically into this beautifully appointed room.

The entire room sparkled, the Thanksgiving table was covered with her mother's cherished handmade lace table cloth, the linen napkins, a gift from Emma Shapiro so many years ago and the de Haviland china, her grandmother's, from the old country. Lilli had retrieved the linen napkins and lace table cloth from the packed boxes weeks before; delicately she washed them gently by hand laying them out on the grass to whiten and dry in the bright October sun. This was a household task taught to her by her mother who had been taught by her mother and Lilli planned to teach this someday to her daughter.

Leaning into the door jamb her head moving slowly left and right, as the memories came rushing in. So many dinners, the scent of heavenly aromas, the sounds of silverware clinking, the sparkle of crystal, the laughter which hung in the air, but mostly it's the faces, smiling, looking right back at her. Her eyes moisten with sadness, but she was enjoying this moment, this was a blessed memory, and she was cherishing it all. She knows they have never left her; they never will.

These memories, this nostalgia she is feeling, will not dampen her mood, she knows that today, this afternoon they were making more memories; creating moments in time, which tomorrow, will become part of this bright glistening mosaic, that was shining on her right now, shining in her dining room not only today but for all of her tomorrows.

Feeling a peaceful sense of calm, she smiled as she turned to walk back to the stove. A melody wafts by her, a catchy tune which she recently heard on their new kitchen radio. The song was by a popular singer, Ethel Waters. Doing a quick two step and swinging her hips to the rhythm of this hit song, she chuckled as she repeated the words, "There'll Be Some Changes Made."

In the distance she heard a knock on the door as Walter shouted," I'll get it." Laying his pipe in the ash tray, he headed to the foyer. This time he sees them, the figures through the amber glass panels, one tall and wide and the other much shorter and smaller. Seeing their silhouettes through the oval glass panels, he smiled and paused before he opened the door. Turning he hollered back to Lilli, "Catisemma and Arturo are here." Opening the door with a flourish he greeted their old friends.

Bending forward, from the waist, Walter offered an exaggerated welcome as he waved his arm in a flourish saying, "Entrez- vous, s'il vous plait." Arturo stepped back allowing his wife to enter first as she smiled and greeted Walter with a peck on the cheek, then headed directly down the hallway to the kitchen. Tilting his head and looking at his friend, Arturo grinned and asked, "So you're adding French to your repertoire Walter?"

Shrugging, Walter sheepishly stepped back, his face opening in a wide grin. He watched as upon entering, the large, muscular form of Arturo filled the doorway.

Quickly Arturo reached out, roughly grabbing Walter's hand as the men offer each other hearty handshakes. Pointing the way, with his loose hand, Walter directed Arturo to the parlor. Then, walking behind his friend, he shook and rubbed the fingers of his hand hoping to bring the circulation back in.

Immediately, walking into the parlor, Arturo assumed a position of authority, in the center of the room. His hands placed on his hips, he tilted his head and surveyed the entire room, quickly appraising, taking it all in. His eyes looked everywhere, with the expertise of a professional, he inspected the finished carpentry, the quality of the plastering, the interior masonry. Smiling he expressed his satisfaction, and approval of the construction of every facet, of Walter and Lilli's home. Looking over at Walter he nodded saying, "Itsa nicely done, good work here, itsa done well." Walter smiled back, thankful, these words meant a lot from his friend.

Arturo had built castles, he had built banks and brownstones; he knows building, he knows carpentry, he knows construction, and he knows quality.

Giving Walter a heavy pat on the back, he reached into his shirt pocket and pulled out two of his most favorite cigars. Handing one stogie to Walter, and taking one himself, he lit them as they both take a seat and relax. For several moments the room fell silent as each man paused, drew in deeply, then in unison, they exhaled, enjoying their cigars and their accomplishments.

Lilli let out a shout of glee, as Catisemma entered her kitchen, holding a huge pan of pasta, meatballs and gravy. Laughing, Lilli said, "Thank you, but I'm not sure if there were meatballs at the original dinner. Catisemma, nodded her head as Lilli continued, "Trust me I know there definitely wasn't sauerkraut." Turning back to the stove she lowered the flames on both the squash and her delicious sauerkraut. Winking at her friend, Catisemma asked in a mocking tone, "So should we try out that butler's pantry door today?"

But, before Lilli could reply, the door knocker was banged once more and now everyone rushed to greet their new guests. Walter reached first and flung the front door wide open, exclamations of joy rang throughout the house all the way down to its foundation, where they settled in forever.

LILLI'S CHAIR

Standing there with a pan of boiled potatoes, jars of pickled beets and a bag of onions was Fred and Florence, with little Marion. She was holding her doll Baaboo, everyone was there for Thanksgiving dinner, everyone.

Walter quickly invited them in as hugs, kisses and laughter were shared throughout, even little Marion was smiling from ear to ear. Her face shone brightly, glowing with contentment and happiness. She loved everyone here; she loved all of them and she knows that all of them loved her. This was her family; they have promised that she is theirs; they have promised that they will all take care of her. She will be staying here, she has her own room here at the Vetterlein's, she has Catisemma and Arturo to visit in East Boston and whenever she wants to go to the farm or to see Fred and Florence she can. She can also ride with Fred on his wagon. She can meet him every Thursday, Florence will come too, and she can give Tippy all the apples she wants. She can't remember feeling this gleeful before, she can't remember feeling this loved before and she doesn't remember ever feeling this glow of warmth that surrounded her, she knows that she has never felt this way ever.

As Fred was rushed into the parlor by Arturo and Walter, he's quickly offered a stogie and a comfortable chair is pointed out for him to sit and relax. Offering, the upholstered chairs to his guests, Walter happily takes the rocking chair by the fireplace. Florence, Catisemma, Lilli and Marion head out to the kitchen, as Marion passed the dining room table, she counted the table settings and smiled noting that there are eight settings, one for each of them, including Baboo.

Slowly rocking back and forth Walter smiled inhaling the unique blended scents of stogie cigars and Thanksgiving dinner all rolled into one. Then he looked around his parlor, he was sitting with friends, who have become family. He was sitting with new and old friends. These friends, have come from different parts of the world, to build a new life in America, as he and Lilli did. They are all Americans now, and today, together they are celebrating and sharing in a hallowed American holiday.

Taking a deep inhale on the stogie, he remembered back to those years so long ago, when he first came to America, feeling alone and apart in this country, which he had adopted as his own and which now had adopted him.

He remembered wondering if he had done the right thing, leaving Germany. He remembered being concerned about losing his German heritage. But here he was, sitting in his parlor, with friends, who like him, represent different countries, friends, who traveled from distant lands, to come to America for a chance, an opportunity, a promise.

They all brought with them their stories, their heritages and their traditions, they haven't forsaken any of that but they have blended their history with their own new American story. And now, they will add a new story to their lives, they have added Marion and her story will blend with theirs.

Lilli poked her head into the smoky parlor and coughed at the heavy cloud of smoke swirling over the men's heads; laughing she told the gentlemen that dinner was served and that they were to leave their stinky stogies in the ash trays on the tables and open the parlor windows. Grumbling manly grumbles, they drew in quick deep inhales as they obediently followed her orders.

Everyone took a seat, Lilli was sitting at one end of the

table and Walter was seated opposite her, at the other. Arturo, Catisemma and Baboo were on the right of Lilli while Marion, Florence and Fred were on her left.

Looking at her guests, Lilli requested that they hold each other's hands, to say grace. Lilli reached out her left-hand to hold Marion's small hand in hers. Marion looked up at Florence and smiling, reached over to hold Florence's hand. As Florence held onto Fred's, he reached over to take Walter's. Walter took Baboo's stuffed mit, while Arturo holds Baboo's other soft cloth hand, reaching to gently hold his wife's. Then Catisemma, turns her head, looked at Lilli and with tears in her eyes, she gently cups her hand over Lilli's, as their fingers wrap together. In unison they all bow their heads, Arturo and Catisemma bless themselves as does Florence, Walter, Lilli, Fred and Marion bow their heads and close their eyes, as they all begin to say grace. Then Lilli stopped and lifted her head, listening to the most beautiful sounds she has ever heard. Florence with eyes closed began her prayer, speaking in Gaelic, "Daor Dia, go raibh maith agat." Catisemma, is praying in her native tongue, Italian, "Caro Dio, grazie." Walter, at the end of the table, prays in the language he first learned to speak, German, "Lieber Gott, danke."

Then they heard it, a child's voice raised proudly above them all. Stopping, they all listened, to her soft, gentle voice as she prayed in her native language, saying, "Dear God, thank you, for my family, thank you for this meal, thank you for this day, I love you, God, oh yes, thank you too for Baboo. God thank you again for my family. Amen"

In unison, all of the adults repeated Marion's words together, saying, "Amen." Hearing the final Amen, Marion looked up and smiled. She felt a bit bewildered, seeing that everyone was looking at her, they were all looking at her, and they were all smiling at her.

Feeling a bit self-conscious, Marion's eyes widened as she looked over to Lilli asking, "Did I do good?" Looking down at this beautiful little girl, Lilli's eyes blurred, as her voice caught in her throat. Trying to hold back her tears, and swallowing through the lump in her throat, Lilli replied, "Yes, my Liebchen, you did good, you did real good."

In him was life, and the life was the light of all people.
John 1:4

38

SILENT NIGHT

The large Scotch pine tree had been placed on the veranda. It laid against the railing, waiting to be brought in on Christmas Eve. Each time the front door opened; Marion inhaled a whiff of its' fresh pine scent; she had never experienced a Christmas Eve like this one. Dressed in her warm red plaid flannel nightgown, trimmed with eyelet around the yoke with ribbon ties around the back she felt like a princess. Lilli had made it for her and every time Marion put it on, she twirled around saying, "I am a princess, a real princess." Tonight, she was so excited, she just couldn't stand still and was jumping up and down begging, "Please tell me again, tell me all about Father Christmas again, Mommy please."

It was getting late and Marion knew that she must go to sleep, especially for Father Christmas to come, but she just needed to hear this story, this amazing story, one more time. Looking up at the woman, she now called Mommy, she beseeched, "Tomorrow morning, really, the tree on the porch will be in our parlor? Father Christmas brings it in tonight?" Breathlessly, she continued, "and tomorrow morning there will be presents under the tree? Some of the presents will be for me? Will they really say "for Marion," on them? The tree will really be inside our house and it will be covered with apples, oranges, sugar angels, and candles? There'll be candy canes too, can I eat them?"

Lilli laughed out loud, as she pulled Marion onto her lap, hugging her and repeating the story of Father Christmas, again, to a little girl who had never had a Christmas Eve like this one before.

Holding Marion in her arms, Lilli began rocking her chair, which was now Marion's chair, since it had been moved upstairs and placed by the window in Marion's new bedroom.

Even before Marion had arrived, Lilli moved it upstairs. Lilli's chair, her gift from Uncle Herman, had already provided her with so much, that she believed the time had come to share Uncle Herman's gift with her daughter.

Lilli understood that behind Marion's smile, joy and loving demeanor, there existed a child, who had been abandoned, violently abused, and had suffered tragic losses. She understood that the pain Marion held was buried deeply within her. She prayed that Uncle Herman's gift, might provide the sustenance that her daughter needed, as it had for her.

Rocking together, they looked out the front window of Marion's bedroom. A light mist of snow was beginning to fall. The gas lamps had been lit by the lamplighter, and there was a soft golden glow shining in the windows. The mixture of the snow and the gas created a golden haze, giving the illusion of halos surrounding the lit lamps.

Marion was tired; she was sleepy, it had been a busy day. She had decorated the house with Walter, baked cookies and little cakes with Lilli, helping to provide desserts for tomorrow's feast. Again, Catisemma, Arturo, Florence and Fred would be coming. They visited often, all of them. Marion saw Fred on every Thursday when he stopped by with vegetables and chickens.

She didn't like it when he had to kill the chickens, that was always when she walked up to Tippy, Fred's trusted pony. She would rub Tippy' s coat and feed her an apple right from her hand.

Marion liked Tippy, she told everyone that when she grew up, she would have a farm too. She would call it, "Marion's Farm" and she would have goats, horses, cows and chickens. She won't kill the chickens though and she won't let any kids run through the chicken coop. She had heard all about that story and how it took weeks for the chickens to lay eggs again, but some, just didn't lay eggs at all, ever again.

Fred and Florence told her that when she grew up, if she wanted their farm, it would be hers. They also told her about their relatives, who had come over from Ireland, and planned to move closer to the city, eventually buying their own home in Charlestown. Everyone was grateful because it appeared that everything worked out beautifully, almost as if it had been planned.

Marion was told that she was loved, for the first time in her life, they all love her, just like a daughter. When she heard those words, her tummy felt warm inside and her face brightened as she smiled. But if you looked closer you could see that her eyes moistened with tears. She knows they mean it; she trusts that they will always be there for her. She knows they love her and she loves them too. But deep down in her heart she was still afraid, afraid, that like before, all this love would disappear too.

But for now, she had a mother and a father, she's going to stay with Lilli and Walter Vetterlein. They have asked her if she would like to be their daughter, if she would like to stay with them until she had grown up and then when she gets married and had children, they will be grandparents for them.

Marion repeated this conversation to herself every night, before she went to sleep, snuggling in her warm bed, she holds onto Baaboo, smiles and nods her head repeating, "Yes, yes, I want to be your daughter, I want you to be my mommy and daddy." She believed them, but still she prays they are telling her the truth, that they will always be her Mommy and Daddy.

The story of Father Christmas had come to an end; Lilli noticed that Marion's breathing had become slower and deeper. Her head rested heavily on Lilli's breast. Bending down, she tenderly placed a kiss on Marion's still damp, freshly shampooed curls. Inhaling this sweet scent, a distant memory returned. This was not a new scent, she'd smelled this scent before, in the deep recesses of her cells this scent had been waiting. It had always been there, simply waiting. She knew that this was not her imagination, she recognized it and thanked God that it waited. Rocking, back and forth, Lilli smiled, as her breathing too, slowed down.

Outside, the sound of Christmas Carolers filled the streets and in Lilli's semi sleepy consciousness, she heard their voices singing. They were singing Silent Night; slowly the chair rocked, back and forth, as the soft sounds of this beautiful Christmas song penetrated through the closed windows. But then, Lilli heard something else, lulled by the hypnotic rocking, she heard individual voices, she heard voices, that she recognized.

Yes, she was hearing the tune of Silent Night, but now the words being sung were not in English, but rather in German, it was Stille Nacht, they were singing in German.

The atmosphere in the room had quickly changed, nothing was moving, everything was still, even the rocking chair had stopped, there were no sounds, it was all silent, except for the voices.

Lilli listened to them as from outside, she heard a tenor's voice, a beautiful tenor's voice. It was her father's voice, he was singing Stille Nacht, but he was not alone. She heard other voices, too. She recognized them; she knew these voices; she had heard them so many times before. Now, she heard her mother's voice; her mother was singing with her father; it was her mother's high soprano voice. Then she heard them, Uncle Herman and Henry's deep baritones. She was hearing all of their voices, each voice strong and distinct. She heard them all, they were together singing, they were all singing Stille Nacht.

As Lilli listened to the voices from Christmas past, the chair remained motionless. Wanting to continue rocking, Lilli gave it a gentle push, but it didn't move, it didn't rock, remaining exactly where it had stopped.

Downstairs, he heard the carolers too, they were outside, rushing up the stairs he called out to Lilli and Marion. He knew that they had wanted to greet them tonight; they wanted to be at the door.

Approaching the top of the stairs he paused, noticing how quiet the hallway was, there was not a sound, it was absolute silence.

He was awed by the quiet, he couldn't remember when he had ever noticed such peace. Thinking that they must be asleep and not wanting to wake them, he quietly opened Marion's bedroom door.

The room was pitch dark, yet he could see their silhouettes, slipping off his shoes, he entered. They were as one, sitting in Lilli's chair. Their heads were bowed together, on his toes he walked over to the bed and picked up a quilt. Recognizing the feel of it, he remembered that Wilhelmmine had made it many years ago. Turning, he covered his two ladies, securely draping the warm, heavy quilt over them, as they continued to sleep deeply.

Then he stood there, looking down, his eyes filled with tears. As slow and quietly as possible, making no noise, he bent over and kissed them both on the tops of their heads. First, he kissed Marion, his new daughter and then Lilli, his wife of over 20 years. They were sound asleep, they were exhausted, and he wouldn't wake them.

Beginning to leave the room, he turned looking back and noticed how the soft golden glow of light from the outside was now shining on them. Curious he thought, I hadn't noticed that before. Then he saw that Lilli had a slight smile on her face, and he was touched by how much she resembled her father. Nodding to himself he's confident that she heard them, she's hearing the carolers, too, he thinks. Carefully, closing the door behind him and on his tip toes, he picked up his shoes, heading down the stairs to the foyer.

Approaching the front door, he heard their voices clearly, they were outside, in front of the house and they were singing loudly. Their voices singing and laughing were becoming even louder as they noisily climbed the stairs. They had been wassailing tonight; they wassailed from house to house, it appeared to be a good wassailing night.

Smiling, Walter opened the door, ready with mugs of hard warm cider as the caroler's tune quickly changed to "Here We Come A-Wassailing." Raising their drinks, they shouted, Merry Christmas! Walter raised his mug in return "Merry Christmas everyone." he responded, thinking yes, it is and yes it will be.

On October 5th 1922, in the city of Boston, the Commonwealth of Massachusetts, 8-year-old Marion was legally adopted, becoming the only child of Walter and Lilli Vetterlein.

On that day her name was changed, from Marion Willett Andrews, a name she had been given, by a mother she did not remember and a father she never knew, to her new name, Marion Lilly Vetterlein.

"I sustain myself with the love of family."
- Maya Angelou

39

IN HER OWN WORDS, BOSTON, 1987

She walked up the brick front stairs and opened the front door leading into her grandmother's home in Boston. In all of the years, she had entered this house, her grandmother's front door was never locked. The house had been in their family, since 1942, when it had been bought by her grandmother's parents. Calling out, she heard no response. This did not concern her, lately her grandmother's hearing had been failing, so it required you to be looking directly at her when you spoke, this way she could read your lips, pretending that she heard you. Turning the corner, she entered the kitchen, and stepped over Bernie, the St. Bernard, whose large body completely filled the small kitchen area, startling both the dog and her grandmother.

Looking up from her newspaper, she placed down the pen and the magnifying glass that she had been using, for the New York Times crossword puzzle. "Oh, hi, sweetie, when did you get here?" "Just a few minutes ago, Nana, my mom dropped me off, she and Jessica are coming back after they do some errands." Replied her granddaughter, giving her a kiss and a quick squeeze. "I guess you didn't hear me coming in. You really, should keep that front door locked, you know."

Her grandmother gave her a look, easily interpreted as, oh, really, you are so grown up now, you're telling me what to do? She responded, "If I kept the door locked, then you wouldn't be able to come in, because I wouldn't hear the knocking. Now, you know that don't you?"

Her granddaughter smiled, shaking her head, as she pulled over a kitchen chair and positioned it directly across, from her one and only grandmother. Sitting down she began, "So, Nana, I have a school project for my English class, I am hoping that you will help me with it."

Smiling back intrigued, she replied, "English, well that was always my favorite subject, I liked History too, but English I liked the most. What grade are you in now?" "I'm in the eighth grade, Nana," and nodded her head. Everyone, all of her grandmother's children and grandchildren knew, that if they used an incorrect verb, noun or predicate in a conversation with their grandmother, or used an adverb where an adjective was required, she immediately corrected them.

"So, what is this project?" she questioned, as Missy opened her note book and took a pen from her school bag. Curiously, watching her granddaughter, she said, "I hope you're not going to be asking personal questions, like my age or if I am pregnant, or anything like that, are you?" Missy looked up, her eyes wide with concern, "I don't think so Nana, but if there is anything you don't want to answer just let me know." Suddenly, Marion became aware, that a deeply buried, sense of caution had risen within her. Now, she sat up straighter, stiffened herself and prepared to be guarded, as she was questioned. Knowing that she wanted more information, she asked, "So, before we get started, what is this again, and what is it all about?"

"Well, Nana, my assignment was to find out background and personal history about my parents or my grandparents. Since, you are much more interesting than my parents, I wanted to ask you." A slow smile crossed her grandmother's face, as she nodded, but her eyes didn't smile, they looked straight ahead, not at her granddaughter but much further into the distance beyond. This could be interesting and tricky she told herself.

Placing a blank sheet of paper in front of her, Missy picked up her pen saying, "I'll title it, The Interview with Marion Vetterlein Baxter, 1987." Then she looked up at her grandmother for approval. Her grandmother looked back, eyebrows raised and said, "Well if you want to use that name you can, but actually, my real name is Marion Lilli Vetterlein Baxter, it's the only name I answer to.

All of a sudden, Missy felt that this interview might not be as easy as she had thought, exhaling, she began with her first question.

"Where were you born Nana?"

"I was born in Tewksbury, Massachusetts in July"

"Did you have any siblings?"

"No, I was an only child and I loved it."

"What family activities do you remember doing?"

"Well, often on Friday nights we went to the movies, back then they were all silent movies, my mother loved them. She thought that Rudolph Valentino was incredibly handsome, I remember when he died, she was quite upset. We did other things too, sometimes we would go on picnics or take long drives. I didn't like the long drives very much, because I would get car sick, but I did enjoy sitting in the rumble seat once in a while. Often, we visited the Teuthorn' s, they lived in Tewksbury, they were old friends and they had a chicken farm. In the summer we would drive to visit relatives or friends, in Maine, Vermont, New Hampshire, Connecticut, and Rhode Island, all around New England. We went to New Jersey and stayed in Asberry Park, right on the ocean. We also went to New York quite a lot, both of my parents had relatives there. We used to go to a huge farm in Schenectady. I liked going there, I played with my cousin Carl, he was a lot of fun. They didn't have a bathroom in the farmhouse, so you had to use out houses or a privy. But you had to be careful, because if the boys saw you going in one, they would knock it over with you in it. I always asked someone to wait outside for me, usually Carl would do that. When we stayed on the farm, I didn't wear shoes the entire summer. We'd run through the fields barefoot. That was really fun, I liked that a lot, but you had to be careful though, sometimes you might run through cow dung. That was nasty, especially when it was warm. But, on some Friday nights, we had to leave and stay somewhere else. People from the big city would arrive, driving long limousines. I think that they played card games and things like that. This was in the mid-twenties during prohibition. I never understood why we had to leave, but I never asked."

Keeping her eyes on the paper, she carefully recorded her grandmother's answers, but then a pause occurred and when she looked up, she noticed that her grandmother wasn't looking at her, she was staring out the window, looking far into the distance. Missy waited before interrupting her grandmother's reverie, then, she asked the next question on her list.

"Nana, did you have to do chores at all?"

Turning her head, she looked at her granddaughter, paused for a moment then replied, "oh yes, I did, my mother was a meticulous housekeeper, she taught me house cleaning, especially dusting. That was my chore every Saturday morning."

It took several seconds as she scribed her grandmother's answer before she asked the next question, she was glad she had waited because after she asked it, her grandmother's demeanor changed.

"Nana, would you say that you ever experienced any hardships or difficulties in your childhood?"

Her grandmother's eyebrows lifted minutely, as her breathing became imperceptible. She stared straight ahead, but she didn't seem to be looking at anything, not a hair moved. For a moment, Missy feared that her grandmother had stopped breathing, but then her eyes quickly blinked, as she turned to look directly at granddaughter. Missy had never seen her grandmother look that way; her countenance had changed; a shadow had crossed her face. There was no smile, no animation, no movement, it was as if everything in her grandmother's body had frozen. After a long, deliberate pause, her eyes staring straight at her granddaughter, but not really seeing her, she replied, "No, no hardships at all."

Needing to swallow and feeling a dryness in her throat, Missy got up to get a glass of water. She asked her grandmother if she would like one too. Exhaling deeply, as her shoulder's relaxed and her breathing returned to her, she replied, "Gosh no, why would I want a glass of water? I'm not going to wash my feet."

Smiling at the strange comment, Missy turned on the kitchen faucet and filled up a tall glass with ice cold water, before sitting down to resume her questions. Then she began.

"Nana, what do you think is different today in how children are raised compared to when you were younger?"

"We were not pushed into adulthood. We played more with toys too, because we didn't have television. Most girls didn't use make up until they were much older. I started using lipstick and some rouge when I was about 14. We also had more respect for adults.

"Do you have any childhood experiences which were memorable?"

"Oh, yes," she quickly replied, "we were coming from New York and driving down a big steep hill, I grabbed the emergency brake on the car and pulled it back, suddenly all the brakes burned out. There was this terrible burnt smell of rubber everywhere. My mother turned and angrily reprimanded me saying, "What the heck did you do that for Marion?" I didn't know why I did it, I just did it. But to this day, I can still remember that smell, that burning smell." Her grandmother paused, then she continued, "There was another time, I remember driving through Connecticut and seeing fields and fields of tobacco, I had never really noticed them before, I had never seen anything like that."

"Can you tell me anything about your Mom?"

"Well, she was very organized, she was a good cook, she was strict but she was a good Mom. When I was a teenager, we had some conflicts, but we became the best of friends when I grew up and especially after I married, and started having children, she loved being a grandmother."

"Can you tell me about your Dad?

A smile crossed her grandmother's face and her eyes blinked several times at the mention of her father. Missy noticed that her grandmother's eyes were moistening, as she replied, "My Dad, wasn't strict at all. I would always go to him whenever I had any problems or questions. I could tell him anything and he always listened patiently. He died when your mother was a little girl, but I remember the last words that he ever spoke to me, those words I'll never forget."

Seeing the very sad and faraway look that crossed her grandmother's face, Missy didn't ask her for those words. However, she did ask, if this was too much, if she wanted to stop or even take a break. Her grandmother replied, "I'm not going anywhere today so if you have more questions then go ahead. I'll let you know when I don't want to answer anymore."

"Can you tell me about your first memory of school?"

"Yes, I recall that easily, my first school was a two-room schoolhouse, it was the Dearborn Elementary School. On the first floor was the first-grade teacher, her name was Miss Walker. On the second floor, was the second and third grade teacher, her name was Miss Willington. I remember that they had a handbell which they rang, telling us to line up for school to start, for recess and for it to end, and we would walk home for lunch too."

"Nana, I know that you have already given me these answers but I had these questions listed so if it's okay may I ask them again? Looking at her granddaughter, proudly, she responded, "Yes, you may, and I am happy to hear that you used the correct verb, because you asked for my permission not if you were capable." Grateful for knowing the difference Missy smiled back.

"What subjects did you like?"

"My favorite subjects were English and History."

"What was your least favorite subject?"

"My least favorite subject was math."

"Do you remember anything special about your high school or the teachers?"

"Yes, I went to Roxbury Memorial High School, the girls and boys were separated by floors and there was no interaction between us allowed. Also, we used to have a swimming pool in the school but the pool cracked so they put an airplane in the pool. I'm not sure if it is still there but I think they used it for a class that the boys took. As far as special teachers, my English teacher, was Miss Winnifred Nash, she was head of the department and she was very a hard teacher, but you learned your English. Actually, I enjoyed her class very much.

Looking at her grandmother she confided, "You know Nana, I like English too, I like to read the classics and to learn vocabulary and grammar. I'm not sure, but maybe I'll become an English teacher someday, just thinking. Responding, her grandmother smiled at her, "Maybe you will Missy, we never know do we?"

"Nana, did you participate in any sports?"

Smiling with pride, her grandmother responded, "Yes, I was on the basketball team and the swimming team until the pool cracked."

Surprised by that answer, from her five-foot, two-inch, grandmother, Missy tried to hide the smile that crossed her face, as her eyes twinkled. She imagined her grandmother on a basketball court, but the image that came was her 73-year-old grandmother running up and down a basketball court, in her flip flops, and flowery house dress. Missy decided not to ask what position she played, so she went on to the next question.

"Nana did you participate in any clubs or organizations while in school?"

"Quite a few," she replied, and she began to list them, "I was in the debating club. I received a certificate for that, I really liked debating. I was a member of the Latin Club. Also, I was a member of the American Red Cross, I did the Latin and the Red Cross Clubs, because I wanted to go into medicine and become a nurse. I participated in Girl Scouts and I was a member of the Order of the Rainbow for Girls organization, affiliated with my church. My mother was an Eastern Star member and my father was in the Masons. I also attended the Christian Education Program which was part of the programs offered at our church, The Dudley Street Baptist Church. "

"Nana, of all of your accomplishments in school, what was your proudest?"

"Of everything, I am proud of graduating, you needed to have 100 points to graduate, I had 102 points. But also, I was proud of receiving an award at graduation for having perfect attendance for one year, and of becoming a lifetime member in the Roxbury Memorial High School Alumni Association.

"Is there anything you regret about school?"

"Yes, I wish that I had applied myself more, I know I could

have done much better than I did. I was interviewed by the newspaper upon graduating, that was an experience."

"Nana, when school would get out, was there anything you did after school?"

"Of course, my friends and I would stop at the local drugstore and get frappes or milk shakes." That sounds like fun, her granddaughter replied. Her grandmother smiled, "Yes, and they were really good too. I have always had a sweet tooth." she confessed.

"Nana, do you remember any school pranks that you did?"

"My friends and I did do some pranks and frankly I have forgotten most of them but, yes, I do remember one day vividly. I played hooky, because I didn't want to take a Latin test. I didn't think I was prepared enough, so I went to school, but I hid in the girl's locker room. I sat in a gym locker, in the girl's locker room, all day trying to avoid that one class. I spent the whole day hiding and being afraid that a teacher would come in and find me. Well, I knew that the Latin teacher usually left the building with her friends, when school ended, but this day she remained a little later. She was leaving just when I left the building. She saw me and knew right away, that I had skipped her class. She was very upset; reprimanded me and gave me an absentee note to give to my parents. I didn't give it to them, I ripped it up on the way home. I never did tell my parents."

"Will you tell me about your friends, particularly your best friend."

Missy noticed the huge smile which crossed her grandmother's face at the thought of her dear friend.

"Yes, her name's Josephine, her nickname's Josie and we are

still in touch, we are still friends, even though she lives way out in the western part of Massachusetts."

"Did you have a best friend of the opposite sex?"

Missy's grandmother took a breath, as a wistful smile crossed her face. Her eyes glistened, and she swallowed before she replied, "Yes, Missy, his name was Bill Baxter. I called him "Billy," he was the best friend I ever had. You've heard about him; your mother has talked about him I know. He died before you were born, he is your grandfather."

Missy paused for several minutes before beginning to ask the next question, but just as she began, her grandmother began to push herself away from the table, as she told her that she needed to get up for a moment, but would be right back. Missy waited patiently, while several minutes passed. She heard her grandmother blowing her nose and coughing slightly. Then she heard the faucets running in the bathroom and the toilet being flushed, before long her grandmother appeared, her face glistened and dewy from the water that had just been splashed on it.

"Nana, other than Billy did you have any other serious boyfriends?

"I did, his name was John Joseph, but I called him Joe. I met him when I was in the 11th grade in high school. He gave me a Hope Chest, it's up in the attic next to the one that Billy gave me."

Again, Missy saw that her grandmother had turned to stare out the window. Patiently, she waited until her grandmother turned back, and looked at her expectedly.

"Nana, you loved English, but you went into nursing. How come?

"My mother always loved nursing, she believed that it was a perfect career choice for a woman. When she was older she volunteered for the American Red Cross and worked at the VA Hospital just down the street. She believed that nursing was a good career especially, if you wanted to get married and have children. I had thought about teaching English but back then, if you were a teacher and got married, you had to give up your job. Married, female teachers were not allowed to teach in schools, those jobs went to the men. Besides I loved babies, I always have loved babies. I wanted to be a nurse that worked on the hospital floors where the babies were treated. I went to Mount Auburn Hospital in Cambridge, it used to be called Cambridge Hospital. It was a teaching hospital affiliated with Harvard University. I did well there, until my very last semester. That was why in high school, I took Latin classes and joined the American Red Cross as preparation for nursing. The Latin helped in studying medicine and medical terms."

"I know that I asked you this before, but looking back do you remember any hardships at all?"

"None."

"Do you have any advice for young women who want to go into nursing now?"

"Yes, why not become a doctor?"

"Nana, do you keep a daily schedule now that your children have all grown up?"

"No schedule, I do pretty much as I damn well please."

"Is there a particular time of day which you like the best?"

"Nope, none in particular."

"What is your favorite season?"

"I have always preferred the summer."

"Why?"

I don't like being cold, sometimes if I get a chill, it is hard for me to get rid of it. So, I prefer the weather to be nice and warm."

"But do you mind the hot, hot weather at all?"

"No, not at all, I just don't like the cold weather, never have."

"Nana, what do you enjoy most doing in the summer?"

When Wally, Chick and Jeri, were little, we would go to the beach, a lot. Living in Uphams Corner, Carson or Tinean Beach, were close, so we would go to the ocean. But then, when we moved to West Roxbury, we went to a pond for swimming. We'd pack your mom, Susie, Billy and Bobby in the station wagon and head to New Pond. I remember that was in Norwood or Westwood. It's not around anymore, because the Catholic Church, bought the land and built a church there. I think it's called St. Timothy's Church. I was disappointed when the beach was closed, we always enjoyed it there. I liked having cook outs with my family too, especially impromptu ones.

"Nana, I know that you like nature. What is your most favorite nature thing of all to watch?"

"Most of all I love sunsets, I find them incredibly beautiful. You know if you're here, I would call you to come look at it too. I also love looking at the moon, especially when it is a full harvest moon. Sometimes, I have called your mom, telling her to go outside and look at the moon. I enjoy watching the trees bud in the spring and the flowers budding. Let's see, I enjoy watching the birds and hearing them sing. But lately, I noticed that I'm not hearing them as much, I guess they're not singing like they used to. My father loved nature, when he and my mother first moved here, he enjoyed sitting out, on the side of the house, feeding the squirrels and enjoying the view of the Charles River across the road. But that was a long time ago. Houses and businesses have been built now, blocking that view. That was one of the reasons they bought this house, because of the view.

"Do you remember any bad experiences with the weather, like with storms or something like that?"

"Oh yes, at the time we didn't know it, but in 1938, I was coming from my mother's house on Forest Street and heading to mine, carrying a 5 or 6-month-old infant. Suddenly, we had what became known as the first hurricane in this area. I had gotten off the bus, holding Wally and it was incredibly windy. A man had to actually help me to cross the street and just as we got crossed, a chimney next door fell down. We still didn't know what was going on. It was really frightening."

"Wow, well Nana you are 73 how do you take care of your health?"

"I eat nourishing foods, and look at life optimistically."

"What is your favorite food?"

"None. I like most of them."

"What is your least favorite food?"

"Lima beans."

"What modern convenience do you appreciate the most?"

"All of them."

"What is your favorite club, sport or hobby?"

"Well my favorite club was the Rainbow Girls. But now, I enjoy listening to the Red Sox, especially when they win. I've always enjoyed knitting too. Do you remember the pale green coats I made for you and Jessica? You both looked adorable in them."

"I do remember them, Nana, I think my mother gave them to Aunt Susie for Erica, when we outgrew them."

"Nana, do you think arts and crafts are important to life?"

"Yes, I do, and photography."

"Do the Rainbow Girls still exist Nana?"

"Of course, they do. Do you think they went out with the cowboys and Indians?"

"Nana, where is the farthest that you traveled?"

"Ohio."

"How did you travel out there?"

"Missy, you know the answer to this one, we all traveled in an RV."

"How would you describe that experience?"

"I thought it was a lot of fun."

"What do you remember most about that trip?"

"I remember everything about it, but I guess it was Laura and Rick's wedding itself and the party afterward, it was wonderful. Everyone in the family was there and it was the first time I had seen your Uncle Chick's and Aunt Jean's house. I really enjoyed that time. It was a great time."

"What was your favorite part?"

"Being with my son in law Kevin, your Dad, my daughters, Susie and your mom and of course my two wonderful granddaughters, you and Jessica. We were all together in that RV traveling from Boston to Sylvania, Ohio and then back again.

"What do you enjoy doing the most with your family?"

"I enjoy just being with them, especially surprise get togethers

"Nana, would you tell me the most interesting experience you've had lately?"

"Well, lately, I haven't had any interesting experiences, which is a bit disappointing, come to think of it."

"Do you have any advice for how to get along with people?"

"Missy, everyone has a good side to them, and instead of looking at their bad sides, look at the good sides."

"Who do you think is the greatest person of this century?"

"Me! No, really FDR, he did a lot for the people of this country."

"And of past centuries?"

"Abraham Lincoln."

Looking around her grandmother's kitchen Missy noticed so many items which only a quarter of a century ago didn't exist, prompting her to ask this question.

"Nana, there have been so many inventions during the 20th Century, in your judgement, what was the most significant one."

"Anything to do with television, telegraph, and telephones, there is so much instantaneous communication available now."

"What do you think of schools today?"

"I believe that they are too big, there isn't as much personal interaction with parents, teachers, or the children like there used to be."

"What is your philosophy of education?"

"Children need to be told that going to school is like training for their future and they should conduct themselves for the professional world. It's very competitive out there."

"Nana, I know that you went to nursing school, when did you graduate?"

"I didn't, and speaking of graduation, I will tell you exactly what happened. It was in the last semester of my senior year. We were staying in dorms and the curfew was 10:00pm. I was in my room getting ready for bed, when the girl in the room next door, rapped on the wall, saying she was starving and did I have any food? I had an orange, so I opened my door and rolled the orange next door to her room. The floor supervisor saw me open my door. That was against regulations, and she suspended me on the spot. I had to go home for several days as punishment. I decided then that if they wanted to suspend me, I would show them, I didn't go back, they could kiss my arse for all I cared. I think, if someone doesn't want me, then I don't want them, I've felt that way most of my life. It all worked out though, maybe I wouldn't have met your grandfather and then you wouldn't be here."

"Nana, I didn't know that story, that's terrible. Thank you for telling me." "Well, Missy, there is often much more than meets the eye, much more. Sometimes, you just have to ask, but then you need to listen and you have been an amazing listener today. Do you have any more questions? Do you want something to eat? I'll cut up an orange, or you can have some cookies from the cookie jar." "No thank you Nana, but I just have a few more questions. By the way, you really are much more interesting than my parents." Her nana smiled, a sphinx like smile, and nodded her head.

"So, what do you think is the United States biggest problem now?"

"Without a doubt, international conflicts. I believe that the

U. S. should mind their own business, a little more than they do."

"What can each citizen do to help?"

"Let the government know that people don't want to be involved in other countries so much. I believe that's what the majority feels right now."

"What old time values should be kept and honored?"

"Children should be allowed to be children and not rushed into the adult world, when they are still only kids, really."

"Nana, what did you learn from your parents and experiences that you would like to hand down to kids today?"

"I believe that we should all attend a church, synagogue or mosque, whichever we belong to, that should be our foundation. And also, we can have a lot of fun with the opposite sex, without getting into sex and not be promiscuous."

"Any other advice?"

"No, just be good kids, that all."

"So, Nana, on a scale of 1 to 10, what are kids today?"

"I'd say, most kids are good kids, on a scale from 8 to 9, basically good kids."

"So, Nana, you had 7 children. And you have, I think, is it 24 grandchildren? Who is your favorite of all?"

"Missy, are you serious? How can I pick one out of 24 grandchildren and 7 kids? You know that I can't, each one of you is special, I have no favorites at all."

Laughing, Missy agreed, "Sorry, that wasn't a fair question. Ok, how about this last one?"

"What's your most favorite holiday of all with your family?"

This last question, caused her grandmother to reflect for

several moments. Then as a look of serenity crossed her face, she answered.

"Christmas Eve, with Father, I mean Santa Claus, the Christmas Tree getting decorated, all of the kids, presents everywhere and everyone, just everyone together.

"Nana, thank you so much. I really enjoyed asking you all of these questions. Was there anything I missed or anything you want to add?" Her grandmother looked pensively, as she glanced out the window and appeared to want to say something. Then she turned to her granddaughter, her head nodded slightly and she said, "You have it all, everything that was important."

Missy gathered her pile of papers, and placed them in her folder. Then, she put her pen back in her school bag. Looking up at her grandmother, she saw that once again she was staring out the window. She didn't understand what her grandmother saw that was so interesting out there, it was just another house with a car parked in the driveway. Getting up to leave, she startled Bernie, for a second time, this time he lifted his head, letting out an annoyed "woof" and then heavily laid it down again.

Before she left, she went over to hug and kiss her grandmother good bye. Knowing that she would walk to the door with her, and wave good bye as she watched her granddaughter leave. She also knew, that her grandmother always did that to guarantee that no one locked and securely closed the door behind them. Missy heard her mother's car pulling into the driveway. They wouldn't be able to stay, she had a cheering practice that evening.

As Missy was leaving, she looked up the street, and saw

coming around the corner, holding a large pan of pasta and gravy, was her great grandmother Catisemma. Quickly running over, she kissed her on the cheek, as she inhaled the flavorful aroma of Catisemma's homemade pasta. "I'm bringing this over to your grandmother, this isa her supper." Missy smiled, wondering how she had an Italian great-grandmother but wasn't Italian.

Missy's mother and sister jumped out of the car to greet everyone. "How did it go?" her mother asked. "Good, I liked asking Nana about her life, I'm glad I have her story now." "Me too," her mother said, as Marion and Catisemma smiled at each other and then waved good bye to the departing car.

*"For all that has been, thank you,
For all that is to come, Yes!"*
- Dag Hammarskjöld

EPILOGUE

Lilli's chair had been put in the attic, the rockers had broken off, the lion's noses had been painted bright enamel red by an artistic child, and the wood seat was scratched and scraped from toy metal trucks, wooden blocks and standing children.

The chair sat silent, motionless; it no long-rocked back and forth, the rockers were gone, they were missing; no one knew where they had gone, or even what had happened to them. They were just missing, that's all, nothing important, no big deal, they said. The chair was broken and old. No need to look for the rockers, they had probably been thrown out long ago. It wasn't important, they repeated, don't bother, they were just going to toss the chair out too; it was going into the dumpster with the rest of the old furniture, the old rugs and everything else that was no longer wanted or needed. They told her that no one wanted it. "I do." she said," I want it."

"But it's broken," they answered, "the chair was broken, pieces were missing, it's an old chair, it's no good anymore."

"No," she said," that was not happening." She couldn't let that happen, not to this chair, this chair was special. She reminded them that it had been their grandmother's chair. She had been told that it was a wedding gift, from her grandmother's favorite uncle in Germany, his name was Herman. He was in the elite guard to the Kaiser, a long time ago. When she was a little girl, she carried the chair up the stairs, and into her bedroom. She had rocked in this chair by herself. She had held her baby sister and rocked her in this chair; she had held her baby brothers, as all three of them rocked, they were twins. It was crowded with all three of them rocking. Sometimes, they rocked too far back and forth and the chair tipped over throwing them out and crashing onto the floor as they laughed and laughed. Their mother would call up the stairs asking, "What are you doing up there? You are making too much noise. Quiet down."

Well, the house was quiet now, it was empty, the pictures had been taken off the walls, the de Haviland china packed and given to a granddaughter. The antique lace table cloths and napkins had become rags, from being thrown into a washing machine and agitated. Any remaining furniture had been distributed among the many family members, everything except the chair. It was left in the attic. It stood alone, in a corner, in the empty dusty attic.

"Even without the rockers I want the chair," she told him. I will find the rockers, he promised her, and he did. They carefully put the chair in the back of his truck, and gently, laid the rockers next to the chair. They brought it home, to their home.

They looked for a craftsman to fix it. No one knew how, they were told the chair would never rock again. They were told it was broken, some of the pieces were missing and it was old. They were told they should probably throw it away.

But they wouldn't, they kept it, they would not throw it away. Then one day he found him, an artist; a skilled creative talented artist. He came to their house. They told him the story of the chair, she told him about her grandmother, about the uncle's wedding gift and about finding the chair in the attic with the rockers broken off, missing until he found them.

The artist looked at the chair, he placed his hand on the back of the chair and he smiled, he said it was beautiful, it was special and yes, of course, he could fix it.

Then gently, he lifted it up and carried it, he put it in his truck, he laid the rockers next to the chair and brought it all, all of the pieces into his shop. He cleaned the red paint off the lion's noses; he refinished the seat and polished the wood. Then, at last he secured the rockers. He replaced the pieces that were missing, and then slowly one at a time he fixed the rockers. The chair was whole again, it was strong and solid and it rocked back and forth, back and forth. He looked at the chair and smiled; gently he placed his hand on top of the lion's heads, holding it there, as the chair rocked, back and forth, he was pleased, proud of his work and he smiled, as a sense of peace and calm washed through his body.

He called them; he said he was bringing it home, back to their home. Gently, he lifted it out of his truck and carried it into her kitchen. When she saw it, her breath caught in her throat, and her eyes filled with tears. She reached out and touched the chair's arms, felt the smooth seat and rubbed the clean smooth noses of the lions. She was so thankful; she was so grateful. She told him you've done such a beautiful job; you've made this chair new again. It looks like it did when I was a little girl. You are an amazing artist, thank you so much, his face lit up as he smiled.

She wanted to pay him, this was his profession, he was a skilled craftsman, he was an artist, and this was his trade.

She saw no invoice on the table, no invoice on the chair; no envelope in his hand. She looked at him asking, "How much do I owe you, let me pay you, please let me pay you.

Shrugging, he shoved one hand deeply into his pocket, he lowered his head looking down at the chair, then he gently placed his other hand on its' back, as the chair slowly began to rock, back and forth.

Smiling, he tilted his head to the side, as he again looked at the chair, then he looked up at her. His head shook left to right, "No," he said, his eyes glistening, there was no invoice, there was no bill. He told her, "I don't want any payment for what I did. Thank you for asking me to fix it. It was a beautiful chair; it was my pleasure."

Then he looked at her and said, "This is your chair now, it is a gift; a gift from your grandmother to you."

The End

REFERENCES AND SOURCES

1. Mah, Adeline Yen, "Watching the Tree," Broadway Books, pgs 202
2. "Seventh Son of a Seventh Son," Wiki2 Republished, Wikipedia
3. A Historic Look Back at Brooklyn's Atlantic Avenue – Curbed NY 2/3/2017, Wikipedia
4. The Brown Building, (Manhattan) Internet Search 3:02, 4/13/2018, The Free Encyclopedia, Wikipedia,
5. Eugene de Salignac, #18 A one legged newspaper boy and other "newsies" on Delancey Street on December 26, 1906, Courtesy NYC Municipal Archives
6. In Focus, Historic Photos from NYC Municipal, The Atlantic, Archives 4/27/2012
7. American Dream, History, 19th Century 2/2/17, Wikipedia
8. Pogroms, 7/13/17Internet Search, Wikipedia, 11:02pm

REFERENCES AND SOURCES

9. Brooklyn, one building at a time Images, (internet search)

10. Langer, William L. (compiler and editor) An Encyclopedia of World History, Houghton Mifflin, Co., pgs 686 -687, 1940, 1948 and 1952

11. Franco-Prussian War, 1870-1871 Wikipedia

12. Haste, Heather, "Heather's Homilies, My Take on Our World," posted by Heather Hastie on 12/28/2014 Britain & Europe, History, Religion/Comments, Internet Search 4/8/2018, 9:03 p.m.

13. Gardes du Corps, Internet Search, Wikipedia

14. Edgar A. Guest, Harbor Lights of Home, The Reilly & Lee Co. Chicago, 1928, Bride and Groom, page 85

15. Josephine Morris, Household Science and Arts, The Homemaker's Duty to Herself, pgs 197 - 201

16. Josephine Morris Household Science and Arts, page 11 Dust

17. Nursery Rhyme Lyrics, Origins and History, "Wash on Monday," Internet Search 1:44, 3/27/2018

18. Emma Lazarus, The New Colossus, Wikipedia

19. Evan Hadingham, Photographs by Jeffrey Gusky, "The Hidden World of the Great War," pgs. 116 – 128, National Geographic, August 2014,

20. Lord's Prayer-German-The Lord's Prayer-www.Lords-Prayer-words.com/Lord_German-Translation.html 3/24/2018 Google Internet Search,

21. Neil Swidey, The Muck Affair, Globe Magazine, The Boston Globe, pgs. 16 – 29, November 5, 2017

22. Anti-German Hysteria in City during WW1 by Jeff Seuss, jseuss@cincinnati.com, published Cincinnati.com. Part

REFERENCES AND SOURCES

of The USA Today Network March 11, 2017, Google internet search 3:47 p.m. to 4:02p.m. 4/6/2018

23. The Spirit of 76 (1917 film) Internet Search, Wikipedia 8:25pm 4/10/2018

24. The WW1 Home front: War Hysteria & The Persecution of German Americans, Google Search 4/6/2018 3:29pm

25. Day, Harvey, 100 The United States WW1 Centennial Commission, The Tragic Plight of Germans in America During WW1, Via the Daily Mail Online Web Site, Internet Search 4/10/2018 @11:50am

26. Chateau-Thierry the 69th Infantry Regiment, NY. 4/10/2018, Wikipedia, @4:33pm

27. Duolingo, Internet Search, Come here, Kommen sie hierher, 1:46pm, 4/15/2018

28. Times Square, The Official Website NYE History & Times Square Ball, The History of The Times Square Ball Internet Search, 3:25pm, 4/15/2018

29. Elizabeth Barrett Browning (1806-1861), How Do I Love Thee, Sonnet 43, Poets.org 5/1/2018 12:39pm.

30. Gilmore, Joseph H. "He Leadeth Me," Timeless Truths, Free Online Library, Internet Search, 9:09pm, 5/4/2018 copyright status Public Domain

31. Lasater, Judith Hanson, PH.D., P.T, "Relax and Renew, Restful Yoga for Stressful Times," page 42

32. Memory Typer, the easy way to memorize stuff, Internet Search 9:33, 5/23/18

33. Playback.FM, Top 100 Charts in 1921, The Fabulous Ethel Waters and Her Orchestra, singing 'There'll Be Some Changes Made, "Internet Search, 5:25pm 5/21/2018

REFERENCES AND SOURCES

34. Farmer, Patricia Adams, Embracing a Beautiful God," pgs.148 & 155, Estrella de Mar Publications

35. Franz Ferdinand of Austria, Archduke, Wikipedia, The Free Encyclopedia, Internet Search 7/1/17, @10:15

36. This Day in History, June 28th, 1914, Archduke Franz Ferdinand Assassinated, Internet Search, 7/1/2017 @ 10:06

37. The New York Times, 6-28-2016, Franz Ferdinand, Whose Assassination Sparked a World War, Internet Search, 7/2/2017

38. Anti-German Sentiment, WW1, Liberty Cabbage, Wikipedia Internet Search, 7/7/17 @10:19pm

39. Christoph von Schmid, IHR Kinderlein Kimment, 1811 – English Translation, "Oh, Come Little Children"

40. Langer, William L. (compiler and editor) An Encyclopedia of World History, Houghton Mifflin, North America, p. 792

41. Cohan, George, Michael, Google Search, "Over there, "song written and sung by George M. Cohan, Wikipedia, 6:20pm, 2/25/18

42. The 69th Infantry Regiment, (New York) The Free Encyclopedia, Wikipedia, 4:59pm 2/26/18

43. Kilmer, Joyce, American Writer and Poet, Google Internet Search, Wikipedia, 3:13pm, 3/3/18

44. Prinzing, Debra, The Fascinating Life of a 1917 Flower Show Trophy, Google Internet Search, 1:43pm, 4/29/17 & 3/6/18

45. The Lord's Prayer, Lord's Prayer-German, www.Lords-Prayer-words.com/Lord_German-Translation.html   3/24/18, 10:05pm, Google Internet Search

REFERENCES AND SOURCES

46. Long, Matt, Landlopers, Discovering Esslingen, Germany's Real Medieval City

47. Esslingen am Neckar, 19th Century to Date, Wikipedia

48. Journeyman, Wikipedia, 2/5/17

49. Boyd, Neva Leona, The Social Welfare History Project, Charles Loring Brace, The Social Welfare Project, VCU Libraries, 7/9/17, 9:19pm

50. Dismore, David, The Feminist Majority Foundation, 5/2/13, Teddy Roosevelt Gives a Speech at the NY Metropolitan Opera House Supporting Woman's Right to Vote

51. Dismore, David, The Feminist Majority Foundation, Feminist Daily Newswire, 1/17/2018 @9:34pm

52. Dismore, David, https://feminist.org/May-2-1913 TR Speaks Out for Suffrage

53. Lewis, Susan Ingalls, Women's Suffrage Supporters march 20,000 strong in New York City Parade with half a million onlookers, Internet Search, 7/9/17

54. Scholastic Teachers, Important Dates in US Women's History, 1912, Suffrage supporters join NYCV parade while a half million onlookers watch.

55. World Digital Library, Suffrage Parade New York City, 5/6/1912, Library of Congress, 7/10/2017 @10:13

56. The Castle in the Clouds, The Free Encyclopedia, Wikipedia, 7/11/2017 @ 2:16pm

57. Langer, William, L. (compiler and editor) Western and Central Europe, June 12, 1900, The second German Navel Law, pgs. 690 - 692, 693. An Encyclopedia of World History, Houghton Mifflin Company, Boston

58. Industrial Revolution, Editors of Encyclopedia Britan-

REFERENCES AND SOURCES

nica,5-2-2017, see Article History Encyclopedia Britannica Website, 6/18/17

59. Langer, William, L. (compiler and editor) International Relations, 1870 -1914 pgs. 695, 763, An Encyclopedia of World History

60. Bachman Uxbridge Worsted Company mill complex at Uxbridge had been a hub of manufacturing for Bernat, once based in Jamaica Plain, MA. The town of Uxbridge was the site of Bernat's main manufacturing unit in the late 20th century. Wikipedia, Internet Search, 7/13/17 @ 9:45pm.

61. Harness, Jill, February 16, 2013, Mental Floss, 100-year-old photos of people delivering mail, Internet Search 2/1/2018 @ 4:16pm.

62. Climatological Date: New York Section General Summary, Vol.XXVI, Ithaca, NY 12/1914, No. 12, Internet Search2/1/2018 @ 4:16pm

63. Restad, Penne, History Today, Christmas in America, (OUP 1995) Lecturer in American History at University of Texas, Austin, TX

64. Christmas in Germany-Christmas Around the World, https://www.whychristmas.comcultures/germany.shtml, Internet search, 1/24/2018 @ 10:33pm

65. The Christmas Truce, 12/24/1914, Wikipedia, Internet Search, 1/29/2018 @ 10:33pm

66. Siegel, Robert, Silverman, Art, NPR, During WW1, Why U.S. Government Propaganda Erased German Culture, April 7, 2017, 6:00pm, Internet Search, 2/2/2018 @ 11:37am

67. What do Jewish people call God? Google Internet Search, 2/2/2018 @ 5:02pm

68. Rumeana, Johanger, BBC News, WW1 Sinking of Lusi-

REFERENCES AND SOURCES

tania recalled, 27 March 2015, WW1, Google Search, 2/9/2016 @ 11:23pm

69. This Day in History, WW1, May 7, 1915, German Submarine Sinks Lusitania, Google Search

70. Baxter, Herbert, Original copy of U. S. Citizenship Certificate 1902

ACKNOWLEDGMENTS

In 2016, when I began to write Lilli's Chair, it felt as if I was trying to put together a giant puzzle. One with many unique, and diverse pieces, but also a puzzle with missing pieces, large, important ones. Combined, all of these pieces, covered a time span of more than one hundred years. Each piece was different, some were large, some small, some oddly shaped, some not. There were the anchor pieces, binding everything together and then the border pieces, keeping everything straight. There were pieces that just didn't seem to fit at all, and then there were the missing pieces, large pieces.

Studying each piece, I tried to determine which ones were connected, I checked for time periods, and relevant events. For clarity, I placed all of the similar ones together, the beginnings in one section, the celebrations in yet another, the legal documents in another and finally, the more recent ones, bolder and clearer still in their own separate grouping. But then, there were those pieces which somehow didn't seem connected to the puzzle, those I put right in front of me, as I waited for a hint or a clue as to their unique and strategic location, but again there were the gaps, those critical pieces, which I would never find.

And so, for many years, that was how it was with Lilli's Chair, many pieces, some connected, some not and some standing all alone, by themselves.

Growing up, I knew that my father's mother had died when he was a young man, I had a step grandmother. I understood that, my widowed grandfather had married for a second time, his new wife had also been widowed. They had recreated a family connected by loss, love, and faith but not DNA.

On my mother's side, we had Nana and Grampa Vetterlein, they were her parents. I had been told that I was named after my mother's mother and my mother's middle name was also after her mother. I remember, finding a picture of my grandmother as a young woman, I asked my mother, "Do I look like Nana?" her reply was quick and not forthcoming, "No, Honey, you don't. "As children, we would sit around the chrome and formica kitchen table, listening to my parents as they talked about their lives, family events and childhood experiences. They shared much of their life stories with us. We thought, we had heard it all, but we hadn't. They had a secret. That secret would change everything that we believed and understood.

It happened on what seemed to be an average evening, I was well into my late teens, when out of the blue, my mother said something quite unexpected. Sitting at the kitchen table, across from me, she said, "I want to tell you something about myself, something about my life." I held my breath, not sure what I was about to hear, and not sure if I wanted to hear it, either. Then in a tone, void of any emotion and with no embellishments, she flatly stated, "I was adopted." Well, to put it mildly, I was gob smacked.

For my whole life, I had believed that we were made up of a combination of German, from my mother, and Scottish/ Irish from my father. I had even learned to like sauerkraut. I remember looking at her and suddenly wondering, if I had heard her correctly, maybe she meant that I was adopted, but she repeated it, "I was adopted."

I stared at her, yet not really seeing her, I wondered who she was, who was my mother and who were we? After that disclosure, there was no more information gleaned, my mother wouldn't share anymore, she didn't want to talk about it. Nor did she want to seek out her biological mother or father. She told me as much by saying, "She didn't want me, then I don't want her." My heart broke for her, as I knew my mother's heart had been broken, because I thought, maybe, that wasn't how it happened.

However, there were some things that I did know, Lilli's rocking chair, a wedding gift from her Uncle Herman, a member of the Kaiser's Elite Guard, was in my bedroom. My mother's stories about vacations to New York and New Jersey with her parents. We had all seen post cards of those luxurious locations. The house in Roxbury on Forest Street, the schools, especially Roxbury Memorial High School, with the airplane in the pool. The incident about the orange and my mother' suspension just before graduation. I now began to understand why she didn't go back to graduate; why she couldn't go back.

I had learned about her piano lessons and her ability to play an octave, even though we never had the opportunity to hear her play; we didn't have a piano. She had shared how important it was for my grandfather, her father, to be able to sit in his back yard the sun shining on his face, as he watched the Charles River and saw the sun set. But I also learned what his final words were to her and the difficult decision she had to make that day. I had often wondered, why on Sunday mornings, my parents, would pile the entire family, all 9 of us, into the Ford station wagon, and drive all of the way to Tewksbury. We were told that we were visiting friends, my mother's friends, who had a chicken farm. This was before any major highway routes had been constructed, we were never told the connection. And then there was Catisemma, my Italian grandmother, who appeared to have known my mother most of her life.

At one point, I asked my mother, why she hadn't told us sooner, she replied, "Your father and I were afraid that you wouldn't accept my parents as your grandparents." We loved them, they loved us and they loved my mother, but my mother wasn't going to bet on that.

So, combined with the stories and the memories there were the tangible pieces ,those I spread across my dining room table, a wedding certificate for Lilli Holzapfel and Walter Vetterlein, pictures of my mother as a little girl, an adoption certificate, a ticket from a social at the Baptist Temple dated April 19, 1897, a picture of my grandmother sitting in a rocking chair, faded birth certificates of Lilli and Walter. A baptismal certificate from The Dudley Street Baptist Church, a RMHS Yearbook, class of 1932, with a graduation certificate boldly stating 102 points. A copy of a Record of Birth for my mother, indicating that Walter and Lilli Vetterlein were her parents, a notice to petition the courts for the adoption of my mother and a formal Adoption and Change of Name, signed and dated by all parties involved.

So many pieces, some uniform and similar, others with no apparent connection to the next. But eventually, most of the pieces came together like a beautifully created quilt, sewn by hand, seam by seam, they blended, connecting one to the next, as the story, "Lilli's Chair," evolved.

But still pieces were missing, it was there, that I wrote what I believed may have happened, conversations I believed that may have been said, experiences and events, as I imagined may have occurred. But I also believe, there were times, when my fingers typed words and conversations, I hadn't prepared, words I hadn't thought about, conversations I hadn't created. The narrative was already there, it had already existed, I was simply the conduit, the scribe, translating it, as it was being told to me.

The Irish poet, author, and priest, John O'Donohue wrote, "Is there a place where our vanished days secretly gather? The name of that place is memory...... We need to retrieve the activity of remembering, for it is here that we are rooted and gathered." I believe that is exactly what my assigned task had been.

There are so many people I want to thank. While many of them are no longer here, I will include their names, because each one was important, each one made a difference, as together Lilli's Chair was written. All of us, we all are kindred spirits, like Marion was with Walter and Lilli, this family, Marion's family, was not created solely by DNA, but by loss, faith and the infinite power of love.

So, thank you to my grandparents, Walter and Lilli, to Catisemma, Mr. and Mrs. Teuthorn, and to you, Uncle Herman and your beautiful gift to Lilli.

Thank you, to my friends and family who read the rough drafts of Lilli's Chair, and encouraged me to continue writing to completion, Victoria and Chrissy Sibley, Jeri Mulvey Murphy, Sylvia LaSelva, Jeanne Hufnagle, Muriel Humora, Amy Osband, Cheryl Wigandt Baxter, and Margaret O'Brien. Thank you, Laura Baxter Riggs, for your continuous encouragement, to my step daughters for your enthusiasm and support, Michelle LaCasse, Christine Jacobs and Kimberly Doyle. Thank you to my sister, Susan Baxter for your heartfelt guidance and questioning, throughout the entire journey.

Thank you to my daughters, Melissa Moran Stampfl, for your decision to interview your grandmother instead of your parents, (smart choice) and to Jessica Moran MacAleese, for your diligent efforts to help find those missing pieces, and finally, to my husband Francis Doyle, for your continuous support, guidance and love.

But most importantly, thank you to my mother, Marion Lilli Vetterlein Baxter, for granting me permission to tell your story. The story that you had kept secret for so many years. I now believe, that it was your hands that guided me when I did not know where I was going; they always have. I trust, that you now know, you were loved; you always were and always will be, I love you Mom.

ABOUT THE AUTHOR

Lilli's Chair is my first historical fiction novel. I wrote and did the research for this novel at the same time when several members of my family had been diagnosed with cancer. As I wrote Lilli's Chair, I was guided to find the fortitude and courage to believe that we would make it through this frightening and life-threatening time.

Writing about the strength, perseverance, and resolve of those who came before me, I knew that the shoulders on whom we stood were strong and supportive, providing a foundation of love.

I believe in the profound power of love. It is exactly that power which never dies. It continues forever, passed down from one generation to the next, breathing faith, resilience, and courage from one generation into the next.

Made in United States
North Haven, CT
06 October 2021